OFF BALANCE SERIES

DISMOUNT

LUCIA FRANCO

Dismount by Lucia Franco

Book 5 in the Off Balance series

Copyright © 2020 by Lucia Franco

Second Edition

Edited by Nadine Winningham
Proofread by Amber Hodge
Cover Design by Okay Creations
Formatted by Jersey Girl Designs

OTHER TITLES BY LUCIA FRANCO

<u>Standalone Titles</u>

You'll Think of Me
Hold On to Me
You're Mine Tonight
Tell Me What You Want
Irresistible Stranger

<u>Hush Hush Series</u>

Hush Hush
Say Yes
The Proposition

<u>Off Balance series</u>

Balance
Execution
Release
Twist
Dismount
Out of Bounds

Dear Reader,

The Off Balance series is a continuation series. The novels must be read in order to follow the story.

This story is purely fictional and does not reflect real-life events.

Each novel in this five-part series follows a heavy May-December romance between a gymnast and a coach. If you consider this subject and any related content disturbing, then the Off Balance series is not for you.

Gymnastics is a hands-on sport that involves hours of close contact with a coach. My goal was to focus on the beauty of the sport in detail, show the emotional aspect of an athlete's dedication, and show how two people can cross forbidden boundaries and evolve together.

This story will push you, question you, and take you outside of your comfort zone.

The Off Balance series is intended only for readers 18 and older. Reader discretion is advised.

-Lucia

To every Off Balance reader who stayed with me through the good and the bad, who never gave up on this series and begged for more...
Thank you.
Dismount is for you.

She's standing on a line between
giving up and seeing how
much more she can take.

— Anonymous

GLOSSARY

All-Around A category of gymnastics that includes all the events. The all-around champion of an event earns the highest total score from all events combined.

Amanar A Yurchenko-style vault, meaning the gymnast performs a round-off onto the board, a back handspring onto the vault with a two-and-a-half twisting layout backflip.

Cast A push off the bar with hips and lifts the body to straighten the shoulders and finish in handstand.

Deduction Points taken off a gymnast's score for errors. Most deductions are pre-determined, such as a 0.5 deduction for a fall from an apparatus or a 0.1 deduction for stepping out of bounds on the floor exercise.

Dismount The last skill in a gymnastics routine. For most events the method used to get off the event apparatus.

Elite International Elite, the highest level of gymnastics.

Execution The performance of a routine. Form, style, and technique used to complete the skills constitute the level of execution of an exercise. Bent knees, poor toe point and an arched or loose held body position are all examples of poor execution.

Giant Performed on bars, a swing in which the body is fully extended and moving through a 360-degree rotation around the bar.

Full-In A full-twisting double back tuck, with the twist happening in the first backflip. It can be done in a tucked, piked, or layout position and is used in both men's and women's gymnastics.

Free Hip Circle Performed on the uneven bars or high bar, the body circles around the bar without the body touching the bar. There are both front hip circles and back hip circles.

Handspring Springing off the hands by putting the weight on the arms and using a strong push from the shoulders. Can be done either forward or backward, and is usually a connecting movement. This skill can be performed on floor, vault, and beam.

Heel Drive A termed used by coaches to inform the gymnasts they want them to drive their heels harder up and over on the front side of a handspring vault or front handspring on floor. Stronger heel drives create more rotation and potential for block and power.

Hecht Mount A mount where the gymnast jumps off a spring board while keeping their arms straight, pushes off the low bar, and catches the high bar.

Hop Full A giant to handstand. Once toes are above the bar, a full 360-degree turn in a handstand on the high bar.

Inverted Cross Performed by men on the rings. It is an upside down cross.

Iron Cross A strength move performed by men on the rings. The gymnast holds the rings straight out on either side of their body while holding themselves up. Arms are perpendicular to the body.

Jaeger Performed on bars, a gymnast swings from a front giant and lets go of the bar, completes a front flip and catches the bar again. Jaeger can be done in the straddle, pike, and layout position, and is occasionally performed in a tucked position.

Kip The most commonly used mount for bars, the gymnast glides forward, pulls their feet to the bar, then pushes up to front support, resting their hips on the bar.

L-Grip One hand is in the reverse grip position. This is an awkward grip and difficult to use.

Layout A stretched body position.

Layout Timers A drill that simulates the feel of a skill, or the set for a skill without the risk of completing the skill.

Lines Straight, perfect lines of the body.

Overshoot, also known as Bail A transition from the high bar facing the low bar. The gymnast swings up and over the low bar with a half-turn to catch the low bar ending in a handstand.

Pike The body bent forward at the waist with the legs kept straight; an L position.

Pirouette Used in both gymnastics and dance to refer to a turn around the body's longitudinal axis. It is used to refer to a handstand turning moves on bars.

Rips In gymnastics, a rip occurs when a gymnast works so hard on the bars or rings that they tear off a flap of skin from their hand. The injury is like a blister that breaks open.

Release Leaving the bar to perform a skill before re-grasping it.

Relevé This is a dance term that is often used in gymnastics. In a relevé, the gymnast is standing on toes and has straight legs.

Reverse Grip A swing around the bar back-first with arms rotated inwards and hands facing upwards.

Round-off A turning movement, with a push-off on one leg, while swinging the legs upward in a fast cartwheel motion into a 90-degree turn where legs come together before landing on both feet. The lead-off to a number of skills used to perform on vault, beam, and floor.

Salto Flip or somersault, with the feet coming up over the head and the body rotating around the axis of the waist.

Sequence Two or more skills performed together, creating a different skill or activity.

Shaposhnikva A clear hip circle on the low bar then flying backward to the high bar.

Stalder Starts in handstand with the gymnast moving backward and circling the bar with legs straddled on either side of their arms or inside their arms.

Stick To land and remain standing without requiring a step. A proper stick position is with legs bent, shoulders above hips, arms forward.

Straddle Back An uneven bar transition done from a swing backwards on the high bar over low bar, while catching the low bar in a handstand.

Switch Ring Performed on floor and the balance beam. The gymnast jumps with both feet, lifting their legs into a 180-degree split with the back leg coming up to touch their head.

Tap Swing Performed on bars, an aggressive tap toward the ceiling in a swinging motion. This gives the gymnast the necessary momentum to swing around the bar to perform a giant or to go into a release move.

Toe On Swing around the bar with body piked so much the feet are on the bar.

Tour Jeté A dance leap where the dancer leaps on one foot, makes a full turn in the air, and lands on the other foot.

Tsavdaridou Performed on beam, a round-off back handspring with full twist to swing down.

Tuck The knees and hips are bent and drawn into the chest. The body is folded at the waist.

Twist The gymnast rotates around the body's longitudinal axis, defined by the spine. Performed on all apparatuses.

Yurchenko Round-off entry onto the board, back handspring onto the vaulting table and Salto off the vault table. The gymnast may twist on the way off.

CHAPER 1

I faded in and out of consciousness, my thoughts befuddled and muggy.

I drew in a breath and smelled the pungent scent of chemicals, like a mixture of antiseptic and iron. I tried to move my fingers, but they only jerked. My skin pulsated from the top of my head to the tip of my toes. I felt like I was retaining gallons of water, my body was so swollen and stiff.

I tried to open my eyes, but they were heavy, laden with exhaustion. I took another breath, though it was tighter this time. My brows twitched. I wasn't sure where I was, but I knew I wasn't in my condo.

Alarm was a low vibration under my skin trying to rouse me, but, God, I was so tired. Warmth surrounded me like a cozy blanket, cocooning me in its embrace. Darkness called me back with open arms, and I moved freely toward it. Toward that sublime state where I felt no pain in my body and my heart didn't feel like it was breaking a thousand times over. I felt nothing as I was suspended over the clouds. I wasn't sad anymore.

I only felt one thing—freedom.

"Adrianna, can you hear me?"

A voice I didn't recognize called to me, followed by a beeping sound. My first real thought was that my kidneys had failed, but it was gone just as quick as it came. I was too lethargic to move, to care, to open my eyes.

"Adrianna."

I didn't respond. For a brief moment I wondered if I even could. I nestled deeper under the blanket of serenity, yielding to its pull. All I wanted to do was go back to sleep.

"Adrianna, do you know where you are?"

The question sounded like it came from an isolated location far, far away. I reached for it, but exhaled a heavy, drained breath instead.

"ADRIANNA."

I stirred. The voice was closer this time. My eyelids fluttered as I struggled to open them, curious of the commotion I sensed around me. What was going on? My breathing seemed to grow denser, and that annoying beeping sound was back. It intensified as I fought to wake.

"She may not be ready to wake up just yet," another voice I didn't recognize said. "She suffered internal injuries and a concussion. She needs time to rest."

Someone was holding my hand. I tried to move my fingers to let them know I was okay, but nothing, no response. I waited and tried again. Willed them to move, twitch, anything. I wanted to convey that I was here. I was okay. But again, nothing.

I released a breath through dry lips. My eyelids felt so warm, like when I had a fever—a telltale sign I was sick. I swallowed thickly, my throat burned. Too tired to fight the pull of sleep, I was ready to drift off when a light shined in my eye. The brightness gave me an instant headache and I moaned in pain under my breath.

"Adrianna, follow my voice."

I wasn't sure I wanted to. I was completely immobilized but content. The exhaustion was too much and the warmth was winning. All I wanted was to go back to sleep and stay in this layer of protection and security without a worry in the world.

I released a tired breath and let myself be pulled under again.

Someone was crying. The whimpering was soft and quiet, as if they suffered in anguish and didn't want to be heard.

Something wasn't right.

I squeezed my eyes tight and tried to figure out where I was. I took in the sounds around me, the sterile smell, the hushed voices. But my mind was still too jumbled to sort it out.

My first thought was to not move—something that had been ingrained into my head since the first time I stepped inside a gymnastics facility. If I'd gotten injured, I could make it worse by moving, especially since I couldn't feel anything.

Slowly and carefully, I started with my feet when I heard that incessant beeping again. A groan vibrated in my throat. I managed to curl my toes, not too much because they were stiff. They moved, though, and then I tried to wiggle my fingers again. Finally, they moved too.

A soft sniffle caught my attention, pausing my movements. My forehead creased as I took in the sterile scent again, then it hit me. I was at the doctor's office.

When did I go to the doctor? I didn't have an appointment scheduled.

Inhaling a deep breath, it lodged in my chest from pulling too hard. I noticed my breathing was different, like I'd been hit by a truck. I was breathing heavier and I expelled every ounce of air like it was my job. My nostrils flared. There was a cool draft of air around my nose. My arm was dead weight as I reached up and blindly felt around my face. A plastic tube was attached to my skin leading to my nose. I was on oxygen. I froze.

A tremor rocked through me. My dry eyes opened, and I squinted, trying to take in my surroundings. I briefly glanced down my body then lifted my gaze to look around the room. Everything was blurry, but I got the gist of it.

There were tubes attached to me that were connected to machines I didn't know how to read. I heard the whimpering again and turned to see a woman sitting with her head tilted toward the floor. She was alone and crying. My heart dropped, and that stupid beeping sound accelerated. Then it all came roaring back.

Kova.

The pregnancy.

Dad.

The fight.

Blood… So much blood.

I wasn't at the doctor's office, I was in the hospital.

The last thing I remembered was flying across the room. I'd landed on the coffee table and had taken everything with me when I fell to the floor. Then my world had turned black.

My brows creased. I vaguely remembered shattered glass. Had I been cut?

A memory of lying in a pool of blood flashed into my mind. A loud gasp parted my lips. Panic surged through me at a hundred miles a minute. Blood. Was the blood from getting scuffed up in the altercation between Dad and Kova?

Or was it from the baby?

I glanced around, disoriented. My head was a little hazy and my vision still blurry, but I finally recognized the woman sitting in the corner.

"Sophia?" I said, trying to sit up.

Tears filled my eyes as bile rose to my throat. My eyes widened in alarm. I felt like I was electrocuted. I looked down to find my right arm in a sling. What the hell happened to me?

Another memory filled my head. Dad had twisted my arm in anger. Was it broken?

A sharp pain sliced through my chest and I covered my mouth with my free hand. Sophia moved into action like she knew what was going to happen next. She jumped up from the chair and grabbed a trash can, holding it for me just in time.

After a few more embarrassing rounds of retching, Sophia took the can from me and walked toward the bathroom. She returned with a plastic cup of water.

"Thank you," I said as she handed it to me. Shit. My throat was raw.

Our gazes met. Her green eyes were bloodshot as they beheld mine. The look in them was both relieved and terrified to see me. I wasn't sure what she knew, or how much she knew, but she seemed so sad, and that upset me.

I averted my gaze and looked down. There was an IV inserted and taped down to the top of my free hand. The inside of my elbow was stressed with shades of blue from injections I didn't recall having.

From the corner of my eye, I saw Sophia take a step.

"Wait," I choked out and she stopped. I had a feeling she was going to get my dad. I wasn't ready for him.

"What's wrong?"

I shook my head, the pain making it unbearable to speak. My arm wasn't in a cast, so it must not be broken. But I prayed my dad hadn't fractured it either.

"How did I get here?" I asked, my throat still scratchy. Maybe I should've asked *when* I had gotten here.

I took a small sip of water and handed her back the cup. The last thing I wanted to do was throw up again.

Sophia placed it on the tray at the foot of the bed. Her brows furrowed. "You don't remember?"

I blinked. "I just remember Dad…" I hesitated, and her lips flattened as she gave me an empathetic look.

"Your father fighting with Konstantin?"

My teeth dug into my bottom lip. I glanced away, nodding subtly. "How long have I been here?"

"Two days."

My brows shot up and I looked back at her. "Two days?" I repeated. "How?"

Sophia took a small step toward me. She fidgeted with her fingers. The chipped paint on her nails caught my attention. I could tell she was being cautious. Worry prickled my arms. The more the anxiety grew inside me waiting for her answer, the faster the machine behind me beeped.

I'd been asleep for two days. Two whole days.

"I think I should go get your father for you, then you guys can talk."

"Wait. Why are you here?"

She tensed and I instantly felt guilty for my choice of words. I didn't mean to blurt it out and make her feel bad, but I didn't understand what was going on either.

Where was Kova?

"I'm sorry. I didn't mean it like that," I said. "I'm just confused. That's all."

"I can imagine you are." I looked at her, waiting for an answer. "Your father and I…well…we had seen each other earlier in the day." Her voice was soft. "He called me when you were taken in the ambulance. I met him here and have been here ever since."

My frown deepened.

"You were unconscious and bleeding. Frank didn't know if you'd hit your head or where the blood was coming from. He said he tried to wake you up and when he couldn't…" Her voice trailed off, too stricken with emotion to finish. "Well, you know the rest."

Her words replayed in my head. My chest rose higher and faster. My dad hadn't known where the blood came from?

I glanced down at my arms. White gauze bandages were wrapped in various places, including around my arm in the sling. They probably covered injuries I'd sustained when I crashed into the glass table and took down the décor with me. I remembered hitting my head. I remembered feeling warm blood pool around me. At the time, I'd assumed it was from the shards of glass. Now, I wasn't so sure. There had been too much blood.

Tears blurred my eyes and my jaw quivered. Gripping the starched white bed sheets in my hand, I trembled as I fought with myself. I didn't want to pull the sheet back and see blood. If I did, then that would confirm my worst nightmare and I'd know the truth of what had really caused the bleeding.

Sophia walked over to me and placed her hand over mine. I swallowed hard and looked up at her. I could see the indecision in her eyes and how this was the last thing she wanted for me. I could tell she really wanted to help me but was hesitant as to how. What role in my life would she play?

My breathing grew ragged as I fisted the blanket tighter. I didn't have to ask, and she didn't have to answer. It was a given that if she was here, then Dad had told her everything. My chest strained with raw emotion as the look in my birth mother's eyes confirmed my fear. Her face slowly fell.

Silent tears streamed down my cheeks as the truth set in. Sophia's gaze filled with sympathy. I wanted her to hug me, to tell me everything would be okay. I shouldn't feel a sense of loss, and I shouldn't be upset since this is essentially what I wanted.

But I was, and I did.

I'd had a miscarriage. I'd lost my baby.

I didn't need anyone to confirm it for me. I felt it.

Placing a hand over my stomach, I closed my eyes and tried to feel for something, a signal I was wrong and just being paranoid. There was nothing. Had I felt one before?

I didn't want to answer that.

While I may not have intended to have the baby initially, up until I walked into a clinic and had the procedure done, the choice was not final and still mine to make. Mine to keep a child, mine to say goodbye to when I was ready. Then there was Kova's choice too.

But instead this was what I got—my karma. My punishment for wanting an abortion was not being allowed the opportunity to say goodbye.

CHAPER 2

My baby was gone.

I may not have been ready to be a mother, but that didn't lessen the loss for me.

I guess history does repeat itself. I had a child taken against my will, and so had Sophia.

Warm tears blurred my vision. I rolled my lips between my teeth and bit down, fighting the emotion. Sophia took a seat at the edge of the bed. She was on the verge of tears too. My heart felt so damn empty as my world crumbled around me.

Without thinking, I leaned into Sophia's shoulder and rested my head on her. She turned to look at me. I needed someone who wouldn't judge me, but instead help me carry this burden.

She embraced me with open arms, and I closed my eyes. For a split second, it almost felt like this was what she'd wanted, for me to come to her. Her hand ran down my hair in a maternal fashion and I sniffled, bringing her close to me.

"Your dad really wants to see you, Adrianna," she said, her voice soothing. "He's worried."

I hiccupped and pulled away, suddenly feeling weird. "I'm sorry," I whispered.

"Please don't apologize."

"I'm sure he's—"

The door to my hospital room opened and Dad waltzed in. He found me in a seated position and halted, his brown eyes widening. My heart dropped into the knotted mess in my stomach. Considering how we'd left off, I was expecting the worst.

"Adrianna!" he cried out.

My lips parted as he rushed toward me. I wanted to throw my arm around him and tell him I was sorry and that I never meant to upset him. The last thing I wanted was to drive a wedge between us.

Reaching my bedside, Dad put his arms around my body and hugged me like he never had before. An acute shooting pain like a bullet streaking through fire ricocheted through the length of my suspended arm. I gasped in agony, feeling instantly lightheaded from the vicious ache pulsating through my veins.

Dad pulled away and looked down at me as I clutched my arm in the sling. He visibly paled. "Did I hurt you?"

A whimper escaped my cracked lips. I hugged myself to hold in the pain as he cupped his mouth, his eyes filling with regret.

"What happened to my arm?"

My breathing grew dramatically dense, my chest rising and falling at an amplitude that was borderline heart attack inducing. If I couldn't move my arm, how was I going to do gymnastics? Looking into my dad's guilt-ridden eyes, I softly pleaded, "Tell me, please."

I could compete with kidney disease. I could compete while pregnant. I could compete with an Achilles injury. But I couldn't compete with an arm that felt broken.

"Your elbow is dislocated." Shame colored his cheeks. "You're going to have to wear that sling for a while. In a few days you can begin working on little exercise movements to get you back up and running. The doctor said it could take four to six weeks to heal completely."

Four to six *weeks*? I shrunk back. "I have the biggest competition of my life in ten days. I'll take it easy today and tomorrow, and maybe the day after, but I have to be able to regain movement quicker than that in order to compete."

Dad stared at me like I'd grown two heads. His challenging gaze made me feel defensive. My elbow was dislocated because of him.

"You're going to be in excruciating pain, Adrianna," he said. "It's going to be next to impossible to practice so soon."

"I'm sure it's nothing I haven't experienced already."

"You're going to be on bed rest regardless," he countered.

"Trust me, I can handle it. If I'm brushing up against death's door with stage four kidney disease, I can handle a dislocated elbow."

Dad's mouth set into a grim line. "Even so, I can't imagine you're going to be able to practice for a couple weeks, at the very earliest."

My heart sank into my gut. A couple of weeks before I could begin practicing again. No. Not possible. I didn't have fourteen days to spare. I would take a few days off, then start with a day or two of light stretches. Give myself five days total, then after that, all bets were off the table and I was going full steam ahead.

"Other than your elbow, how are you feeling?" Dad tried to change the subject.

How was I feeling? Angry. Hurt. Lost. Empty and totally gutted. I wanted to riot in the streets and then cry alone in my bed. There was a lot to talk about and I wasn't sure where to start or how he was going to react.

"I've been better."

Dad studied me, his eyes flickering through an array of emotions from love to disgust. This was as uncomfortable for him as it was for me.

"I think we need to talk about the extent of your injuries right now and the type of recovery you will be going through."

I swallowed hard. "Okay."

Dad pulled up a chair to my bedside. I glanced toward Sophia standing by herself near the window watching me.

"Aside from the dislocation, and some small cuts and scratches, you have a concussion." He clenched his eyes shut. "Adrianna, you will take the proper time to recover from that, which is around three to five days, and no sooner." Dad lowered his voice to a warning. "I will not take no for an answer."

"I'll take a few days for my head and elbow. I can't really miss more practice time than that."

I knew not to be too defiant when I was still very much in the wrong. I could work through pain, but a concussion was serious. I didn't have a death wish, despite everything.

Dad remained quiet for a long minute, which did nothing to ease the anxiety mounting in my veins. He exhaled a weary huff and leveled a stare at me that made my stomach twist.

"Adrianna," he said, and I knew what was coming next. "You'll be coming home with me."

I didn't respond.

"You'll get the proper rest and recovery there where I can watch over you."

I had no leg to stand on to defend my actions, but this wasn't just any situation where I was caught red-handed and had to pay the price. There were too many separate lives involved that could be ruined if one wrong thing was said. This was entirely different, and I was sure none of us knew what to do next.

"No, Dad, I'm not." His eyes rounded. I spoke low and slow, making sure I made my case clear despite my shaky voice. "I have the Olympic Trials in less than two weeks. I'm not going home. I'm staying here and I'm preparing for it. I didn't come this far just to walk away because of a little elbow issue."

He looked right through me. "I've already made arrangements to have the condo cleaned out and your car returned home. Once you're discharged, you're coming back to Savannah with me. End of discussion."

My throat was tight, I could barely swallow. I'd resent him for the rest of my life if he made me go home now and forfeit a once-in-a-lifetime chance at the Olympic Games. My pulse was pounding so hard it was going to explode. I didn't have much to barter with, so I had to play my cards right. I couldn't let him take this away from me.

"Do you want me to have a personal bodyguard to watche over me and takes me to and from practice? Live with me? I'll do that. Anything you want. But I *am* staying here and I *am* going to practice." When he didn't say anything and continued to stare right through me, my jaw began to wobble in despair. "Can you please at least consider the consequences after this competition? We're talking about the Olympic Trials, Dad. Let that sink in for a second."

I began to feel frantic. There was an underlying tremble in the pads of my fingers. Didn't he understand how huge this was? That every single practice mattered?

Dad's silence simmered like little bubbles of tension in the air. He let out an unnerving huff. His eyes hardened, even though I saw the empathy in them.

"Imagine my shock when that— When he—" Dad's body trembled. "When I learned you were pregnant. Then we get here and the doctor tells me you had a miscarriage and would need to have a procedure done." My cheeks flushed and I looked down in embarrassment. "Do you know they had to use some type of vacuum device to get the baby out?" He paused until I looked back up at him. "And you want to tell me what to do? That's not how it works in the real world, Adrianna."

I squeezed my eyes shut, letting the warm tears fall down my cheeks. My lips were firmly sealed together as I silently cried to myself.

A fucking *vacuum*? The visual made me nauseous. I hadn't known that was how an abortion was done. Not that it mattered now. I knew in my heart I'd had a miscarriage before he'd confirmed it. But hearing it from my father first and in such a way broke me. There was no compassion. Just stone-cold truth that seeped into my bones like black tar and embedded into me forever.

"Was it *his*?"

No. Why'd he have to ask that?

I squeezed my eyes tighter, tears filling them once again. The machine spiked behind me.

"Was the baby Konstantin's?"

I pressed my lips together and my cheeks flushed. There was no way I would answer that question honestly.

"I'm going to ask you one last time." Dad's voice was controlled and quiet, alarming. "Was the baby his?"

Holding my breath, I exhaled through my nose and shook my head.

CHAPER 3

I knew how it looked.

And I knew what Dad was thinking.

I denied the obvious truth, which made me look foolish.

A white lie never wears well.

From the corner of my eye, I saw Dad turn his head to look away. I probably disgusted him and that made me so sad inside, but I couldn't tell him it was Kova's baby. I never would.

"You're barely eighteen and you had a miscarriage."

"It wasn't his," I said low, my voice cracking. I'd rather him think I'd been with more than one person than to know the baby was Kova's.

Dad sniffled and I popped my head up to glance in his direction. Lines pulled tight around his eyes and his jaw subtly shook. I felt his despair a mile away, and a small breath hitched in my throat. My gaze shifted to Sophia, who was watching him with sadness. My shoulders sagged. It broke my heart to see how many people I'd hurt with my lies.

I looked away, unable to handle any more added heartache.

"So that's the reason you'll be coming back. You were heavily sedated and had a minor procedure on top of your concussion. You have to let your body rest."

"You can't force me to go home."

Dad whipped his head toward me. His eyes were as large as I was sure mine were. A mocking laugh bellowed from his chest. "Yeah? And how will you live? What money and connections do you have, Adrianna? Everything you have is because of me."

I sat up a little taller, humiliation burning under my skin. "I'll take the prize money and forfeit competing in college. I can support myself on that." I paused, hoping to seal the threat. "It's not like I'll be in any condition to compete anyway, not when I'm close to kidney failure as it is. I'll even sell my car if I have to."

Dad squinted his eyes and crossed his arms in front of his chest. "Fifty thousand dollars isn't enough to pay for dialysis and a transplant surgery. Now you sold your car but you can't get to treatment. What are you going to do?"

I ground my molars together, fighting back the angry tears. I didn't have anything else to barter with and he knew that.

Dad's gaze didn't waver. How could he hold my illness over my head? I was scared it would consume me before I had the chance to live and he knew that. It hurt almost as much as the vacuum comment he made.

"Don't test me, Adrianna. I have years of experience under my belt that you can't compete against."

"I'll figure it out."

He shook his head. "Not this time. How do you expect to practice when you're bleeding?" he jeered.

My emotions closed in on me. The way Dad was staring made me angrier by the second. Anything I said, he had an answer for. That wasn't fair. None of it was fair. I averted my gaze just as a fresh tear rolled over my cheek onto my arm. I looked down and my brows drew together. My emotions were on severe overload.

With my teeth, I pulled the tape back from the top of my free hand. I needed fresh air. I needed to get out of here.

"Stop it, Adrianna," Dad yelled and placed a hand over mine. I tried to shove him away. I was on the verge of losing it. My chest ached with sharp pains. Everything in me hurt.

"Leave me alone," I cried.

"The sooner you accept it, the better you'll be," he said, wrestling my hand away. I didn't have much strength and he knew that.

"I'm not accepting it," I responded. "I'm staying here. I'm an adult. I'm not missing that competition!"

"That just proves how naive you are. You can't support yourself, and you won't be able to support yourself to get to the competition." He paused and his eyes turned nearly black. "You have nothing."

God, I wanted to scream at the top of my lungs. This was never supposed to happen. None of this was supposed to happen. A concussion, dislocated elbow, and a fucking miscarriage.

"Do you have any idea how sick I am over the fact that he took advantage of you? Someone I trusted. He raped you."

"No, he didn't," I spat back. "He didn't touch me."

Dad glared at me, his eyes wild. "I almost beat him to death." He gritted the words out through his teeth. "He has your fucking initial cut into his chest, Adrianna." His hot breath blew over my face. "Care to explain that?"

"He didn't touch me," I said, as my breathing turned erratic. I was losing control. "He didn't touch me."

Oh, God. I was going to have a panic attack. Christ on a fucking stick.

"You'll never convince me otherwise. You might as well just tell me the truth, starting from the beginning."

For a split second I debated with myself whether to tell him or not. Of course, I wanted to get it off my chest to clear the air, but I knew deep down it wouldn't help the situation. If anything, it would make things worse.

"He didn't rape me," I whispered. "Kova didn't touch me." *Not in the way you think,* I wanted to add.

Dad stood straight. He peered down at me. "You sound like a typical victim," he said full of disgust.

My eyes closed in defeat and I dropped my head back onto the pillow. I shook my head, my voice soft. "I know the difference. I'm not a victim."

I looked up at the blinding white ceiling wondering where I'd go from here. Fat tears streamed down my temples. I laid in a freezing hospital room with my heart breaking.

Dad's hand enveloped mine. Something inside me broke, and suddenly, I wasn't an eighteen-year-old girl anymore with dreams and aspirations. I was just a child who wanted her dad.

Without giving it another thought, I sat up and leaned into Dad's side. I tried to be strong and push for what I wanted, but my heart could only hold so much. My forehead fell into the crest of his neck, and his arm came up to gently wrap around my shoulders. Dad hugged me despite everything. I sobbed softly as he rubbed my back.

I was so embarrassed, sad, filled with sorrow and longing. The anguish was too much to bear

"I'm sorry, Dad."

"I am too, sweetie." God, I hated the remorse in his voice. "What happened that night… Adrianna—"

"I know you never meant to hurt me, Dad."

He held me a few minutes longer as I cried on his shoulder. I pulled back and he reached for the tissue box on the tray.

"When I entered the condo and took in the scene… Saw what little you were wearing, the state of undress Konstantin was in, and that fucking A on his chest… I've never been filled with so much rage. I lost it."

I took a tissue and dabbed at my puffy eyes.

"Then you lost consciousness. You were bleeding and we couldn't wake you up. Konstantin yelled that you were pregnant. I grabbed my phone and dialed nine-one-one." Dad was quiet for a moment before he spoke again. "How long did you know you were pregnant?"

I swallowed. "I'd only just found out a few days before. When we got home from the competition, actually. I was so sick."

"Did you plan to tell me?" I shook my head and stared at the stark white bedsheet. I couldn't look at him. Dad released a strangled breath that eviscerated me. "You were going to have an abortion," he stated.

"Yes," I whispered.

"Adrianna, I wish you would've come to me. I could've protected you better."

I licked my lips. "There was no reason to come to you. I didn't need protection because he didn't touch me like you think he did."

"I thought you were dying." He paused. "I thought you died." He corrected himself, and I finally looked at him. "Do you have any idea what that does to a parent? You wouldn't wake up. You were as white as a ghost. There was blood everywhere."

Fresh tears fell from my eyes. "I'm sorry, Dad." I didn't know what else to say.

"When the paramedics arrived, we gave them a quick rundown of your health and the medications you were on before they carried you out on a stretcher. I thought that was the last time I was going to see you. The police asked questions…" His voice trailed off.

"Police?"

"Yes." He held my gaze. "That's what happens when you call nine-one-one. The police show up too. I told them Konstantin and I had gotten into a scuffle and you tried to break it up but were hurt in the process." He paused briefly before adding, "Then they took him away."

I stared at him in confusion. I'd been wanting to know where he was, but I was afraid to ask.

"I don't understand. What do you mean they took him away? Why?"

"He's been arrested."

Arrested.

I froze, unblinking.

I couldn't move.

I only focused on one thing.

Kova had been arrested.

CHAPER 4

I held my stomach and bent over.

My heart pounded at the thought of Kova behind bars. The stupid machine behind me beeped erratically.

"Arrested for what?"

Dad was unfazed. "Rape."

"What?" My lips parted in shock. "But you just said you told the police you guys got into a scuffle. I don't understand."

"When the police asked what the fight was about, I told them he'd raped you and got you pregnant. Konstantin didn't fight it. He went with the police willingly."

Oh, God. I was going to be so sick.

The one thing I'd been concerned about was Kova getting arrested and the gymnastics committee finding out about us. If this got back to them... I shuddered. I didn't want to think about it.

My gaze flickered around the room aimlessly, overwhelmed by a million and one thoughts. I needed my phone, but I wasn't sure where it was. I needed Avery to do some digging for me, like arrest records. She was the only person I could trust.

"Kova didn't do anything." My voice was barely above a whisper. "You need to tell the police that, please."

He didn't bother to grace me with a response. My jaw trembled from holding back the scream trying to erupt from my throat like fireworks.

"Is he still in jail?"

Please say no.

"It's where he belongs."

"But he didn't rape me!" I gritted the words out through my teeth. There went my restraint.

I couldn't handle anymore. My pulse was skyrocketing; my shattered heart was on the verge of bursting from my chest any second. I was moments away from having a stroke, and the stupid machine wouldn't shut the fuck up. This wasn't Kova's fault, and I wasn't a victim of anything. Nothing. For a fleeting moment I thought about airing the truth and telling Dad it was all me.

Screw it!

I leaned forward with fire in my veins ready to burn down the world.

"It was me. I went after him. I chased him. He didn't do anything I didn't want. It's not Kova's fault." Dad hardened to stone. He looked like he was going to explode. "None of this is his fault. I purposely enticed him until he couldn't say no, and I didn't give a shit that he had a girlfriend. That's the real truth."

"That's still no excuse. He's a grown man. He knew better."

"Just like you knew better with Sophia? Like Xavier knew better with Avery?"

"Adrianna Francesca!"

I bowed my head and closed my eyes. I didn't mean to drag others into it my mess.

"He had no *right!* He never should've let it happen. He was your coach, a teacher. He was a friend whom I trusted to watch over you. Not to manipulate you and get you pregnant." Dad stood and pushed the chair back. He glared down at me and pointed a shaking finger. "You'll never see him again."

My jaw dropped to my stomach. "I love him!" I shouted as I shook like a leaf on a tree blowing in the wind. I couldn't control it. "I love him," I repeated. "I love him, and there's nothing you can do about it. You'll never be able to change that."

Dad reared back. Repulsion filled his face. "Puppy love, Adrianna. You're just a child. You don't know the difference."

I rubbed at the ache across my chest, unsure whether the shooting pain was from the tension in the room or my kidney disease. It bothered me that he could disregard my feelings so easily when I'd told him the truth.

"It's not rape when I willingly gave myself to him. I'm eighteen. I'm telling you the truth," I implored him to believe me.

"I don't want to hear another word," he responded with a wave of his hand. "It's making me sick to my stomach to hear this. Say another word and I'll kill him for touching you before any inmate can get their hands on him. You know prisoners hate child abusers. Don't test me, Adrianna."

I was taken aback by his harsh tone. I was losing everything that mattered most to me. "It's not his fault." I wiped the tears away and said, "You can't stop me from seeing him. He's the reason I'm not living on antidepressants and rocking in a corner. He was there for me when my world fell to shit—"

"He took advantage of your most vulnerable state!"

Frantically, I shook my head in disagreement. "He didn't. I know you want to think that, but he didn't." I licked my dry lips. "When is he getting out of jail?"

"Not anytime soon, if I can help it."

All the air seized from my lungs until they constricted in desperation. How was this happening? Chills rolled down my arms as I stared at him wide-eyed in complete disbelief. Dad was really going through with this.

The door to my room opened. A nurse strode in and headed straight for the machine behind me. Dad and I glared at each other. He looked like he was going to ring my neck, but I wasn't backing down.

"All right, what do we have here?" the nurse asked.

"Nothing." I glanced away from Dad's lethal gaze and dried my eyes. "I'm fine, just talking to my dad."

She eyed me for a minute. "I'll be back in a few to change your IV. In the meantime, you need to rest." She turned her attention to my dad. He got the hint and stormed out of the room without a word, and the nurse followed him out.

I stared at the door as it closed behind them. A shadow shifted in the corner by the window, startling me. Sophia. I groaned in mortification.

"I forgot you were there. I'm sorry," I said. "I didn't mean to bring up your past."

"Don't apologize. It's an awful feeling when you think the world is against you." One corner of her mouth drooped down. I nodded in agreement. "He's just angry, you know." Her voice shook as she spoke. "He feels like he failed you as a father."

I closed my eyes and released a sigh. What a fucking mess. Quietly, I said, "He didn't."

"No parent will ever see it that way," Sophia said delicately. I looked up at her and she took a few steps toward me. "May I sit?" she asked, pointing to the chair Dad was just in.

"Of course."

"He just needs a little time to cool off. Frank worries about you all the time. His only daughter is extremely ill. Then he found out his friend was having an affair with her that resulted in a pregnancy. It's a lot to handle. When you didn't wake up yesterday and the hours kept passing, his coloring started to fade and he couldn't stop shaking. He was sweating profusely. I was worried he was going to faint that I had a nurse check his vitals. His blood pressure was high enough that they wanted to admit him for observation, but he refused."

My stomach tightened and shame colored my cheeks. I felt terrible he'd suffered like that. I'd always known if Dad had ever found out about Kova and me it would be comparable to at least a category three hurricane.

I didn't expect it to be catastrophic. That was the last thing on earth I wanted, and it made me feel like garbage because of it.

"Kova didn't rape me. He didn't take advantage of me. It wasn't like that."

Sophia gave me a knowing look. "Has your dad ever told you how he and I met?"

I shook my head. "No, but I haven't had much time to ask him about it. I know you were his assistant."

"We had a whirlwind type romance where the feelings lasted longer than the affair was supposed to. Frank was this big, powerful man, and I was a young girl with big city dreams in her eyes. I'd just graduated from high school early and had plans to attend the community college while working. Frank was this sought after real estate mogul at the time, and he'd happened to be looking for a part-time assistant." She gave me a helpless shrug. "We'd hit it off by accident, really. He would show me properties he was considering investing in, or buildings that were heavily detailed he admired, ones you'd have to have an eye to notice. He showed me the tricks of the trade. It was all very innocent at first.

"I was in awe of what he'd accomplished at his age, and I started talking to him about my future and asking questions and looking for advice. We'd connected and didn't even know it. The more we worked together, the more impossible it was to stop the growing feelings between us." She hesitated. "Frank was married, so I never hit on him, but I couldn't deny what I felt for him either. I wish I could pinpoint when and how, but things just clicked into place one day and we never looked back. We knew this was it." Sophia paused, quiet for a moment as she reflected. "There's a lot of things we would've done differently if we could go back. What I went through alone at the time was one of the most challenging moments in my life. No one understood me. I was labeled a homewrecker. But what people didn't know was that Frank and Joy were already on the verge of a divorce before I came along."

This was news to me. I felt bad for Sophia. She seemed like she had a gentle soul with good intent, yet she lived with so many regrets she still dealt with on a daily basis.

"He was going to leave her until Joy came barreling along and played the perfect part." She sounded remorseful and a little envious. "I don't blame her, though, and I don't hate her. She fought dirty and won."

I, on the other hand, had a fair amount of animosity toward Joy. She didn't just fight dirty, she kicked a dead horse and anyone else who stood in her way.

"I wouldn't say she won if you're here," I said.

A momentary twinkle lit Sophia's eyes, then she said, "Joy never loses."

CHAPER 5

frowned and pulled the thin blanket to my chin. I was so cold and the chills were making their way down my arms.

How could Joy win if they were divorcing? I had so many questions I wanted to ask.

"Why are you telling me this?"

Sophia expelled a heavy breath. It made me wonder if this was harder for her to talk about than she let on.

"My parents were dedicated churchgoers and lived by the Bible. Well, my mom still is, my father passed away years ago. They had reacted in a similar fashion as Frank did with you, except they kicked me out. I was suddenly homeless and pregnant. I only had my sister, and she was sick.

"I know I'm not in any position to tell you what to do or to give you advice, but I want you to know that if you ever need someone to talk to, or a place to run, I'll always be here for you. I remember being your age like it was yesterday. The heart wants what it wants."

She looked at me and I felt like I was staring at myself. It was no wonder Joy hated the sight of me. I must've reminded her of Sophia every day of her life.

"What I'm trying to say is I want you to know you don't have to go through this alone. What happened in my life caused me to fall into a horrible depression I thought I was never going to climb out of. I don't want to see that happen to you. It's a lonely place to be and can destroy you mentally."

I nodded and relaxed into the bed, trying to get comfortable. Over the course of the last year, I'd been in and out of depression and I hadn't even known it until Kova pulled me completely from the black hole I'd been stuck in. He had forced me to face the facts. At the time I hated him for it, but it had also made me love him more because it was what I'd needed in order to move on. That was the day I'd carved a letter into his chest.

Dad would never see it through my eyes no matter how strong I made my case. What hurt the most was knowing nothing I did or said would ever change how he saw the situation. He automatically took me for a victim.

Tears rested on my eyelids. I sniffled. "I don't know what to do. Kova didn't hurt me. He didn't force me to do anything. I swear he didn't take advantage. I know I probably sound young and dumb, but it's the truth and Dad will never, ever believe me. Now Kova is in jail for rape, and Dad wants me to go home with him to rot."

My nostrils flared. I tried to hold back the emotional baggage that came with the territory, but I couldn't. My heart had been ripped from my chest and my future destroyed in a matter of minutes. I wished I had never answered the door.

"Maybe you should take some extra time off for *you*," Sophia suggested lightly. My brows rose. "I think you have a lot going on and need some time to yourself. I did some soul searching after I lost everyone I loved. Frank, you, my sister…even my parents. I'd been kicked out and I was so alone and scared. I hardly had any self-esteem. I wish someone had told me if I focused on myself right then I'd live a happier, longer, fuller life." She paused. "I was too upset to realize that. The most important thing in your life right now is you. That's the only way you're going to get better."

Sophia looked toward the door and back at me, then leaned closer. "I probably shouldn't tell you this"—she dragged her teeth over her bottom lip—"but I think it would help rest your mind." My brows furrowed at her hesitation. "Konstantin isn't in jail for rape. He was arrested for assault."

My jaw plummeted to the floor. "What are you talking about?"

"You have to understand your dad is devastated. People act on emotion first and think later, especially when the situation is dire. Frank only told the police Konstantin attacked him. You're not involved in any of it."

My jaw was still hanging open. I was speechless as a new wave of nausea turned my stomach.

"I don't understand. Why would he let me believe Kova was charged with rape?"

She gave me an apologetic look like she was torn down the middle. "He's your dad, Adrianna. I think if he had it his way, Konstantin would be locked up for the rest of his life." Her eyes roamed my face. "I think rape is easier for him to accept rather than think his daughter willingly slept with someone he trusted…and then got pregnant."

My eyes dropped down to the bed. She was right, and I was sure I'd probably act the same way if I was—

No. I let out a breath. I let that thought go. I couldn't go there.

"I'm going to see if I can get him to think about dropping the charges. I think down the line he'll regret it."

I didn't say anything. I wasn't sure how to respond properly.

"I think he needs to be reminded of how it was for us," she continued. "Then ask himself if he'd want that for you. I'm not saying I agree with your actions, but the situation isn't black-and-white either."

"He's going to say it's not the same thing. He'll never see it like that."

"I can try, right?"

CHAPER 6

D r. Kozol stood before me as he looked over my chart. Dad had called him in as soon as I was admitted.

"I highly recommend bed rest until you leave for your next gymnastics meet. You're burning the fuse at both ends. All you're doing is working against yourself," he said, sounding like my dad.

My eyelids were heavy as I looked up at him. I just wanted to go back to sleep.

"I know," I said. "I'm going to. My arm hurts really bad anyway. There's no way I can even do a cartwheel right now."

His eyes bore into mine and he lifted a brow. "Do not take Motrin for that. If you're in pain, or something is bothering you, I need to know first. Not all medications are safe for your kidneys."

"Okay."

"You're in pretty bad shape right now." He flipped to the next page. "Luckily, your kidneys have leveled out since you were admitted. As for the miscarriage," he continued, and my cheeks heated with embarrassment. "Again, bed rest is an absolute must. If you don't heal properly, you'll develop scar tissue and risk your chances of conceiving in the future. Your body could work against you, causing a flare up on top of that. Anything is possible when your immune system is compromised, as yours is right now."

"She'll get the proper rest she needs, Doctor." Dad reassured him.

Dad made it sound like I was going to be on bed rest for the rest of my life. I'd already decided I couldn't spare more than five days, and even that was pushing it. I was hoping by then my arm wouldn't hurt as much.

"You're cutting it close, young lady," Dr. Kozol warned.

I nodded in agreement. I was playing with fate and I knew it.

Dr. Kozol strolled out of the room and Sophia returned to my bedside, reclaiming the chair next to me. Her fingers fidgeted with the sweater in her lap. I watched her, wondering if me being in a hospital bed brought back memories of her sick sister.

I reached out with my good hand and Sophia took it and gave it a sympathetic squeeze. Her jaw trembled.

I eyed Dad wondering when he was going to tell me the truth about the charges he pressed against Kova. I wouldn't throw Sophia under the bus for telling me, but how long was he going to torture me with his lie?

Dad's cell phone rang. He pulled it from his pocket and looked at the screen.

"It's Xavier. I need to take this," he said, and left the room.

"You're going to listen to the doctor, right?" Sophia asked.

I shifted, trying to get comfortable. "Yes." Maybe I could sleep the pain away during my downtime, then I wouldn't have to think about anything either.

She released a sigh. "Thank God."

"Does me being in this bed remind you of Francesca?"

She nodded, her mouth flat.

"I'm sorry."

"If I could trade places with you, I would," she said, her voice tinged with sadness. Her comment moved me intensely. Joy never would have said anything like that.

"Can you do me a favor and put my hair up for me, please?" I asked. I was hot all of a sudden thinking about Joy and her lack of compassion. Sophia nodded and dug in her purse for a hair tie.

"Francesca had such thick hair like you. I used to wish I had it. She had the prettiest beach waves, while mine was bone straight."

"Thank you." I smiled at her once she was done.

The door to my room opened and Dad strode back in with his phone held out toward me. "Your brother wants to speak to you," he said. I took it as Sophia pulled my hair up into a messy bun.

Bringing the phone to my ear, I said, "Hello?"

"Well, well, well, if it isn't my sister trying to steal the spotlight," Xavier said. It felt good to hear his voice.

"Hey."

"Is it true?"

My smile faded. "Which part?"

"About you being pregnant?" Leave it to Xavier to get right to the point. I didn't answer. "I'll take your silence as a yes."

"I was." I glanced up as Sophia ushered Dad to the other side of the room, giving me a bit of privacy. "I'm not anymore."

"Listen, I know you've gone through a lot these last couple of days. I'm not going to sit here and act like I'm not pissed the fuck off at you and the situation, but I will shut my mouth and save it for when you're able to have that conversation. And, Adrianna, we will be having that conversation."

God, Xavier reminded me so much of Dad in this moment.

"Thank you." I lowered my voice to almost a whisper. "I know I'm in no position to ask for a favor, but I really need something from you."

"Yeah, shoot."

"You have to promise to do it. Say, 'Yes, Adrianna, I promise to do anything you ask,' and then I'll tell you." He repeated after me with a hint of sarcasm that made me feel good inside. "Good," I said. "Now call Avery for me and tell her where I am. I don't want her to worry. I don't have my phone but I'll call her first thing I can, so tell her to be ready for me."

Xavier was quiet for a long drawn out moment. I felt bad asking him to do this considering their history, but I needed him to call her. "Please. I need to talk to her."

He released a deep sigh, which told me him calling her was going to take a lot out of him. "All right, but only because you're my sister and I love you."

I smiled. "Thank you. When was the last time you spoke to her?"

"Oh, months ago. Around the Fourth of July." He was quiet, but I detected the sadness in his tone.

"You're not over her, are you?"

"Avery isn't someone you can easily get over."

I smiled to myself. "Sounds like her. She's hard to forget once she puts her mark on you."

He half chuckled, half huffed. "Tell me about it."

"I better go," I said, my voice small. It was nice talking to him. "I should rest now if I plan to make a huge comeback in just a few days."

"You're crazy, you know that?"

"Yeah, well, what's life without a little madness?"

"A boring fucking life, that's for sure. Stay strong, sis. You got this."

I tried not to tear up. "Thanks, Xavier." We hung up. I sniffled then wiped my nose.

Once Dad and Sophia realized I was off the phone, they stopped talking and walked over to me. I handed his phone back to him.

"Is it okay if I rest for a little while? Alone?"

A shadow crossed Dad's eyes. He shifted on his feet. "Yes, of course. We'll be out here whenever you wake up." He turned to Sophia. "Do you want to go get coffee?" She nodded and they turned toward the door. "I'll just be a shout away," he said right before he stepped out. I thanked him and watched as they exited the room together.

Once the door clicked shut, I waited a few minutes to see if they would return. The silence grew thicker as their footsteps finally retreated. When a fair amount of time passed, I let go and broke down.

I cried for Kova.

I cried for my aching arm and not knowing how the heck I was going to manage when it felt broken.

I cried for the baby I would never meet and the cramps that were eating me alive in its memory.

I cried for all of the hurt I'd caused Dad and for making him feel like he failed as a parent.

And lastly, I cried for my future, for what could've been, but would never be.

CHAPER 7

D ad opened the door to my condo. I held my breath as I slowly stepped inside with Sophia following behind me.

I hadn't been here in three days and I was a little afraid of what I would walk in and see. Would there be broken glass? Blood? Furniture that had been turned over?

I glanced around the space, unprepared for what I saw. My condo looked perfect. It was like World War III hadn't happened here just days ago.

"Your dad and I came by yesterday to clean up for you," Sophia said a little hesitant.

She seemed nervous and I wished she wasn't. That desire to be a mother was evident in her eyes and by the way she spoke to me, but she held back. I had a feeling she was worried about overstepping, but, truthfully, I could use a mother right now.

Glancing over my shoulder, I looked at both of them. Sophia seemed hopeful with the way her large round eyes watched me. Dad, well, he just looked sick and torn.

"It was Sophia's idea," Dad added grimly.

"Thank you," I said, my voice quiet.

All the broken glass was gone. There was a new decorative rug on the floor, but the coffee table was missing. I vaguely remembered hearing the wood splinter when I fell on it and felt a pinch on the back of my arm from the shattered glass.

My pace was small and slow as I walked across the carpet. My stomach had been cramping and any sudden movement seemed to make it worse. I'd had some painful periods in the past, but nothing like this. I wanted to bend over and hold myself, and pray it went away soon.

Instead, I sucked it up.

I walked into my room and came to a halt when I looked at the bed and rumpled sheets. Emotions clogged my throat. The sadness that rocked through me filled me with an immediate heartbreak I wasn't prepared for. My heart actually felt like it was being ripped down the middle.

This was the last place Kova and I had been right after he'd found out about the pregnancy.

I could still feel his strong arms around me, smell his cinnamon and tobacco scent in the air when he told me how he felt about me being pregnant. How he asked me to tell him that I loved him, and I wouldn't. I should have. I wished I had. He was my light when my world had been so dark, and now he was gone before I could really tell him how I felt. He deserved to know, and if we ever got the chance to be alone again, I'd tell him.

Thick tears brimmed my eyes, but I pushed them back. Everything was still so raw. I didn't want to cry in front of Dad because that would open the door for questions he couldn't handle the answers to.

"I don't agree with this," Dad said as he came up behind me. I swallowed thickly before turning around to face him. "In fact, I don't like it at all. I'd rather you come home so I can watch over you closely."

I had thought Dad agreeing to let me return to my condo was a sick joke until we'd pulled into Coral Cove.

Dad placed a hand on my shoulder and I had the strong urge to lean into him. Instead, I bit my lip and drew in a breath through my nose. I was so angry at him for having Kova arrested and letting me think it was for something other than assault. He still hadn't come clean, and he'd said Kova was still in jail. Was that another lie?

"I don't want to ruin your gymnastics career," Dad continued, his voice ragged with guilt. "I don't want to be the one who took that from you." His jaw locked tight. "Your safety is my main priority, and that was jeopardized by someone I put faith and trust in to watch over you."

I waited for him to collect his thoughts. He was never going to believe that I'd played a huge part in mine and Kova's relationship. I had so much I wanted to say but felt I should stay quiet.

"This was an extremely difficult decision to make, and not one I'm entirely sure is a good idea. I don't want to lose you, Adrianna.

You're my only daughter. I just want what's best for you, but this whole thing has sickened me and brought me to a point I can't seem to come back from. I'll never forgive Konstantin for what he did." I opened my mouth to speak but Dad put his hand up to stop me. "Regardless of what happened or how you feel, he knew better." He gave me a pointed look. "You don't love him, Adrianna. You're infatuated with him because he's been to the Olympics and has the connections to get you there. That's all it is. He played on that."

My jaw dropped and my eyes widened.

"Are you suggesting I slept with my coach to move up higher in rank?" My brows creased when he didn't answer me. "That's insane to even fathom, not to mention literally impossible. You can't fake it to make it in sports. You can't sleep your way up the chain, especially in the Olympics. In your world of business and money, yes, but not in mine."

He shook his head, disappointment weighed heavily in his eyes.

"You don't love him," he repeated, and I wondered who he was trying to convince more.

My shoulders dropped. I wanted to argue with him and tell him I did love Kova, but I'd already told him a few times and got nowhere.

"You're going to be watched. Your phone will be monitored. Your truck now has a tracking device. If you so much as even try to contact Konstantin, or go somewhere other than the gym or the doctor's office, I'll know. Your condo was scoured and cleaned, and that pregnancy test you saved was thrown away."

I swallowed hard. I'd forgotten about that.

Dad shook his head, his eyes becoming glossy. "I trusted you." His voice was a broken whisper and it cracked something in my chest. "I put all my cards on you, defending you, insisting you were mature for your age when others said I was irresponsible to allow you to live alone. I'm furious you put yourself in the situation that you did. I raised you better than that. You let me down."

I winced at his blunt words. All I seemed to do was mess up everything for everyone and that truth fed my guilty side.

"Maybe it's my fault for asking him to watch you like I did," he whispered, talking more to himself than to me. "Maybe I brought it on or just made it worse."

Dad was gutted far worse than I understood. I felt like the situation was amplified by ten for him. The way he looked at me crushed me. His eyes were guarded, and there were blue tinted sacks under them.

"Thank you for giving me this last chance," I said.

His eyes bore into mine. "Don't thank me, thank Sophia. The only positive that came from this is I now know what Joy had on you." He was quiet, like he was deep in thought. "It all makes sense, and I know how to handle her now."

"She couldn't have known about the pregnancy, but I guarantee she knew about the affair." I swallowed, then said, "I'd prefer if you didn't talk to anyone about the miscarriage."

"I wasn't planning on it."

His eyes roamed around my room, not really looking for anything, it was more like he was trying to process it all. Dad cleared his throat and I looked away. I couldn't handle seeing the disappointment in his eyes. "Come to the kitchen. Sophia went shopping."

My brows shot up. Sophia was really trying.

Holding my stomach, I followed Dad into the kitchen and found Sophia waiting for us. She bit her lip then shot Dad a nervous glance before looking back at me. "I wasn't sure what you needed or could eat, so we got a few basics for you. I also set up your medications and got you a few feminine products that I placed in your bathroom," she said. I assumed she meant pads and such because of the bleeding. I hadn't even thought of that. I was really thankful she had.

I nodded subtly. "Thank you, Sophia. I really appreciate it."

"Figured you could use some stuff. I didn't think you'd want to drive anywhere."

She was right, I didn't.

Dad turned toward me. "I have to go back to Savannah tonight, but Sophia lives off the highway just two exits from here. She wants to be here, so if you need anything, don't hesitate to reach out to her." He blinked. "It goes without saying you're not to have any contact with Konstantin once I leave. None whatsoever. Do you understand me?" I nodded, my lips flat. How did he expect me to train without my coach? I decided I'd leave it for another night.

Leaning toward me, Dad pressed a kiss to the top of my head and gave me a brief hug. He pulled back and looked into my eyes for a long moment. I wished he'd stop looking at me like I'd failed him beyond repair, like there was no coming back from this.

He exhaled a heavy breath before heading to the door and stepping out, leaving me alone with Sophia. She rounded the kitchen counter and stopped in front of me.

"Anything you need, Adrianna, please just call me." There wasn't an ounce of pity in her eyes. "Even if you just want to vent or cry or have girl questions your dad can't answer. I left my number for you."

I nodded as stupid tears climbed to my eyes again. Joy had never been that authentic with me, like she really wanted to be there and help me at the drop of a hat.

Moving on instinct, I threw my good arm around her and buried my head in her neck. Sophia froze, then her breath hitched as she stepped closer to hug me back. She was only a little taller than me.

"Thank you," I said, my voice breaking.

Sophia nodded her head in response and cried with me.

CHAPER 8

After they'd left, I immediately took a shower and cried my eyes out until the water ran cold.

I couldn't take smelling like a hospital any longer.

I had found my phone in the nightstand and put it on the charger, knowing I would need to call Avery the second I got out. I desperately needed to talk to her.

Not having use of both hands proved to be challenging. My hair had thinned out a lot from the illnesses, but I still had a mop on my head and washing it wasn't easy. Neither was dressing with one hand. I brushed my teeth, then I stood in front of the floor-to-ceiling bathroom mirror and looked at myself. My skin looked ashen, and there wasn't an ounce of life in my green eyes. I looked frail and malnourished. Dehydrated.

I shook my head and stepped out of the bathroom. I climbed into bed and scooted under the covers. The nurse had advised me to take the sling off when I slept. I did a few slow stretches to extend my arm, but I hadn't tried to touch it or move it much before that. The tips of my fingers were numb as I reached, and the ache at the center of my elbow was relentless. It made me nauseous, but I pushed myself to do a few more and deal with it. I didn't want to rely on pain medication if I didn't have to.

Exhaling a heavy breath, I picked up my cell phone and turned it on. All my notifications popped up one after the other. I ignored them.

I pulled up my favorites in contacts and hovered over Avery's number. My thumb trembled as I pressed down.

"Adrianna!"

Jesus. It didn't even ring.

Tears burst out of me and I cried at the sound of her voice. "Ave?"

"I've been waiting for your call!" Avery was frantic. "Are you okay? How are you? What the fuck happened!"

"I'm sorry I couldn't call before," I said in between sobs. "I didn't—"

"It's okay, I don't care about that. I spoke to Xavier and he filled me in. I've been a nervous wreck waiting to hear from you. If I didn't have school tomorrow I'd already be over there."

I rolled my lips between my teeth. "He's in jail."

"No." She gasped.

"Yes. My dad pressed charges."

"What happened? Did he really find you?"

I closed my eyes and pictured his face when he walked into my condo and saw us. I can still feel the shift in the air and his rage.

"Yes. They fought, Ave." I couldn't hide the guilt in my tone. "Well, Kova didn't hit back but I think—"

"Kova would've knocked Frank out cold."

"Yeah, and I think Kova knew that, which is why he didn't fight back. He just blocked everything for the most part."

I told her how Dad was keeping an eye on my phone calls and had a tracker put on my car.

"What's your address again? You need a burner phone. I'm going to have one sent to your condo because this is serious, and when he gets out you need to be able to talk to him so you can get your stories straight."

I hadn't even thought of that. I gave her the info she needed, and she said the phone would be here in two days.

Then I gave Avery a play-by-play of everything, from the news about Katja and the lies she'd told Kova, to how he'd said he was divorcing her, and when we'd spotted Dad and Sophia in that little town. She was shocked that Dad was with Sophia just as much as I was. She asked if they were dating and I told her I didn't know, which was true. I told her how nice and empathetic Sophia had been toward me. I also said how awkward it was too since I wasn't used to it. The worst part was reliving the moment when Dad told me I lost the baby.

"Christ on a stick." Avery was quiet for a few beats. "This is like a soap opera. It's almost too much to believe. Did you really tell your dad everything?"

"I did, including that I love Kova."

"Oh. My. God."

"Yeah," I said, mortified.

"I don't know if I would've gone that far, but at least you cleared the air."

"I went a little further than clearing the air."

"Shit. What did you do?"

"I was dramatic and screamed. Obviously, I wasn't thinking clearly. I do love him, you know that, but I should've left that out. Dad called it puppy love. He insisted I don't love him. Honestly, though, I felt like he was saying that more to himself than to me."

"We'll, ah, just blame your raging pregnancy emotions for going the extra mile. I still can't believe you did that."

"I know, I wish I hadn't." I clenched my eyes shut trying to block out how let down Dad had looked.

She was quiet before she eased her way into the next question. "Did your dad really say they used a vacuum?"

I winced. "Yes."

"That was heartless."

"I don't think he knew what it was called. He just said a procedure was done and the baby was vacuumed out. He was so angry with me, I wouldn't be surprised if he said it on purpose just to be cruel."

"Yeah, but where's his sympathy? Especially since he basically broke your arm. And it's called a D and C. It's not as gruesome as he made it sound. I mean, it is, but it's not. How do you feel otherwise? Have you been bleeding?"

"Nonstop. My shower was all pink and red water. I feel like my insides are falling out."

"That's how I was too. I had severe cramping and had to use a heating blanket. Make sure you don't use tampons or have sex either until you heal properly, not that you'll be in the mood for sex for a really long time."

"The cramping is horrific. I feel like I'm going to throw up. Sophia got me some pads. She picked up all different sizes. Some even look like diapers. I'm not using those. Who wants to sit in blood like that?"

"That's what you say now but they're about to become your best friend at night."

I grimaced. "Really?"

"Oh, yeah. Make sure you put a few towels down on your bed too just in case you bleed through. It's only really heavy the first couple of days, then the cramping will go down and so will the bleeding. If I didn't know any better, I'd say you're trying to copy me. I know I'm amazing and all, but this is just borderline creepy."

"You're terrible." I laughed.

"You know you love me," she said, her voice airy. "Seriously, though, I wish I could be there with you right now."

I glanced down at my white comforter and realized I felt the same way.

I also realized I shouldn't use this blanket until I'd completely recovered.

"I wish you were here too. Who needs high school anyway?" I joked. "My arm is all fucked up and I'm stuck inside for the next few days."

"I can't believe your dad." She blew out a whistle.

"I know he didn't mean to hurt me. His emotions were, like, amplified…" A flashback of the harsh look in his eyes filled my mind. "What am I going to do?" I whispered. "I can't call Kova. I don't know what he's been charged with, or if he's even out. Dad said he was in jail, but he also said he'd been arrested for rape. I don't know what to believe. And what do I tell my teammates when they see me again? Everything is ruined," I said, drawing in a tight breath. "What if I'm not ready in time to go back? What if I can't move my arm and wrist? I'm screwed."

I used the blanket to wipe my tears away. I didn't want to let my mind go there, but there was a good chance I wouldn't be ready. I could hardly flex my fingers. How the hell was I supposed to do gymnastics?

I wouldn't be able to.

I froze.

My throat was closing up, and my body was tightening everywhere. The fingers on my good hand started to tingle. My body lit up like an inferno and I kicked the blanket off.

"Ave—" I gasped, my eyes widening. My heart was beating the shit out of my ribs. "I think I'm having a panic attack."

I felt like my heart was going to explode.

"Aid. Breathe with me. Close your eyes and focus on my voice. Breathe in slowly through your nose." She instructed, and I heard her inhale. "Gently blow out. Let me hear you." I did. "No, you're not blowing out candles. Blow like you're trying to dry your nail polish and not get spit on your nails and ruin them. Do it again with me," Avery said, then gave me the instructions for a new breathing technique she wanted me to copy.

We did a few rounds of these exercises until my body uncoiled and I was crying all over again.

CHAPER 9

I don't know what I would do without you," I said, clutching the phone.

"Yeah, I'm pretty amazing." She was quiet for a moment. "Senior year is a joke. I hardly have to do anything. I wish I could be there with you. Going through something like this is hard, even when you have someone to talk to about it. Sometimes just having someone there makes a difference. Have you considered therapy? I was doing it a few times a week. Now I'm down to one day a week."

My forehead creased. I hadn't known she was talking to someone. "And it helps?"

"At first I hated it because I had to relive every painful memory over and over. I've learned a lot, and it's helping me cope and move on. It wouldn't be a bad thing for you to consider."

I nodded. "I could probably use it after everything that's happened. Then again, it's not like I can tell a therapist about Kova, and he's a large part of this. Wouldn't the doctor need to notify someone?"

Avery mused over my question. "Well, not necessarily since you are an adult now. But then, people talk…" Her voice trailed off. "Scratch that. You can always call me and vent anytime you need to, you know that."

"Don't text me anything about this in case my dad really is checking my messages, not until I get that phone."

"Noted."

"Practice is going to suck."

"What are you going to do when you see Kova?"

"Try not to cry?" I joked sadly. "I don't know. Obviously, nothing because people will be there, but what if my dad really does have someone watching me? The last thing I want is to provoke him into pressing rape charges. Assault is enough."

"He can't press charges for rape."

I frowned. "What are you talking about?"

"We went over this when you first started training there, remember? The age of consent in Georgia is sixteen."

"But I was still a minor. I just turned eighteen. It happened before I was considered legal."

Avery let out a huff. "Doesn't matter," she said, her voice straining. "Sixteen is the age of consent. You could fuck an eighty-year-old the moment you turn sixteen and the law can't say anything. You're legal. That's it. Your dad can't do anything about it. He can press assault charges for himself, but that's about it."

I stared across the room in surprise. Her words sliced me open and woke me up. A thin ribbon of hope blew through me.

"I can't believe I didn't know this," I said, my voice barely above a whisper. It was a startling revelation.

"You did know it, you just forgot. Honestly, bestie, and this is me speaking from the heart, I think the only thing you really need to do is focus on gymnastics. You're down to the wire, so everything else can wait. Don't lose that focus you've carried with you the last ten years of your life." Avery's voice rose in intensity. "It's inspiring. I was looking forward to watching you go all the way so I can say, 'That's my best friend,' when you're doing flips and shit at the Olympics. Plus, I was hoping to find my future husband there too."

I tried to smile, but I just couldn't bring myself to do it.

"It's really hard, Ave," I said. "I'm stuck between a rock and a hard place." I paused as reality stared me in the face. "I have no leverage."

She didn't respond. Shifting onto my side, I winced at the shooting ache in my elbow. I tried to move back to my original position and clenched my eyes shut. I drew in a long breath and counted to five, praying the throbbing would dissipate soon. Even the simplest movement caused a widespread shot of pain to vibrate through my arm. I exhaled, wondering how this was all going to work out.

I glanced at the clock, it was past midnight. My eyes were heavy with fatigue and puffy from crying earlier.

"I would say allow yourself time to grieve, but I think considering what's on your plate right now, that's going to have to wait. It's time to saddle the horse and mount that beast. You got this. Shelve your emotions and feelings, turn on autopilot, and do what you were born to do."

I moved the blanket aside and lifted my shirt. I needed to grieve the miscarriage, but I'd effectively avoided thinking about it since I got home. I eyed my stomach. It didn't look much different, not that it had before. But it was.

I wondered if I'd regret this loss for the rest of my life.

I bit my lip. Avery was right. *So* right. I needed to grab the reins and hold on, I just didn't know if I had the strength to guide the horse with one hand.

"I feel like I don't know how."

"Turn it all off. Don't allow yourself to think about it. You've done it before, you can do it again. You just have to find that moment of clarity and ride with it."

She was right. I'd shut down the outside noise to become successful, but it took an enormous amount of energy from me in return. The thought of doing that again concerned me.

Shutting down had chipped away pieces of who I was as a person that I'd never get back. It had also taught me strength and shaped me into who I was. But doing that was as emotionally draining as it was physical. How much of myself would I lose this time? Would I turn away people I love forever?

Kova had been there to pull me back right before I pushed myself over the edge for good. He had selflessly let me use him to come back from the dark world I'd locked myself in and had lit the way so I could see again.

This time, though, I was on my own.

"It's getting late and you have to be up in a couple of hours for school," I said. "I'll let you go."

"I'm good. I can still hang."

I smiled to myself, grateful for a friend like her "It's okay. I'm going to lie down and hope this pain in my arm doesn't keep me awake."

"Don't forget to wear the diaper."

I groaned under my breath and she laughed. "Talk to you tomorrow. Hey, Avery? Thank you."

"What are besties for? Later, chica."

After we hung up, I did as Avery suggested. I put a few towels down before I climbed into bed. I made sure my alarm wasn't set and added a note in my phone to contact my private tutor to go over my schedule. I was close to finishing high school a couple of months early and only had very minimal left to complete to graduate.

I switched the light off and then pulled the comforter up to my chin and nestled under the covers. I closed my eyes hoping sleep would consume me soon. That way I wouldn't have to think about anything more, or feel the cold tears coat my cheeks.

I WOKE FROM THE FIERY heat of cramps in my belly at 3:00 a.m. This happened the last two nights since I got home.

I'd followed the doctor's orders. I thought doing absolutely nothing for at least forty-eight hours would help me heal faster, but each night it seemed to get worse and worse. Avery had mentioned it was probably because my body had been through a traumatic experience, and while I was physically fine, for the most part anyway, the emotional duress I was under would tighten my body and make everything stiff.

I let out a whimper and turned over onto my side, curling up into a ball. I wrapped my good arm around myself like I had done the last couple nights and clenched my eyes shut while I held myself. There was an ache in my bad arm that never seemed to quell, but it was nothing compared to the cluster of knots in my stomach tightening by the millisecond. The little balls of hell exploded like fireworks gone wrong. They were intense and I couldn't help but focus on them. I held my breath until my lungs throbbed for air.

God, I wished this would all go away already.

After a few minutes of lying still, the cramps weren't as intense. I sat up and reached for my cell phone to pass the time, knowing it'd be a good hour or so until I fell back asleep. I had a bunch of missed texts from Avery.

BFF

You are amazing. Remember that!

BFF

Be confident in your abilities and remember that's what got you where you are now.

BFF

Keep your head up, gorgeous. WE got this <3

BFF

Okay, you need to wake up already.

BFF

I'm gonna send out an Amber Alert if you don't text me back.

BFF

...It's been 84 years.

BFF

Fuck the Amber Alert. I'm just gonna find a new bestie.

I sent Avery a slew of texts. She was dead to the world when she slept, but she'd see them when she woke.

I fell into a routine as the last couple of days at home dragged on. I'd rise to messages from Avery that would either make me cry or laugh, sometimes both at the same time. She would send me texts throughout the day to check on me. I knew what she was doing, and it made me feel so guilty for finding any hint of reprieve because I hadn't done that for her. I got the feeling she was trying to engage with me more than usual because she felt like I was going to break soon. She wanted to be there for me, and the thought alone made me tear up.

I attempted to stretch my arm, my wrist, and elbow, but the ligaments were so tight that I grunted under my breath. I wondered how it would feel if I did a handstand, and if I could handle it. I got on my knees and flattened my palms to the floor. Straightening my elbows, I leaned forward and applied a little weight, and winced as pain shot up my arm.

Screw it.

I retrieved a bottle of Motrin and Tylenol from the bathroom cabinet. I'd alternate between them both. I had given myself two days to get back to my original form. It was time to numb the pain. It was the only way I was going to get through practice today.

I knew to stay away from these types of medications because of my kidney issues. It wasn't that I had a death wish, but desperate times called for desperate measures, and all that jazz.

Other than Avery, Dad checked in regularly. He called in the mornings and at night. We FaceTimed a few times just so he could see me. I felt like I was twelve years old again, but I wasn't going to argue.

The last conversation I'd had with him lasted no more than a handful of minutes, but it had carried enough tension that I couldn't stop thinking about it.

I'd asked him if he'd spoken to my coaches, if anyone knew anything. I hadn't dared mentioned Kova specifically, I didn't want to push it. He'd said he'd spoken to Madeline and told her I had a set back with my Achilles and needed to rest it. He'd informed her I'd dislocated my elbow as well. Before we'd hung up, he warned me again about not engaging with Kova. He had even went as far as threatening to press other fraudulent charges to keep him behind bars.

I was an adult. Dad legally had no say in what I did. I didn't understand why he was doing this.

CHAPER 10

My duffle bag sounded like I had a Costco-size container of Tic Tacs in it with the Tylenol, Motrin, and all my other medications.

I wasn't supposed to use tampons yet, but I couldn't wear a pad during practice. Not with how much I was bleeding. I had tested it out before I left home with a pair of workout shorts and decided it was a no-go. On my way to World Cup, I'd stopped at the pharmacy and bought the biggest tampons I could find. I figured they'd hold more. I just hoped using them wouldn't make the pain in my pelvic area worse or extend the recovery time.

With my bag stowed in my locker, I turned around to leave when Holly appeared in front of me. I jumped, startled. She stood there watching me with inquisitive eyes.

"Adrianna!" she shouted, and threw her arms around my shoulders.

I hugged her back with one arm and forced a smile. She squeezed me hard enough to produce a wince, but I hid it.

"Hey, Holly."

She pulled back and eyed me up and down. "Where have you been? Hayden and I were so worried about you. Hayden said he tried to call you but you didn't answer. Madeline told us you were absent but didn't say why."

"My Achilles was flaring up and I managed to dislocate my elbow." I nodded toward my side where my bad arm hung like a scarecrow. She cupped her mouth and gasped in shock. "It's fine now. It was popped back into place, but it's sore as hell and hurts to do anything, really."

Her worried eyes studied me. "How'd you do that?"

"I went to lunch with my dad, and we were walking back to the car when another car came flying around the corner and almost hit me. Dad yanked me out of the way and dislocated my elbow when he pulled." The story Dad had come up with a couple days ago rolled off my lips.

She gasped again, horrified. I had been just as surprised when Dad came up with that on the fly too.

"But what about the meet? What about…about everything?"

My lips flattened at the rising panic in her voice. "I wish I had an answer. All I can do is push through. What choice do I have?"

Her mouth twisted. "Yeah, you don't really have a choice, do you?" Her gaze traveled to my upper arm and her frown deepened. "What's that bruise from?"

I followed her stare and spotted the black-and-blue I hadn't realized I had. I blinked rapidly and squinted my eyes. I needed to quickly come up with a lie.

I took Dad's story a little further. "When my dad yanked me away, I stumbled over my feet and he pulled harder. My arm twisted and I fell into the back of a nearby car pretty hard." She studied me a bit longer before looking into my eyes again. "We were in a parking garage when it happened." I had no idea why I added that.

"Luckily your arm will only be sore for another day or so, then you'll be good to go. That's how it was for me."

My brows rose to my hairline. Holly confirmed we'd had the same injury. "I was working a new bars routine and added a new skill when I did it, only, I panicked because it was my first time trying it." She gave me a knowing look. "I freaked."

I cringed, hearing the socket pop in my head.

We exited the locker room together. Anticipation filled me as we approached the gym. I wondered how Kova would react when he saw me, if he'd try to talk to me later. I was supposed to receive the cell phone Avery had ordered for me today, so maybe I could call him tonight.

As I stepped onto the blue carpeted spring floor, I felt an energy zip through my feet and realign my center. A sensation came over me and I breathed it in, hoping it would guide me in the right direction. It felt like stars were kissing my skin trying to coax life back into me. I prayed it would give me the strength I needed to get through this.

It felt good to be here.

"Madeline is waving everyone over," Holly said, and I nodded.

There was already a small group of gymnasts sitting crossed-legged in front of her. My gaze took in every corner and square inch of the vast room, searching for the pair of green eyes I loved so much. My excitement started to fade when I scanned over the people again and didn't see them.

Kova wasn't here. My anxiety spiked. If Dad had only pressed assault charges, then why wasn't Kova here? I'd assumed he'd be out of jail by now, unless there was something I didn't know.

My stomach tightened. I exhaled a heavy breath and looked ahead. My gaze stopped on Madeline who eyed us as we joined the group. She observed me closely through narrowed eyes and my breath hitched in my throat. I smiled at her, pretending like it was any other day of practice. I prayed she didn't know the truth.

I shook my fingers out and looked to her right. There was a man standing next to her I'd never seen before. He was stiff as a board. His arms were behind his back, his stance was that of a soldier. If I had to guess, I'd say he was a little older than Kova, and he was built a little rough around the edges. His hair was dark and his eyes were a striking black that led to a sharp, pointed nose. He looked of European descent. I wondered if he was from Russia too.

We sat down and waited while Madeline flipped through her yellow notepad. She had one foot propped on a folding mat and was swaying back and forth.

"We have a full week ahead of us and need to stay on track. Since the Trials are right around the corner, I'll be working with Adrianna closely to prepare her while the rest of the team works with Danilo to prepare for their scheduled meets. He's the new coach Coach Kova recently hired. I'll let him give a brief introduction before we get started."

My brows furrowed. Kova had hired a new coach? When had he done that, and why hadn't he told me?

"My name is Danilo Teglia." The new coach began his introduction, and I was caught off guard by his heavy, stiff accent. "Konstantin has been a friend of mine since we were teenagers, though we did not start out as friends. We were first competitors. Where he represented Russia, I represented Ukraine. I have competed in three Olympic Games and have almost as many gold medals as Konstantin." A smile curved his mouth like he was thinking about something. "We became a challenge to each other at meets, always trying to outplace the other. He was my biggest competitor. I currently own a gym back home that is strictly for elite, but also where the Olympic trainees prepare before the Games. I will be splitting my time between here and the Ukraine."

Holly leaned over and whispered, "What's with the lack of contractions?"

I shot her a fleeting look and tried not to laugh. I shrugged.

Reagan looked at us with a grin. She wiggled her brows. "New eye candy," she said, and turned away.

"I look forward to getting situated here. Konstantin has spoken highly of all his gymnasts. I am excited to see what you are all made of. We have similar training methods, so expect the same from me, if not more."

Madeline gave Danilo a friendly smile, then she looked at all of us. "If you need anything, Danilo and I are here to help. Now, let's get started." Her eyes darted to me. "Adrianna," she said, and waved at me to come to her.

"Where's Kova?" I leaned over, asking Holly. She shrugged her shoulders.

Frowning, I got up and walked to Madeline. Luckily the Motrin was keeping the cramps at bay and they weren't as severe. There was a steady warmth of bloating and pressure, but I could deal with it.

"Hi," I said.

Danilo stood to the side. His hands were propped on his hips and his closeness made my heart skip a beat. He was dressed in a plain white T-shirt and navy-blue basketball shorts.

"Nice to finally put a face to the name. Konstantin speaks very highly of you."

I offered him a nervous smile. I couldn't say the same.

"Kova had you scheduled for a blading session tonight. Dr. Hart will be here to take care of it," Madeline said. I turned to her and nodded. "We'll go over your schedule tonight for the next couple of days as well. How's your elbow?"

Slowly, I stretched my arm out to show her. "Honestly, it hurts. It's really sore, but once I start working out a bit more, I'm sure I won't even feel it."

"Can you move your fingers? Raise your arm above your head?"

I swallowed hard. "I need to stretch first and warm it up really good, then I think I should be okay."

She didn't look thrilled. "I'll have Ethan look at it tonight and see what he can do."

"How did you do that?" Danilo asked, nodding with his squared chin toward my arm.

"My dad was playing hero."

His brows drew in like he didn't believe me. "May I?" he asked, and I nodded.

Danilo got on the floor and instructed me to get down next to him. "Flatten your hand on the floor and spread your fingers out. Slowly apply weight as you try to straighten it."

That's what I'd done this morning and it hurt.

I clenched my eyes from the tightness. Danilo placed his hands on my upper arm and elbow and carefully pressed against it to straighten it out. I grunted under my breath, and he halted and looked at me with his midnight eyes.

"It's fine, keep going."

He dipped his chin once. It wasn't fine.

Danilo applied more pressure, counted to ten and then let up. The muscles and ligaments in my arm screamed in protest. I bit the inside of my lip. He relaxed and then did it again, this time the sharp pain radiated from my wrist to my shoulder. Once he did a few rounds of those, we moved onto another stretch.

"Lie on your stomach and prop up on your elbows. Turn your hands up," he said, and I did. "Take a deep breath, then release."

Placing two fingers on the inside of my wrist, Danilo carefully pressed down until the top of my wrist touched the floor. I tensed and clenched my eyes shut. My arm was straining as he held it for a few seconds before he let up and repeated his actions. Something as simple as this caused a series of hot flashes to tingle through my body.

"Are you okay?"

"Yes," I said through clenched teeth.

"How are you feeling, Adrianna?" Madeline asked.

Sitting on my knees, I moved my arm around in front of me. "It's a little better, still tight, but it should loosen up during practice."

"Let's hope it does because with the time you missed, you don't have a choice right now other than to push through it. Your schedule is pretty intense—there's no room for downtime. You need to block it out and work your hardest."

I nodded in agreement and licked my lips. I was going to have to grin and bear it, and pray to every god that I didn't make it worse.

"Lift your arm above your head," Danilo said. I was still on my knees and raised my arm.

He stood next to me and placed his palm to mine. His fingers wrapped around mine and held on while he very gently pressed down to see if I could handle impact. Danilo held my wrist as he did so.

"Lock your elbow if you can," he said, pushing a little harder.

My stomach twisted in agony. God, I wanted to cry from the excruciating pounding that took my breath away.

How the fuck was I going to do vault? Or swing on bars? Tumble?

"Block it out," he ordered. "Pretend it does not exist."

I nodded furiously, teeth pressing into my lip so hard I tasted blood. Clenching my eyes shut, I held my breath as he angled my arm back to stretch it out. My back arched and he noticed. Danilo used his knee to prevent me from leaning back. The jerk.

"You are going to need physical therapy tonight, warm compresses, and an inflammatory to get you through this. I suggest something like this every morning before practice to warm up the arm and loosen the muscles around the elbow, and then again at the end of the day."

"Great, you can do it for her," Madeline said. "Adrianna, I'll see you at beam while I speak to Danilo."

I stood up, giving my thanks to Coach Danilo, then turned around and made my way to the balance beam. I watched the floor as I walked, listening to the springboard at the front of the vault ricochet and the spring in the uneven bars rebound. A prickly sensation spread across my neck. I reached up to rub it away and glanced around the gym.

I felt like there were eyes all over my body. My brows furrowed. Was Kova here and I just couldn't see him? Maybe Dad really did have someone watching me.

The paranoia festering inside me was starting to eat away at me. I expelled a strained breath and wondered if anyone knew anything.

They couldn't... Right?

I'd been absent from the gym for five days. So had Kova. For someone who was going to the Olympic Trials, that kind of absence was unheard of. The same would be said for Kova, and he still wasn't here. It looked suspicious. People were curious, and for the most part, they weren't stupid. I felt like they were putting two and two together.

Stepping in front of the balance beam, my fingers trembled a little as I placed them on the leather. I grazed my palms on the material as I found my center again. My gaze dropped to my hands. There was an indentation on the edge from when someone slipped and hit their mouth.

An indentation like Kova had left on me.

I mounted the beam. The moment my feet touched the four-inch piece of wood, my mind cleared and I set my focus in place.

I knew what I needed to do and let the rest fade away.

I exhaled everything I was holding on to and visualized my routine. The leather beneath my feet called to me, encouraging me. My heart pounded in my chest and my nerves were back to taunting me. But then I thought about how Kova had once said nerves were good and kept the adrenaline going. Lose the nerves, and you lose the love. His words made sense to me.

Despite the flickering agony in every nerve ending in my body, there was not a chance in hell I was going to let anything, or anyone, take this from me.

I could relax when I was dead.

Warming up with connecting back handspring step outs, I blocked out the pain like Madeline and Danilo said.

That didn't mean I couldn't feel anything.

I was silently screaming on the inside.

CHAPER 11

C ome on, Adrianna." Madeline grumbled. "That was weak going over. You need to excel after you hit the handstand, then you can push it over."

Weak.

That word left a sour taste in my mouth.

I wiped the sweat from my temples as I walked to the end of the track thinking about Madeline's suggestions. I rotated my arms in wide circles to loosen them. I desperately wanted to rub the ache in my elbow, but I didn't want to show it was bothering me. Instead, I chewed the hell out of the inside of my mouth to hide my discomfort.

Madeline had felt it wasn't a good idea to risk practice tumbling on floor with my arm just yet. So, after we broke down my floor routine and conditioned the dance skills for three hours, we moved to the tumble track.

"Your butt is too low and you're going to knock your teeth out if you land like that on the actual floor. Do it again. Stick the landing," she yelled and clapped her hands.

Using the tumble trampoline had been a good idea after practicing all day. Even though I could feel the strain deep in my elbow, I kept going. My fingers started to go numb but I shook it off. I told myself if I could work through an Achilles strain and a kidney infection, then there was no reason why I couldn't work through this too.

"Faster. You need to rotate faster to build power. Do it again. Get that flip moving faster."

I set my eyes on the end of the trampoline and pictured myself doing exactly what she instructed. Inhaling a deep breath, I placed one foot in front of the other and tapped the black netting. I exhaled and looked to my right. I could feel someone watching me.

Black eyes met mine.

Danilo was blatantly staring at me as he worked with Reagan and Holly on bars. My brows twitched. He wasn't observing me with interest, but more in bewilderment.

"While I'm young." Madeline bit out.

My eyes snapped back to hers. I nodded and shifted my feet.

When I glanced over at Danilo one last time, he had his back to me.

Shaking it off, I hurdled into a roundoff, my shoulder tight as I flipped backward two times before rebounding off the trampoline with a grunt. I reached as high as I could to set a twisting double full out. This was a dangerous tumbling pass on the floor because I was twisting toward the ground and could lead to injury faster.

Blocking out the shooting pain in my arm, I rotated as hard and as fast as I could by bringing my fists to my chest. I told myself to keep going, to push and fight for that perfect landing. I could feel the pull of gravity and squeezed every muscle in my body, twisting until I spotted the giant blue mesh matt to open up for my dismount.

Feet together, my toes touched down first on the floor and I raised my arms above my head to set the landing. After an inconsistent day of practice, I stuck it.

"Fabulous," Madeline said, clapping her hands as she praised me. "Let's move on."

Panting, I flopped down on my butt to scoot off the mat. My chest was a little tight but nothing I wasn't used to, I just needed to take smaller breaths.

"Madeline?" I called out.

She walked over to me. "Yes?"

"I was thinking about something you said earlier. Are you going to be training me until we leave?"

Her head tilted to the side. "I am."

"Oh, ah, okay," I stammered from nerves. "I was just wondering where Kova is. I didn't know he'd be gone."

Madeline studied me. My stomach clenched with anxiety, but I didn't show it. I kept a straight face and didn't look away as if I'd asked a completely innocent question. Her eyes shifted back and forth between mine as if to say, "You already know."

Her lips puckered with false pity. "Don't worry about a thing. I spoke with Kova and I've got it covered. He gave me your schedule until we leave. Go ahead and head to bars now," she said, her lips rolled up firmly. She stepped around me and walked away.

I frowned. I guess we were finished with the conversation.

I hid the slight limp as I walked to bars covered in chalk and my hair a mess at the top of my head. For once, I was looking forward to a blading session. It'd been a while, and they always made me feel brand new…once the aftermath wore off.

I reached the uneven bars and Danilo gestured at me with two fingers. I walked over to him and he reached out for my arm. My hand gently rested on his bicep as his large fingers began kneading my aching muscles. I sighed in relief, my eyes closing.

"Feel better?" he asked.

"Yes," I said, a little breathless. It did.

"I could tell you were in pain."

I looked at him and wondered how he'd figured it out when I knew I'd hidden it well. "It feels numb."

His fingers made their way down the inside of my arm, his eyes inspecting my reaction each place his fingers pressed into me. When he reached the crease of my elbow, I tightened up.

"I will not hurt you," he said. His lack of contractions made me think of Kova.

My lips formed a thin line. I swallowed. Danilo laced his fingers with mine, giving them a good squeeze, then he held my wrist with his other hand and rotated it in slow circles. His hand was warm, and what he was doing felt incredible. He got the blood flowing again. It took away some of the tingling in my arm. Almost like it could breathe again.

"Thank you," I said when he removed his hand and let go. Danilo nodded. "It feels so much better."

"All right," Madeline said, tearing my attention from Danilo. I looked into her eyes, searching for something that indicated she knew what really happened with Kova. Anything. But there was nothing there. The tension in my neck loosened marginally. "We want flat hips, a big cast, and a stuck handstand." She was all business. "Beautiful lines would be a plus. Then we'll move on to the release. Think you can do it?"

A full and a half turn release? No, I couldn't do it right now.

"Yes, just spot me."

I HAD NO IDEA HOW the hell I made it through my first day back at practice. All I wanted was to take a hot bath and crash. But I still had a blading session and physical therapy on my arm.

I sat in the cold locker room stuffing my clothes and leftover lunch into my duffle bag while Madeline spoke to Danilo and Dr. Ethan Hart in the hall. I had a few more minutes to spare before I was supposed to meet them in the therapy room. Madeline planned to go over my schedule, down to when we needed to board the plane.

"He was arrested for assault."

I stopped moving. Though Madeline's voice was low, I could still hear her. I wasn't trying to eavesdrop, but the gym had cleared out and their voices easily carried down the hall.

"Tak," Danilo said. It sounded like the word was in the back of his throat.

"Just doesn't seem like Kova to fight someone in a bar," Ethan said. He wasn't convinced. "He doesn't go to bars," he said, sounding even more stumped.

Ethan had a point. Kova wasn't a barhopping kind of guy. I don't think he ever went out to dinner, or really did anything for himself. He either was at World Cup, or at home…or with me. My stomach tightened as I held my breath. His life was devoted to gymnastics and those close to him knew that.

I stood up and tiptoed to the door.

"I'm just letting you know what he told me," Madeline said. "He fought in self-defense, but since no one saw the victim hit him first, he was the only one arrested. Things are up in the air as more charges are possibly pending; that's why he hasn't been released from jail yet. Until then, he asked if we could all come together to help. I think we all can agree Kova isn't the kind of person to ask for help, so when he does, it must be serious."

I clenched my eyes shut.

Kova was still in jail.

CHAPER 12

ick up… Pick up… Pick up.

The first thing I did when I got into my truck was call Avery.
I needed to talk to her.

He's still in jail.

I clenched my eyes shut at the red light feeling so guilty. How was
Kova still in jail? Something wasn't adding up. He should've been
released by now.

Remaining indifferent while I'd been in the therapy room had been
a challenge. I'd wanted to ask questions, but felt that would've been
too suspicious in itself. So, I'd kept my mouth shut while Madeline,
Danilo, and Dr. Hart had engaged in small talk.

I lifted my foot off the brake and pressed down on the gas to
merge into the next lane. My arm felt a little better. I had more
flexibility in my fingers, and they didn't tingle when I flexed them
anymore. Ethan had finished up my session with a full-body, deep-
tissue massage, and it was exactly what I didn't know I needed. My
body was in worse shape than I'd realized. He'd kneaded every knot
and had made sure I wasn't as tense before I left.

While I was there, my mind had run wild with thoughts of Kova
and how he was doing.

"Besties 'R' Us," Avery answered.

"Ave." I parked the truck and sat back.

"Shit. What happened?"

I repeated what I'd heard at the gym.

"Why is Kova still in jail? Shouldn't he have been out by now?"

I feared the worst. With how distraught my dad was over the whole
situation, I wouldn't put anything past him. I had a gut feeling if
Dad could get away with murder, he'd attempt it.

"I don't know why he's still in when the charge was so small,
honestly."

I pulled the keys from the ignition and grabbed my duffle bag.

"I wish there was a way to look this info up," I said as I climbed down from the truck.

I glanced to my left; the sun was dipping behind the rippling water. The salty sweet scent of the ocean calmed me. Memories of when Kova and I lounged on the beach watching the sunset blew into me. I wished I could go and sit there now, replay the moment when he'd said he was already missing me even though I was in his arms.

"You can," Avery said.

"What?"

"You can look it up. There's a specific website you can use to see when he was charged and if he's out."

My brows shot up. "Really? How'd you know that?"

"Because I don't live under a rock, that's how."

The corners of my lips twitched. "Can you do the search for me?" I asked. "I'm just walking into my condo and I need to take my medicine."

"Already on it, powering up my laptop now. How've you been feeling? How was practice today?"

There was a brown box waiting in front of my door. I picked it up and realized it was the phone Avery had ordered. Hope bloomed inside of me. As soon as I was off the phone with her, I'd charge it and call Kova to see for myself if he was out. I stepped inside and shut the door.

"Well, I felt like my arm was hanging by a thread and going to fall off today. The period cramps suck. They're the worst ever, and I had to use tampons today when I'm not supposed to. I plan to soak in the bathtub tonight. Figured it might help. Overall, I'm just peachy."

"Try to use tampons only if you have to. You don't want to risk anything. I don't know what could actually happen, but since you have such shitty luck, I'd say proceed with caution."

I walked into the kitchen and flipped on the light. I immediately went for my medication. "You make a good point." I chuckled and uncapped a bottle

"All right…" she said, her voice trailing off. I put all my pills in a little bowl, then grabbed a water bottle and took a sip. "Oh, dayum. Fish lips gives a good mug shot."

I perked up. "I want to see."

"FaceTime me and I'll show you."

I did, and she flipped the screen so I could see what she saw. I leaned against the kitchen counter.

My heart skipped a beat looking at the picture of Kova from the shoulders up. His green eyes lacked vitality, and he had a purple fat lip. His hair was disheveled, and there was a small cut near his eye. A series of pangs thumped in my chest. I still couldn't believe Dad had him arrested.

I stared at him, feeling his torment crash over me in waves. There was anguish in his gaze, though resigned, like he deserved this.

This was all my fault, and I would fix it. I just hoped he didn't hate me for this.

"What does it say?" I asked, my voice a little shaky.

Avery scrolled. "He was arrested the night you were admitted to the hospital. No bond has been posted…" Her voice trailed off, then picked back up. "It says he hasn't been released."

Chills coated my arms. I stared in confusion. I didn't know what to think.

"Ah, Aid?"

My heart dropped at the dread in her tone.

"He wasn't arrested for assault, he was arrested for *aggravated* assault *and* simple battery."

"What! What does that mean? Is that worse? Why are there two charges? Are you sure?"

"Yeah. That's what it says." Avery sounded like she was in a state of disbelief herself.

"How long do people stay in jail for something like that?"

"No clue. Let me see what I can find." Avery placed the phone in her bra so I could watch while she opened a new tab and typed. "Aggravated assault charges in Georgia…"

She grew quiet. I couldn't see what she was reading no matter how hard I squinted.

"Okay, there's a couple different things… I could be wrong, and don't quote me, but it's a felony. He could face one to twenty years in prison, plus fines and restitution."

"What makes it a felony?" I asked, my voice low.

"Let me see, hang on."

I held on for what felt like an eternity.

"…with intent to murder, rob, or…" Her voice trailed off again. "Or rape someone." She spoke so low I almost missed what she said.

Chills raced down my arms. I moved to a chair and took a seat.

"So your dad did file charges against him," she said more to herself, her voice full of sympathy.

I nodded as if she was sitting in front of me. My mind flickered like a strobe light with thoughts flying to every corner. How had he managed to file rape charges if I was eighteen?

My heart plummeted to my gut. He must've lied. Again. I bet Dad had told the police I was seventeen since I was unconscious and couldn't speak for myself.

This was all sorts of fucked up.

"And simple battery?" I whispered. "What's that?"

I almost didn't want to know the answer.

"It's a misdemeanor," she said a little brighter. "He'd serve up to a year in jail and some small fines, could be elevated to an aggravated nature if…"

Avery stopped speaking and I leaned forward. I wasn't sure how much more my heart could take.

"What is it?" I asked.

"If the victim…" She struggled to get the words out, and cleared her throat. "If the victim was pregnant…"

The silence was deafening.

Neither Avery nor I spoke for a solid minute. This must've been what Dad had meant when he threatened to press other charges against Kova if I didn't keep my distance.

My dad went there. He really, really went there. If Dad couldn't get Kova for rape, he'd get him for something else.

"Want my theory?" Avery offered, breaking the dreary silence.

"Sock it to me."

"My theory is your dad told the police you were seventeen. He'll later say he forgot you just had a birthday because he wasn't thinking clearly. He'll put on a show and they'll buy it. They'll also drop the charges because your relationship was consensual. Plus, you're legal and you'll never press any."

I was momentarily speechless and a bit proud of Avery for coming up with that.

"Not bad. But what about the simple battery? Kova didn't touch me, and Dad already admitted he told the police I got hurt trying to break up their fight," I said, curious to see what she'd say next.

Avery mused over the question. "Daddy doesn't have a leg to stand on. Even if he lied to the police and told them Kova hit you and that's how you got hurt, you can easily set the story straight. The truth is your dad's emotions got in the way and he lost it."

A pulsing throb began in the side of my neck. I needed a moment. I needed air.

I walked across the living room and slid open the sliding glass door. Beach air breezed around me as I stepped onto the balcony. I inhaled and closed my eyes. The ocean was the place I found comfort in many times growing up.

"I'm sorry, bestie," Avery said, her voice soft and apologetic.

I opened my eyes and kept my gaze focused straight ahead on the horizon. The sun had completely disappeared behind the ocean.

I didn't want to face the music that my dad had taken this as far as he had, but the spasm in my heart forced me to wake up. The fact he'd purposely lied about my age to keep Kova and me apart as long as he could topped everything for me.

Dad knew exactly what he was doing. If this did actually go as he hoped, Kova would miss everything we'd worked so hard for.

The Trials…

The Olympics…

A breath rolled off my parted lips.

I was sick to my stomach at the thought of Kova missing it. That's not how it was supposed to be, that wasn't the plan. Kova deserved to be there just as much as I did.

It wasn't fair.

I took a deep breath, my lungs tight as I struggled not to panic. How was I supposed to do this without him?

I shook my head. I couldn't. I needed him. Kova was my everything.

I swallowed thickly. Tears rose to my eyes at the possibility of that being the outcome. It killed me inside.

"Are you sure there are two charges?" I asked, needing confirmation.

"From what I'm reading, if this is his first offense, they'll release him on his own recognizance." She paused. "Is this his first time?"

I shook my head, overwhelmed. "I... I don't know. I assume so, but I guess I really don't know. I'm guessing since he's still there it's not. Unless my dad said something and wants to actually go through with the other charges without speaking to me, but he can't do that. So, the only issue really is my dad's charge. And," I continued, drawing out the word, "I'll say I don't know who hit who."

My body started to overheat. The last thing I wanted to do was call Dad and talk about this, but I realized I had no choice. Not because I wanted to beg him not to press charges, that was a given, but because Kova had to be at the competitions with me. His absence would raise red flags, and without a doubt, it would hinder my performance.

Dad didn't like bad publicity brought to the family name, so I had an idea.

"Ave? I have to go. I need to call my dad."

"Oh, my God. What are you going to say to him?"

"I have an idea; I'll tell you if it works."

"Just remember that regardless if you wanted the dinosaur dong or not, Kova was wrong and that's all your dad is going to ever see. Try not to overreact, but I know that's easier said than done."

It was wrong of me to laugh, but I couldn't help it. "Always trying to find a way to lighten the situation."

She smiled from ear to ear, proud of herself. "I try. Text me when you're done."

"Will do. Thanks, girl."

After we ended our FaceTime session, I went into the bathroom and splashed water on my face. I needed to get my thoughts straight and think about my questions before I called Dad.

Expelling a heavy breath, I decided to sit down first and open the box containing the new cell phone. Maybe the website Avery had used hadn't updated their records and he was actually out. Once the phone was all set up, I immediately tried to call Kova hoping he'd answer.

Please. Please. Please.

"*Allo?*"

I stiffened at the sound of Katja's voice. If she answered his cell, then that could only mean he was in fact still in jail.

"*Allo*?"

I bit my lip.

"Is anyone there?"

"Goddammit!" I yelled after I disconnected the call. "Fuck!" The word came from deep in my chest.

The new phone rang and I nearly dropped it when Kova's phone number flashed across the screen. I held my breath and hit the "fuck you" button. In that moment, I was so grateful Avery had gotten me the burner phone. It rang again, and again. I finally turned it off when the ringing wouldn't stop.

Once I didn't feel so shaky, I reached for my actual cell and dialed Dad's number. I steadied my breathing as my emotions and hormones combated each other. I didn't want to explode on him because that would only work against me. However, with the simmering anger inside me, I couldn't make any promises.

"Hello, Adrianna," he said, answering the phone.

My throat swelled. "Hi, Dad. Do you have a minute to talk?"

"That depends on what you want to talk about."

CHAPER 13

My stomach cramped. Shit. I already had a bad feeling.

"Now, I know you don't want to talk about—"

"Adrianna—"

I sucked in a breath. "Dad, just listen to me, please, for a second," I said quickly.

"How dare you call me and even attempt to talk about this issue. You have some nerve, young lady."

Clutching the phone in my hand, I dropped the niceties and demanded answers from him.

"Kova wasn't at practice today. Why wasn't he there?"

"Of course he wouldn't be there," he responded. "He's in jail where he belongs."

My nostrils flared and I forced myself to breathe calmly. "He has to be here. He's my coach, and I need him." *Steady breathing… Steady… Breathing.* "How long will he be in there? Why do you have to press charges anyway? Why can't you just drop them so he can leave?"

"It's what he deserves for what he did." He ground the words out bitterly. "You have no right to call me and question me on the whereabouts of the lowlife who took advantage of you. Keep this shit up and I will press further charges on that disgusting piece of shit," he shouted.

I was quiet as my anger took ahold of every part of my body from the words he just spit out.

Then I lost it.

"You can't press rape charges because I'm eighteen!" I yelled into the phone and it silenced him. My heartbeat double-timed, I'd never spoken like that to him before. "People are talking. They know he wasn't at a bar fighting a drunk guy. That's not who he is. They know it's just a cover. They know we were both gone during the same time. People are going to put two and two together." I stressed.

"Not my problem. Maybe the world needs to be aware of what kind of man he is."

"I know you lied to the police. If you don't drop the charges, I'll walk into the police station with a photo ID and have them dropped."

I wasn't too comfortable with confrontation, but I was beyond frustrated with the situation and the lies being told. I guess everyone had a breaking point.

Dad didn't respond, and I knew it was because I'd hit a nerve.

"I know what you did. The charges won't stick if I walk in there. Drop them, please. I'm begging you."

I heard an intake of air from the other end of the line. "Adrianna." My name was a warning on his lips. "Do *not* push me or I will withdraw any and all of your assets. You'll have *nothing*. You may have been living on your own, and legal in the eyes of the law, but you can't support yourself or pay for gymnastics. You have no idea the amount of money I've funneled into your gym career, or for you to live like a princess."

"Dad, I know I have no right to ask you." I tried to heed the warning, afraid he would follow through with his threat. "But please think about it. Kova needs to be here. He *has* to be here. The Trials are my last chance at a shot at the Olympics before everything is over." My jaw wobbled. "I need my coach."

"Maybe you should've thought about that before you spread your legs for him."

I flinched, unprepared for his cruelty. "So, this is out of spite? Because you're mad at me?"

He ignored my question. "You have everything you need, including top-notch coaches, to go to the competition. You don't need anything else. You *want* something else, but you're not getting it. If this isn't generous enough of me, then walk away. I'm going to keep you two as far away as possible from each other. I'll do whatever I have to do, just like any father would when a grown man touches his daughter. This is ethically wrong, and not to mention, disgusting. You're too young to understand the ramifications of his revolting actions."

Tears slid over my flushed cheeks. His venomous tone pinched at my skin. I blinked, wondering how he could say such hateful things without an ounce of remorse.

"He's my coach and I need him," I said a little too passionately. "If he doesn't show, people will dig and ask questions, wondering why the former Olympian isn't with his gymnast at the Olympic Games. Is that what you want? Because then the truth will not only ruin everything I've worked so hard for, but it'll expose you too. You won't be able to hide it."

"Fake crying isn't going to get you anywhere, and neither will your idle threats."

I clenched my hand into a fist. "I'm not threatening you. People are going to figure out why he's nowhere to be found. They're nosy, and with a few simple searches, the pieces will fall together. People will discover the fight took place in one of your buildings. Then they'll dig further and find I live here because it's already been registered with several meets. The wheels will start turning. Assumptions and lies will be spread about all of us." I paused. "All it takes is a quick internet search, and *boom*."

Dad stayed quiet. If it wasn't for the sound of the ice from his drink sloshing around in his glass, I would have thought he hung up. His continued silence made me seriously edgy. I took a deep breath and broke down, adding one final thing.

"I'll just say this and then I won't bring it up again. In a few months, all of this will be over and behind us." I reminded him softly, my voice cracking. "I'll have to walk away from gymnastics and never look back. You have no idea what that realization does to me. Gymnastics is what makes me feel alive and happy, because even though I tell everyone I'm okay, I'm really not. I haven't been for a while now unless I'm practicing. In a couple of months, the only thing I'll have to look forward to are endless doctor appointments and a brew of pills and tests. Please," I begged, "let me just have this one thing."

A quiet gush of emotion escaped my lips. I couldn't wipe away the tears fast enough. My lips were trembling and swollen. I drew in a lungful of air and hoped he saw I was bearing my soul to him.

I hadn't lied, but I did get a bit more dramatic than I probably needed to. Though, I didn't feel bad this time. Everything I said was spoken from my raw heart and needed to be said.

"I know I've lost your trust. I know you don't believe a thing I say, but please consider dropping the charges so Kova can come back. Don't make me walk into a police station and do it. Kova has to finish this with me. Not as anything other than my coach, I swear. If you never believe anything I say again, just believe that. I need him by my side to get me through it. He is the only one who can help me."

"I'm sorry, Adrianna, but this time I can't give you what you want." Dad hung up.

I sat there in a daze. Dad hadn't shown an ounce of compassion even though I brought up his lies. I opened myself up and proved I didn't have any ulterior motives. It got me nowhere. I wished he could see it was more than just childish lust, and that Kova and I actually worked well together when it came to the sport. Kova understood my fears and turned them into positives. He saw me as a person and helped me overcome my internal battles while standing by my side. I needed him now more than ever. Two people like us didn't find each other by accident. Kova was my other half. No one in this world could ever replace even an ounce of him.

I let my phone slide to the couch. Tears leaked down my cheeks and dripped on to my arm. I used my shirt to wipe them away only for fresh ones to bloom right after. I had a horrible feeling I was never going to see Kova again, at least not any time soon.

A sob burst from my lips like a dam breaking free. I cried, and cried, and cried, letting it all out in the loneliness of my condo.

I cried for what Kova was going through.

I cried for our unborn child that was taken away from us with no choice.

I cried for Dad and what I was putting him through.

I wished I could reverse time for a split second so I could rectify this. So many "if only" moments went through my mind.

If only Kova had been wearing a shirt.

If only I hadn't answered the door.

If only I hadn't fallen in love with my coach.

If only…

I yawned. I was so, so tired.

Grabbing the closest throw pillow, I hugged it to my chest and leaned down to curl up on my side. My heart was raw for the taking and I missed Kova so much. I longed to feel his arms around me and tell me it was going to be okay. My emotions were inflicting such destruction on me that I was physically sick from them.

I didn't know how I was going to recover from this—the miscarriage and arrest—or if I ever would. I needed the comfort of someone, anyone with empathy, but I wanted it only from Kova.

My stomach warmed with cramps and a new wave of lightheadedness took over. I curled up tighter, holding myself as I cried alone for the loss of so much more than just my heart.

My eyes fluttered closed as I began to doze off, sinking into a deep, dark hole. I moved my hand to my stomach and held myself where the life we'd created used to be. That was the last thing we had together, and it was gone now…just like he was.

CHAPER 14

I feel like I haven't seen you in years," Hayden said as he sidled up to me. Practice was over and I just stepped out of the locker room.

He wrapped an arm around my shoulder and tugged me to him, giving me a friendly little kiss on the top of my head. I leaned into him, soaking him up with half a smile. I didn't have it in me to fake it today.

Bittersweet dreams had kept me suspended ever since the conversation with my dad. Night after night, my mind had played the worst-case scenario. I'd dreamed I'd never see Kova again. I'd dreamed he regretted meeting me and our time together. I'd dreamt I wouldn't be called to stand as a gymnast for the United States women's gymnastics team.

There was nothing more or less I could do. Walking away wasn't an option, losing wasn't either. I'd have to compete without my rock so I could achieve my dream, even if it took every last breath from my body.

I would succeed.

If Kova couldn't do this with me, then I'd have to do it for him.

"It's been a minute," I said, giving Hayden an apologetic look. "Things are just a little hectic right now, you know. I barely have time to sleep." He knew how hard I'd been working in the gym and where my focus was.

"Tell me about it." He paused. "Do you think it's strange Kova hasn't been here?" Hayden eyed me, and I stood up a little straighter.

"Don't look at me. I don't know where he is. Maybe he has something personal going on with his wife."

"He was gone the same week you were, and now he's missing the Trials."

I nodded, keeping my gaze forward. "I do think it's odd, and I wonder why he hired a new coach. But I'm in the dark. Speaking of the new coach, how do you like training with him?"

Danilo was a good excuse to switch topics. I knew exactly where Hayden was headed with that conversation, and I wasn't in the mood to hear or see his disappointment.

"He's going to be a hard ass, probably more so than Kova. I'm kind of glad I'm leaving for college soon." He laughed lightly. "Nah, he's good. Seems angry all the time though."

I laughed. "Like Kova."

"No wonder they're friends," Hayden said. "I can't believe you're leaving for Trials tomorrow. I'm going to be watching and rooting for you, you know."

A sad smile formed on my lips. Tomorrow I'd be on a plane headed to California for a two-day competition that ended with the Olympic team selections on the final night. The upcoming meet would be the most taxing one in several ways but also a learning experience too.

"It's surreal, isn't it? This is what so many of us dream about, and I'm actually doing it," I said. "Sometimes I feel like I don't deserve it."

"Only the stubborn survives."

I shrugged one shoulder. "I guess."

"How are you feeling otherwise?" he asked, gesturing to my arm. My fingers were a tad swollen and my arm wavered between light tingles and itching numbness.

Shaking my head, I grimaced. "Honestly, it hurts so bad that I just want to cut it off." I joked, and he laughed. "The last five days have tested me in every way possible. I'm kind of nervous about this weekend."

"I think you're going to surprise yourself and shock the gym world. You may be older than most of the girls, but they don't have the same passion. It's clear watching you compete. Your dedication shows. I'm placing bets on you. You're sturdy out there, someone they can rely on."

I gave him a friendly bump with my shoulder. "Thanks. How much am I worth?"

He laughed and I found a real smile tugging on my lips.

"Make sure you take a moment to yourself this weekend and realize how far you've come. Soak it up. Think about what you had to do to get where you are, because you may not think you deserve it, but you do. This could be your only time at the Olympic Trials. Enjoy it while you can."

"You're going to make a great father one day, Hayden."

Hayden let out a loud chuckle as Holly stepped out of the locker room. She was wearing a pair of khaki shorts and a crimson shirt with a white A on it and the words "Roll Tide." She finally heard back from Alabama. While she hadn't received a scholarship like she'd hoped for, Holly had been picked to be on their gymnastics team.

Hayden was headed to Michigan State, and Reagan had been accepted to the University of Louisiana on a partial scholarship.

"What's so funny?" Holly asked as she joined us in the hall.

"Hayden was giving me fatherly advice. Very inspiring."

She sighed like she was relieved his advice wasn't for her. What he said was thoughtful, and I actually planned to do exactly what he suggested. Hayden didn't know this would be my only chance at the Olympics, but he was right. I needed to take in the moment because it would all be over before I could blink.

That was going to be my new motto: it's all going to be over soon.

"Better you than me," Holly said, taking me away from my depressing thoughts.

"Someone has to watch out for you," he said to his sister. She rolled her eyes.

"I can't wait to go to college."

"Why? It's not like I can't text or call you," he said.

"You're so annoying. You're going to make an annoying husband one day."

Hayden looked at me with faux shock written on his face. "See what I have to deal with?"

"Go away, Hayden. Let me talk to Adrianna."

"Don't leave before I say goodbye to you," Hayden said. I nodded, and he headed into the locker room.

Holly waited until her brother was gone before turning to me. "I wish we could've had more time together before you had to leave. When you get back, I'll be gone."

I pursed my lips together and pouted. "Me too. Time always feels like it's moving slow but it's actually flying by. Maybe we can visit each other during the summer."

She frowned. "Where will you be?"

Inhaling a deep breath, I exhaled and my shoulders fell. "I haven't decided yet."

"Have you reached out to any schools?"

"Yeah, I actually had some inquiries, but I haven't had much time to look into them with so much going on. Maybe I can next week. Unfortunately, I'll be postponing the college experience. I need to take a year off to get my health in order."

"How have you been doing?"

I beamed at her. "I have a donor."

Holly's eyes lit up and she pulled me in for a bear hug. The last time we'd spoken about my kidney issues, I hadn't found one.

"Best news ever! I've been worried sick about you and was thinking about getting tested."

My lips parted at her generosity. Tears tried to rise to the surface but I pushed them down and mouthed "thank you" to her.

"Avery is a match, actually," I said after a few seconds.

Her eyes widened. "That's kinda cool."

"Yeah, she's excited about it while I'm terrified. So much could go wrong, you know? What if my body rejects it? Then we're both out of a kidney. I'd feel bad for the rest of my life."

She grimaced. "I think that thought is normal for anyone in your position. So, you've been talking about it more, then?"

I shook my head. "No, actually, I haven't. No one here knows anything except for Kova and you."

"Speaking of…"

I averted my gaze. Like brother, like sister. "You haven't told Hayden anything, have you?"

She shook her head, her eyes large. "Not a thing. I swear."

"I didn't think so, but he asked me about Kova too. I know you're leaving soon and will have a new life, but please don't ever tell anyone, okay?"

Holly looked me directly in the eyes. Her brows furrowed in offense.

"I'd never do that. Is everything okay, though?"

I looked away again and swallowed. "Everything is fine," I lied. "Normal, nothing new." I glanced over my shoulders and around us to see if anyone was within listening distance. "It's good," I said, keeping my voice low. "We're both just focused on gymnastics and keeping our distance. It's better that way right now."

Holly was studying me closely. I made sure to wipe my face clear of any hint of emotion as I spoke. I didn't want her to put things together in her head about me and Kova and our absences.

"I'm always here if you want to talk about anything." It was all she said, and I was so thankful. "You can call me anytime. I'll always pick up your call."

I laughed. "I'm going to hold you to that. Don't forget about me when you kill it in the collegiate world."

Holly opened her mouth to respond, but Reagan spoke before her as she walked toward us.

"For someone who is hopping on a plane to head to the freaking Olympic Trials, you don't look so happy."

"Always a pleasure, Reagan," I said. "I am happy."

Her eyes glowed with sincerity and her lips twitched from the smile she was trying to fight. She was going to remain that mean girl she loved to be until the very end. I was okay with that. Reagan wasn't being callous, she was just being her snobby self.

"Hey, girls." Madeline rounded the corner. "How about one final picture of the elites before they leave us to move onto the next chaper of their lives?" Her voice cracked a little even though she was beaming from ear to ear like a proud parent.

We all turned toward her as she pulled her cell phone from her pocket. Hayden rejoined the group just in time. Standing side by side with Holly, Reagan, and Hayden, we looped our arms around each other and pulled in close like we were the best of friends. Because in a sense we were. There was this softness in my heart for them that surprised me. I joined their little family late in the game, and while there were some heated arguments along the way like every family has, we'd all gotten extremely close.

Plastering on smiles, we said "cheese" and Madeline snapped a few pictures. Hayden made a joke and Holly told him to be quiet.

Reagan leaned in closer and whispered in my ear, "Good luck, Red." She winked at me. "I mean that."

LATER THAT NIGHT AFTER I'D packed my suitcase and taken my medication, Madeline texted the group of us a picture from earlier. Holly and Hayden were playfully mocking each other like typical siblings, and I was looking at Reagan with heartfelt tears in my eyes while she gave me the realest, kindest smile she could.

If a picture was worth a thousand words, I'd say this one was roughly worth seven hundred and fifty thousand of them.

I immediately saved it to my phone.

I couldn't wait to see where the future would take them.

CHAPER 15

My heart was heavy as we checked in at the airport.

It was five in the morning, and our plane was set to depart in just under two hours. Dad had told me he was traveling the entire way to the meet and back with me, and had made sure we were both on the same flight. It wasn't enough that I'd be flying with Madeline, he'd insisted he be there too.

I was hoping I could get a little shut eye on the flight to California. Last night I hadn't slept more than two hours, give or take. I couldn't get comfortable because of the little aches pinching under my skin. Motrin was a joke. I'd considered taking one of the stronger prescribed pills I had left over from when I had the kidney infection. I didn't, though. I disliked the drugged up feeling.

My arm ached, and the cramps were worse at night, but I had the notion a lot of what I was feeling was because I was missing someone. The bone-deep heartache was taking a toll on me physically. It was killing me that he wasn't going to be by my side.

Once we cleared security, Dad and Sophia wanted coffee.

"Can we get you a cup?" Sophia asked.

I nodded my head. "Yes, thank you."

I never said no to coffee.

"Any food?"

"I'm good. Thanks."

"If you want to go sit, you can," she said and pointed toward the gate.

I walked to the somewhat empty waiting area and sat down in an open row of chairs and placed my carry-on at my feet. Dressed in a World Cup sweat suit, I pulled my hood over my head and folded my arms together so I could use them as a pillow to rest my head on.

I closed my eyes and tried not to think of how Kova should be here by my side. My entire being was missing him something fierce. It was like a sickness I couldn't shake—lovesick was real. I was already craving the inspirational words he liked to give me before competitions. I wouldn't get them or see the look in his eyes when he told me to be strong.

I clenched my eyes shut, pushing the emotion back. It wasn't fair, and if I had even the slightest feeling I could sway Dad, I would. But I knew there was nothing I could do at this point. Not after what he'd said to me. He'd made his decision clear and that was it. Plus, it was too late anyway.

Curling up into a ball, I tucked my knees under me and covered my face with my hood to block out the light. I was prone to migraines these days, and the blinding light inside the terminal didn't help the pounding on the side of my skull. I drew in a lungful of air and my back tingled with awareness. I shifted in my seat and it happened again, this time stronger. My brows furrowed. It felt like a warning. My arms prickled, and my nose twitched from the faint scent of something familiar.

I felt a presence wash over me, but I hadn't heard any footsteps approach. Maybe I was more tired than I thought. I was in an airport with hundreds of people and my mind was playing with my emotions. I was too delicate when it came to him and his absence. It was the harsh truth, and after this weekend, I was going to try and stop mourning him so much. I didn't have the strength to let go right now. I needed to put all my focus into the sport. It was what Kova would've wanted.

Something in the air shifted and caused the rate of my pulse to increase. I flushed, and warmth pushed through my veins. Electricity danced around me like it was mocking me.

My cheeks bloomed with heat. I was hyperaware of someone watching me.

I held my breath.

The warmth in my chest made my heart speed up with anticipation.

I prayed this wasn't a cruel trick that my subconscious was playing on me.

I took a deep breath, then another, and another.

I knew before I opened my eyes...he was here.

I was terrified. I was scared of what I'd see, or what I wouldn't actually see.

Inhale, exhale.

Every fiber in my body said Kova was here.

Would he be angry with me? Would he resent me and never want to talk to me again after all this was over?

No, he wouldn't. He loved me. He'd told me he did countless times. Love didn't make people feel hate.

My heart was fluttering harder than ever as I slowly opened my eyes…and I stilled.

The first thing I saw was his hand hanging between his spread legs. I blinked to see if it was real. He was moving, pushing his palm toward the floor to signal me. He did it twice, silently telling me to stay. There was a small black duffle bag near his booted feet.

My heart catapulted into my throat. I popped right up and pushed my hood back as my frantic eyes took in his sorrowful ones. My lips parted in disbelief.

Konstantin Kournakova was at the airport.

"Kova," I whispered under my breath. My hands grabbed the armrests. I wanted to jump from my seat and run to him, but I knew better.

"Stay, Ria." He issued the command quietly.

My brows furrowed as I stared at him. I watched him closely, afraid he was going to disappear. His eyes lifted toward something over my shoulder.

My stomach tightened. Kova was eyeing Dad. My fingers tightened around the armrest and I gripped it to steady myself.

There were dark scalloped circles under his guarded eyes as he watched my dad closely.

A vicious ache slashed through my chest. My heart was burning for him.

"Keep your eyes on me," he said. I nodded subtly, my heart hammering against my ribs.

"You're here?" I said quietly.

Tears blurred my vision and my jaw quivered. I didn't want to get caught showing any kind of emotion toward Kova and ruin this, even though I felt like I was breaking inside. That would be like putting us on a platter and handing it to Dad along with a carving knife. I needed to pull myself together.

Anxiousness flickered in my stomach. My nerves were making me edgy again.

I drank him in from head to toe; the demanding need to know what he was thinking and feeling rushed through my blood. He was wearing dark distressed jeans, and I tried to think of a time when I'd seen him in them. All I could remember ever seeing him wear were dress pants or gym shorts. The black military style boots were loosely laced, and the hem of his jeans were haphazardly tucked into them.

My gaze made its way up his body and stopped on his knuckles. They were scraped and bruised, cut with deep red stitching over the creases. It reminded me of when I fell off my bike and skinned my knees. I frowned, wondering if that happened with Dad or while he was in jail.

"Are you okay?" I asked, keeping my voice low.

Enigmatic green eyes bore into mine. There was no half exposing anything in his gaze. He let go and aimed straight at me.

"I am now. And you?"

His eyes dropped to my mouth.

"I'm fine." It was an automatic answer these days, but he knew the real meaning behind the word. "How are you here?" I whispered.

My gaze lowered. His black cable knit sweater looked cozy. I wanted to curl up and burrow myself into him. I needed to feel his arms around me. He seemed so calm and relaxed on the outside, and it made me second-guess what he felt for me on the inside. If he held me, I'd be able to tell.

My eyes traveled back up to his. Kova didn't bother answering me. He didn't need to. His expression told me everything I needed to know. He held my gaze with a depth that wrapped around my entire being. He was asking me to hang on another second, yet to the outside world he remained aloof.

Then he dropped the shroud, and I knew him.

I felt him.

I saw him.

He was anything but cool inside. He was emotionally distraught. He was raw, ribs ripped wide open, bleeding love and despair.

Air expelled from my lungs.

Kova's gaze dropped to my stomach. My nostrils flared and I covered myself, looking away. I felt protective of what was no longer there, protective of my initial choice, but more so protective of my emotions because I didn't actually get a choice in the end. Neither did he. My biggest worry was that I was going to be blamed for the miscarriage. I didn't want to be blamed.

From the corner of my eye, I could see Dad and Sophia walking over to us. I stilled, panicking at the thought of how this would turn out. Did my dad even know he was here?

I turned my attention back to Kova to see if he'd noticed, but he hadn't. The light remaining in his eyes dimmed lower, his gaze staying where my hands were on my stomach. He wasn't angry at me like I'd worried he would be.

He was dying inside, like I was.

I swallowed hard, wishing it wasn't like this, fearing this would change us forever.

I heard their muffled voices before they came into full view.

Dad's eyes were fixated on Kova, glaring at him with hostility. I stiffened. Judging by how tense Dad's shoulders were, I could tell he was irritated, but I also knew he wouldn't make a scene in public. I sat up straighter, my heart beating a little faster. Different scenarios flashed through my mind wondering how this would go as Dad sat down stiffly next to me. Sophia reached over to hand me the coffee cup, then she quietly took a seat next to Dad.

Kova didn't move his head, but he lifted his gaze and nailed Dad with it.

"Konstantin."

My eyes widened.

Kova continued to eye him.

"Don't forget what we spoke about and the reason why you're here. Unless it's regarding gymnastics, there will be zero communication between the two of you. You're here solely for her benefit in the sport, and *nothing* more. Do you both understand?"

I held my breath, waiting. Kova didn't reply, and that only skyrocketed the friction between all of us.

I nodded subtly and worried my bottom lip. Kova's eyes softened with guilt as he turned my way. A flash of regret shadowed his eyes before he turned cold. My chest deflated on a hushed breath. Kova grabbed his duffle bag and stood.

My heart stopped.

Gripping the armrests again, I watched him walk a few chairs down. He flung his bag to the floor then dropped into an empty seat. With one leg bent and the other extended, he slouched back and folded his hands behind his head and looked up at the ceiling.

This was hell on earth for us.

Not seeing Kova for nearly two weeks affected me in ways I couldn't explain. Missing him left a profound ache in me that worsened with every second that passed. I thought about him every day. With him sitting so close, I wanted desperately to run to him and never let go.

God, I hoped he felt the same way.

I stared at him, not caring if Dad or Sophia were watching me. Our love was real, but something in my gut pulled on the knots tighter the longer I watched him. He didn't look my way. I stared at him, willing him to look at me. We'd have to choose between being in love and simply breathing. I knew it in my heart we would. We wouldn't get both.

Kova always said timing was everything. He failed to mention our timing would never, ever be right. I looked away. Love and breathing went hand in hand for us. He exhaled and I inhaled. That would never change for us.

I loved my dad. I never wanted to hurt him. But if loving Kova meant I was stabbing Dad in the back, then I'd take the knife and have Dad face a mirror to watch me do it. This weekend was an important one, and I wasn't going to hold back just because he was here and watching like a hawk.

I was elite gymnast Adrianna Rossi, and he was gymnastics coach Konstantin Kournakova. We were going to do our thing. Together.

I allowed a small smile to bare my heart.

"UNDERSTAND THAT I'M AGAINST THIS," Dad said, leaning over his shoulder to me. "Him being here doesn't change anything. Do you understand me? You'll still be watched, and you will be coming home after this meet."

We were sitting in first class while Kova and Madeline were in coach. She almost missed the flight but luckily made it just in time before the doors closed.

We hadn't talked about Kova showing up. Of course, it was on the tip of my tongue to ask every question that popped into my head the moment we took our seats. By the grace of God, I stayed quiet. Dad obviously knew Kova was coming, otherwise his reception would've been entirely different. So, I patiently waited.

It wasn't until I'd fallen asleep and woken before our expected arrival, did Dad finally decide to speak to me.

"I've thought a lot about the things you said to me the other night. It stuck with me," he said, angling his body toward mine. He held a glass of whiskey in one hand. Sometimes he was nicer when he drank alcohol. "I've spoken to Sophia about it too. I'm sure she's ready to sew my mouth shut." I smiled at him, though it was small. "She reminded me that girls' emotions are heavier and deeper than boys', that your heart beats differently when you're…in love." He stopped and glared out the window, then looked back at me. "Adrianna, do not mistake him being here for anything other than him coaching you at a gymnastics meet. *Nothing* more. Sophia is not encouraging you to be around Kova, but she is a huge reason why he's here. I can't say that I don't agree, but I don't like it."

All I could do was nod my head furiously. Dad was finally telling me all the things I'd stressed about in my head.

"I'm not okay with this," he continued, "and I never will be, so don't forget that. I'd rather *he* not be here or within a thousand-mile radius of you, but I also don't want to be the one to ruin this opportunity for you by changing up your usual schedule. I thought having any coach with you wouldn't change a thing, but after speaking with Madeline too, she made it clear it's not the same."

I wondered when he spoke to Madeline and what they spoke about. Did she call him to say I wasn't giving my all this week? She couldn't have said I slacked, but I was a little slower…and I was withdrawn and feeling really far away mentally. Being my normal self required too much from me at the moment. I was suffering inside, and I didn't have the energy to fake it, so I didn't. I just kept to myself and tried to turn off everything else. I needed to stow my energy wisely. I had more than an injury and an illness trying to pull me down. I wondered if that was what she told him and why he had a change of heart.

"Does she know about the lupus and kidney disease? And…and what happened?"

I waited with a tight breath.

"No. She just updated me on how your arm was doing, among other things."

I exhaled. "Thank you."

Dad took a sip of his drink, finishing the contents, then signaled to the flight attendant for a refill. "Adrianna… That night, with your arm…"

Instinctively, I hugged my sore arm closer to my side.

He regarded me with grief in his eyes, then turned his gaze forward. "It makes me sick to think of the real damage I could've caused. I hate myself for it. I could've broken your arm." He dipped his chin and angled his head toward mine. "What you said about having to walk away from all of this for good struck a chord with me." Dad paused. "You've worked hard, you deserve this. What you're about to accomplish with your health in the state that it is, is monumental." His eyes softened with pride. "Despite the things I've said to you lately, and what's happened, I want to see you smiling out there, doing what you love to do. We only get one life, Adrianna. I don't want to lose you."

Tears threatened to spill as I took in my father. There were prominent lines around the corners of his mouth, and dark circles hung beneath his eyes. He'd turned so haggard looking from this nightmare. My illness, my relationship with Kova, everything, it had all thrown a curveball his way.

I leaned into Dad, wrapping my free arm around him. He reciprocated the hug. Sometimes less was more, and in this moment, I felt that.

"Thank you, Dad."

CHAPER 16

Yawning, I stepped from the car in my World Cup sweat suit and laid the duffle bag strap across my chest. It was day one of competition and I started it with a low-grade fever, stiff joints, and a lot of shit on my mind. I had a hotel room to myself, which Dad hadn't been happy about. Thankfully, Madeline had reminded him of the rules. Gymnasts weren't allowed to communicate with family or friends the night before. It helped to prevent outside noise from messing with our heads before the meet.

I stepped over the threshold into the main arena. Cool air enveloped me, invigorating each fiber in my body. My eyes were everywhere, trying to take in the room all at once. The place was gigantic and easily housed thirty thousand people. There were massive rectangular banners hanging across the second floor in the middle of the room from the previous years. I blinked in disbelief, not quite grasping I was at the Olympic Trials. So many great hopefuls were in this room. I was among the best of the best in the entire country. I inhaled a deep breath and drew the trace of chalk into my lungs. I held it and smiled to myself. My love for the sport was finally overcoming the shitstorm in my head and taking over.

Following Madeline, I maneuvered through a maze of leotards and slicked back ponytails to look for Kova. I wouldn't deny the fact that seeing him spurred a trail of excitement through me. I'd hoped to see him, or at least talk to him last night, but Dad had quickly doused that with his threat to stick a piece of tape on my door to know if I'd snuck out.

"This is such an exciting day for you. Kova mentioned changing the dismount on one of your routines because of the recent rule change."

I nodded… Then I spotted Kova before he saw me.

His head was bent as he scribbled something onto a yellow legal pad. His wide stance and beautifully carved shoulders combined with his commanding aura capitulated my heart into my throat. He was in the zone and I loved that. It did strange things to my heart. Would the sight of him ever get old? Or would it increase over time?

"Adrianna's here. I'll see you in a few, Kova. I'm off to get an updated schedule of events," Madeline said, then sprinted off in the other direction.

I drank him in, not worried in the least that someone would see the way my love for him shone. His hand slowed, and he stilled. I chewed on my lip waiting as a veil of familiarity brought me home.

He lifted his eyes, and I caught the faintest curl at the corners of his lips.

"*Malysh.*"

WARM-UPS HAD BEEN TOUGH, BOTH physically and mentally. By sheer determination and stubbornness, and a strong bout of tunnel vision, I got through them. Anytime my hips had swiveled a little more than necessary to one side, shooting pain would spear my pelvis, robbing me of breath. And the pressure and pounding my elbow had taken with every tumbling pass or vault felt like someone had taken a hammer to it. The pain had been nauseating. But I'd grinded my teeth and kept going.

Now, as the competition was in full swing, I watched all the young gymnasts who seemed free from restraint and moved as fluid as water, and it messed with my head a little.

"Where did you go?" Kova asked, breaking my thoughts.

I shook my head and stared down at the floor. I think what he really meant to say was, "What the fuck happened out there?"

"Nowhere. I'm just thinking."

Friction radiated off him over my mistake, though he didn't say anything. We walked side by side toward the end of the runway for my second vault of the evening. The first attempt had ended with me on my butt, which would cost me big time. The blind landing was already difficult to begin with, but when I didn't get enough air and dropped my hips and then opened too late, there was no saving it.

"Your form was loose, and you did not block hard enough. Is it because of your arm?"

I shook my head and tapped my feet in the chalk. I curled my toes under to crack them.

"Give me," Kova said.

I glanced up wide-eyed. "Give you what?"

"Your arm. Give it to me." He waved his fingers.

I gawked and moved my arm behind my back. His eyes lowered like he was aggravated.

"Give me your arm, Adrianna," he demanded. "We do not have much time."

I shot a paranoid glance over my shoulder, then raised my arm to him. Kova took it and held me with only the touch of a professional. His thumb pressed on the muscles and joints, then he applied pressure to the crease. He hit a sore spot and I clenched my eyes shut, wincing. My arm was so swollen. Kova extended my arm and made sure my elbow was locked straight.

My teeth dug into the inside of my lip.

"Breathe." He commanded. I hadn't even realized I wasn't. "Flex."

He pushed on my palm and arched my fingers back, then rotated my wrist while holding the inside of my elbow so I couldn't bend it. My fingers were a little tingly and my hand was shaking.

"Do you have extra sports tape with you? If not, I will find some," he said, and I nodded in response. "This is what we are going to do. I will tape your arm after this rotation. It will not completely erase the pain, but it should help. In the meantime, you are going to put everything you have inside of you into that second vault. Give it your all. Do you understand me? We did not make it this far only to crumble when shit gets tough. When you are done, you are going to walk off and come to me like it does not bother you." He paused, then said, "Tonight after the meet, we will do therapy on it. Your father can stand over me and watch for all I care."

I nodded again robotically.

Kova let go of my arm but he didn't move back. He propped his hands on his hips and exhaled a tight breath.

"Talk to me. You have been so quiet."

"I don't want to do anything that will provoke my dad," I said under my breath. I was embarrassed to admit it.

"Believe me, I understand your fear more than anyone, but that is going to cost you everything you have worked for. Do not do that to yourself. I am not telling you to go against your father, but right now, this is about *you* and no one else. You worked hard for this, Adrianna. Do not let anyone or anything take it away from you. Your father knows this, and it is why you are here. Stop overthinking and do what you were born to do. You will live with regret if you do not. You are not reigning champ on vault for nothing."

He had a point.

The warning bell sounded to let us know it was time to go.

Our eyes met. My lips parted.

I watched him exhale, and he watched me inhale.

"Make it count," he said.

Kova turned around and walked to the end of the vault to double check the springboard was in position and the height of the apparatus was correct. He stood off to the side then looked down the runway at me. He dipped his chin to let me know I was good to go. I padded some chalk onto my palms then clapped my hands together. A small cloud appeared in front of me.

I moved to stand behind the taped white line and then stepped back another foot, needing the extra momentum.

Kova was right. I needed to reset my focus. Adrenaline surged through my body as I rolled my toes under me until they cracked, a nervous habit of mine. I raised my arms to salute the judges, then zeroed in on the vault and leaned up on the tips of my toes.

I got this.

I took long strides, building up the power, and envisioned myself flipping over the vault and completing the two and a half twists cleanly.

Fingers spread wide on the floor, I turned my roundoff over, and feet slamming into the springboard, I rebounded backward and reached for the horse to block as hard as I could. Pain ripped through me, but Kova was right. I had worked too hard for it to fall apart now.

Rebounding off with as much force as I could grasp, I soared through the air as tight as I could, twisting and rotating at the same time.

Everything I'd learned from Madeline and Kova flashed through my mind.

I could hear them whispering in my ear where to open up, and I listened, hoping the blind landing was perfect.

The arena came into view as my feet met the blue landing mat. A gush of air exploded from my lungs as I raised my arms to salute the judges. No hop. No bent legs. Just a perfect, stuck landing. The crowd erupted as fans cheered on. From the corner of my eye, I could see Kova's excitement as he clapped his hands and yelled.

Heart racing, I blinked repeatedly…and smiled.

I landed *and* I stuck my vault!

Stepping off the floor and down the steps, I wasn't even thinking when I ran into Kova's arms. It was so automatic and what we'd always done—what so many coaches and gymnasts do. He picked me up and squeezed me to him. Feeling how proud he was of me made me feel so damn good. That told me I'd done my job correctly.

"Magnificent!" he said in my ear, then put me down. Kova high-fived me. My heart bloomed with happiness. "There is the focus you need. That was flawless and what everyone knows you are capable of."

All I could do was smile at him. "Thank you," I said, keeping my voice low, only for him.

"Boy, you had me worried there for a second, Adrianna." Madeline approached us, her eyes twinkling. "That first vault was so unlike you, but this one had your name written all over it. Good job."

I grinned at her. "Thank you," I said when the crowd erupted again.

The three of us turned around to glance up at the scoreboard knowing that was the reason for the cheering. My score had been posted and there was only a third of a tenth deduction.

My eyes widened in shock at the nearly perfect. Madeline tugged me into a quick hug, said a few things to Kova, then walked away. I felt like she was always on the run going somewhere.

Without a worry of who was watching us, Kova stared down at me with a tenderness that synced my heart with his. There was so much love and pride in his eyes that I could hardly handle it. Words weren't always needed to show someone that you cared for them. Sometimes just a look said enough.

One side of his mouth lifted into a crooked smile. My cheeks blushed and I glanced down.

"Come. Let us wrap your arm. It is not going to bring a miracle to you, but it will help a little bit."

"I'll take anything at this point."

"I will work it out with each rotation as much as I can, but expect some pain."

I followed Kova to the seating area where he conditioned my arm, then applied the stretchy sports tape. My fingers weren't as numb, and I was glad about that since I had bars next. I had read online numbness was a cause of nerve damage associated with dislocations. I hoped that wasn't the case, and that this stinging ache that never seemed to go away was because I hadn't allowed myself enough time to heal properly and nothing more.

"Prepare to rotate. I will be back shortly."

CHAPER 17

G et the white tape."

I dropped my bag and rummaged through it. I handed the tape to Kova. He began wrapping my wrists for added support and laced some of my fingers with tape too. He applied another layer of tape to my injured arm, saying it may help with the straining. Once he was finished, I took over and slipped on my wristbands and grips then buckled them. Flexing my fingers, I shook my hands out.

"Good?" Kova asked, and I nodded. "Go chalk up."

I turned around and walked over to the stand holding the bowl of chalk and submerged my hands in it. I powdered my inner thighs and then the tops of my legs. Bars was another specialty of mine and one that I usually medaled in. I was confident, but still I visualized my routine and focused solely on that. I sprayed water on my palms, then glanced over at Kova who was spraying the bars with water and then rubbing them down with chalk for me. It provided an added grip. It wasn't something we did often but given how the inside of my elbow was stinging, Kova wasn't going to take a chance.

I walked over to him and eyed the high bar where he applied the chalk.

"Do you want me to spot you?"

"Yes."

"Strong core and stay tight," he said. "Drive your heels way down on the first tap and then drive them again just before the release." I nodded furiously, adrenaline spiking my pulse. I was getting excited to perform. "Hollow through the swing." He instructed by imitating what I needed to do and pointing to his chest. "Just a little longer, then drive to initiate the rotation."

"Got it."

"Straight lines. Stick your handstands. This is your event, Ria. Do not let anyone take it from you. Own it."

Kova clapped my back and then moved to stand parallel to the uneven bars. Piling on a bit more chalk, I blew on my palms and a cloud of white dust appeared before me. I stepped in front of the low bar with my foot pointed in front of me and shook my fingers out. I met Kova's eyes to center my balance, and I inhaled, pulling the air deep into my stomach, then exhaled.

The bell sounded. He dipped his chin.

It was go time.

Mounting the low bar, I did a kip cast to a handstand and let muscle memory take over. I performed my heart out, free flowing from bar to bar in my own element, making sure I stuck my handstands and I had clean lines. As I geared up to release to the low bar, Kova stepped into the side and put his arm out to spot me.

Gripping the bar tightly, chalk dust floated in my face as I came down swinging into another kip, then to a free hip circle before I let go and twisted backward to reach for the high bar. I moved quietly, flowing freely into a handstand. I stuck it, then fell backwards, rotating with only one arm—my bad one—and held on for dear life as I swung around the bar to stick my handstand. This was a skill worth more points than most and it had to be executed perfectly to get the value for difficulty, otherwise it would be all for nothing. My fingers gripped the bar while I gritted my teeth from the strain in my ligaments.

Kova took another step closer to spot me as I completed a pirouette. I rotated my hands once more before I fell forward, tapping into a giant, then tapping again like Kova said to, and reached for my release.

I whipped my hips for momentum to take flight and flew backwards in a pike position, reaching for the bar. My heart stopped for a split second as my toes glided past the bar and I came down. Kova made a fist and pumped it in excitement, then moved out of the way and back to the waiting area so I could complete my routine. I had two more releases that took my breath away before I was circling the high bar to complete two giants. I'd worked on this dismount long and hard with Kova to know when I had to release.

Coming down on the second rotation, I waited until my toes were parallel with the bar and I released my hold. The bar ricocheted violently behind me as I twisted two times with a straight body to complete a double twisting double layout. This dismount was one of the hardest dismounts to complete. It required a straight body going against pressure, and I'd worked endlessly with him to perfect it.

Spotting for the ground, my arms came out in front of me. Feet together, I landed on the mat with only the tiniest hop. Before I could raise my arms, I heard Kova yell his excitement, followed by Madeline shouting. I smiled from ear to ear as I saluted the judges, then I ran off the podium to my coaches. I hugged both and waited with them for my score to post.

I went into this routine with a different mindset than I had vault. I let myself go, living in the moment and loving the sport that had captivated my heart from a young age. I didn't hold back. I didn't worry. I just let my body feel.

I knew it had a lot to do with Kova. It was always him. He sensed my reluctance, my fears, my worries. I had to wonder how I would do without him by my side. I'd like to think I'd perform the same, but honestly, I wasn't sure.

I pulled my buckles back and slipped my grips off.

"How's your arm?" Madeline asked.

"Killing me," I said, panting. "It was the reverse grip and the back giant that did it. I thought I was going to end up tearing my shoulder all the way down. I'm going to need to ice it tonight to compete tomorrow."

"I'll make sure you have everything you need when you go into physical therapy."

Luckily, I had brought a small bottle of Motrin with me. I planned to pop six pills the moment I got back to my hotel room. I couldn't tell anyone, though. I'd probably get yelled at, but this was one of those desperate moments that required it.

I exhaled a heavy breath. I had no idea how the hell I even got through that routine.

"Thanks, Madeline," I said when the crowd erupted.

We glanced at the black screen high above us and looked for my name. With only a few deductions, I was still in second place with a large margin separating me from third. I couldn't believe it. I stared, afraid it would all go away if I blinked. Falling on that first vault was going to cost me today, but I knew in my gut going forward I'd excel from here on out. That was what I hoped anyway.

"Fantastic," Madeline said, smiling. "Keep it up."

She pulled her notebook from under her arm and strode away, writing in it as she did. Probably making a note of the items I'd need for therapy.

"How do you feel?" Kova asked. His hands were clasped behind his back.

I peered up at him and lifted one corner of my mouth into a smile. "Aside from my dangling dead limb, I feel good. Really good, actually. More confident than before."

"Good. I am glad. You should be happy while you are here. You earned it. Pack up and let us move onto beam."

Kova turned to leave, but I called his name.

"Wait."

Anxiety swirled in my blood. I should've waited, but I had to say something. It was stupid to feel this way when I'd been alone with Kova before, but I was too nervous to ask him to meet me tonight. We hadn't had a chance to talk and I really wanted to. We needed to.

I bit my lip, and his eyes fell to my mouth. "Do you think we can talk tonight?"

Kova drew his lower lip between his teeth. "Come on. Let us go."

A blush crept into my cheeks. I felt like a weight had been lifted from my chest just asking that simple question.

The balance beam had passed much quicker for some reason, thank God, and now I was on my last event—floor. Fortunately, I was still in second place after beam. I'd only had a few wobbles, but nothing to knock me down to third place.

Madeline was rubbing my arms, warming me up. She bent over so she was eye level with me and took my hands in hers, shaking my arms out.

"I want you to go out there and have fun, you hear me? Smile and show this arena who you are and that you're a force to be reckoned with."

My cheeks flushed. Sometimes I was shy. "I'll try."

"No, you *will* do it."

I giggled. "All right." I was high on life right now and really, really happy. I felt like I was bursting with sunshine, something I hadn't felt in a while

She let go of my hands and said, "You're up! Knock 'em dead."

I saluted the judges, then walked up the steps and onto the blue carpeted spring floor. This was a favorite event of mine. My classical routine had a lot of spunk and charm woven through it that had been choreographed specifically to fit my personality and aptitude. It was a lot of fun to perform, a total crowd pleaser where fans of the sport clapped their hands and joined in.

Right before I stepped into position and took my stance, I glanced over my shoulder and searched for my good luck charm.

He was already looking at me.

That was all I needed.

CHAPER 18

So," Avery said, drawing out the word, "how'd you do today? Tell me everything!"

I chuckled at her excitement.

"I need to know if my bestie is going to the Olympics so I can tell everyone at school tomorrow. Then I'm gonna book my ticket so I can watch you in person."

I smiled, my heart beating with so much love for my friend. "It was unreal, Ave! The crowd was so loud the entire time, and there was this big extravagant opening to introduce the gymnasts today. The lights were turned down low while this video montage played above. Each one of us walked onto the floor one by one waving to the people while these huge smoke bombs in red, white, and blue erupted behind us. The announcer said which state we were from and the gym name. We were given matching USA sweat suits too. I can't wait to get a free minute to watch the replay." I hadn't realized how cool the introductions were until I told Avery. Funny how it was a blur until now. "As for the team, I'll know tomorrow. I have one more day of competition, and that's when the team is picked."

"Shit." She groaned. "I must've gotten the days mixed up. I thought it was today. Anyway, that sounds so damn cool. I wish I was there to see it. I'll have to check before I go to school when it'll be on television so I can record it. Make sure you tell me ASAP after tomorrow. Do you think you'll make it? I think you will."

That was the million-dollar question.

"I think I have a good chance, but I'm trying not to get my hopes up even though I'm dying to make it." I chuckled. "I may have placed at Worlds and other major comps, but you just never know. There are so many amazingly talented girls here too. My coaches think I have a chance."

"You mean Madeline?"

I perked up. "Oh, my God. I didn't get a chance to tell you. Kova is here."

"Shut the fuck up!" Avery gasped.

"No, I know. I couldn't believe it myself when he showed up at the airport."

"No shit. Did your dad flip?"

"No. I'm not sure of the details just yet, but my dad knew Kova was coming. He just didn't tell me. Can you believe it? Kova just showed up at the terminal and sat across from me."

"How did he look?"

"Like a wreck, honestly. Horrible. He looked like he hadn't slept in days."

"He probably hadn't."

I told Avery about Kova and how it'd been preparing for the meet without him. I told her I felt as bad as he looked. She made a comment, concerned about how much time I spent thinking about him. I reminded her a gymnast needed her coach. The coach was the only person who understood an athlete's mind and where it goes during competition.

I didn't deny my attachment, I loved him, but I hoped she didn't confuse it for anything more than what it was. When the coach becomes all you know for nearly fifty hours a week times three hundred and sixty-five days a year, a connection is formed that's nearly impossible to break. He knows me better than anyone in the world.

"I'm seeing Kova tonight, but I kind of feel bad because of how much my dad is putting aside for him to be here."

Avery made a sound under her breath like she agreed. "I'm assuming he'll be back at practice. You could always talk then. I wouldn't risk it right now. It's not worth it, and tomorrow is a big day for you. Do you have an alibi in case anyone comes by your room and you're MIA?"

I chuckled. I hadn't thought of needing an alibi, but aside from that, Avery made a good point. I didn't want to risk anything. Even though Dad was putting everything to the side at the moment, it didn't mean I wasn't on thin ice with him. One wrong move and I knew he would take this away from me. I had to decide if it was worth risking everything I loved for him.

There was a light knock on the door. My brows drew together as I stood up from the small chair facing the window. No way would Kova blatantly come to my room like that, not when there were eyes and ears everywhere right now on the floor where all the gymnasts stayed together.

"Someone's at the door," I whispered into the phone. "Let me grab this and we'll talk tomorrow."

"Text me ASAP! I'll be on the edge of my seat waiting. Good luck! Love you!"

After thanking her, we hung up. I placed my cell down on the dresser then walked to the door to look through the peep hole. I was surprised to see Sophia standing on the other side.

When Dad had told me she wanted to come to the competition but wanted to make sure I was okay with it first, I'd been both stunned and secretly elated. It was nice to be supported by a mother who wanted to be there. I had to remind Dad this was a huge competition and they would likely be captured on camera in between rotations since I was competing. I thought he might be concerned to be seen with someone other than Joy. He insisted he wasn't and that I shouldn't be either.

"Hey," I said when I opened the door.

She gave me a hesitant smile. "Hi. Do you mind if I come in?"

"Not at all." I shook my head, happy to see her.

I stepped aside and opened the door wider for her to enter, then shut it behind her and gestured to the little round table by the window.

She took a seat, placing an item wrapped in brown paper she brought with her on her lap. I took the opposite chair and regarded her. It was strange looking at someone who looked eerily similar to me.

"How are you feeling?" she asked.

"Aside from the fact I'm competing on less than half my kidney function and with a gimpy arm, and I'm dead tired, I'm honestly fine for the most part. I have a headache right now, and I'm feeling stiff since everything is settling for the night, but nothing new there."

I scratched the side of my head anxiously, wondering if there was a reason why she was here. A piece of hair got stuck around my fingernail when I pulled my hand away. I glanced down. There'd been so much hair surrounding the drain when I took a shower after I'd gotten back to the hotel room. I'd tried not to read too much into it. I lost hair all the time, but this time there had been clumps. I hadn't lost clumps before.

"I just wanted to thank you for allowing me to come here with you. It was incredible to be able to watch you. I've followed you over the years, and Frank always gave me updates, but witnessing it in person is something I can't begin to explain. You made it look so easy."

My eyes softened. I took that as a compliment. "I'm glad you're here. It's nice to have someone besides Dad who's supportive and actually wants to be part of this."

"I know things are probably a little strange right now with me suddenly in your life. If it's something you don't want, please just let me know. Frank insists you'll be okay with it, but I had to say it myself." One side of her mouth tugged up into a half smile. "I don't want to step on any toes or give unsolicited advice. That's the last thing I'd want. I'll do anything at your pace to be in your life."

There was no way to explain how much that meant to me. Every girl needed a mom, and the only one I'd ever known never wanted me. I didn't want to yell and scream "Yes, please, be in my life," but it was exactly how I felt.

"It was a shock at first." I laughed lightly. "I had no idea you guys were even talking, let alone seeing each other." I paused. "I kind of wished I'd known sooner, but then again, I guess things happen for a reason… I never would've guessed I had someone else out there." I began to ramble and needed a quick subject change. "So, why did you stop by? Something you wanted to talk about?"

Whatever it was, it had to be very important for her to sneak over here to talk to me. I wasn't supposed to have family in my room or talk to them before a competition.

Sophia sat up straighter. She had a small frame like I did and looked petite in the chair. She placed the wrapped item on the table and passed it to me.

My brows angled toward each other. "A gift?" I glanced up to meet her eyes. "You brought me a gift?"

"Yes. It's not much. It's something I was given once and it helped me find my way. Go ahead and open it. I thought you may be able to use it."

I peeled back the brown craft paper to reveal a book. Holding the glossy cover, I flipped it open and glanced down the front, reading over the blurb.

"It's technically a self-help book, but I don't like to call it that. People tend to stray from those." Sophia waited a moment, then said, "I read that book during a chaotic time in my life, and it stuck with me ever since. I was angry at the world and I hated myself because nothing I did was right, only I didn't know it at the time. That book taught me to be gentle with myself, to focus on what I needed in order to be happy, that I needed to put myself first. But more importantly, it taught me how to embrace every part of me."

I looked at her. She seemed a little uneasy. This was the first time she was trying to give me real advice and I think it made her nervous.

"Just say it, Sophia," I said in a friendly tone. "I can tell you're holding back. You don't have to with me."

We smiled at each other.

"Based on what Frank's told me, and what I've seen, I thought it might be helpful for you to read in your downtime, if you ever get any." Her airy laugh caused my smile to broaden. "You're dealing with more than most kids your age, on top of your health issues. Even if you weren't dealing with the other things, you're at the Olympic Trials. That's huge. Do you even realize how big this is? There's a lot for you to process."

I grinned, and looked at the book again before I met her gaze once more. "It'll probably hit me when I get home, and probably at the worst time too. Seems to be how my life is going at the moment."

Sophia took a deep breath. "There's a light at the end of the tunnel, you just have to truck through the mud first to see it. I hope the book is encouraging for you the way it was for me. When you do get time to process everything, it'll all come roaring back and hit you at once."

I'd yet to have time to process what happened that day in my condo, or the days proceeding. My world had crumbled in a matter of minutes and I had to shelve it because I had more important hurdles to jump.

There was a part of me that didn't want to think about it anyway. How many tears could one girl cry? Just thinking about it knotted my stomach. I was better off not having to think about it, but the other part of me knew I'd have to come to terms with it eventually, whether I wanted to or not.

"Thank you, Sophia," I said, feeling slightly emotional. "This means a lot to me. I may start to read it tonight, actually."

I planned to meet Kova down the street at this coffee shop after the sun had set. I could flip through a few pages when I got back while I was lying in bed.

"Can I be frank?"

We both chuckled. She wasn't talking about my dad. I nodded.

"Like I said before, I don't want to overstep, so if you feel I am, please just tell me and I won't say anything." She paused and locked eyes with me. "I saw the way you looked at Kova today." I stilled, and the color drained from my face. "I feel like I need to say it's not a good idea to act on it."

CHAPER 19

My jaw wobbled as anxiety filled me.

This was why she came here. Dad must've sent her.

Or was she saying this on her own?

I wasn't sure where to start without looking guilty or feeling suspicious.

"I wasn't going to do anything."

Her eyes softened at my lie. "Maybe not tonight, but eventually you will, and no one will be able to stop you." Sophia gave me a sad smile. "You're a young woman in love. I see it because I was your age once and in love too. I remember the feelings and emotions like it was just yesterday. Your eyes light up when you look at Kova. It's not one-sided either, that's what is concerning."

I was stiff as a stone even though my heart was hammering against my rib cage threatening to break free.

"Did my dad send you here to talk to me about this? Like a warning or something? Because I already know the consequences, he made them quite clear."

Her face fell and I instantly felt bad. I wasn't angry, but my words came out a little more aggressive than I intended to.

"No, he didn't. I promise. He has no idea I'm talking to you about this and he never will. He thinks I just wanted to bring you the book." I caught a flash of boldness in Sophia's eyes. "In Frank's defense, though, it took a bit of convincing to get Kova here. I feel like you should know he's trying extremely hard. When he got off the phone that night with you, he was a disaster, stuck between right and wrong. It's taking every ounce of self-control he has for Kova to be here, to allow him near you, to touch you." I opened my mouth to speak but she placed her palm up to stop me, and continued, "Frank knows Kova touches you only with a coach's hand right now, but that doesn't matter. The damage is already done and that's all he can see. You have to know any father would feel this way, right? How Frank is with you, and what he says to me, are two totally different things. He's holding back for your sake, and he's trying really hard, Adrianna."

Her face twisted like she was carrying a burden on her shoulders. The concern she had for my dad was touching. There had been far and few moments where Joy had showed concern toward him in the manner Sophia was. Almost like she actually truly cared about him.

Now I felt like crap for even attempting to see Kova.

I glanced away, and responded softly, "I know he's dealing with a lot right now. I wouldn't want to upset him more than he already is. Why are you telling me this? Why now?"

"I was kicked out of my house when I got pregnant with you. My sister was so sick that my parents pretty much forgot about me anyway. No one knew what was wrong with Francesca at the time, only that she was ill. I think it was easier for them. They had one child to support instead of two with one on the way." Sophia paused like she was hurting inside. It seemed like any time she reflected on the past she drew sadness from it. "I was young and impressionable. There was no parental figure around to advise me when I needed it the most. I just want to remind you I'm here any time you need to talk. I'll never judge you or be angry. Even with guy stuff, been there, done that." She chuckled then sobered up. Large green eyes peered back at me. "I missed out on so much of your life. Now we finally have a real chance to have a relationship, and it kills me to see this web you're stuck in. I want you to know I'm here if you ever need me." She cleared her throat as a way to disguise the emotion filling her eyes. "Anyway, I was going to give that book to you tomorrow, but it seemed like you might be able to use it tonight."

I glanced down at the book again, curious about the pages inside. Sophia was offering her guidance when I'd never really been given any from either parent. Dad was always working. I'd assumed most fathers were like mine since I hardly ever saw any dads at practice, it was always just moms. Joy was another story entirely and not someone I ever asked advice from.

Listening to Sophia brought on a wave of melancholy. A longing. I'd never say I was neglected. I most definitely wasn't, but I had been easily overlooked by both parents with their assumption that I would figure it out. The thought of having a parent figure to come to with questions would've been nice. I mean, just one who wanted me around would've sufficed. I would've taken anything, really.

The creases between my eyes deepened. Even if I'd had that type of relationship with my parents, would any ounce of advice have stopped me from loving Kova?

No. The heart wanted what the heart wanted, and it gave no fucks about anyone's feelings or objections.

"I don't know what to say. I feel like thank you isn't enough. This is more than a book you're giving me."

Her eyes glistened with relief and that made me feel good inside. "You don't have to say anything. Despite your maturity, you're still young. Not that I'm doubting what you have with Kova isn't real, but you should live your life and experience every age while you can." Her eyes narrowed into a knowing look. "I bet you're really consumed with him and you think about him all the time and wonder what he's thinking. Like you have to be with him and can't imagine a life without him." I tried not to squirm. "Find what *you* love and what *you* hate. When you're involved with someone, we tend to think only about what they want and need. It's easy to forget ourselves in the process. Put what you want first. Go to college and attend parties. Stay up until two in the morning with your girlfriends and burn a pizza in the oven. Don't lose out on this time in your life. You'll regret not living it to its fullest. I know I do." She pointed to the book. "Check it out when you can. It might be more useful than you think."

Sophia stood. I placed the book on the table and stood with her. "No one's ever told me that." No one ever spoke to me like that. What she said to do sounded kind of fun.

"Me either, but I think it's something a teen Sophia needed to hear." She waited. "I thought you may too."

I glanced at the book again and reread the tagline. *Don't let this life pass you by.*

"I'm going to read a few pages tonight while I ice my arm. Thank you, Sophia."

"Frank is waiting for me, so I'm going to head out. Regardless of the outcome tomorrow, I'm proud of you. I can't wait to watch you. Thank you for allowing me to be here." Affection swirled in her eyes before they glossed over with remorse. "Francesca would've loved to be here to see you."

While I never got to meet my aunt, the emotion clogging my throat was real. I was so much more sensitive than I used to be.

Nodding, she walked to the door. Right before she left, she looked at me.

"I'm not going to tell you to not see Kova because that'll only make you do it more. If you do, I want you to consider not only those affected, but yourself too. Think about you and your life and the opportunities you have. Take advantage while you can and create your happy ending."

Sophia opened the door and stepped out quietly. I glanced back at the book, debating whether I should open it up and read a few pages now, or go see Kova like we'd planned. Listening to what Sophia said stirred my interest and swayed my decision a little.

Not being able to experience life to the fullest had been a fear of mine since I was diagnosed. I didn't want to lose out and have regrets about things I could've and should've done. The thought scared me.

What Sophia said to experience, I wanted to do. I just hadn't allowed myself to think about it because my focus was on this moment right now and getting through the heartache and pain my body dealt with every day. I didn't allow myself to look ahead, and anytime I had, I assumed Kova would be there. Yet, all those moments she mentioned—college, parties, late nights with friends—sounded like so much fun to me, and he wasn't there.

Gymnastics had always been, and will always be, the love of my life, but it would be naïve of me to not realize it was going to be over soon. I needed to decide what I wanted.

And what did I want? My fingers grazed the cover. What did I truly want?

Thoughts flickered too quickly through my mind like an old film. Some involved Kova, some involved Avery, of course my family, but most of them were of me alone. Happy, but alone, and constantly searching for something no one could give me but myself.

I was angry at the world and I hated myself.

Did I feel the same way as Sophia once did? My skin prickled with realization. I tried to push it away, but...

My breathing labored. My heart started racing. The more I thought about it, the more it hit me that my feelings were nearly identical to hers.

It didn't just hit me. It slammed into me.

I *did* feel the same way. I *was* angry at the world, and I *did* hate myself.

I hated myself for so many reasons, but mainly for how sick I was. I hid it from everyone who cared about me, and in turn, I pushed my body to the brink of total destruction to prove to myself there was nothing wrong with me. Everything about what I did made me angry and filled me with hate, not only for myself but for everything around me, except gymnastics. Becoming sick wasn't anyone's fault, but I couldn't help but wonder if I had listened to my body in the first place, would I have caught the illnesses before they grew into something more? I was stubborn and had assumed it was from overtraining, but I think in the back of my mind I always knew something wasn't right.

A fire burned inside me just thinking about it. Tears burst from my eyes and I covered my mouth. I wondered when my heart hardened and why I became like this, or if I was always like this and I just didn't know it. Tears dripped down my cheeks and my knees shook. It hurt me that I was like this.

An unexpected quietness settled in my chest. It forced me to become aware of the truth, and damn did it hurt. I realized I needed to let go of the resentments I'd built, and the only way to do that was on my own.

The things Sophia said, words of wisdom, were all things I'd been seeking without even realizing it.

My knees buckled and I fell into the chair behind me. After the meet today, I'd done therapy with the other gymnasts to help speed up recovery. Some were getting full-body massages, others were cupping or doing various chiropractic stretches, or wearing vibrating sleeves to increase blood flow. All so we'd be ready for the beating our bodies would take tomorrow for the chance to hold a coveted spot on the United States women's gymnastics team. The faster we healed, the better we'd perform. Lactic acid in the muscles would only hinder the performance and make the joints stiff. It had to be released and that's what we'd focused on. A recovery that would normally take a week for any normal person to heal would take one night for a pro athlete.

I glanced around my cold, small room with two twin beds, and stopped when my eyes landed on the ice pail. I got up and walked over to the black bucket. I checked to make sure I had my room key before grabbing the bucket to go fill. I was supposed to meet Kova in just over an hour. I wanted to, I missed him terribly, but my gut told me to stay in the room and open the book. It was a feeling that resonated within my soul and I couldn't ignore.

I wasn't going to give up Kova, that was virtually impossible. What I needed for myself right now was to rest my body and ice my aching arm.

Maybe cry a few more tears too.

What I really needed to do was heal my heart and learn to love myself again.

CHAPER 20

t was a quiet, somber morning.

Madeline didn't say much, but neither did Kova. My guess was that we all were going through the motions and preparing for the long day ahead of us.

I'd worked my ass off to finish in the top five yesterday, but that didn't mean anything today. Today was a new day with new scores and new routines.

Once the meet was officially over, both days' scores would be taken into consideration along with previously required meets standings. Then the Olympic committee would convene in a private, soundproof room, while all fifteen gymnasts were placed in a separate room, watching the clock turn as we overanalyzed our routines, wondering where we could've been better. Everything we all worked so hard for came down to that moment. Only four would be chosen plus two alternates.

It was such a mind game.

Later this evening, the final women's team would be selected and prompted to stand in the center of the floor of the arena. Chills raced down my arms just thinking about it. For that reason alone, I was a ball of nerves today.

I hadn't told Kova I wasn't going to meet him last night. I just didn't show. I couldn't contact him, and he had no way of contacting me either. I felt bad. He'd probably waited for me. I imagined him looking for me every time the door opened, getting his hopes up. Eventually he'd realized I wasn't going to show. He hadn't said anything about it, and it made me wonder if that was why he was all broody and quiet this morning.

The book Sophia gave me was an oddly interesting page-turner. I wasn't sure I'd like it at first. A self-help book definitely wasn't my style. But I gave it a shot and found myself having to force it closed to get proper rest for today. The author offered a thought-provoking approach to finding yourself that strangely resonated inside of me. I had to ask myself a lot of open-ended questions that kept going and going. I was oddly excited to read more once we were on the plane ride back home, tempted to try out the different methods to finding inner peace. I had a lot of turmoil left inside me.

"Does being here bring back memories?" I asked Kova, breaking the silence.

A distant smile touched his lips as he wrapped up my wrists for bars. "Yes, it does, actually. Some happy, some bittersweet."

It took me a moment to realize what he was talking about. Kova had been to two Olympics but had to withdraw from the third one because of his mom's declining health. If I remembered correctly, she'd passed away shortly after the Games that he'd missed.

"Is that why you're moody today?"

"I am not moody. I do not get moody."

A laugh gushed from me before I could stop it. He moved onto my other wrist. His movements felt mechanical. "You're the moodiest man I have ever met."

The corners of his mouth curled but he still felt a distance away. Why did he have to smile like that? So sexy and so relaxed and so at ease. Damn him.

"How many men do you know?" he asked, humoring me.

"A lot." I teased. He quirked up a brow. "I know many men."

It took effort not to laugh or smile. I knew no men.

"That so, *Malysh*?"

Blush decorated my cheeks. My heart fluttered with warmth at the sound of the nickname that caused a torrent of feelings inside me. Kova lifted his eyes to mine as he tore a piece of white tape with his teeth. The look in his gaze flooded my thoughts with memories of us together. Doing things I shouldn't be thinking about. It took me back to the day in my condo when the hurricane had hit and I'd carved the first letter of my name into his chest.

Using my other hand, I boldly tapped the left side of his chest twice with my index finger, right over the letter. His hand automatically reached up for mine. My heart sped up and I held my breath. Our eyes locked. Kova held onto my thumb while my fingers softly curled around his knuckles. I didn't have to say anything, and neither did he.

"*Malysh…*"

"I know."

I was his, and I always would be. The same went for him.

But we couldn't act like this in public.

His callused finger stroked the space between my thumb and forefinger. Something so simple pulled on my heartstrings. It was just us until a bell sounded in the background and broke the moment. I prayed no one took notice of us.

"Are you mad about last night?" I asked ever so quietly. He dropped my hand.

"Not at all. But now is not the time for that. Now is the time to show them why you are a valuable player for the team."

My eyes fluttered shut. I knew Kova supported me, but it still felt good to hear it at the eleventh hour.

"The United States is the number one team in the world right now. You know why that is?"

"Because we're the bomb dot com?" I joked. He wrapped one last piece of tape around my wrist.

"You are one of four reasons why that is. Do not forget that. Vault and bars are a given. You are the best out of them all and why you are the reigning champion. You know it too; you just do not like to admit it. Remind them why they need you on the team. Win the crowd over with your beautiful smile and love of the sport."

My lips pursed together. Luckily, I was wearing a leotard and it covered the blush creeping up my chest to my neck. Kova had said really sweet things to me before, but this time his words made me feel a little bashful. He spoke like he was confident of my abilities, and that ignited my adrenaline.

"You ready?" he asked once my grips were on. I nodded and bounced on my toes to get moving. "We are almost to the finish line."

I exhaled and flexed my fingers. All the days that had been filled with tears and aches and hopelessness, the same thing over and over, my diligent coaches who pushed me to the brink of insanity, it was all coming to an end. This was it, and the feeling was something I couldn't describe. Now it felt like it got here so fast.

"It's kind of crazy, isn't it? We've waited for this moment for what feels like forever, and it's finally here."

"It is yours if you want it."

"Are you?"

My lips rolled between my teeth, embarrassment flooding me. I briefly squeezed my eyes shut wishing the ground would swallow me whole. I hadn't meant to say that. Not now at least.

His eyes bore into mine. "I think you already know the answer to that."

The bell sounded again, which meant one more gymnast before I took my turn. Steadying my breathing, I said, "I'm going to chalk up. You're going to be there, right?"

He nodded.

Relieved, I smiled, then made my way to the big chalk bowl and submerged my hands. One event down, three more to go.

I closed my eyes as my fingers shifted through the dry, white powder. I regained control of my inner self as my hands moved over the little chunks of chalk left unbroken. My entire body was swollen from head to toe despite taking all my medications like usual. I wasn't going to let that get in my way. I knew once today was over I could crash hard. It'd be worth it.

That's what I kept telling myself, anyway.

"LADIES, PLEASE FORM A SINGLE file line and follow closely."

All fourteen of us got in line wearing our matching USA sweat suits to make our way to the back.

Fourteen now, not fifteen. One of the gymnasts landed wrong on her vault dismount and snapped her knee in half. I wasn't squeamish, but seeing a person's knee inverted and protruding from their leg made my already nauseous stomach churn higher. I felt so bad for her as she was carried off the floor in a stretcher. She covered her face with her hands, hiding her tears and missed opportunity. She was so young, just barely of age to make the Olympic team from what I'd heard. Hopefully, she wouldn't lose faith and would come back fighting ten times harder. She was incredibly good, and constantly trailing my scores.

Day two was in the books, and now we were headed to the waiting room while the Olympic committee met in another room to discuss the team. A man holding a video camera followed closely, making sure to zoom in as we walked by, but he wasn't allowed in the room with us.

I wasn't sure which was worse, the anxiety or the adrenaline pulsing through me knowing that within the hour, six of us would be called to the floor to represent the United States. The anticipation was making me crazy. I didn't want to get my hopes up, but damn it, I really hoped my name was called.

While the meet went exceptionally well, that didn't necessarily mean anything at the end of all this. Gymnastics was so political behind closed doors. I knew from the beginning I needed to prove myself time and time again at the meets. And I had. At least I hoped I had. I prayed it showed that I worked well under stress, because they were looking for that too. Mistakes could be made, but the committee had to believe in you, had to see you come back with upgraded routines that were more difficult than before. They wanted to see that you were one of the few and strong who could handle the pressure of wearing the red, white, and blue.

Given my secrets, I felt like I was equipped to handle it.

There was nothing I could do now except wait. I'd finished in first place for both vault and bars, fourth on balance beam, and second on floor. My fate was in their hands.

Quietly, we made our way down a chilly, narrow hallway and through a set of double doors. The material of our uniforms swish-swashed as we reached a room with a sign taped to the door that read coaches and athletes only. Ushered inside, we took a seat on the floor and crisscrossed our legs while all of our coaches talked softly amongst themselves. Leaning back on my hands, I glanced over my shoulder and eyed Kova. He seemed to know I was looking for him and glanced at me from the corner of his eye. We exchanged a brief look. He was leaning one shoulder against the wall with his arms crossed in front of his chest as he spoke to another male coach that looked roughly his age.

I looked back at the girls. My nerves were so bad I felt like I was going to vomit any second. I was sure we all felt that way judging by the look of panic written on everyone's faces.

"Is everyone replaying their routines in their head wondering where they could've been better?" one of the pixie girls asked.

We nodded in unison, giggling here and there. The small talk did nothing to hide our jitters.

"Does anyone else feel like they're going to throw up any second?" I asked. Most nodded their heads, and giggled again. Using the back of my hand, I dramatically swiped it across my forehead pretending I was glad it wasn't just me who was a damn wreck.

Time passed painfully slow. Just as we were starting to soothe our nerves, the door opened and five people strode in, three of whom were the Olympic coaches. They carried six large bouquets of roses and sunflowers. It was what the team held in the air once names were announced.

My stomach dropped. I felt like I was going to have a heart attack. My pulse was in my ears and I started sweating. A nervous energy filled the room. There was no denying each of us—including the coaches—felt it. I wanted to unzip my jacket and shake my arms out. I glanced around looking for a bucket because I was sure I was going to vomit any second.

We all came to win, but tonight was the end of the road for eight girls in this room. They'd go home in tears, debating whether this backbreaking lifestyle was worth enduring another four years to achieve Olympic glory.

I knew where my road led if I wasn't chosen.

The door shut with a click, and Romanian Coach Elena, who I last saw at the training camps, held a piece of paper in her hand that sealed our fates. Voices decreased and each of us waited with baited breaths to see who'd been chosen.

CHAPER 21

adies and gentlemen…"

Chills kept pebbling my arms. I closed my eyes and listened as the president of the gymnastics committee spoke to the crowd. The team had been selected and announced in the private waiting room, and now the four were just waiting to be individually called to the floor.

The air in the room was packed with tension, anguish, and exhilaration. Tears fell for those whose road came to an end tonight, and for those whose dreams were only beginning. The anticipation was wreaking havoc on all of us. For me, it was a bittersweet ending.

"How does my mascara look?" I heard one of the girls ask another as she hiccupped.

After the team was announced, my stomach had been a disaster of emotions and still was. Now I knew why coaches were brought into the waiting room too—they had to console us after. My knees had buckled, and my heart had crashed to the ground in shock. Kova had been right there when my vision became spotty and I almost fell over. He grabbed me immediately and took me into his arms.

He'd comforted me as I cried on his shoulder, then held my face between his palms and kissed my forehead. It had been both heaven and hell for me.

Heaven, because this was it and what I'd worked so damn hard for.

Hell, because I knew what came after.

I took a deep breath and sniffled, and watched the rowdy crowd with blurry eyes through the tiny window. Coaches were sent to the floor while the rest of the gymnasts stood behind the double doors, waiting. I could see Kova standing next to the other head coaches with his arms crossed in front of his chest as he wavered back and forth on his heels. They were standing near the floor. His black dress pants were custom tailored and fitted to form around his butt and thighs, and the polo World Cup shirt made his biceps stand out. He wore a massive smile, one I rarely saw unless I was alone with him. I loved seeing him like that, though it had been a while since I had. A few feet down were the members of the men's team in matching sweats that'd been selected and announced before us. We'd only been standing there for three minutes max, but it felt like three hours.

"The United States is the number one team in the world…"

My pulse hammered in my chest. I took a deep breath and exhaled. I looked ahead through the narrow windows of the doors and tried to locate Dad and Sophia in the seats. I thought they were somewhere on this side of the building, but I couldn't find them. I probably looked right at them and didn't even notice. Dad was probably on the verge of a stroke waiting for what felt like forever. Even the parents were left in the dark as to who made the team. Any minute, names were going to be called again. And any minute, the tears would start up again.

"I'm sweating right now!" I heard one girl say. I chuckled, so was I.

"It is with great pleasure, I announce the four women who will make up the United States women's gymnastics team…"

The crowd went wild. They were so loud I could barely hear the first name announced.

The double doors were pulled opened by two people with earphones and microphones. Cue the tears. They waved with frantic hands instructing us to hurry up. The coaches turned around and my eyes immediately locked with Kova's.

I didn't hold back the smile on my face. Neither did Kova. The pride in his eyes made everything we'd gone through together worth it. He was so happy.

I pulled my lip into my mouth and bit down. It was hard to believe we were finally here. My chin trembled and I sniffled again. After all the tears and rips, the aches and pains, aggressive coaching and daunting practices, we were finally at the moment we'd worked so hard for. There'd been so many days where I didn't think I could handle another second, yet, somehow, I didn't give up. Sometimes I was surprised myself that I didn't give. I'd made mistakes along the way. A lot of mistakes. There were a few meets where I'd let the nerves get the best of me, but I'd gone into the next meet challenging myself ten times harder to be better, proving to myself and my coaches and those watching that I had what it took.

And it had paid off.

"Go, go!!" one of the employees said.

I drew in a shaky breath as tears filled my eyes again when the second girl was called to the floor. I watched as her arm went into the air and she waved to the crowd, then covered her mouth as she cried and sprinted onto the floor. We were advised to wait before the next name was called.

My teeth chewed into my lip.

"Reigning world champion on vault and bars..." I sucked in a breath and thought my heart was going to burst from my chest "... The third member to join the women's Olympic gymnastics team, Adrianna Rossi from World Cup Academy of Gymnastics!"

There was no stopping the full-blown tears when my name was called next. They hit like a punch to the gut. Suddenly all eyes were on me. A bouquet was pressed to my arms as I stepped back into the arena. I crushed it to my chest, the clear plastic wrap holding the flowers couldn't even be heard over the roar of the crowd. My eyes frantically searched the packed room.

Elena, along with the other two Olympic coaches, believed in me enough for me to represent the United States.

I can't believe I really did it.

All I saw were smiling faces and clapping hands and my country's flag being waved in the air. Emotion flooded every ounce of me. Happy tears poured from my eyes. I was too overwhelmed to really see anything except Kova and the steps I was about to walk up.

My dream had come true.

I made it to the Olympics.

I'd never forget the way Coach Elena had pronounced my name in the small waiting room in her thick Romanian accent to tell me I'd made the Olympic gymnastics team as a specialist for bars and vault, and possibly floor. I practically fainted. Kova was immediately at my side joking that I was in shock and hugged me to him. I *was* in shock and I couldn't stop crying. My hands had been shaking and I was a huge ball of feelings. Luckily, I hadn't been the only one like that. The others named had reacted the same. We all wanted our name to be called, but the real possibility of that was so slim. Being the oldest named to the team with a slew of health issues that were kept under wraps, the odds were not in my favor. Still, I had been optimistic and tried so hard.

My gaze met the two other girls—my new teammates. We all had the same pink rimmed eyes and puffy cheeks from happy tears. Once the final girl was called after I was, and then the two alternates, we stood in a straight line next to each other.

It wasn't real. It had to be a dream.

"Give another round of applause for your 2020 women's gymnastics team!" the announcer said enthusiastically, and the crowd erupted.

Flashes from multiple cameras flickered in front of my face. We raised our wrapped bouquets of flowers in the air as red, white, and blue paper confetti exploded from the ceiling. The national anthem played in the distance. Streamers crisscrossed the air above us. I glanced up and smiled as the colors fell around us like snow. It was the coolest thing ever that I giggled to myself. I couldn't believe I'd made it. I was still in shock.

The men's team, who'd been selected earlier, were welcomed to the stage. We all exchanged hugs under the blowing confetti and congratulated each other. Group pictures were taken, then we were finally disbursed to find our loved ones and coaches.

I walked over to Madeline and gave her a massive bear hug. She was like a proud parent and that made me feel so good to know I made her happy. There were tears in her throat as she sang her praise. Happiness burst through me. She worked with me just as hard as Kova did. She earned this too.

One of the people from the committee came over to speak to Madeline. Just before she left, she looked up and spotted someone behind me. Brows creased between her eyes, she pointed at me, nodded her head, then quickly turned away. It was chaos on the floor and she was gone in the blink of an eye.

I turned around, and through the people crisscrossing in front of me, I realized she was talking to Kova.

Our eyes locked, and something clicked into place. I weaved through the crowd, my feet carting me to him automatically.

Without a care in the world, Kova got down on one knee and I walked straight into his arms. I cried again. His strength I'd needed to get to this point embraced me immediately. Kova gave me a real hug. His hand cupped the back of my neck and his fingers gently pressed into my skin. I drew in a breath, and softly let go, crying into his neck. I'd—we'd—been through so much for this moment, and I wanted to live in it with him for as long as I could. My heart felt full as he held me to his chest.

"*Malysh, pozdravlyayu,*" he said over and over only for me to hear. When I'd finally caught my breath, he said, "Let us find your father." I nodded.

Releasing me, Kova looked at my face. We were eye level. He used his thumbs to wipe away my tears, then without thinking, he took my hand and guided me to where Dad and Sophia were standing. The moment I spotted my parents, I blindly handed Kova my bouquet and then ran to the tall wall that separated the athletes and coaches from the fans.

My father's eyes were glossy, which caused my lips to tremble again. He was beaming from ear to ear like he was going to burst. Saying he was ecstatic was an understatement. I'd never seen a smile like that on his face, one that screamed how proud he was of me and that he loved me. He held his arms open, waiting. I jumped on the white folding chair against the wall with one foot to reach him and wrapped my arms around his shoulders. My eyes closed. He hugged me like he never wanted to let go. His back shook as he squeezed me, and his head was in the curve of my neck. I could hear the clicking from the cameras next to us and my name being called. I felt his hot breath as he released his emotions. Dad gave me a long hug. Despite all the despair we'd both endured lately, none of that was a thought in our minds. It was all forgotten as we celebrated this uphill battle together.

Dad pulled back and that was when I realized he'd shed a few tears himself. My eyes watered. I softened even more.

"Adrianna, I can't believe it!" He laughed somewhere between being happy and filled with so much emotion that he clearly wasn't used to. "I was on the edge of my seat waiting. Congratulations, sweetie! I can't believe it!"

I grinned. Dad was in shock.

"Thanks, Dad."

"How do you feel?"

I shrugged, the massive smile still decorating my face. "I think I'm in shock. I don't really know what to feel yet."

"I'm so proud of you. This is by far the best day of my life. Well, the best day since you and your brother were born."

Giggling, I glanced to my right and caught sight of Sophia. She wore a bittersweet expression that made my heart hurt a little. I stepped onto the next chair and reached for her. She embraced me immediately and I felt the same thing with her as I did when I hugged my dad. Her back was vibrating with feelings.

"Congratulations, Adrianna," she said ever so softly. "I'm sorry for crying," she said, and I laughed lightly.

"It's okay. Thank you," I said in return, smiling sweetly.

I used the back of my hand to wipe under my eyes. I was sure my mascara was leaking everywhere but I didn't really care. Sophia straightened her back while Dad stepped closer to her side. He wrapped an arm around her petite shoulders, pulling her to him. She went willingly. I watched with a gentle smile as they looked at each other like honored parents. Their eyes glistened and my heart felt the longing between them. Sophia closed her eyes as Dad leaned in to kiss her temple. It was so sweet that I stared at them, unable to look away.

From the corner of my eye, I saw Madeline walk over to us and speak to Kova. Behind her, the confetti still floated like something out of a fairy tale. Kova stepped back and gave Madeline a deep nod, then turned to me. She strode away with a clipboard secured to her side.

"We have to go. You are required to take team photos and do an interview with the news station."

I glanced at Dad and Sophia. "I have to go—"

"Go," he said with a nod of his chin. "We'll see you guys for dinner tonight."

I was momentarily caught off guard. Dad answered my questioning gaze.

His eyes glistened with love despite everything. "Dinner with you and your coaches. Both of them."

My nostrils flared as I fought to keep the tears at bay. Flattening my lips, my jaw trembled as my vision blurred. I was overcome with heartfelt gratitude. He didn't have to do that. Dad was extending an olive branch and I respected the hell out of him for that. My heart was pounding so hard. I was relieved this wasn't as tense as I thought it might be. I gave Dad one last goodbye hug, then I climbed down from the chair and turned around and met Kova's emotive gaze.

"Adrianna will be back later," Kova said to Dad.

My eyes widened. That caught me by surprise. I hadn't seen them exchange more than two words since we flew here.

"She has obligations for the team that must be met before she leaves tomorrow," Kova added.

Dad's expression gave nothing away. I knew it wasn't easy for him to speak to Kova, let alone look at him, but he was, and he was doing it for me.

Agreeing, Dad smiled and applauded me one last time.

"Let us go."

Kova opened his palm up to me and I took it without another thought. We walked through the flurry of confetti together toward the double doors with smiles etched on our faces.

There was no turmoil, no heartache, no secrets.

It was just us, together, living my dream.

CHAPER 22

The interview ended up being a lot of fun.

We giggled and smiled the entire time. Our coaches watched nearby but they spoke amongst themselves. I was sure none of us even made sense half the time when we responded to the questions, but the reporters went along with it anyway. There was a blanket of euphoria in the air. Nothing could ruin the biggest moment in the world for me.

Once we were finished, we were ushered into a room for hair and makeup and given new matching leotards. A photographer came in and we were staged and prepped, taking what had to be hundreds of team pictures to use for promo. We tried acting serious and tough, but we were really laughing and giggling the whole time.

There were butterflies in my stomach. My heart was filled with so much joy that I couldn't stop smiling. Happiness was an understatement and I was sure anyone could see that within a five-mile radius. I wasn't the only one who felt this way either. Each of us wore matching expressions and had shaky fingers. We shined and glowed and laughed like we'd been best friends since we were toddlers.

This was, without a doubt, the best day of my life. I never wanted it to end.

Now I was back in my hotel room repacking my belongings to drop them off in Dad's suite before dinner. I still couldn't get over the fact that my dad was going to have dinner with both of my coaches. He was doing it for me, but I was curious to see how he'd be able to sit there without wanting to strangle Kova.

My cell phone rang, and I smiled to myself and quickly zipped up my bag. I walked to the dresser where my phone was charging. I assumed it was Avery, but when I picked up my phone, I saw a name I hadn't seen in a really long time.

My heart froze. The smile vanished from my face. I was stuck, staring at the screen, wondering if I was imagining things.

Mom's cell

Joy?

Why was she calling me? Creases formed between my eyes and my pulse accelerated as I stared at the name on the screen. I hadn't spoken to Joy since that awful Easter day, and before then, it had been so far and few in between that I couldn't recall when she'd reached out. My first thought was that something had happened to Xavier.

Hesitantly, I accepted the call and brought the phone to my ear.

"H… Hello?"

"Ana."

I cringed. My eyes closed. I hadn't heard that nickname in ages. I'd always hated the way it felt on my skin when she said it, and hearing it again brought a flood of emotion back to me.

"Hi," I said softly. "How are you? Is everything okay?"

"I'm well, thank you for asking. Are you available right now?"

I frowned. "Well, I'm actually at a gymnastics competition right now so—"

"I'm aware." She was curt, then she cleared her throat. "I'm here too and thought I would see if you have a free moment before I have to leave for the airport."

My stomach sank and my frown deepened. "What? You're here?"

Paranoia instantly enveloped me. I was literally across the country and Joy flew to the Trials when I hadn't seen her or spoken to her in months?

That was uncharacteristic of her.

My first thought was that she had a motive. While Joy had been the doting mother attending practices and meets, it'd been a façade and a deal she'd secretly made with my dad. She'd considered me a chore, and once I'd discovered the truth, she stopped caring altogether, which was why I found it so nerve-wracking she was here at all.

"I can stop by your room," she suggested.

I nodded as if she could see me, I was still stunned. "Ah, okay. Do you know which hotel I'm at?" Joy said she did, and that she was actually in the same hotel.

"I'll be there shortly," she said after I gave her my room number, then she hung up.

I stood motionless, staring at my cell phone wondering what twilight zone I was living in that warranted a call *and* an appearance from Joy thousands of miles away like this. She had never come to see me when I lived in Cape Coral, so this visit was an extremely peculiar one.

Quickly, I shot a text to Avery telling her Joy was stopping by and I'd fill her in when I got back home. At least she'd know about me if anything happened. Not that I expected anything would go awry, but seeing Joy put me on edge and caused a severe bout of anxiety to rush through my veins.

A few minutes later, there was a knock on my door. I gave myself a little power talk and then expelled a breath before walking across the room. I reached for the knob, and my spine stiffened as I opened the heavy hotel room door. Joy stood on the other side dressed in a white sleeveless body-fitting dress with matching high heels. She wore a rich navy-blue knee-length coat.

Hard eyes stared back at me. "Hello, Ana."

"Hi," was all I said. "Come in."

Joy stepped inside with her clutch gripped between her fingers. She slowly glanced around the room, her eyes taking in every square inch. I licked my drip lips and shut the door. When I turned around, Joy was sitting in a chair at the little table near the window. I walked over and took the seat opposite, regarding her with confusion as I faced her. Her blond hair was flawlessly styled, but her face seemed different…tighter. Like she'd gotten more Botox in her forehead and cheeks.

"I'm surprised to see you," I said.

She placed her purse on the round table and expressed an exaggerated sigh. "Contrary to what you or your father might think, I do care about you."

My brows shot up. I could easily refute that statement with plenty of examples, but I chose not to. There was a reason she made an appearance, and I needed to know why.

"How long have you been here?"

"I flew in two days ago."

"Two days ago? Why didn't you call sooner?"

She lifted her shoulders in a nonchalant shrug like she couldn't be bothered. "We haven't seen each other in a while. I remembered the rules about parents not visiting before a meet, and I knew how important this competition was for you." She paused. "Congratulations on making the team. I have to say, I'm surprised. You've come a long way, and seeing you perform was…an experience." She grew quiet as she observed me. Her eyes were a little misty. "You really did it," she said, a small smile tried to tug on her over plumped lips. "You made it to the Olympics. I thought it was just a dream that all little girls have, but you made it happen. They say when you're stubborn enough anything is possible."

My eyes widened, brows angling toward each other. Stubborn enough to put my health on the line for it.

"You were there? You watched? Why didn't you tell me?"

"I've been to all your big meets over the year. I just didn't tell you."

My lips parted. "But why? Why wouldn't you? You're my mom."

Her eyes flared with a mixture of sadness and regret. "You shouldn't call me that. I'm not your mother. I did try, though. It may not seem like it, but I did."

She looked away. Her guilt hit me square in the chest. I wouldn't say she didn't try, because she had, it was just toward the end that her heart had hardened and her dislike for me became transparent. To Joy, I was the reason she and Dad split up.

"I'm not equipped to be a mother." Her voice splintered with emotion as she looked back at me. "I never wanted kids, let alone wanted raise another woman's child, one who was the product of an affair my husband had, no less. But I tried for Frank because I loved him. I even gave him a son before you came along. I would've given him anything if only he could've stayed faithful to me."

I pulled back, my chest was tight with hostility. I couldn't disguise the hurt etched on my face. Callous words from a callous woman. She never wanted to be a mother. Who said that to the child they raised? She was the only mother I'd ever known, yet she'd completely discarded me in the blink of an eye.

Taking a deep breath, I shook my head. I couldn't stop the words from flying from my mouth. "Other than to remind me how unwanted I am, why are you here? I know what you did. Dad told me everything. Is that why you've been to the meets and didn't tell me?"

Joy stilled. "Well, if you weren't sleeping with your coach, then I never would've had to do anything."

"You told him out of selfishness and not out of concern for me. You did it to get back at him and nothing else."

She looked me dead in the eyes. "I did. There's no reason for me to lie, but I did. Little did I know what my PI would find once I hired him. I was appalled, disgusted by what he found out about you and Konstantin."

"But why? Why did you go to the length that you did?"

"Regardless, Frank needed to know what was happening. Konstantin was his friend."

"That's not why. You used me as blackmail to get what you wanted."

Joy was quiet. She stared out the window again and it bothered me that I felt bad for her. No, I didn't feel bad. I pitied her. She could wear all the makeup she wanted, but it wasn't going to hide the melancholy that flickered too often in her gaze. The fine lines around her eyes and mouth were taut with anguish. She went with her claws out taunting Dad with evidence to get what she wanted out of him for feeling so deceived. Only she hadn't thought it through, and her plan bombed on her.

"I guess that saying rings true," she said more to herself. "Hell hath no fury like a woman scorned," she said with a fleeting smirk. "I'm sorry I couldn't love you the way a child needed to be loved. It wasn't fair of me to try when I knew all along I never wanted to be a mother in the first place. I sometimes wonder if that's why Xavier behaves in the manner he does..." Her quiet voice trailed off. "You're finally getting what you wanted, though. Frank and I are officially divorced."

My head tilted to the side. I frowned, offended she could ever think that was what I wanted.

"That's not what I wanted. I never wanted that. All I ever wanted was for you to want me the way a mother is supposed to want her child. To be happy for me and not pick on me for every little thing I did. To support me and not body shame me. I tried so hard, but nothing was ever good enough for you no matter what I did. Do you have any idea what that did to me?"

Chest rising and falling, my emotions were getting the best of me and I didn't want to give her that. She didn't deserve my tears anymore. She didn't deserve to see me in pain ever again. I think she'd enjoy that even though her guilty body language and remorse was plain as day.

Joy ignored my truth. "Well, you have a real mother now to give that to you."

I shook my head in disbelief. Joy was hurting. I knew she didn't come here to act bitter toward me, but I could feel it in her words. She was such an insecure woman. I'd never understand her.

"Why are you here if you're just going to continue your mean girl mentality? Why did you want to see me?"

Joy stood up. She straightened her dress and picked up her purse. With a dignified look, she said, "I wanted to congratulate you and tell you I am proud of you, regardless of our relationship and what's occurred. Anyway, I won't attend the Olympics, but I'm looking forward to watching you. What you did, so few can do." There was an awkward pause as tears filled her eyes. "It wasn't right of me to take the issues I had with Frank out on you. For that, I'll forever be sorry."

Standing, I meant to follow her to the door but she shocked me in place with her apology. Right before she opened it, Joy turned around and looked at me. Really looked at me.

"Is that why you came? To apologize?" I asked, my stomach tight with apprehension.

An apology was never something she gave easily. However, there was no resentment in her eyes and her shoulders weren't stiff. The mask was gone, and I saw a woman living with a black conscience covered in guilt and lies.

I saw a person with feelings. Her jaw wobbled and it made my heart ache for her. "Yes. I truly am sorry. I never wanted this for you despite my inabilities. A few times I wished I'd paid more attention to you when you performed. You're incredible, Ana, and I felt like you needed to hear me say that in person."

My lips parted. Her eyes watered and she wiped a tear away that slipped out. I was speechless that she allowed herself to be so vulnerable.

Joy opened the door and I held my breath.

Goodbyes were never easy, and that's what this felt like. We had eighteen years of history together that were coming to an end.

I watched as Joy walked out with the door quietly closing behind her.

In my heart, I knew this was probably the last time I'd ever see her again, and I wasn't sure how to feel other than cry.

CHAPER 23

The first day we flew back to Georgia, I slept the entire day.

In fact, I'd slept for three days straight.

The consequences of pushing myself had set in and I was out for the count. My body kept spasming. Everything tightened up and my body fought against me, trying to take over and bring me down. All I could do was wake up to my alarm going off as a reminder to take my medications, eat something small, and then go right back to sleep. I only had a week until I would be shipped off to Texas again, and my body needed to heal. I may be stubborn, but I wasn't an idiot. Recuperating was an absolute must, or I wouldn't stand a chance. For once, I listened to my body's warnings.

I had yet to speak with Kova privately. After I saw Joy, I went to dinner with both coaches and then back to Dad's suite where I'd stayed until we checked out the next day. Dinner had gone surprisingly smooth and luckily short. No words were exchanged between Kova and me after that night and I hadn't seen him since.

Now, I was back on Amelia Island with no way of talking to him. I could use my burner phone, but I didn't want to risk calling him after Katja had picked up that day, so I stored it in a hidden place in my room where it wouldn't be found. It was so tempting, but somehow, I'd managed to resist.

I didn't want to hurt my dad again either. Something about what Sophia had said when she gifted me the book twisted my stomach with guilt.

Still, my heart yearned for Kova. The longing that was caged inside my chest wanted to break free and run to him. I ached for him, his touch, his words, the look in his eyes when it was just the two of us. I fucking missed him so goddamn much. If this was what a real breakup felt like, then I never wanted to experience it again. It hurt.

While I had to drive down to Cape Coral to pack, there still wouldn't be time to see each other. We were flying together to Texas to train and prepare for the Olympics, but it wasn't going to be possible to talk to him during that time either. It definitely couldn't happen on the plane, and there'd be too many ears around for the type of conversation at the training facility too. We needed time, and we didn't have it. I wasn't sure what the status was of his arrest, or if he was charged with anything.

After I finally climbed out of bed, I showered and ate a normal meal, then I texted Avery to tell her I was in town only to get a ton of angry emojis in return because she was away for a cheerleading competition. She congratulated me on making the team. I hadn't told her—apparently Xavier had. When she got back, I'd be in Cape Coral and then Texas. We promised to fill each other in when we got a chance.

Walking into Dad's office, I asked, "Where's Xavier? Is he here?"

He moved the phone away from his face, and mouthed, "Pool house," and pointed a finger toward the window.

Nodding, I turned around and made my way outside and down the walkway to his mini house.

I knocked on the door and waited. I didn't want to barge in on him; who knew what he was doing and with who. It didn't take more than a few seconds for the door to fling open and his bright smile to greet me.

"Hey—"

My brother pulled me into a bear hug and squeezed me. "Sleeping Beauty finally wakes," he joked. Laughing, we separated, and he invited me into the house. "Dad said not to bother you or he would take my credit card and my truck, so I stayed far away."

I beamed up at him. Xavier's truck was his pride and joy.

"It's all good."

I glanced around. It had been awhile since I was here. His pool house looked nothing like what Avery had described when she told me their breakup story. It looked...livable.

"I really needed the rest. I can't believe how much I slept." His eyes softened with empathy and I pointed a finger. "Don't look at me like that, you loser."

Xavier grinned from ear to ear. "I'm just saying for someone who legit slept for days straight minus five hours, you still look like shit."

I rolled my eyes and took a seat on his couch. "I don't feel like it, though. I did when we first got back and my body locked up. I was throwing up like crazy, but I'm way better now."

Xavier studied me. His honey brown eyes took in my face down to my toes. He grabbed a cigarette out of the pack on the beat-up coffee table and lit it between his thumb and index finger. He took a long drag and exhaled.

"Do you mind?" he asked after he lit it, and I shook my head.

I frowned. His hand holding the cigarette shook, and I wondered why.

"Why are you shaking like that?"

His eyes dropped to his hand. "Alcohol withdrawal. I need a fucking drink."

My brows shot up, surprised he was being so honest. Every once in a while, I had seen his hands shake but I never thought anything of it until now. I had no idea it was alcohol related. Kova loved his vodka, but he never shook.

"But it's so early," I said, stating the obvious. It had to be around noon on a Thursday.

Xavier shook his head and brushed it off. "Nope, we're not going there. We're going to talk about you and how you made it to the fucking Olympics. Do you even know how cool it is to say my sis is going to the Olympics?" He paused, and took another drag. "We have a lot to catch up on."

I let out a light laugh. "What if I say we're not going there?" His eyes turned to stone and I stared right back. Of course, I was going to tell him. I smiled and that seemed to loosen him up. "I'm just playing. What do you want to know?"

"Well, for starters, how the hell do you feel? Your arm okay? Healing…everywhere else?" He used his hand to gesture toward my empty stomach.

I moved my arm around, slowly stretching it. "It aches here and there and it's a little sore, but it's much better. Not nearly as bad as it was. I should be good to go by the time the Games start."

"I couldn't believe when Dad called me. I know he didn't tell me everything because he's concerned about my 'anger issues.'" He sounded annoyed. "I almost drove down there to murder Kova and kick Dad's ass for hurting you. I want the truth, Adrianna. What happened? What's been happening? Has your coach been abusing you this whole time? Did he rape you? Why didn't you come to me? Why didn't you tell anyone?"

My stupid brother had already assumed the absolute worst and it was going to be hard to convince him otherwise. The last thing I wanted or needed was him worrying too.

Xavier's nostrils flared, and the hand that wasn't holding the cigarette tightened into a fist. His knee started to bounce furiously. By the rapid succession, I'd swear he had the questions stored in his mind ready for when he saw me. I don't think he even took a breath. His sudden anger struck a slice of panic through me. Stress cramped my stomach. I hoped I wasn't the reason he needed a drink.

I softened with compassion. I wanted Xavier to see that I was going to be honest with him, but make sure he knew that nothing bad had happened to me. I didn't want him to worry about me like that, or think I wasn't protected and left to be abused. This was going to be tricky because I could already taste his rage.

I sighed and pulled my knees up and crossed them under me. I reached for the blanket on the back of the couch and covered myself. His house was freezing yet he was sweating profusely.

"It's not like that. I know what you're thinking and what Dad told you, and I swear on my life that it's not. I know it's hard to believe, but it's the honest truth. I wasn't raped, Xavier. I wasn't abused. I wasn't taken advantage of. Nothing like that ever happened."

He stabbed his cigarette out in a glass ashtray. "Then what the fuck happened? Because I've been thinking the worst over here ready to go on a murder spree."

"It's not pretty."

"Life rarely is."

I was a little unsure what to do. Xavier threw his hands up before I could even think. He had no patience.

"Well? I'm waiting."

Closing my eyes, I began.

The story took nearly an hour to tell, and during that time, I purposely left the sex out. He knew I'd had sex with Kova, he didn't need the details. I told him how Kova had pulled me from the meet, then he'd gotten married without telling me. How I'd hooked up with a guy from the men's team to spite Kova. I wouldn't tell him who, though. Xavier was shocked over that one and said he didn't expect that from me. I told him how his mom had played a part in the whole charade to get back at Dad, and how she'd roped Katja into it. I'd tried to focus on how Kova and I'd connected through gymnastics and personal stories so Xavier could see it was so much more than lust like Dad had said. Kova and I had a mutual attraction and the chemistry didn't need any friction to begin with. It was already there the moment we'd met.

Just about every little aspect of my illicit relationship with my coach, Xavier now knew. He let me speak, but that didn't mean he wasn't fazed by it.

It was the complete opposite. His eyes rarely left mine, but his body emitted a trail of rage I could feel. Quite a few times I'd wondered if this was what Avery had been talking about because it scared me too. He was like a volcano ready to erupt. His knuckles were screaming white and when they weren't, it was because he was chain-smoking cigarettes. He got up and paced the floor, sat down and grabbed his head and pulled on his hair. I felt bad and stopped a few times only for him to wave his hand in a circle for me to keep going. When I was done, we both sat there for a long moment without saying anything.

I was second-guessing my decision to tell him so much.

"It's kind of similar to you and Avery, you know," I said, breaking the silence.

His head snapped up. Elbows on his spread knees, he dropped his hands and gawked. Wild eyes stared back at me.

"You can't possibly say that."

I frowned. How did he not see that? "But it is."

"Aid—no, it's not. Not even close. He's a fucking adult, what he did is illegal. There's a huge difference."

My jaw slackened. "He didn't do anything wrong." I pleaded with him to understand. "How can you sit there and say that after I told you I pursued him too? I told you I love him. How can you sit there and say otherwise? Who cares about the ages?"

He put his hand up. "Stop. I can't stomach anymore. I'm disgusted. All I can picture is his hands on you, and I want to fucking break them."

Xavier stood and marched into the kitchen, each step louder. I followed him and watched as he yanked opened the freezer and pulled out a bottle of vodka by the neck. He didn't bother with a glass. He uncapped it and took a long swig. I grimaced. How gross. That stuff tasted like rubbing alcohol.

"Xavier, please. I thought you'd be understanding."

He put the bottle back and wiped his mouth on his bicep. "Well, you thought wrong. There's no excuse, honestly." He glared at me, refusing to back down. "There's not."

Hurt laced my eyes as anger ignited inside of my heart. "Avery told me she went after you too. And you're an adult."

He let out a haughty laugh. "Yeah, she's fucking lying, but I'm not surprised. That's all she's good at anyway." He shook his head. "Fucking lies. She's filled with them."

My eyes lowered, and the flame of anger inside of me rose higher with how he spoke about my best friend he'd screwed over. Avery wouldn't lie to me, not after our pact.

"I knew she wanted me, so I chased her until she caved because I wanted that sweet ass too. Only it kicked back and I got attached. Who knew—little fucking Avery." He shook his head again like he was in a state of disbelief. "Karma got me, though, when she got rid of our kid."

"That's right. You got her pregnant then fucked her over and left her."

CHAPER 24

is eyes widened and all I could see was white.

"Don't even go there!" he yelled in my face, spit flying. I pulled back because I wasn't going to take his aggression. "You have no idea what you're talking about."

"You're a drug addict and an alcoholic. She couldn't handle that and tried to help you. I know about all the overdosing too. You were spinning out of control. You shoved her away to hook up with someone else in front of her. You fucked her over and left her and then ignored her while she was going through the worst time of her life. You used her. I knew you would too, and had I known what was happening, I would've stopped it the first chance I got."

It wasn't fair of me to say that, but I was mad and couldn't stop the pent-up aggression from coming out of me. Damnit. A tear slipped from the corner of my eye. And then another. I couldn't tell if it was because I was angry, sad, or just frustrated with everything.

"Don't start with the waterworks. That's the same stupid shit she used to do, and it won't work."

"You're such a dick," I said and wiped them away. "You got my best friend fucking pregnant and then walked out of her life like she didn't exist. How can you sit there and get mad at me and want to kill Kova when you're no better?"

I thought he was going to explode. Xavier put his index and middle finger in the air along with his thumb. It reminded me of a gun. His hand trembled and from that trembling came his wrath that spread throughout the room.

"You better stop, now," he said. His voice was quiet, barely in control. I wasn't afraid of him. He'd never physically hurt me, but I'd never seen him this worked up before either. "You're so far off that I'm about to fucking lose it. What happened is because of her, not me. I didn't do anything wrong but worship the dirty ground she walked on. She fucked us up."

"Famous last words from a junkie," I spat out and then immediately wished I could take it back.

His chest rose and fell fast, and his eyes flared. "Seriously, Aid? How fucking dare you compare me to your sleaze-ball coach and then call me a junkie. What Avery and I had was really not the same at all. I don't care if you stood in front of him naked with your legs spread willing and ready, he should have walked away. Dad trusted him. He was supposed to look after you, not fuck you." He seethed. "I can't believe Dad didn't kill him."

"He almost did."

"Good. I wish he had. I wish that fucker was six feet under and rotting. I wish I could pull each fucking limb from his body."

My jaw trembled violently. Before I could stop them, tears gushed from my eyes. This was not what I wanted to happen when I came in here to see him. I didn't want to fight with my brother. I missed him and wanted to talk to him.

I covered my face with my hands and cried, sobbing quietly. A loud sound erupted in the room, like an explosion, and I jumped. Glancing up, I saw Xavier had punched a wall. There was a massive hole.

He stalked over to me and I stepped backwards quickly. My heart was racing. His knuckles were bleeding and when I stumbled, he grabbed me by my elbow.

"Get the fuck over here," he said, and hauled me to his chest.

Xavier released a deep, slow sigh that was dripping in regret, and hugged me. I broke down, crying hysterically against him.

"I'm sorry for calling you a junkie." I whimpered. "I didn't mean to. I know you're not."

"Just shut up. I am one, and I got pissed. I'm your big brother. I'm supposed to protect you and all I ever do is fuck up every damn day. I'm not mad at you, I'm mad at myself and feel like all I do is let people down." Cupping the back of my head, my brother held me, letting me cry as much as I needed to. "I wanted to kill him, sis, when Dad told me what happened. He had to hold me back because I fucking lost it and I was ready to get my boys and go after him. I feel like I let you down and didn't protect you when you needed it most."

His apology wasn't helping my emotions because all I could do was feel the weight of his words and the regret lining them. I clenched my eyes shut trying to hold in the tears. We both felt bad. Maybe we both had shit built up inside we had to get out, and it just happened to be with each other.

Guilt ate away at my heart. All I did was hurt people and sometimes I didn't even know I was doing it.

"I promise, Xavier, I promise nothing like that happened. I swear." I sniffled. "I have no reason to lie anymore. Please believe me. He—Kova—he was sick over it when it happened. I didn't care that he was, and I found myself purposely tempting him and trying to be around him."

Xavier pulled back and lifted the hem of his shirt for me to wipe my tears. I tried to smile but I couldn't bring myself to as I took it and dabbed my eyes. I was hurt, but so was he. God, I wished we could go back and redo this conversation from the start.

Exhaling a large breath, I glanced up and was taken aback by the way he was looking at me.

Xavier was in a bad place. I had a terrible gut feeling no one knew just how messed up inside he was. His pointed nose flared. His dirty blond eyelashes framed the glowing amber of his eyes. He was going through some deep stuff too.

I didn't say anything. All I could do was hug my brother. He was emotionally suffering just as much as I was, possibly more, and maybe, just maybe, he needed this more than I did.

My heart pounded against my chest for him. Squeezing my eyes shut, I prayed that whatever he was dealing with inside would get better.

Xavier rested his head on top of my shoulder and we stood in silence as tears streamed down my flushed cheeks. He dipped his head and I felt his back shaking. It was a subtle shake, but I could feel it.

After a few good minutes of us dealing with our struggles in quiet, I said, "I know you're mad at her, but I hope you can come to terms with what happened between you guys. Not only is she my best friend, but she's my match, Xavier. She's always going to be in my life."

"I know. What are the chances that would happen?"

Xavier seemed much calmer now that he released whatever he was holding in.

"I was just as shocked. She surprised me on my birthday with the news."

"I know. She told me," he said, and I glanced up with my brows drawn together. He answered my puzzled stare. "When she got the news, she was bursting to tell you. I'm sure you know she's terrible with surprises. So, she told me and talked my ear off for days and said she was going shopping for you."

A dim smile tugged at one corner of my mouth.

"She got me some really funny things," I said, thinking of the shirts and mug. "I loved them."

"Yeah, I saw them. I helped her pick them out."

Surprise was written on my face. She hadn't told me they'd spoken or that he'd helped her, but I guess that didn't really matter in the grand scheme of things anymore.

"It'll never work out with her," he added, his voice as far away as his stare. He was looking at something over my shoulder, but I could see he was lost in his thoughts.

"You don't know that."

He looked back at me. "No, I do."

"Do you love her?"

His long silence was my answer and I didn't like that. It was like barbed wire around my bleeding heart.

"I don't want you to worry about me and her. Everything'll be fine. I'll be real with you that I still fucking love her even though I want to wring her tiny goddamn neck. I know she feels the same way. But sometimes love just isn't enough, some things just can't be forgiven."

"Crazier things have happened."

He ignored me. "The last couple of years have been really… disturbing, but I'll always be here for you. I love you, but you better not ever think about hooking up with that man again, Adrianna, because I will kill him."

A sad chuckle rolled off my lips. I knew he wasn't serious. At least I didn't think he was.

"I love him, Xavier. How does one stop loving someone when it's killing them? I don't want to let go of him, and I know he feels the same way about me."

"Even with everything he's done to you, you still would hold on and love him?"

Before I answered, I took a hard look at him. Something in my gut said he was asking more for himself than to question me. I had a feeling this had to do with him and Avery.

"I do." I looked in his eyes and told him the truth. "If it's worth it, I have to forgive to move on. Kova's worth it." I nodded. Xavier didn't say anything. He seemed surprised and slightly hopeful. "Please, *please*," I said, stressing the word, "don't tell Dad. It's the honest truth, though."

He lifted my side braid and ran his fingers over it. Still looking at my hair, he said under his breath, "When you find out how to stop loving people when it's killing you, let me know."

CHAPER 25

'd almost forgotten I had to see my doctor for a full checkup before I left.

Lupus brain fog was real.

I drove south to Cape Coral the day of the appointment.

Before I'd left, Dad told me Kova had called him and said he needed to speak with me because a couple of colleges had inquired about me. I had been thrilled, thinking I could put my focus on my next goal to keep my mind busy, but Dad had been reluctant. He didn't want me going back to World Cup for anything without him, especially where Kova was involved. But he also knew how important it was to discuss this matter. As gradually as I could, I'd reminded him Kova wasn't going to college with me.

With a little over an hour before I had to see my doctor, I was currently sitting in Kova's office with Madeline next to me. They'd already been in his office waiting for me when I walked in wearing light denim skinny jeans and a boho chic top with my leopard flats.

Looking at him but not being able to touch him, physically hurt me. I was getting to the point where I was unable to tell the difference between heartache and the tightness from my illnesses anymore. Both hacked my chest open with bare hands. I swallowed, wondering if he felt the same. I thought this would be easy—come in, have the conversation, leave.

But it wasn't like that at all.

The anguish in my chest at seeing him again in his element consumed my heart and took over all feeling. His fingertips tapped the top of the wood desk and my eyes dropped to the motion. Memories of us in his office flashed through my mind. My eyes lifted to the wall he took me against when Hayden had walked in and found us. I looked back at the desk he was still tapping, and I pictured myself hidden under it naked when Katja had walked in.

I shot a quick glance over my shoulder to look at the couch where we had shared many intimate moments together and did a double take. My stomach plummeted.

It was a direct blow to my gut.

The couch was gone. My brows knitted together and hurt lacerated my tender heart. I wondered when he got rid of it, and why. My instincts told me it had to do with us, but the bigger part of me fighting for us was more optimistic about it.

I turned and faced forward. Madeline was still writing stuff down and checking her phone while she did, mumbling to herself. Kova was peering straight into my eyes with a helpless look.

I needed him. I needed to touch him, to feel his arms wrapped around me. I needed him to demand I tell him I love him so I could say I hate you. I just needed him to breathe against me and I'd know how he felt about us.

Absence did not make the heart grow fonder. It made the heart ache for something that might never be.

I didn't believe in soul mates. I thought the saying was cheesy, it made me laugh, but I got it now. I understood it, because I felt the two words come together.

Not attempting to see Kova later was going to be a struggle. I was trying to respect my father's wishes and not hurt anyone else, but when my stomach was in knots and my heart was screaming out for him, it was difficult to consider anyone else's feelings but my own.

I looked at Kova. Our eyes met and he took my breath away. His hat was missing—I loved seeing him in it. The half-moon crescents under his eyes and drained expression told me he hadn't been sleeping much. I briefly wondered if he was writing his thoughts away or finding solace at the bottom of a vodka bottle. Sometimes he did that when his thoughts were dark.

My gaze drifted further down and I noticed Kova wasn't wearing his wedding ring anymore. I glanced away, trying to think back to the Trials and whether or not he had it on then, but it was all a blur. I wanted to believe he hadn't worn it, but I just couldn't remember.

"It's good to see you, Adrianna," Madeline finally said. She looked up from the binder she'd been writing in. "It felt strange not seeing you all week."

I gave her a sincere smile and cupped some loose strands of my hair behind my ear. "It was strange not being here, actually. I didn't know what to do with myself. All my schoolwork is done. I finished early, so I just slept the whole time."

Her gaze softened with a knowing look I didn't like. She knew why I'd slept the week away, I was positive she knew. Though, it became a question with multiple choice answers. Did she know about both diseases? Or about the abortion—could I call it that if I'd already started to miscarry?

I didn't want to think about it.

"What did you do with your medals?" she asked me.

Now I was grinning from ear to ear. "I hung them up in my room at my dad's house along with the flowers. I placed the bouquet upside down to dry so I could keep them forever."

"That was such a great idea. You can spray them with hairspray and they'll hold."

"Thanks. I'll do that."

Just as I looked at Kova, Danilo walked in. Glancing over my shoulder, I watched as he took a chair that looked too small for him to sit in and pulled it right next to me. He was a beast of a man and looked like someone on steroids. I bet he crushed soda cans between his meaty hands for fun.

"As you know, Danilo is now with World Cup," Kova said. "I felt he should sit in with us to go over a few things as he will be the new head coach."

I frowned, and looked back at Kova. Head coach? But what about him? Or were there two head coaches?

I studied Kova's gaze, trying to see what he meant by that, but he gave nothing away. Zero. Was he going to have to go back to jail? The thought made me queasy and now I had even more reason to talk to him privately…if we ever could, that was.

"Congratulations, Adrianna," Danilo said, putting my attention back on him. His Ukrainian accent was stronger than Kova's Russian.

"Thank you."

"Yes, let us get started," Kova said and stacked a few papers together. "A few universities have interest in you. They are top ranking division one schools in gymnastics. Now, while we are unaware as to what you plan for your future, it would behoove you to consider their offers, and to do it soon."

My lips twitched at the way he said "behoove.".

Kova continued. "They are aware you are a member of the Olympic gymnastics team and that you may postpone for one year. This is very common. Should you commit to a school, you have a place on any of the teams whether you postpone or not, except for one."

I was curious. "Which schools?"

Kova's eyes scanned the papers. "University of Florida, UCLA, University of Georgia, and University of Oklahoma. They are all offering full gymnastics scholarships. The head coach at UCLA feels she can work with you enough on beam to have you as an all-around gymnast, and not just a specialist. Georgia and Florida want you as a specialist on vault and bars. The difference between them is Florida wants you to commit this year. They will have to reassess you the following year. Oklahoma wants you as a specialist on vault, bars, and floor." He paused and looked me in the eyes. It was hard to focus on his words when I was looking at him. "You have options."

"All the schools are the absolute best. You can't go wrong with any of them," Madeline said. I turned toward her and she smiled. "I'm partial to Florida—Go, Gators!—since I went to school there." She put her arms out and did the gator chomp. It made me smile bigger.

"I have no preference," Danilo added blandly, and I stifled a giggle. He just shrugged when I looked at him. "I am not familiar with any university here."

I sat for a moment thinking as I looked back to Kova. Madeline and Danilo gave me their opinions, but Kova hadn't and I was curious what he thought.

"What do you think?" I asked him.

Kova's opinion mattered most to me.

"It does not matter what I think. The choice is yours to make."

My brows furrowed, my smile faltering a bit. I was overcome with emotion. Uncertain which choice was right, grateful that I'd been offered at all. I swallowed, feeling a little stressed out but happy. If we were alone, I would ask again and make him tell me.

"When do I need to make a decision by?" I asked.

"Your commitment will be announced after the Olympics so you can focus. I believe the schools will be emailing you and your dad with documents to review."

Being offered a place on the team from any of those schools was an honor. I was flattered they recognized me. Kova had said they were watching, but I never believed it when there were so many other athletes better than me.

"You have a big decision to make," Madeline said. "You'll have to weigh the pros and cons and really think about where you want to call home for the next four years or so."

Danilo added, "They will do a full medical sweep on you as well and check you for ailments. It is wise to be honest and up front before any contract is signed."

I nodded reluctantly, aware of what he was hinting at. Eventually I'd have to share my secret and pray the school wouldn't withdraw their offer. Until then, I couldn't worry about it. I had enough on my plate as it was.

"Before you leave today," Madeline said, "you'll need to clean your locker out since you won't be returning to train here."

I was quiet. It never occurred to me that I needed to take everything with me, but she was right. I would never train at World Cup again. Tomorrow I would leave for Texas, and then I was Olympics bound. After that, I was going back home to Amelia Island.

I glanced down at my hands. My palms were dry, and the skin was ripped a little. A bittersweet sensation climbed to my eyes. I hadn't grown up in this gym training, but I spent enough time here to consider it a home. I matured as a person and athlete. I formed friendships and relationships within these walls. I cried and laughed.

I'd take the memories with me and hold them close to my heart. This was another chaper of my life I was about to finish.

"You didn't realize, did you?" she asked softly. I shook my head.

Still looking at my hands, I said, "I guess I'll be saying goodbye, then."

"Take all the time you need."

Madeline and Danilo rose to their feet. "Make sure you come say goodbye before you leave. The girls are waiting on us, so we need to get out there."

Danilo stared down at me a moment, then said, "Second place winner is first place loser. Bring home the gold." My lips lifted at his words of wisdom.

I sniffled back my emotions and thanked Danilo, then told Madeline I'd find her. The door shut behind them as they left, leaving Kova and me alone.

The moment I'd been waiting for had finally arrived.

The air in the room became dense, that awkward silence filling the space between us. It was just the two of us, a ticking clock, and many, many words left unspoken.

I blinked my eyes rapidly trying to fight the tears when I decided to stand. I needed to get out of here, but I wanted to ask Kova questions. My pulse kicked up a notch and beat like a drum in my throat. I was jittery, feeling too vulnerable at the moment. I wasn't prepared for these emotions when I came here and now that they were baiting me. I needed to leave or I was going to cry any second.

"I'll see you later." My throat tightened and my words sounded mumbled.

I couldn't even look at him.

Saying goodbye to World Cup meant saying goodbye to Kova.

My heart was not ready for that.

My. Heart. Was. Not. Ready.

I couldn't breathe. Oh God. My chest was so tight. I struggled to get air into my lungs.

"Wait," he said, but I was already at the door and reaching for the knob. "Please." His hand appeared in front of me. He held the door closed, and I immediately dropped my hand.

We were alone. He was right next to me. My eyes closed shut as my breathing deepened. I could feel the warmth of his presence, the smell of his sultry cologne, the dire need pulsing through me to reach out for him. I couldn't walk away when we were made for each other.

I shook my head before he could say anything. My eyes were filled with tears now. There were pieces of my heart embedded here that I couldn't take back with me. How was I supposed to leave?

Kova didn't say anything.

I didn't say anything.

Did he know how much I needed him right now? How close I was to breaking inside?

Of course, he did. Because he was Kova, and I was Ria, and we understood each other in ways no one else could.

He reached for me…and that was all it took.

Kova cupped my arm and pulled me to him. I went willingly and let out a cry against him. My hand found his chest and I fisted his shirt as soft tears fell from my eyes. I hugged him so tight, like I was afraid to let go, because I was. I was scared to let go because I wasn't sure what would happen to us next.

"Ria," he whispered. His fingers brushed the hair away under my ear and draped it over my other shoulder. He tried to tip my face back to look at him, but I shook my head. "Please, I need you to look at me."

"I'm so sorry." I whimpered. "For everything. I wish I could take it all back."

"No," he said on a strangled gasp. "Do not say that. I do not regret a thing, and I know you do not either."

Taking my wrists gently into his hands, he brought them up and over his shoulders so I had no choice but to hug him, and it broke my heart even more. He let go then placed his hands under my shirt and on my hips like he needed to feel me. Kova hugged me to him. A sigh rolled through my lips at the touch of his warm flesh on mine.

Kova needed me too.

Rising up on my tiptoes, my heart beat wildly against my ribs. With trembling fingers threading through the hair at the back of his neck, I finally looked up.

My heart was in his hands.

CHAPER 26

wanted to kiss him and tell him that I did love him, that I was going to do whatever I could to fix this and make it right, but something felt so off that it caused a tide of anxiety to wrap around my heart and hold back.

I could hardly breathe. Kova's eyes were on mine, but he wasn't looking at me. He seemed distant even though he was right in front of me. My chest rose and fell, tight with the panic that he no longer wanted me in his arms.

"What...what's wrong?" I asked.

I'd never felt him like this, so withdrawn from even himself. It scared me.

"Nothing," he said under his breath. "I just want to look at you."

His hands squeezed my hips, his fingers clenching my twisted shirt in his hands now. Kova was nervous. I didn't like the feeling closing in on me at seeing him like that. It made my stomach ache, like a negative intuition I feared to acknowledge. It lit up through me, but I doused the paranoia and pressed closer to him. I wasn't supposed to hurt when I was in his arms, and I was going to prove to myself it was all in my head.

"Kiss me," I said quietly. I wanted his lips on mine, but I wanted more to see his reaction.

Kova let go of my shirt and placed his palm around the side of my neck. My knees were weak with him this close. Something so simple caused a surge of feeling to rush through me. His thumb caressed my jaw, and his lips parted, but he didn't move. All Kova did was look at me like he was suffering inside.

If he wasn't going to kiss me, then I would kiss him. I would show him that despite everything, I was still his and he was still mine and we would get through this.

I leaned into him and felt his palm press against my chest.

My breath hitched in my throat.

I blinked, and frowned.

Kova. Stopped. Me.

My frowned deepened.

Kova didn't want to kiss me.

I reared back, my eyes as round as a full moon. I stared at him. Surprisingly, his gaze didn't waver, but he was sad and confused, filled with indecision.

We'd come so far. This didn't make sense. He wasn't supposed to look at me like that.

Oh, God.

I was going to be sick.

It wasn't supposed to be like this.

He was supposed to crush his stupid fish lips to mine and kiss me like I meant everything to him. He was supposed to tell me we'd get through this. He was supposed to tell me he loved me, damn it.

My hands fell from around him and I stepped back. My legs shook. A numbing low vibration spread beneath my skin. It made me jittery as hell. I needed to get out of here before I threw up. Kova didn't want me anymore, and I wasn't sure how to handle it.

"I have to leave," I said.

A string of Russian flew from his lips as I reached for the doorknob behind me. Kova's arms flew up to the sides of my head and caged me in. I looked up at him, confused, and held my breath. He couldn't tear his eyes from mine. Kova stepped closer until I was forced to press against the door. I was confused, yet I couldn't stop myself from relishing the feel of his body on mine. A gush of air rolled off my lips. He was touching me, he was right in front of me, and yet he wasn't, but now he wasn't letting me leave.

Kova pressed his forehead to mine and let out a shaky sigh. He was struggling and I hated that after we'd come so far.

"Do not ever second-guess my love for you again," he said, then smashed his lips to mine.

Tears climbed my eyes. My jaw trembled and I broke down seeing the insult in his wounded gaze. I couldn't help but cry against his mouth. I felt guilty for doubting his love after he'd told me countless times how much I meant to him. The first opportunity to question him, and I slipped into a coma of insecurity.

"Please, do not cry," he said, then kissed me again. Kova's lips were on mine, but he wasn't there.

"Then kiss me like you mean it," I begged.

"Devil, strike me down," he whispered so low that I almost missed it.

His lips stroked mine with despair, but his tongue didn't penetrate. He breathed against me, and I begged for any ounce of proof that he still loved me.

Kova tugged my top lip between his as he wrapped his arm around the small of my back. He pulled me flush against him and held on to me with his warm body. I wanted so badly to take the lead, but I needed some sort of signal from him that we were okay so I could put those thoughts to rest. I needed to see if what I was fearing was all in my head, or if my worst nightmares were true, and I was losing him."

He proved me wrong.

Kova's tongue licked past the seam of my lips with a sigh. He leaned into me and let go of whatever he was holding on to, kissing me like he meant it. His tongue fondled mine, his teeth were sharp nibbles on my lips. He made sure his mouth consumed every breath of air I had. He took and took and took, and I loved that he did because I loved his fiery passion and the way it made me tingle everywhere. His shaking hands gripped every inch of skin he could touch, his nails dug into my skin as he lost himself in us.

This was my Kova. The Kova my heart beat fiercely for.

His hands slid down to the back of my thighs. Kova lifted me up and pressed my back to the door. I melted against his strong chest, loving how he held me in his arms. Sex with Kova was electrifying, but kissing Kova was something entirely different that I wasn't sure how to put into words. A kiss was more intimate. A kiss was unspoken words tangled with raw feeling. It brought you closer to someone. It was how I learned to understand Kova.

We needed this moment to know that we still had each other to get through this.

My legs wrapped around his waist as he deepened the kiss and made love to me this way, telling me he was still there when I thought for a moment he wasn't.

"I missed you so much," I said in between kisses.

His hand came up to press against my throat. I swallowed, remembering how much he liked that. Vibrant green eyes stared back at me before roaming over every inch of my face. His jet-black lashes lowered, his thumb smoothed over my neck and jaw, then to my lips, like he was finger painting them. His tongue dragged over his bottom lip as he leaned in to steal another kiss from me.

"Not more than I missed you," he said.

"I thought you might hate me for what happened."

His eyes snapped to mine, his brows angled toward each other. "Impossible."

"Where's your wedding ring?"

His callused thumb was still on my throat like he wanted to feel me talk. "I do not know." When I didn't say anything, he said, "I threw it out the window while I was driving." His voice was low, guttural when he spoke. "It is of no value to me and a reminder of the mistake I made."

"Oh." I wasn't expecting that.

"I know you have your appointment and a few things to wrap up here, but I need to hold you for just a moment longer." He paused and carried us to his desk where he sat on top of it with me wrapped around him. "We have to talk."

Dread coiled inside of me.

Four words, that when put together, could quintessentially make or break a relationship. I tried not to think the worst like I had earlier, and hoped for the best.

My head fell forward and rested on the honey curve of his neck.

"When we arrive in Texas tomorrow, there will be a full health scan by the Olympic coaches and the governing bodies. They look for all unauthorized medication that enhances performance." He tightened his arms. "I know you do not want anyone to know about your health right now, but they will discover the medications in your blood. They are going to question you."

I stared at his neck, unblinking. "What if they think I'm using steroids or something?"

"They will not. I have already checked all of your medications against the list."

My brows furrowed. Lifting my head, I looked at him. "How? You don't know them."

His fingers twirled a lock of my auburn hair. Tugging on the strand he was looking at, he said, "When I called Frank and spoke to him about the universities, I mentioned this issue as well. He gave me a list and we both agreed that you need a printed copy of your medical records from all doctors. I informed him that the Olympic doctors and media news stations will learn of the kidney disease and lupus. They will no doubt talk about it."

I swallowed hard. "What do you think the worst is that can happen?" My fingers rubbed over his skin. "I'm nervous now. I didn't even think about them finding out."

One corner of his mouth twitched. "Nothing other than you will most likely have more cameras in your face than other gymnasts, and more questions to answer. Probably more screenings. I do not want you to fear the worst or think that you will be treated any differently when we get to Texas. Believe me, the coaches will not go easy on you and they will not feel bad in the least. They have a one-track mind and all they see is gold. They will demand your blood and sweat. But I want you to be prepared beforehand to talk about it."

"Thank you for warning me. You know I don't like talking about it. It makes me feel like a walking disease. I mean, I am, but I feel like all eyes are on me now and I hate that feeling. I think this might be harder for me than the actual Games."

Kova eyed me cautiously.

"I want you to think of it as a story of both survival and inspiration, nothing else," he said, but his voice was too distant again for my liking. "That is what you are, Adrianna. You are an inspiration. You may not see it now, but one day a young gymnast will look up to you for your strength and fight, using your story as her motivation. Do not get caught in your emotions thinking the worst. Not only did you make the team, you made it while having lupus *and* kidney disease. That is not something to just be proud of, but to wear with pride. People will talk regardless. Who gives a shit? Do not let that take away from what you are about to do."

My lips twitched for a second. He said shit with a heavier than usual Russian accent.

"Why didn't you give an opinion when I asked about colleges? You know what you think matters to me. I want your insight."

He kissed the top of my head. "I don't want you to make a decision based on what I say."

"I won't. I'm just curious. I'm sure you know more about the schools than I do anyway."

Kova sighed deeply. "UCLA is a fantastic school, the team is top-notch. The head coach is someone I could see working well with you. She is known for bringing out the best in gymnasts and giving them time to find where they shine most. However, after all you have been through, what you will undergo soon, I am not sure competition on all four events is wise. You hate balance beam. Why waste your time and energy on something you dislike when you can spend it on something you love and excel at?"

Kova made a valid point, but I also liked to challenge myself. Plus, if I was taking a year off to recover, then I could possibly do all four events.

"Florida and Oklahoma are both neck and neck," he continued. "I personally love watching you on floor. Yes, vault and bars are where you outdo every competitor, but you come alive on floor, so I am leaning toward Oklahoma. With that all being said, given your health, Florida is an ideal choice for you."

My finger traced back and forth over his collarbone. I noticed he didn't suggest Georgia. My intuition told me he didn't want to make it seem like he was asking me to stay back and that was why he didn't bring it up.

Goose bumps prickled my skin as I touched him. Kova rested his cheek on the top of my head. I realized this was all it took for me—a stolen moment with him that settled my nerves.

CHAPER 27

I think your best option at this point is to forgo dialysis and schedule the transplant surgery immediately following the Olympics."

Puzzled, I sat staring at Dr. Kozol as if he'd just spoken a foreign language and expected me to understand *and* respond to it. The plan was originally to begin dialysis so I could allow my body time to rest and heal from gymnastics before I jumped into surgery. I knew eventually I had to get the transplant, just not so soon.

"I don't understand," I said, confusion shifting through me. I thought I was doing okay, better than I had in a long time. I felt okay, not worse. "I was going to move after the Olympics, possibly to another state. I thought I would continue our treatments there, just long distance. Now I need to schedule surgery immediately? What happened to dialysis?"

While I hadn't had time to give it thought considering how fast my life was moving lately, I knew accepting a place on one of the college teams was next on my list. If I had surgery, the offer might be retracted. A decision needed to be made soon even though I'd only just learned of the proposals.

It'd be what I worked for, my incentive to get better.

Not to mention, Avery had to prepare too. Was there even enough time for both of us to get on the same schedule? Anxiety gripped me. This was getting more real by the minute.

Avery was going to college. Did that mean she needed to take a leave of absence? I couldn't do that to her, especially not her freshman year. Maybe a summer surgery would work. That way we both could rest and heal properly. This summer was too late, it would have to be next year.

Clearing my throat, I continued. "Were my test results not what you expected?"

"They're not where I hoped you'd be at this point. You're responding to the medication, but your body is fighting it, and though the decline is slow, it's steady. The longer you go without surgery, the more wear and tear you're doing to your body even though you can't physically see it. You need to really consider surgery immediately upon returning. You don't want to get to the point where you'll be too far gone."

While Dr. Kozol had seen me when I was in the hospital, he hadn't been able to run the tests he typically did. When I got here, he had vials of blood drawn and tested in his office, some sent out to the lab, along with X-rays and ultrasounds on various organs. He left no stone unturned. I'd sat for hours in his office thinking he'd tell me one thing only to surprise me with something else.

I glanced down at my lap. My fingers were twisted together, my nailbeds a pale pink. This was not what I was expecting. That changed a lot for me. I wouldn't be able to do that *and* move at the same time.

"How would this work if I move out of state?"

Dr. Kozol stared at me for an uncomfortable moment. "Where are you planning to go?" I listed the schools I was offered a scholarship to and told him the training hours were not nearly as grueling. His bushy brows rose. "So, you're going to continue with gymnastics?"

I nodded, and his eyes bore deeper into mine. I felt like he was silently ridiculing me, that I was reckless for my choices. He wasn't happy with me.

"If it's possible, I'd like to. It's really the only motivation I have right now."

"Have you considered speaking to a psychologist?"

I grimaced. "No, I don't want to do that."

The last thing I wanted to do was tell some stranger my problems and have them give me more pills to take. I was already on a daily cocktail of medication. I didn't want to add more.

"I'm concerned the illnesses have skewed your vision. You're not making wise decisions, Adrianna. Maybe you should really consider speaking to someone. You do realize you won't be able to do gymnastics this year if you have surgery, right? It's not physically possible."

Of course, I was aware of that. I was aware of everything against me.

I wasn't going to answer him. If I could do dialysis, then I'd be okay for a little while. He had to know that was the door I was going to walk through. At least that way everyone can get prepared and adjusted. That's what I told myself, anyway.

"Wherever you decide to live, I'll put a team together for you. Everyone knows someone in this field, but I'll make sure I'm personally part of the new team, if you like." Dr. Kozol grimaced as he stacked the papers together. "Medically speaking, however, it's not wise. I just don't see how you're going to be able to come back with the thunder you need to train, even if the hours are less and the routines are not as demanding. Transplant recovery is going to take months for you to heal. Then you have to build yourself back up, and then start training. I'm concerned you're going to break your body back down and we'll have to start over. We don't want that. We only want to go up from here."

"But it's doable?" I asked, hopeful.

"I can't recall seeing anyone do it, but that doesn't mean it's not possible." He paused. "I just have to ask something." I nodded, curious about what he wanted to know. "Is gymnastics really worth risking your life for? Really think about that question. You're young. Why are you trying to destroy yourself? You wear yourself down by playing a sport. Once you reach stage five, which you aren't far from, that's it, Adrianna. You can kiss gymnastics goodbye and live out your days in a hospital bed." He studied me. "I don't understand why you want to do that. You'll make your life so much harder."

My eyes dropped to the floor. I didn't have a death wish. I guess I just didn't like my life and strived for a better life. It bothered me that something that couldn't be seen could dictate so much in my life.

"If we're not going to schedule your transplant right after, then we need to start you on dialysis. I want you on a plane back here within two days after the Olympics. Otherwise, I'm going to have to resign as your doctor. The risk is too great, and you've not yielded to the treatment I've devised for you. I've done everything I can for you up until now—I've waited long enough."

If I did what he said, that meant I wouldn't be able to do the promo tours with the Olympic team after. My heart crumbled a little.

"I'm not trying to be defiant and I don't want to die. I guess it's the one thing I have control over. It's the one thing that truly makes me happy. Without gymnastics, I don't know who I am. I don't know how to live or what to do."

"That's because you haven't given yourself time to live," he said sympathetically. "Give yourself time to recover properly and then weigh your choices. After that, you can decide what you want to live for. You'll have all the time in the world during recovery to find who you are and what you want to do."

Quietly, I said, "I don't know how to live without gymnastics if I quit. Gymnastics is who I am."

"You don't have to quit. There are other ways to be involved in the sport. You need to get better first and then sort out your future. But with these kind of results after months and months of powerful medications"—he tapped the paper—"you're knocking on death's door. Your kidney function is already extremely low. You're pushing the limit. If you drop to fifteen percent, you'll need emergency surgery. Just attending college is going to be difficult in general with the side effects of dialysis. You need to seriously weigh your pros and cons."

I nodded. "I have a question. Realistically, say I start dialysis shortly after I come home, and say I respond well to the treatment, how long do I have before I would need a transplant?"

Dr. Kozol chuckled under his breath. "I feel bad for your future husband," he joked, which made me laugh. "If, and that's a big if, you have a positive response, I'd say no more than two years to be safe. Four would be ideal, but given where your health is right now, that's highly unlikely. We'd rather be prepared early. I hesitate to tell you this because I don't want you to focus on that."

I perked up. I could work with a two-year timeline for both Avery and myself. Even though she was selflessly giving me a kidney, I had to take her time into consideration too. I wasn't going to chance my life like everyone around me assumed I was. I felt in my heart of hearts I'd get better enough to compete again, and that's the kind of mentality I went with. I could hire a personal trainer and do light workouts while recovering with dialysis that way I didn't lose what I'd worked so hard to attain.

Biting the inside of my cheek, I said, "Let's schedule the dialysis now. I'll be here with bells on first thing when I get back." I stopped when something dawned on me. "Wait, I'm supposed to be going back to Amelia Island after the Games."

"That's not an issue. I have an office about thirty minutes west of there. I'll make sure your file is transferred and everything is in place when you come in. In the meantime, once you decide where you will relocate to, let me know so I can put together a reputable team. How long will you remain in Georgia?"

"I'm not sure."

Dr. Kozol began writing while he asked me questions. Since I was deferring school to recover, I had roughly nine months before school started again, which meant I had about six or so to prepare for the collegiate team, and three months to get my health in order.

"Right now, you're retaining fluid in your feet, which isn't good."

"Is that why they felt stiff and swollen this morning? I almost had to change my shoes."

"Yes. Luckily, it hasn't reached your face. Any nausea or confusion? Irregular heartbeat? A change in urine?"

I shook my head. "Honestly, no. I've been feeling really good. Other than the usual joint pain and more hair loss, nothing out of the ordinary. My headaches have been pretty bad, but I think those are due to the fact I'm stressed out and running on anxiety because of the training camp and the Games."

His eyes met mine above the rim of his glasses. "Don't ignore what your body is trying to tell you."

"I'm not."

The room grew quiet as Dr. Kozol made his notes. I wasn't too thrilled about starting dialysis.

"You're going to be monitored for heart disease since you already have severe kidney damage that's progressing. I'm going to switch out one of your medications for a stronger steroid. This'll help with the wear and tear. I implore you to take the medication exactly as it's stated on the bottle. You cannot miss a dose."

I sat up straighter. "I'll fill the prescription, but I need to see if it's on the list of banned medications before I take it. I'm going to be given a full health screening by the Olympic Committee, so I'll need a full copy of my file."

"I spoke with your father and already have it prepared for you. I've included my personal phone number for their physicians. Everything is right here," he said, tapping the thick folder next to him. "I also told Frank I'd be willing to attend just to be safe. He felt like it was a good idea."

A huge sense of relief washed over me. I smiled, actually liking the idea. There would be doctors chosen by the Olympic Committee, but they didn't know me, and if I was cutting it as close as I supposedly was, maybe this was a good thing.

I hadn't made it this far just to collapse now.

CHAPER 28

E veryone is going to know." I whined into my cell phone.

"Why is that a bad thing?" Avery asked.

"When you found out, how did you feel?"

She was quiet for a moment. "I guess I was really sad and just felt so bad. I started thinking about all the negative things. I got really down inside and cried."

"Exactly. I don't want that. I don't want anyone to feel that way about me. I'm fine. I'm not going anywhere anytime soon. Now people are going to look at me differently. They're going to be like, 'Oh, that's the girl with lupus and kidney disease,' or 'Why doesn't she look sick?' What if they call me names for pursing my dream instead of getting better? Then the digging starts, and the questions follow. Then there's the pity looks. I just don't want to be made to feel any different, because I'm not. I'm just a little sick. Others have it worse than me. I'll be fine."

I was in my room packing for my early flight and stopped to sit on the bed. Lying back, I stared at the celling.

I started to panic about one thing, then all the little things followed that didn't bear a thought in my mind before this. The walls of my chest began to feel like they were closing in and then the pressure started. I didn't like when my pulse pumped harder in the next beat. It shook me up. My hand flew to my chest and I closed my eyes, inhaling through my nose and exhaling through my mouth. My fingers shook and my body began to warm all over.

"Yeah, but they're not going for gold either." Her tone softened and I opened my eyes. "Maybe it won't be such a bad thing. Talking about it is good, chica."

I let out a dramatic sigh. "I can't believe I didn't see this coming."

"I can't believe I get to go to the fucking Olympics and watch my bestie!" Avery said.

I chuckled and sat up. Glancing over my shoulder at my suitcase laid open on my bed with clothes and leos strewn across it, I reached for my favorite leo and fingered the material. I'd gotten this one shortly before I went to World Cup. It was all black with tons of fuchsia Swarovski crystals in different sizes across the chest. It was the leo I wore to warmups right before my big meets. Joy had gotten it for me.

"Will it be weird with Xavier there?"

"I don't have an issue with him, he's the one who hates me. You know that."

"True, but didn't he call you when he found out I made the team?"

Her giggle made me smile. She was giddy. I was surprised when I found out Xavier had called Avery and told her the news considering how he supposedly felt about her.

"He did. He's so excited for you. I honestly hadn't heard him like that in so long." She paused. "It was good to hear him so happy for a change."

"Do you think you'll talk to him, like hang out at night? You know I have to room with my team, so I won't be able to stay with you."

"I'm not worried in the least. If he wants to chill, I'm cool with that. If not, then that's fine too. I figured I'd walk around and check out the eye candy. I know all"—she drew out the word—"about the Olympic Village and what goes on. I read online that over a hundred thousand condoms were ordered just for the Village, and nearly five million for the whole city. That's a lot of fucking for just two weeks."

A loud laugh burst from my throat. The Olympic Village had super tight security to protect the athletes and help keep them focused on their events without distraction. That meant no reporters or parents or friends were allowed behind the gates. Only those competing in the Games. With a variety of ages and bodies primed, and all the tension and stress, athletes needed a way to let loose. From what I'd heard, nothing was off limits and anything was possible. There had been numerous rumors surrounding the last Games about orgies and dating apps used for sex. Honestly, I couldn't imagine doing any of that.

"So, what do you think you're going to do? Just sneak inside and people watch?" I laughed picturing her walking around like a little kid in a candy store. "Are you going to walk up to a dude and say take me for the night, no name needed?"

"Aid… Stay innocent. I know a lot of the guys visit bars and venture outside the Village after they're done competing. I just want to see them in all their glory. Nothing more. Look, but don't touch."

"Right," I said, not convinced in the least. I placed my cell on my shoulder and held the phone with my ear. Folding my leos and gym shorts, I stacked them in my suitcase. "Make sure you tell my brother first. I bet you won't make it through the hotel doors."

"He won't care."

"That's what you think."

I thought back to how he acted over her while I was home. Fat chance she was doing anything without him. Xavier could deny all he wanted that he was done with Avery, but after speaking to her and him, they were both so totally head over heels for each other still. It was too bad they were hiding their pain and not dealing with it together.

"You're so crazy."

"And you love me for it."

"True." I smiled to myself as I walked into the bathroom to place my toiletries into a separate bag. "So, I had to see my doctor today before I could board the plane tomorrow."

"And?" she responded quickly, her voice tight. "What's wrong?"

Now it was my turn to laugh. "Nothing is wrong. He did a thorough body check." I paused, swallowing hard for what I was about to say. "He wanted to plan the surgery after the Games—"

"Let's do it!" I frowned, caught off guard by her response. "Tell me when and where and I'm yours."

"I told him I would start dialysis instead."

She groaned under her breath. "You know, if you were in front of me right now, I would shake you. Why did you do that?"

I walked back into my room holding the little Louis bag. "You'd have to take time off from school your freshman year of college. I'm not doing that to you, and he said I could probably get by two more years with dialysis. Maybe even four. I figured if it all goes well, that's what we'd do."

Avery made a sound under her breath. "I don't understand you. I'm willing and ready now. You are well past ready and needed a damn kidney a week ago. What's the hold up? Are you scared your body is going to reject it? Because I'm not. I think it's going to be a success."

I sat on the edge of my bed and slid down until I was on the floor, and pulled up my knees. My lip rolled between my teeth. I picked at the carpet, feeling that gloomy sense of despair swirl around my chest again. I hated when I got down and out like this. It was hard to breathe, hard to focus, hard to just think because of the guilt I was dealing with inside. Avery would have to give up a lot for me. She'd have to alter her life for a while for mine. I really felt like I needed to let my body cool down from all the intense training before jumping straight into surgery. They all seemed to say otherwise.

"I'm not going to take away your first year of college like that. The recovery time is long. Plus," I said, hesitating, "it would have to be well planned and more organized since I won't be here. I don't even know which doctor will be doing it. It's not that easy."

Was I trying to convince her, or me?

"What do you mean you won't be here? Where are you going, and why am I just now hearing about it?"

"You're going to need months off. A summer would be ideal."

"Aid," she said. "What do you mean you won't be here? Where are you going?"

Exhaling a strained breath, I told her about the offers I received from the colleges and broke it down for her. "They couldn't have come at a better time," I added. I truly believed that.

"Hold the phone. Florida wants you, and you're going to say no? Are you serious? But that's where I'll be going, and we always planned to go to college together." She mock whined. I swear I heard her stomp her foot.

My shoulders slumped forward. "I don't know. I feel like I know, but I don't. I'm really so torn."

"Ugh. You'd rather live with tornados or earthquakes?"

I paused, unblinking, trying to figure out what she was saying when it dawned on me. A small laugh rolled off my lips.

"Well, when you put it like that, neither. Seeing as my gym future is so uncertain, I have to think about where I'd want to go to school if I don't end up doing gymnastics. Where I'd be happy living and possibly one day having a life there. The plan is to have a place on the team, but there's a good chance I won't be able to handle it in the end."

She was quiet. "Yeah," she said softly, agreeing with me. "What about Kova?"

My eyes closed. Her question was a straight shot to my gut. I tried not to think about him when I thought about my offers, but the truth was, I did. He was very much sewn into the layers of my heart. He always would be, and I'd be lying if I said living near him wasn't high on my list.

"You're going to leave him? I find that hard to believe."

"I can't walk away from him."

"Then what will you do?"

I contemplated my answer. I had a feeling that what I wanted to do, was not what I would do.

"How do you walk away from someone you love?" My jaw began to tremble at the thought of leaving that I had to stop talking for a second. "It's impossible."

"What?" Avery yelled, though she'd pulled the phone away. She gasped. "Be right there! Can I call you back in a few, Aid? My dad literally just said my ass is grass, so I have to go run and hide now."

A slow smile curved my lips. "Ave," I said. "What did you do?"

She snickered into the phone, which made me laugh in return. "My brothers were pissing me off. They got what they deserved."

I shook my head. "Which was what?"

"I put that temporary hair dye that's all the rage in their shampoo. Now Connor has electric blue hair, and Michael's is corn yellow. Or maybe it's the other way around. Either way, they deserved it."

I covered my mouth. Xavier would straight up murder me if I did that to him. He was all about the hair right now, which was probably why her brothers were too.

"Text me later," I said, then we hung up.

Rising to my feet, I finished packing everything except for a few things I'd add in the morning. It wasn't late, but the flight departed very early, so I figured I'd just go to sleep since I didn't have anything else to do. I was always tired anyway.

Lifting my suitcase off the bed, I spotted the book Sophia gave me. I reached for it. I gazed down with the sudden need to flip through it, wondering if this was a sign too.

I climbed into bed and pulled the blanket over me. I read countless passages about stepping forward into growth and that I was to trust in myself to see my true beauty. How I had to train my mind and heart to be stronger than my emotions or I'd risk losing myself. That I needed to prove myself to me, because I mattered most to me. Then there were the reminders that I'd been given this life because I was strong enough to live it.

Sometimes I didn't feel like I was strong enough to live it.

There were so many motivating pages that I connected with. Who knew words could breathe inspiration into me like this, like maybe I was strong enough to handle anything.

It wasn't until I read the last page of a chaper that it really hit close to home.

When you change within yourself, the world around you will follow suit.

I had to close the book otherwise I would cry. The words rang with too much truth. Somewhere along the way I'd felt the change and had been trying to fight the pull, not accept that it was okay like the book suggested I do. I *was* a different person, and that meant I would have to let go of who I was comfortable with to find the new me. Accepting this also meant there would be a domino effect of change coming into my life. Was I ready for that?

I placed the book on my nightstand and turned off the light. I'd had enough reading for one night. Going to sleep sounded more appealing than mulling over my thoughts. Curling up on my side, I was on the verge of dozing off when my cell phone rang and startled me. I reached for my cell and frowned.

"Avery?" I said. She was sniffling into the phone. "What's wrong? Are you crying?"

"I'm just so happy for you. I only want what's best for you, and I feel like you're starting to finally see your worth and what you're capable of. I'm so happy you're my best friend."

I nestled the phone closer to my face and smiled. "You're so corny. I love you."

"I know. I just had to say it. Wherever you end up, it's where you're supposed to be. Even if you are hundreds of miles away from me," she added. I could hear the smile on her face. "I can't wait to see you soon."

We both hung up and I drifted off to sleep, feeling much more optimistic and truly fortunate that I had a friend who'd stuck by me through all the shit I'd been through.

CHAPER 29

Kova kept to himself as the clouds passed by. His blank stare was reflected in the glass, a look I couldn't recall ever seeing in his eyes. He seemed lost. Usually there was a feeling in his eyes, or an emotion he was trying to hide that I could typically see through.

This time there was nothing. That's what worried me the most, because he was the same exact way when we flew to the training camp a couple of weeks ago.

When we had first arrived at the Olympic training camp, I thought Kova's distance was due to us keeping everything strictly professional. We hardly spoke during then, not that we had time to. It'd been more intense than the last time I was there.

I wanted so badly to reach out and take his hand and just ask what's wrong. He didn't look at me very much, and when I did actually catch his eyes on me, he'd quickly look in the other direction. It bothered me to see him hide his emotions from me when he rarely ever held back before.

I knew it was the last thing I should've been concerned about, but before life had flipped upside down, we were in a really good place. I wanted to go back to that time. To when Kova had picked me up from the training camps and took care of me. I'd been in rough shape, probably having flare ups if I could remember properly. Funny thing, though, the camp I attended this year made Nationals feel like a walk in the park. Located in a secluded area of woods with hardly any cell phone reception, the coaching had been borderline emotionally and physically abusive. Food had been carefully calculated and washed down with laxatives once again. I'd forgotten how much I hated that part with a passion until my stomach had cramped in the middle of training from the pills. We had been weighed every day. I knew nothing about my new teammates except for the injuries they'd hidden and been forced to train on. Not one girl was in working order, each one of us brought something more painful to the table. One gymnast had trained on a foot that had broken bones. Another girl had landed wrong and fractured her back, resulting in an alternate taking her spot. Still, we hadn't complained as our bodies were manipulated during the day and therapy was applied at night. We were brand new come morning.

Those two weeks were probably the most intense weeks of my life and I hadn't even realized it at the time. Not only had I trained with a whole new team, but I'd been nervous about my medical file. The tests had come back clean like I knew they would, but I'd started to harbor animosity from the constant interrogation into me regardless. Each time I was interviewed, the anticipation mounted inside of me. I kept thinking the next question would be about Kova.

The doctors couldn't comprehend how I was training like the others who were relatively healthy, let alone hid my illnesses the way I had. Kova had reassured them it was under control. I'd told them I trained like I always had because I didn't know any other way, and Kova added that I actually challenged him as a coach while he was training me to see how far I could go. They'd seemed to like that and told me they could recall only three other athletes with health issues similar to mine who persevered against the odds. That gave me hope. But the two weeks after we arrived until now, was where things really started to shift.

It was crazy to me that I could be sitting right next to Kova yet feel miles and miles apart from him. Even crazier was it happened in the course of a month where we worked so near each other. The change in his demeanor left me confused. He was here, but he wasn't. Detached. He stood in front of me, but I couldn't feel his essence surround me like I usually did. Kova was never rude. On the outside he looked normal, like every other coach here. But when he looked at me and our gazes actually had the chance to meet, Kova appeared depressed for that brief moment. I tried to tell myself that we both were in the zone and he probably didn't even realize it. I had no real reason yet to believe otherwise since we hadn't talked.

My heart could only believe so many lies until it started to weep for the truth.

Reaching for the bag near my feet, I rummaged through and pulled out the notebook I got just for documenting my life once I had made the team. I'd done a little writing here and there, just not as much as I had hoped. Now I had time to kill.

I flipped open the notebook and ruffled some pages. I hoped the sound of the papers would make him curious to see what I was doing. At least initiate a conversation. But it didn't. Kova just stared ahead at the clouds, stuck in his thoughts. The look in his dead eyes made my stomach clench. This would've been the perfect opportunity to push him like he'd once begged me to, if only we weren't on a private plane filled with Olympic officials and athletes.

I wrote for a little while. Mostly things about Kova, and the feelings I was dealing with inside. How I fell for his flaws, my fears of the future and what I was up against. Where we would end up—yes, we. There was no fooling myself—I knew in my heart I would be wherever he was.

Closing the journal, I put it away safely hidden and took out the book Sophia gave me. I didn't want to be lost inside of my head anymore, and lately these words were an escapism for me. They gave me cause and a drive to be a better me.

I read for a little while then started to nod off. Kova still hadn't looked over at me, so I put the book away and shut my bag.

I couldn't stand another second of seeing his head pressed against the glass any longer. Lifting the divider between us, I pushed it between the seats then pulled my legs up under me to get comfy. Without asking him, I leaned against his arm to rest my head on him.

That got his attention really quick.

Startled, Kova sat up straighter and immediately looked above my head. The tension in his shoulders loosened as he glanced around. I took that as a hint and nestled closer to him. Kova's gaze fell on me. Seconds ago, his eyes were vacant, now they were overflowing with turmoil.

I held my breath hoping he wouldn't shake his head or push me away. Kova slouched at an angle in his black dress pants and stretched his legs out. His crisp, white long-sleeved shirt that'd been rolled up at the sleeves was wrinkled from sitting in the same position for so long. A few buttons were left undone and the collar bunched around his jaw. Muscular thighs filled out the material of his pants, and I couldn't help but notice his bulge when he shifted again. His length strained against his pants and it left nothing to my imagination. I stared longer, picturing how his cock looked bare and how it looked right then. My cheeks flamed and I clenched my eyes shut. I felt like I'd looked too long.

When I opened them and met his gaze, his eyes were a brilliant green from the way the golden sunlight was reflecting off them. A breath caught in the back of my throat. He studied me for a quiet moment, his softened gaze taking in every inch of my face. Truthfully, I was afraid I was going to lose him.

Kova turned slightly to the side and pulled the screen down to block the light. He reached for the blanket hanging off my chair and surprised me by fluffing it out before draping it around both of us. Kova raised his arm that I was leaning on and wrapped it around my shoulder. He snuggled me as close as he could get me until I repositioned myself. I was lying on half his side and half of his chest, so we had more of each other now.

I closed my eyes, and for a good moment, I didn't move. My thoughts were on him, how I felt at peace in my soul while in his arms, the way his warmth spread through me. I was secure and safe. His fingertips pressed into my upper arm and it just solidified how I felt. His body relaxed against mine and I heard him let out a long, relieved sigh under his breath.

We both held still for a long while. Together.

To my complete surprise, Kova's other hand slipped under the blanket. I stilled as he laced his fingers on top of mine and then curled them over to bring us to rest against his stomach. Kova exhaled slowly and I felt him unwind. Without moving, I lifted my eyes just enough to catch a glimpse of him. His eyes weren't squinting, and his jaw wasn't so tense. He looked…almost at peace.

I molded against the length of his body. Something in my stomach was warning me this was the calm before the storm. I blocked it out, not wanting to ruin this moment we both needed by overanalyzing it.

Kova shifted ever so slightly.

"I still love you, *Malysh*," he whispered, his lips brushing the shell of my ear. "Forever."

We stayed like this for the remainder of the flight and didn't move.

CHAPER 30

his is what you worked for. Are you ready?" Kova asked, running his hands up and down my arms. I nodded, blinking a little faster and breathing quickly through my nose. "Look at me."

My eyes snapped to his. I was feeling a little frantic. Kova was kneeling on one knee in front of me. For once I stood a little taller than him. We were standing in the back where only coaches and athletes were allowed, waiting to be called by country for introductions.

"Now take a deep breath and exhale."

I looked right into Kova's unwavering eyes and showed him how nervous I was. He glared back and shook his head, silently telling me to let it go. His gaze didn't waver until he felt I had. I expelled a tight breath and rubbed my chest.

The nerves from being in the Olympic arena were impossible to ignore. The moment I stepped off the plane, I felt the eagerness in the air. So much hope was packed into the city of Athens that would host seventeen days' worth of sporting events. It had been decorated and cleaned for the arrival of those participating and those who traveled to watch. There were rainbows of colors everywhere, each participating country brilliantly represented, and attendants walked around with massive smiles. The Olympics were the one place where every nationality came together and let bygones be bygones.

"Do not let this experience pass you by like most of us do. This is your moment and you need to enjoy it. You trained, you worked hard to get here. Nothing, and no one, can take this away from you. You may not realize it yet, but you are an inspiration to me and to people of all ages. So, take this moment in as much as you can, and let your body take over and do what you were born to do—perform. Do not let up here"—he pressed a gentle finger to my temple—"take away what is in here." He laid his finger over the left side of my chest, right over my racing heart. "You bloom under pressure where most crumble, Adrianna. You are so incredible to watch. Believe me when I say, the world is waiting to see you walk out there today."

His eyes bore into mine. I could tell by how tight his words were and how stiff he spoke that he wanted me to believe him and trust what he said.

Like I'd done many times in the past, I trusted him.

Behind the glitz and glamour of one of the most esthetically appealing Olympic sports, were hours and hours of tears, blood, and sweat I'd put in for this moment. All the preparations, the mistakes I'd made that brought on a series of ups and downs, the rigorous long training that sometimes made me want to give up, outrageous coaching methods that ended with positive results because my coach demanded nothing less than perfection, it all came down to this. This was it. This was what it had all been for.

"Gymnastics is seventy percent mental, thirty percent physical. Your body already knows what comes next. All you need to do is have trust in yourself." His brows rose. "Prove yourself to you," he said, and it reminded me of what I'd read in that book Sophia gave me.

I nodded again.

"Talk to me, Adrianna. Tell me what is on your mind."

Taking another deep breath, my shoulders fell when I exhaled. I looked at him and said, "I'm nervous. I can't concentrate. All I keep thinking about is what if I mess up. I think about my routines. Who my biggest competitor is on each event. My mind is all over the place."

I clenched my fingers into a fist and felt how swollen they were. I was beyond anxious from the moment I opened my puffy eyes in the tiny room I shared with one of my teammates in the Olympic Village. My bones ached, my skin was tight and inflamed.

When I woke up, I'd immediately taken all of my medications, then I ate a banana. I wasn't supposed to have them, but it was all there was in the room since the cafeteria was too far to walk to with the little time I had to get ready. This was the first time I didn't have to hide the bottles, and it felt good.

My teammate didn't stare at me like I was contagious while she watched from her bed. She didn't question me. She didn't even bat an eye when I threw back eight different pills, and dramatically said,

"Make way world, here I come." She just laughed. She was a freshly turned sixteen-year-old, but she looked twelve. She was also the alternate who'd been given a chance.

The four of us had decided to get ready in one room this morning. My chest had been so tight that I couldn't even get in a proper deep breath. Nerves hung in the air like black dripping tar. We joined hands to form a circle and prayed together silently to our higher ups, preparing to take on the biggest event of our lives. The confidence shone brightly, quietly, as we bowed our heads and closed our eyes.

The United States had won gold in the last two Olympics. The pressure was on. Determined to take the prized medal home, we dubbed ourselves the Phenomenal Four.

After our prayer session, one of the girls had played Beyoncé's "Run the World (Girls)" and the mood instantly changed. Giggles and smiles replaced the distressing fear. Our hair was intricately braided into stylish ponytails topped with spray glitter, and our makeup was naturally done. Sports bras and bloomers were tucked in and hidden, hairspray was applied to our butt cheeks and thighs so the leos didn't move too much. After shedding a few more tears, we took turns posing for pictures solo and grouped together.

The most emotional part of the morning had been when I stepped into my leotard with USA stamped on the back. There were swirls and swirls of red and blue crystals against a white background. I ran my hands down my flat stomach and then over my long sleeves, feeling the decorations under my palms. I had allowed myself to take in the moment and smiled, hugging myself.

Nothing, and I mean nothing, could describe the feeling that had rushed through me as I pulled up the sparkly, stretchy material for the first time.

I had done it.

By some miracle, I had made it to the Olympics.

"It is not only about how good you are as a gymnast physically, it is about how good you are here, too," Kova said, his fingertips back on my temples, pulling me from my thoughts. "You have shown there is no limit to your dreams. You rose to the challenge. It has been a privilege to coach you. Watching your growth in the sport has been the highlight of my career. You are my biggest accomplishment. You withstood the pressure and odds and proved everyone wrong. I am proud of you and cannot wait to watch you out there."

Damn it. Tears filled my eyes. I blinked rapidly, trying to hold them in, but his words, they were spoken from his heart and not because he was trying to encourage me. I knew by his intimate tone that Kova meant them. Without another thought, I wrapped my arms around his shoulders and leaned down for a hug.

It was hard for me to talk. I wanted to say something back to him, but my emotions were too strong and I couldn't find words good enough for him. I'd only been with Kova and his gym for a few years now, but it felt more like a lifetime when we worked so closely together. He motivated me. He critiqued every little thing I did to help me perfect it, knowing I wanted nothing less. Kova helped me see that I could resist the fall that so many easily succumbed to on this journey.

This was our last competition together. The final show.

The last time that Kova would stand before me and make sure I was mentally prepared.

My heart pounded against my ribs so hard, I could feel it in my throat.

It didn't hit me until right now that this truly was the end in so many ways. Even if I hadn't wanted to train in college, I wouldn't be walking into World Cup again to prepare for another Olympics.

While I could mentally handle the training, my body could not physically endure another four years. I didn't want to ever admit it, but the truth was, I was too weak to continue. I'd maxed out. Stubbornness, willpower, ambition, call it what you wanted, it's what got me here to this moment, but I didn't have a death wish. I knew that after the Olympics this really was the last time for us.

One last squeeze, I missed the comfort of his arms so much. If only after the competition I could end the night with him just like this. Kova meant so much to me, he gave me more than he realized. Without him by my side, I don't think I would've made it this far.

Sniffling, I pulled back and looked at him. Before I could wipe away my tears, Kova's thumbs were already there. He dried his hands on his pants. I expelled a tight breath, trying to exhale the nerves and shook my fingers out.

My jaw trembled as our eyes met. My teeth dug into my lip as I fought the surge of feelings flushing through me. There was so much commotion around us as staff instructed the athletes where to line up and where the coaches needed to be. We were just getting ready to walk out to be introduced.

"This is our last competition together," I said.

Kova's tongue ran over his bottom lip as he studied my eyes. "Let us make it the best one yet."

I nodded, and he stood.

Bending down, Kova picked up my duffle bag and placed it over his shoulder. Just as he was about to walk away to stand with the other coaches behind us, I reached for his wrist. Kova glanced down.

"Thank you...for everything," I said.

Kova shifted his hand over mine and gave me a little squeeze.

I dropped my arm then turned around to find my place in line. My teammates and I bounced on our toes waiting to be announced in our matching royal blue sweat suits with USA printed down the spine in white and then over the left side of our chest in red.

This was my proudest moment.

I drew in a deep breath and closed my eyes, taking it all in as I tried to steady my racing heart.

"Team USA, they're ready for you," someone yelled. She had a microphone attached to her head and a clipboard glued to her chest. She dipped her head then waved her hand at us.

I exhaled slowly and a smile that I wasn't prepared for spread across my face.

I still couldn't believe I'd made it.

CHAPER 31

Double doors were held open as the four of us walked behind an employee who held a white sign high in the air that read USA in black, bold letters.

The crowd exploded the moment we stepped inside the stadium. It was loud. A massive smile split across my face at the jolt of excitement it gave me. The fans had to reach an octave that was earsplitting. It was really cool and made me feel alive. My eyes ran over the crowd in a blur. The fans stood waving flags, air of enthusiasm surrounded all of us, welcoming us... I was still in shock. I couldn't believe after all the hard work that I was actually here. We followed the woman in a straight line to the floor. Walking up the three steps, we stood next to Team China on one side, and Team Romania on the other. My eyes skimmed the gymnasts. Some exchanged smiles, some didn't. I smiled brightly, though, feeling the thunder of adrenaline course through me. It was empowering to look around at the faces of girls who gave up so much of their youth to be here, fighting for a dream just like I had. We may not have a lot in common, but we had that, and it connected us for a moment in our lifetime forever. I may have missed out on football games, high school dances and prom, making memories with friends, but I didn't regret it because nothing could top this moment. How often did one get to say they went to the freaking Olympics?

Music blared through the speakers and my smile grew larger, happiness taking over me. The crowd clapped and shouted as introductions were made by team before we departed to the first event. I was eager and couldn't wait for the Games to begin.

The countries were split up on the four events, with USA starting on the balance beam. Considering my nerves were already wired, I was both thankful and anxious as hell to start with this event. I'd rather have started with bars, something I had more confidence in, but maybe this was a good thing. That way I got beam out of the way and I could loosen up a little.

I wasn't supposed to compete on beam, but when my teammate fractured her back during the training camp and the alternate was chosen, the committee made a decision between the both of us. After some deliberation, they chose me to compete on beam, which meant I was competing on all four events now while she had two. My routine had the higher execution score, but hers had the difficulty.

Because of the governing rules, the Olympic coaches were not permitted to be on the floor while gymnasts competed, only their coaches were allowed. However, they could instruct from the seats. Each of us had our coach with us and we were allowed a quick warm-up with them before the competition began.

"I know you were not prepared to compete on beam, but the coaches believe in you. They believe that you also have the ability to help carry the team to gold."

I nodded as I powdered my feet then stomped on the floor.

"Look at me." I looked right into Kova's green eyes. "Center your focus. Concentrate on your routine and know you have what it takes. I want you to take a deep breath before your connection series, and keep your chest high when you execute your jumps because those completed in a clean succession will increase your score. Keep that ankle locked in your turns."

Expelling a tight breath, I nodded. "I got it." I paused. "I can do it." I paused again. "I got this." Balancing for ninety seconds on a four-inch piece of wood. I could totally do it.

Once we took turns warming up and it was time to begin, we came to stand in a close circle. We placed our right hand out in the middle of us, and yelled "Phenomenal Four" just as the bell sounded letting us know it was time to start the first event of the Olympics.

I watched as my teammate stepped onto the podium and walked up to the balance beam with her shoulders squared back. There was something exhilarating about watching this tiny little fairy-like girl mount the beam and dominate it like a queen. She was inspiring, and she was also the front runner with the highest difficulty of the meet. The only other gymnast who was capable of executing a routine similar to hers was a girl from the Ukraine. The Ukrainians were trying to make a comeback after not winning any medals since the nineties.

I couldn't sit still, none of us could. We paced the floor and cheered on our teammate in between doing various stretches to keep our muscles warmed up. When she stuck her dismount and the crowd cheered, my heart dropped a little. Now it was my turn.

I powdered my feet again and applied more chalk to my palms and the tops of my thighs. Kova stood behind me, massaging my shoulders and arms to keep me warm. My heart was fluttering and my fingers shook. I drew in a large breath and inhaled the chalky air, coughing when I exhaled. That made my lungs burn. I swallowed, wincing because of my sore throat.

I could do this.

"Stay focused," he said, turning me to stand in front of him. "Positive thoughts. It is just like any other meet."

"Only it's not." I half joked, eyeing him.

Kova smiled halfway, but I'd caught it. "Your biggest competitor is yourself. This is you living your dream, and me living it with you."

It was only us in the arena despite the thousands of beating hearts surrounding us. *Let me live with you*, was something I'd never forget he said. It was woven into my soul for eternity. The happiness I felt was a seed soaking up his words and blossoming inside of my chest.

A smile slowly, contentedly, fell over my curved my lips. I knew what he was doing. I made a mental note to remind myself of what he said so I could write it in my journal. I wanted to remember it forever and explain in detail how I felt, that way when I looked back on this day many years from now, I'd get that same feeling again when I reread the words.

"You better go," he said. There was a spark in his eyes. He seemed content, and that pleased me.

Turning around, I walked over to the stairs and took a deep breath. Then I proceeded up the three steps and made my way toward the sixteen-foot piece of wood that was either going to make me or break me. Right in front of it sat four official judges wearing matching navy-blue suits and unsympathetic stares ready to critique every little thing I messed up on.

I stopped in front of the apparatus and breathed in positivity. Before I saluted the judges, I looked over my shoulder and made eye contact with Kova. He gave me a deep nod, and mouthed, "You can do it."

That was all I needed. Turning back to face the judges, I drowned out all the noise around me and let the countdown begin.

I raised one arm to salute them with a thin smile on my face. Fingers twinkling over the beige material, I mounted the beam into a straddle press handstand and swiveled my hips until my split legs were parallel to the balance beam. Clenching my stomach, my inner thighs helped center my hips as I balanced over the beam with every muscle squeezed in my body. I arched further to stand and finally took a breath. It was so easy to forget to breathe during competition. However, if I breathed even the slightest breath at the wrong time, I could easily slip up.

I sashayed across the apparatus from one end to the next, staying focused on only what I was attempting and what came next. Muscle memory kicked in and I completed turns on my toes with finesse. I completed a double back handspring full-twist like a silk ribbon floating through the air. Then the courage came and I felt confidence bloom through me.

I lowered my arms; I was almost finished. After another exhale, I gracefully stepped into a succession of jumps with turns, adding a back tuck straight into a bonus jump. My arms came down and I prepared for a standing back flip twist. I looked at my clear painted toes between the four inches of wood and tried to center my hips. If I went backwards, I could swing my arms behind me to gain the momentum I needed to flip back and twist at the same time. If I went forward, I didn't have the arm swing, and I could only hurdle so far into a front flip twist. Going in a different direction was what made it so difficult and upped the score.

My routine had me flipping forward.

Inhaling, I stepped into the barani and pushed off the balance beam into the front flip full twist. I came down and felt the leather scrape against the arch of my foot.

Eyes wide, my heart dropped.

No.

My heart sank.

I clenched my muscles and curled my toes around the four-inch piece of wood, my entire body fighting to hold on. I stiffened, pushing against the pull of gravity. If I fell off completely, I would lose one full point. If I could save it, even if a little messy, it would be a lesser deduction.

Digging deep, I pulled it together and raised my arms in the air to attempt to save it. *Thank God*, I thought to myself. I blinked and realigned my focus once again. I thought I saw stars for a second there.

I made my way across the beam in a series of required dance skills, then straight into a standing back pike that I landed with ease. Stepping toward the edge, I glared at the apparatus, determined to make it mine. I wasn't going to lose, not after I'd come this far.

I licked my bottom lip, then stepped into a roundoff back handspring, then into a double twisting double back. Fists pulled tight to my chest as I rotated backwards, double twisting at the same time, I spotted for the ground.

My feet landed together, my stance steady as I raised my arms and stuck my dismount. A massive smile filled my face. I held my landing for a moment longer and then turned and raised my arms to the judges to salute.

It was the longest ninety seconds of my life.

I turned around and found Kova's thrilled face immediately. I skipped over to him quickly and threw my arms around his shoulders as he caught me from the steps. He pulled me into a swift embrace then released me.

"Excellent dismount and routine."

My eyes narrowed. "Aside from the slip, you mean."

Kova smirked but he didn't get a chance to respond as my teammates came over to congratulate me with hugs. We were all smiles and hopeful eyes. My score went up pretty quickly and the crowd yelled with enthusiasm. I gasped and my brows shot up. A shot of electricity zipped down my spine as I stared up at the television screen with my name next to the flag.

It was my first Olympic score, and it wasn't bad.

The two other gymnasts from my team took their turns. Each time one finished, we congratulated her, praising her and lifting her spirit regardless if she needed it or not. It brought morale to our small group and helped quiet our loud thoughts. We we're panicking on the inside and going through the same thing together, we just didn't talk about it.

One gymnast from my team had more balance checks than I had, while the other had a near perfect score. Both had high scores in difficulty, which made a difference. Along with my score and after the first rotation, Team USA was currently in second place, a tenth of a point from being in third.

CHAPER 32

Beam was just a warm-up. Now you get to show the people one of the reasons why you are here," Kova said. "The Amanar." Vault.

I smiled proudly. I was one of the few who attempted this skill. I'd worked hard to perfect it.

"Remember," he continued, lifting one arm to demonstrate, "when you block"—he arched his chest and tapped it—"get to the front and middle of the table to gain proper flight with a vertical takeoff."

I listened closely as I put on my wrist guards then flexed my wrists and fingers. The block was going to hurt. For the most part, my elbow had healed from the dislocation. It was still tender here and there, but not all that bad. I was careful during qualifications, but I knew after this event it was going to be sore. All my power was going into my block that required straight arms and a strong pop throughout the arm. I was going to put everything I had into this block.

"Strong run, low and long, we want power when you take off."

"Got it."

I did. I had it. I imagined myself doing exactly what he said.

I was the last to take my turn for this rotation. The other athletes from my team had competed already with USA dropping to third, just a fraction of a point that separated us from second. It wasn't due to my teammates, though; they hadn't made severe mistakes. It was quite the opposite, actually, and they'd done very well. The other countries were just better in that rotation. Plain and simple.

I didn't want to let my hope slip, so I stayed blindly optimistic. My vault would be the deciding factor if we'd go up to second or stay in third. I was confident enough to carry my team to second.

I pulled back the Velcro to loosen it for a moment so my hands could breathe. I woke this morning to swollen wrists but ignored them. I could crumple when I got back to the States.

Not today, kidney disease, not today.

"Go chalk up," Kova said. "I will adjust the springboard."

"See you on the flip side."

I turned around to walk in the opposite direction but halted when I heard Kova laugh under his breath. I glanced over my shoulder and saw that he was already watching me with genuine pride in his eyes. His hands were propped on his hips and his expression radiated with content. He was looking at me.

My lips twitched. Turning back around, I walked to the end of the runway. I bounced lightly on my toes and shook out my fingers, my head bobbed from side to side. I refused to look into the stands and only kept my eyes on the vault and my coach. Bring on the tunnel vision. My fingers felt a little numb, so I retightened my brace. I swung my arms around in circles and shook my legs out. The green light was given, and I took a deep breath.

This was it.

Exhaling, I drowned out the sound again and pretended I was the only person in the room. I looked down and double checked I was standing eighty-seven feet back. I lifted my right arm to salute the judges then looked only at the vault and exhaled again. My heart was pumping so fast it was all I could hear. I had one chance to stick this dismount and only a few seconds left to complete it as perfectly as I could. I stomped my feet in the chalk once more, then tapped one pointed toe in front of me and lifted my arms in front of me.

Inhale, exhale.

Rising up on my toes, I licked my lips and swallowed. I leaned forward and drew in a lungful of air, then took off running as fast as my legs could take me. The room grew eerily quiet as I neared the apparatus, the cool air kissed over my skin.

Kova's last-minute suggestions played back in my mind. I heard his voice and applied what he said. My body moved of its own accord the moment my feet slammed into the springboard, rotating back onto the horse. Chest arched and hips flat, my legs were glued together as I blocked the hardest I possibly could manage, grunting from the impact. I took flight and reached as high as I could for maximum height and began twisting while I rotated two back layouts at the same time. After thousands of hours of practicing this skill, my body could do it on its own. I stayed tight and timed the right millisecond to open up, praying I got it right.

Core muscles tight, I opened my arms as my tiptoes touched the landing mat. Knees bent slightly for impact so I didn't hyperextend them, I stuck my landing perfectly and raised my arms in the air, holding my position to prove no hop was coming next.

The crowd exploded and a huge smile spread across my lips. I was so ecstatic that I almost started to laugh. I saluted the judges once more then turned and spotted Coach Elena in the stands behind a wall where the Olympic coaches were, right behind where Team USA was currently sitting. She was pumping her fist and shouting her happiness and showing the first smile I'd ever seen her give me.

My cheeks burned with joy as I made my way down the stairs into Kova's bear hug. He kissed my temple and said a slew of things in Russian that I assumed were praises before putting me on my feet. My teammates rushed over, squeezing hugs and cheers and clapping from all around. They were already dressed in their sweats to rotate.

Glancing over my shoulder, I turned around waiting for my score when I spotted Kova standing on his tiptoes talking to Coach Elena who was bent over the railing. She looked my way as she spoke to Kova, who nodded his head in return. He tapped the railing twice with his palm and pushed off, walking back toward me with determination. Before I could ask him anything, my score was up.

My jaw dropped in total shock. Not only was it nearly perfect, I had the highest scored vault of the competition so far. Only two tenths away from perfection. I'd take it.

I was still in shock when the girls gave me a group hug, springing on their toes. Gymnastics was an individual sport as much as it was a team sport.

Giggling, I covered my mouth with my hands and shot a glance around the room. Home flags waved though the air, faces were painted various colors, and signs raised above heads to show support for a sport that easily created so much doubt. It was my first real time looking at the beaming faces who'd traveled across the world to be here. I took it all in, appreciation invigorating my heart. I still couldn't believe I had made it to the Olympics.

Since I really wanted to compete in the all-around tomorrow, I had to compete on vault twice today. One for the team, the other to qualify for the all-around.

"Number one, Ria," Kova whispered, patting my shoulder after I executed my second vault and finished with nearly an identical score. "Get your bag and let us go to floor."

I grinned. I was first in vault by a large margin. A few steps and I was grabbing my duffle and quickly speeding up my pace. Coach Elena was hanging over the ledge and put her hand out when she saw I was coming her way. I smiled and rushed over to her, slapping her palm with a high five.

"Excellent job, well done," she said, her words stiff through her Ukrainian accent.

This was the best day of my life. I wondered if I'd ever feel anything like this again one day.

Still trying to catch my breath, I skipped over the black wires on the floor and met up with my team that was now on floor. I dropped my bag, and Kova squatted next to me. He leaned over and unzipped it, rummaging through it for my sports tape. He pulled it out and I turned toward him to give him my ankle.

"How is your foot?"

I thought about his question for a minute. "It's fine. Nothing I can't handle for a few more days."

He smiled but was looking at my foot as he taped my ankle. Once he was done, he ran his hand over the kinesis tape on my calf and Achilles. He nodded to himself, pleased. He was checking to make sure it was still on good.

"You are incredible to watch. The crowd loves you."

My cheeks blushed. I playfully rolled my eyes. "They love everyone, Kova."

"True, but they are much louder for you."

"You're just saying that."

"No. I am not. They see what I see."

My teeth dug into my bottom lip. Kova stood up, and I asked, "And what do you see?"

He studied me for a moment, then placed his hand out to help me up. His jaw flexed, my gaze fixed on his full, kissable lips.

"I will tell you tomorrow night." My brows furrowed, waiting for him to explain. "Tomorrow night, Adrianna. Now go warm up. Elena altered a tumbling pass."

Nodding, I squinted at him as I walked up the steps to the blue carpeted floor. I had questions, but I didn't want the thoughts to be stuck in my head for the rest of the day, so I shut them out and placed the questions in a drawer for tomorrow.

Each team was given a specific number of minutes to warm-up with tumbling passes. I stepped closer to the corner and looked ahead for Kova who was standing in the opposite corner ready to spot me.

He looked both ways then waved his fingers for me to come.

I turned over my first tumbling pass with Kova spotting right next to me. He halted my body with the palm of his hand so I didn't over rotate.

"Good. Delay the twist for another second and a half the next time," he said, and I nodded.

This was another last-minute change from Elena. I only knew this because I'd had the same passes for almost a year. They were just a little more difficult, especially on my endurance and lack of kidney function. I tried to remain calm as I drew air into my lungs, but they were so tight that it caused me to breathe harder. I stomped in chalk and powdered some on my palms. Kova reached the other corner and it was my turn again. I waited, watching his eyes, then he turned to me and waved.

I swallowed back my nerves and sprinted halfway across the floor. I hurdled into a front handspring, flipping over and punching my feet together into the floor to rebound into a hand-free roundoff, then finally double twisting backwards to land. My feet pounded into the spring floor and I felt the impact grind down my spine. Kova was right there to catch my chest from leaning forward too much. A gush of air rushed from me and I started coughing.

"Are you okay?" he asked, a slight shadow of concern in his eyes.

"I'm fine," I said out of breath. I winced and grabbed the inside of my elbow. I knew vault was going to make it hurt. "I'm just a little out of breath. I'll be good."

Kova's eyes were fixated on mine. I shook my arm out like it didn't faze me, but the truth was, there was a burning pain shooting up my arm. "Okay, because you will need to add a front tuck to the end of the pass for bonus. You will also switch your first tumbling pass."

This time I returned the concerned look. He was adding a bonus front flip and changing my tumbling pass. I waited for him to tell me which new tumbling pass I would do.

"Coach Elena believes that after she watched the other countries perform, if we increase our difficulty right now, it could push us to first."

CHAPER 33

The four of us stood in a circle with our hands in the middle again. Each coach told us what to do and where we needed to make small tweaks to our routines. Some coaches even suggested pointers to the others. We knew the risks involved with a last-minute change even though we were still prepared if it came to this. Stepping out of bounds, twisting an ankle, over rotating. Anything was possible if your body is out of sync for even a millisecond. We came together and discussed what we had to do in order to take gold.

"Ready, girlies," the smallest one said with the brightest eyes. She sounded like she still hadn't reached puberty even though she was fifteen. "On the count of three."

"One… Two… Three."

"Phenomenal Four!"

We split up and I stood to the side, cheering on my teammate. I was third to go in this rotation.

The music started and I watched as she began, holding my breath when she executed her first tumbling pass like it was second nature to her. I could breathe.

There was something about seeing someone else do a trick first that brought a sense of relief to me. Now I knew I could do it too. Seeing her skip and leap across the floor to the other corner and then complete another extremely difficult tumbling pass, one that even I couldn't do, made me feel even better the second time. I was eager to get out there and perform.

"Is it true?" one of my teammates asked. "Do you really need a kidney?"

I blinked, confused for a moment until I remembered that the world knew about my secret now.

I nodded hesitantly. "It's true. After the Games are over, I'm on a flight back home to start dialysis immediately."

Her eyes softened, but not with pity like I expected. There was a sparkle of admiration that caught me by surprise. My head tilted to the side.

"Wow," she whispered. "You're, like, really tough."

My cheeks warmed and I laughed, feeling slightly embarrassed. "I wouldn't say I'm tough, just hardheaded."

"Do you hurt? Like are you in pain now? You don't look like you are."

"Not really right this minute, but once I sit down and unwind is when I'll start to feel the side effects. Everything tenses up and the pain sets in. It makes me feel like I'm an eighty-seven-year-old and strips me of me. Doing gymnastics numbs that feeling. It makes me feel like nothing is wrong with me."

She stared at me for a long minute like she was trying to figure me out. "When I heard the news, I didn't believe it. I honestly thought it was a hoax to drive attention. There was no way, not after I saw how hard you trained at camp with everyone. And then seeing you here? I still didn't believe it even though I'd read about it numerous times. Sorry if I'm being rude, but I had to ask. You just seem so…normal."

I am normal, I wanted to say.

I wasn't sure whether to smile or not, and that was because I wasn't sure how to feel. She wasn't pitying me, she wasn't being cruel about my illness, she was genuinely curious and somewhat in awe. It was kind of a…normal conversation.

I glanced at my chalky toes and allowed the smile I wore to hide the imperfections and sins of my personal life tug into a real one. I looked back at her.

"You're not being rude. I was just caught by surprise is all. I've kept it a secret for what felt like forever and then suddenly everyone knows overnight."

Her eyes widened. "Yeah, I can see that now." She began to frown.

"Don't feel bad," I said, trying to reassure her. "Really, I don't mind."

"You seemed out of breath when we were practicing earlier."

My cheeks warmed again. "I was. The shortness of breath is daily for me and kind of annoying. I'm missing like seventy percent of my kidney function which means I'm depleting all my stored energy and oxygen at a much quicker rate. Sometimes it's hard for me to catch my breath when I'm in the zone, my chest gets all tight and sometimes I get nervous thinking I'm going to have a panic attack from it."

She stared at me, a little disturbed. I averted my gaze to the floor where a gymnast was completing her final pass. "Well, that escalated quickly." We both laughed. "As you can see, I don't talk to people a lot about this."

I was so awkward about it. I'd have to work on my rambling if I was going to respond to questions from others.

"It's all good in the neighborhood."

"When I crash tonight in the room with a pillow over my head, don't worry. I can breathe just fine, so don't pick it up. I'll be recharged by tomorrow, well, ah…" I hesitated. "If I make it that far."

She gave me the thumbs up and smiled. "Done. And you totally are, at least for vault anyway."

The classical music we all performed to ended with a round of applause.

"Wish me luck." She smiled over her shoulder.

"Good luck," I said enthusiastically.

Just before her routine ended, Kova strode over to me. His arms were crossed in front of his chest as he watched. She'd completed her last-minute adjustments with ease and perfection too. I was next.

"Excited to watch me?" I asked, the implication was obvious. I was in a really good mood.

Kova tried not to look at me, but I could tell it was a challenge by the squint in his eye. I knew Kova liked to watch me perform on the floor. He dropped his arms behind his back and grabbed his wrist.

"You think changing the tumbling passes will really help?"

He wavered back and forth on his toes and heels. "I do. USA is very close to being first. We may not make it there in this rotation, but with everyone's upgraded skills, I believe we will in the last event." He paused for a moment, then lifted one shoulder. "Well, I am sure we all here believe that," he said more to himself.

I cracked my knuckles. The floor music ended and my heart beat spiked. Butterflies swirled in my stomach and I inhaled slowly. I loved floor, but it'd always caused me a little trepidation. There were many risks involved in doing gymnastics, but I didn't really ever feel like I could become paralyzed on the other events as easily as I could with floor.

"This is for you, Kova," I said, and stepped up the stairs to the floor. I saluted the judges then walked to the center of the floor, taking my stance. I positioned my arms like a delicate swan out to my sides and exhaled before I bent over and dropped my head dramatically.

Five seconds later, I began. I lost myself in my element, flouncing from one corner to the next in a sequence of whimsical leaps and delicate jumps. There was no faking the smile on my face—I truly loved performing on the floor. I danced the way I felt, so alive and free. As I made my way to the corner for my first tumbling pass, I took a deep breath and turned around, counting the music in my head. My heels met the edge of the tape and I brought my hands down and rose up on my toes. With my last-minute change, Kova stood in the corner that I was running to simply for peace of mind.

I turned over my roundoff, punching my feet out of the wide back handspring and set the first flip, rotating in a snug twist. I decided midair I wasn't going to add the bonus leap like Coach Elena wanted.

Spotting the ground, I landed with the force of ten times my weight into a graceful lunge and smiled from ear to ear. Or, as Kova had once put it, "Become a gentle ripple in the ocean when you lunge." I'd made fun of him for that one.

My arms spread out as I danced to the next corner like a feather billowing through the air, my toes hardly touching the floor. I could see Kova from the corner of my eye make his way to the opposite corner to spot me again. It was silly, if I really thought about it. The comfort of a coach triggered bravery for the athlete to attempt something outright intimidating. A lot of gymnasts chose to have their coach nearby. It was the psychological part of the sport. Kova couldn't step onto the floor, but just knowing he was there made all the difference.

Kova dipped his chin once. I counted the music beats in my head and hurdled into the center of the floor to do the front flipping tumbling pass I warmed up earlier. Forward flipping was more terrifying for me, not to mention, exhausting. It took a lot of energy out of me. I stepped into a front handspring and dug deep. I pushed away any type of mental and physical fatigue and ran on autopilot, releasing every ounce of energy I had left in me. I knew this series of flips were worth more if executed properly. It was why I didn't do the bonus jump a few seconds ago. I wanted to conserve my energy for this tumbling pass.

My figure breezed through the air, defying gravity with completely straight body twists every three seconds until I reached the corner. I paid attention to the tightness of my muscles and centered my hips in rotation. Feet punching the ground in the blue spring floor, I immediately rebounded with the bonus jump and then stepped into another front handspring without taking a breath and into a roundoff, a full twisting layout, and then flipped to the other corner in a series of back handsprings to complete a double layout.

Rippling like a wave, I smiled and let out a huge gush of air as my fingers fluttered for effect. I could faintly hear the crowd clapping and cheering, but I wasn't sure for who. My lunge was completed with finesse and ease and then I was skipping around the floor until my last tumbling pass came. It was a simple one, a double twisting double back.

Counting down the beats, I drew in a breath and leaped to the center of the floor to finish my floor routine with a flare from the ground, my body contorted like a pretzel. My heart was racing so hard my chest physically hurt.

As the music came to an end. I exhaled and held my position, then I was standing up to salute the judges twice.

Panting, I spun around and clapped my hands excitedly as I exited the floor. Coach Elena was waving her flag in the air. Her excitement was contagious and I found myself smiling in return. Guess she wasn't too mad I skipped out on the extra points. All those around her watched her cheer with the crowd, her pride obvious. Floor was always so much fun to watch.

I stepped down right into Kova's arms and pulled my feet up behind me. The smell of his cologne lured me closer to his neck. I wished I could give him a little kiss on the lips to the ending of a great routine. I'd performed my heart out for him and I could tell by the way his fingers pressed into me that he was indebted by the gesture. He hugged me tight to him as he took a few steps. He said something in my ear, but I didn't catch it.

Kova released me and my teammates came running. As much as I loved training at World Cup, it would've been nice to have camaraderie like this when we competed together. The girls got dressed to rotate to the final event, but my body was too warm to put clothes on just yet.

My breathing labored a bit. I took huge breaths when I knew I shouldn't because I just couldn't help myself. I paced the floor waiting for my score while holding my neck. Time always slowed waiting for the numbers to populate. Inhaling, I could feel the low-pitched wheezing sounds in my chest as I struggled to pull air into my lungs.

I stared at the screen and I didn't blink. Goose bumps broke out over my body as the black, bold letters finally appeared.

My lips parted. I held first place for vault, and now I was in third highest overall for floor too. Now I had medals for two of the four events.

A sated smile split across my face. Now that I had the third highest floor score of the entire meet, Team USA was only five tenths of a point away from gold.

Easy peasy.

Maybe Kova had been telling me the truth all this time. Maybe I do work really well under pressure.

CHAPER 34

Once we rotated, I sat down on the floor to remove the tape from my ankles just as Kova squatted in front of me.

He didn't speak. He was waiting to wrap my wrists for me. After I balled up the tape from my ankles and dropped it into my bag, I glanced down at my hands and my brows furrowed. Kova reached for my fingers and turned my wrists over. He inspected them the way I had. He pressed gently and flexed a digit back. They were much more swollen than normal, and my fingers were puffy. This could've easily been from how much of an impact my bones took today, though.

I took my hands back and shook them out. I looked ahead, acting like it was normal, then gave Kova my wrists again with steadiness this time.

Kova ripped a piece of tape with his teeth. I asked, "What did you say to me when I got off the floor? I didn't catch it."

He was quiet for a moment. Kova didn't raise his head to look at me, he just kept winding fresh white tape around my wrists.

"What did you say?" I asked again, leaning closer to him.

"Nothing."

"Yes, you did. I heard you."

His nostrils flared. "It was nothing."

Now wasn't the time to push, but I had another idea. "What's tomorrow night?" I whispered.

"Tomorrow night," he said, more so under his breath, "is when you and I are going to be alone to finally talk."

Somewhat accepting of that response, I glanced around wondering how he was going to pull that off with my family here.

I shelved that thought for later. I was starting to get a headache from everything I'd been shelving lately.

This was the final rotation, and then we'd know if we got back what we put in. We were holding the silver, and as much as I wanted gold, I was still very pleased with second place.

"I can't believe it's almost over," I said, wonderment in my tone.

Kova's lips twitched. "It goes by fast. All that time and work for one day."

"Yeah."

He wrapped my palms up next. "How are you feeling otherwise?"

"Great," I said, and shrugged. "I'm really great."

I *was* really great, and happy.

I drew the chalky air into my lungs for it to revive me one last time. Kova finally lifted his eyes to mine. My thoughts were quickly forgotten when I caught view of his smile. His lips were pressed together and there was a flirtatious glow that surrounded him. I found myself giggling just as a photographer took a picture of us. There was news media everywhere we turned, but they weren't allowed to interview us or call our names. All they could do was video record and take photos.

"Why are you laughing at me?" I asked.

Kova shook his head. "The way you said that, I am not sure what I found so funny. Maybe it was the sound of your voice." He paused, then said, "Great. I'm really great," the way it sounded to him, and I erupted with laughter. "You did not respond like I expected."

My smile widened. "Oh, and how's that? Like I'm going to talk about how stressed I am? We both know that. How my nerves are totally shot and I can't stop shaking on the inside. I don't want to be a broken record today."

He studied me, then he stood and held his palm out. I pulled on my cotton wrist wraps and Kova guided the grips to my ring finger and middle finger, slipping them through the little holes.

"Everyone is going to be watching you," he said, engaging in a conversation.

I was the last one to compete on the team, with my routine being the highest in difficulty. Once my score was added into the team's final score, we'd know what place we'd finish in, but that didn't mean it was the medal we'd receive. If we did.

"I know," I said softly.

"You should be proud of what you accomplished to get here, and that your routine is the hardest one here." He nodded and spoke with his lips hardly moving. "The others who competed before you had either the same starting score as you, or were close to it. From the looks of it, the one who was in the lead, her routine was adjusted at the last minute, or she lost the difficulty points during execution. Which means, you are a full point ahead of her."

My eyes lifted to his.

"I could take the lead in bars."

Kova's hands stilled. We both understood the magnitude of this moment and didn't look away. My chest housed a wild frenzy of heartbeats at this realization. I couldn't contain the smile that started spreading on my face.

I licked my chapped lips. "I can do it. I know I can."

Kova moved onto my other hand. "I do not want you to think when you are out there. I just want you to let your body take over—it knows what to do, trust it. Do not overthink it. We will do our standard warm-up like always."

I glanced around his body. The other girls were warming up with their coaches. We would be up soon.

"Okay. Okay. Okay. I got this."

He looked into my wide eyes. "If you secure this event, you will be headed into the all-around tomorrow. Too many mistakes on beam from gymnasts after you that you are surprisingly still in the running for a spot tomorrow. Between vault and floor, I have a feeling bars is going to be another medal for you."

My brows shot up. "What makes you so sure?"

Some of the gymnasts were already granted entry based on other qualifying requirements that I hadn't been able to meet at previous meets. That made the entry margin even smaller for me.

"I have been keeping track. I firmly believe you will secure a spot."

It was all Kova said. Like he was so sure of it and I had to accept what he said.

I was at a loss for words and smiled to myself. I was so giddy inside I couldn't stop smiling. Shrugging, I said, "Sweet."

After my grips were on and tightened, Kova and I warmed up on bars, loosely running through the routine and practicing some release skills. A few handstands and pirouettes, then my dismount. A couple of quick pointers, Kova reminded me not to overthink and just let my body do what it was made to.

"Let gymnastics live with you," he whispered from behind me.

I didn't move. I just nodded my head. We both knew what those words meant.

Be still my sick heart and listen to him already.

Within five minutes, I was standing in front of the low bar preparing to mount it. This would be the last time I would compete wearing a red, white, and blue leotard, and the final time I'd compete at the Olympics. Kova was right—I was going to let gymnastics live with me in my final performance.

Drawing in a deep breath, I looked over at Kova who stood to the side of the apparatus prepared to step in and spot me like we'd agreed. I was the last one to compete now. Team USA was teetering back and forth between gold and silver, only a tenth of a point away from slipping into silver again. I would either lead us to victory or we'd become first place loser, as Kova had put it once and Danilo had reiterated the last time I was at World Cup.

Funny how I didn't feel like a first place loser anymore like I once had. Not after the struggle I was forced to bear this past year.

"You got this," Kova said, focusing solely on me. "Do not think, just feel," he said, using his hands.

I exhaled and felt the crowd's enthusiasm around me. I used what they were giving as my reason to be strong and help my team take home gold. I had this.

My teammates cheered my name from the sidelines where they stood, just like we had for each one before me. I chalked up one final time on my palms, thighs and feet, and then, I saluted the judges.

One minute and thirty seconds, and it would all be over.

My hands reached for the low bar, my hips swinging forward into a kip cast to a handstand. I stuck it for a second with my hips flat and toes pointed, then swung down into a back hip circle straight to a handstand again. I did this once more then brought my body down and around the bar for a second time. At the angle I'd been trained to release the bar, I did. The bar ricocheted as I reached for the high bar and swung up to a handstand. Switching my grip so it faced backwards for added difficulty points, I fell forward into a full giant and closed my eyes, feeling the wind against my cheeks and tasting the chalk in the air. I knew Kova would be standing right to the side ready to spot as I completed another pirouette holding my body stone still.

I swung down into a giant to gain momentum as Kova stepped closer. Tapping at the right timing, I hollowed out my chest and swung my body around, bringing my hips parallel to the bar and then whipping them as hard as I could into the air as I released the bar at the same time to fly backwards and over it in a pike position. Kova's arms went up as my body came down. I gripped the bar with all my might and moved swiftly into another release skill that we'd worked hard on. Nothing mattered but this routine and the way I felt as I soared through the air from bar to bar like a snowflake delicately drifting in the wind. My heart was on display, my undying love for bars and this sport, it was all there as I performed my routine. I did a total of three releases back-to-back when Kova stepped down and let me do my thing for a couple of seconds until he was standing there again, this time gearing up for my dismount.

I took a quick breath. This was it.

Licking my lips, I spotted the landing mat that had clouds of chalk on it.

My mind went back to my first day at World Cup.

To the excitement and hunger for this moment.

To the pain.

To the anger.

To the betrayal.

It all lead to right now.

My fingers tightened around the bar. Stuck handstands with flat hips and pointed toes, I could vaguely hear the exploding crowd as I circled the bar two and a half times gearing up for my dismount.

And then…

I let go.

CHAPER 35

The sudden silence from the crowd was thrilling. It was as if they held their breath with me. Slowly, like in slow motion, they came into view with every rotation and twist. They stood motionless as I squeezed my body and completed my last half twist. My heart spiraled as I descended and spotted the ground.

Feet together and knees slightly bent, I extended my arms in front of me and closed my eyes, knowing immediately how this would end.

Chalk floated up around my ankles as I squeezed every muscle to stick my dismount. The crowd erupted, breaking the quiet. I opened my eyes and raised my arms to salute the judges twice. My chest rose into the air as I dragged in a ragged breath, and I turned toward my team with a massive smile splayed across my face.

I knew in my heart that we had done it.

All three girls were waiting for me, jumping and chanting as I ran toward them with open arms. I was enveloped in group hugs and happy tears.

The four of us spoke at the same time, and we giggled.

"Do you think it's enough?"

"I'm going to be sick."

"What's taking so long?"

Our questions and worries flew out of our mouths. We were currently holding first, but only by a thread. If I was given the full points for difficulty, my score would make it almost impossible for another team to beat us.

Tears streamed down my cheeks, and I held my breath, waiting, praying that we wouldn't get bumped to second. My score lit up the screen and my jaw dropped. Shock rendered me immobile.

I couldn't move. I was stunned, unable to do anything but stare and feel the chills wrack my arms. The fans exploded in a wild frenzy, and that got me in motion. My teammates and I hugged each other as happy tears fell down our cheeks. We were in a state of disbelief and total shock. Of course, we'd hoped and dreamed, but never imagined it would actually happen. It was absolute mania where we stood. The screen changed to show the current standings.

I blinked, and blinked, and blinked.

My jaw plummeted to the floor.

Team USA was in first place by a full three points now.

I looked around frantically, unable to control the abundance of feeling rushing through me. Happiness. Disbelief. Shock. My heart was in my throat. Cameras were everywhere. Their flashes reminded me of fireworks as excitement in the arena spread. There were still gymnasts who hadn't competed yet. The remaining teams were now fighting for silver and bronze, and they were aware of it. No team would be able to take the gold from USA.

I always thought the girls looked a little maniacal on television when they realized they'd won. Now I got it. This moment was worth every ounce of heartache I'd gone through. Whether it was from those I loved or due to my health, it was worth it.

I'd wanted this my whole life.

Gold. Team USA would win gold. *I* would win gold.

I held my chest. This wasn't real. It was too good to be true. I tried to catch my breath and slow down my heartbeat when someone pulled me into a hug.

I didn't have to guess who it was. I knew the moment his hand touched me.

A smile spread across my lips. I threw my arms around his shoulders and jumped into him. My feet kicked up behind me as he snuggled me to his chest and hugged me tight. His happiness surrounded me.

Being in Kova's arms while Team USA took home gold was how it was meant to be.

My arms tightened around his shoulders, and my heart pounded so hard I was sure he could feel it against his chest. No one thought I'd make it this far, but he did. Reluctant at first, Kova was the only one who thought I had a fighting chance if I put the work into it. And I had.

My tears continued to flow as I cried in the curve of his shoulder. This moment was more than just winning gold.

"Congratulations, Adrianna," Kova whispered in my ear.

I clenched my eyes shut. Normally I'd step from his arms so bystanders didn't give us nosy stares, but I didn't care who saw us this time. This was something I never wanted to forget. I wanted to remember how this moment felt for me, Kova, and us. Plus, we were at the freaking Olympics! No one was going to say anything, especially when we looked just like other coaches and gymnasts.

"Is it real?" My voice shook as I asked. I didn't want to look and see that I'd made it up in my head.

Kova chuckled under his breath. "It is real, *Malysh*. Team gold, and you move onto the all-around tomorrow with the highest vault and bars scores of the Olympics. I think you will take floor too tomorrow."

My head popped up and I looked at him. I probably looked a little crazy with how wide my eyes were.

All I could do was respond with a dropped jaw.

Kova nodded, his gaze falling to my mouth then back to my eyes. He released me, but neither one of us moved. We were so close we were still touching.

"You did it," he said. There was a soft smile behind his eyes. "Even when the world was against you, you showed them how resilient you are. That is bravery not many are granted with. It is one of the things I love about you, you know. You are steadfast in the pursuit of your dream. You are so much stronger than you realize. Your willpower makes me look weak, but I aspire to have the heart and drive you do one day. I hope you are proud of what you have accomplished. I know I am."

I blushed. Kova made me sound like such a strong person, but I was only as strong as those I surrounded myself with. He was my strength. He was the reason I pushed myself so hard. He pushed me to push myself because he knew I could handle it. He loved the adrenaline and so did I. He evoked motivation in me and made me want to be a better gymnast and human. I had learned a lot from him in these few years I'd been at World Cup, and probably even more than I realized until years from now when I look back on my experience.

Kova made me the best version of me, the elite gymnast I only ever wanted to be. He dedicated countless hours of selflessness and coaching because he believed in me.

"Where do you think I learned it from? It's a reflection of you."

His eyes softened. "Get dressed. We have to go."

Nodding, I turned around and went to my duffle bag. I quickly pulled on my sweat suit and strung my bag over my shoulder. I sped up to rejoin my team, and Coach Elena and the entire U.S. Olympic Committee held their hands out over the railing again. I slapped them all with a giant smile on my face, grateful that they also believed in me enough to give me this chance.

Most days I was my own worst enemy because I knew what I was capable of in my heart. When I didn't meet my own expectations, I beat myself up. It was an incredible feeling to see that I had people supporting me all along.

"IN THIRD PLACE, WINNING THE bronze medal…"

The crowd gave a vivacious round of applause. Third place at the Olympics was a huge accomplishment, but I knew those girls felt defeated inside and my heart cried out to them.

Second place was announced next, and my pulse skyrocketed as I awaited our turn. My knees shook and happy tears climbed my eyes for the millionth time. I was an emotional mess. Every time I dried my tears they started right back up.

"Ladies and gentlemen," the announcer said, his voice booming through the speakers, "please welcome your Olympic gold medalists, Team USA."

I stepped up onto the center platform with my team and waved toward the crowd. Chants of "USA! USA!" came from the stands. My jaw trembled as an abundance of happiness filled me. I couldn't stop smiling.

A woman came forward holding an open box with four shiny gold medals. They lay flat with the multi-colored ribbon folded underneath. They were brighter close up and beautifully engraved with an image of Nike, the Greek goddess of victory. The woman was met by a member of the International Olympic Committee who reached for the first medal then draped it over my teammate's neck as the announcer called her name.

"Adrianna Rossi."

I sniffled when my name was announced next. The IOC member lifted a medal and I bent at my waist. Carefully, she adorned my neck with the surprisingly heavy accolade.

"Thank you," I whispered.

I straightened and stood tall, drawing in a deep breath and exhaling. Glancing down my stomach, I picked up the award and held it in my palm. I had the strongest urge to take a bite. It reminded me of a gold wrapped chocolate coin I got one Easter.

Of course, I didn't bite it. I'd do that in private.

I gave it a little toss to feel the weight in my hand. I'd given up so much of myself for this, and it was so worth it.

After the last medal was placed around my teammate's neck, another member of the Olympic committee came forward to hand us small bouquets custom to Greece. Bushy olive branches cupped the beautifully bloomed orange, red, and yellow flowers. I smiled down at the bouquet then bent my knees to receive the laurel wreath on the crown of my head. The interlocking olive branches represented victory, power, and glory. I was proud to wear it.

I searched for Kova, but he was lost in the sea of faces. Then the three flags representing the medaling countries rose high in the air, and "The Star-Spangled Banner" began to fill the room.

My eyes glistened at the sight of the flags. I was in awe. I couldn't tear my gaze away. This night was emotional on so many levels. Everything I'd worked hard for was all for this moment in time that would live with me for the rest of my life. Being in a room surrounded by hundreds of thousands of people who loved this sport just as much as I did was no better feeling in the world. These were my people.

I peered down at the medal again and held it closer wondering if I'd feel the same way if we hadn't medaled. I realized I would because it wasn't about winning. It was about the journey and the drive to achieve my dream. My determination had completely overtaken every molecule of air in my body, making the chase worthwhile.

A soft smile moved my lips. I wasn't going to lie to myself anymore. I was going to be open and honest with myself and accept what I couldn't change.

I looked up at the American flag and stared. I was proud of myself. I didn't feel like there was a crushing pressure on my chest anymore, or this need to improve myself all the time. There was freedom that came with this moment. I was free from the restraints of myself.

Standing underneath the gleaming lights, I felt different. Older, newer. On the mend. I felt that after today, I could take on anything my future held.

Gymnastics made me strong. It made me brave, and if I really let myself think about it, gymnastics prepared me for the next phase of my life by pushing me to fight for something I really wanted. It gave me strength.

I thought I'd be bursting with joy standing on this podium, but what I felt more than anything was a sense of relief.

I could breathe again.

As the anthem drew to an end, we raised our flowers in the air to give one final salute. I smiled as rainbow colored confetti shot from the high corners of the room and balloons fell upon us like fresh snow.

CHAPER 36

After the Team USA celebratory dinner last night, I didn't get to talk to my family for more than a few minutes before I was ushered to the village for therapy, then sent back to my room to decompress and prepare for today. I'd stuck to the same schedule of eating and meds, hoping to relive what I did yesterday.

Not even twenty-four hours later and it was a totally different sporting event.

Inhaling a deep breath, I looked down at the leotard I was allowed to design myself for this competition in preparation of making it this far. Every gymnast did. Over two thousand jade Swarovski crystals in several sizes were attached to the deep mahogany material in fiery flames, overlapping each other. It was a color I didn't typically wear.

Yesterday I was decorated in stars and stripes that represented independence and freedom. It took two years for that design to mature at the imagination of Coach Elena, all for one day of glory.

But today's leotard was by far my favorite for two reasons. The base was a color that complemented my dark red hair and sun-kissed dusting of freckles on the bridge of my nose. The green was for Kova's eyes, a color most redheads just so happened to wear too.

Intertwining colors. Strength in darkness.

I smoothed my hands down the front, my palms catching the three-dimensional stones. He didn't know what I'd done, and I wasn't sure if I was going to tell him.

I glanced at Kova standing next to me. He seemed focused. Almost too focused. My eyes raked down his body. He was dressed similarly to yesterday, only this time he wore a black polo shirt with his dress pants. The shirt strained around his biceps. I moved my eyes upward and found Kova still deep in thought.

I bit my lip, then said, "Where's my pep talk?"

He didn't hear me, so I gently backhanded his arm. He jumped and glanced at me with confusion.

"What is wrong with you?" he asked.

I almost laughed because he was genuinely confused. "Did you hear what I said? Any last-minute pointers?" I paused. Now I was worried. "Are you okay?"

He stuffed his hands into his pockets and turned his body toward me. "There is nothing wrong, I am sorry. I was focused on trying to read Coach Elena's lips. There are no last-minute pointers today."

I looked over at her. She was waving frantically, trying to get his attention. I tapped him and lifted my chin in her direction. He glanced her way and nodded, then held up one finger.

"How come you're not saying anything positive today?" Kova smiled at me, and I continued, "It's almost like tradition for us. I'm trying to recreate my past meets. I'm feeling a little superstitious I guess…"

Kova chuckled. "You are as far as you could possibly go. Today is about you, your talent, and your accomplishments, and being awarded for them." He paused, then smiled and said, "But if you want me to tell you what I am thinking, I will."

My cheeks bloomed with warmth. "I do."

"Do not beat yourself up tomorrow for any mistakes today. Of course, the goal is not to make any," he said, and my lips twisted. "But try to remember that you worked really hard to get here and this competition itself is a gift. You made your dream a reality, and you took it a step further. Not many people are able to say that. That is a beautiful thing to witness."

He didn't say that to appease me, Kova spoke from his heart. If it wasn't for his nostalgic tone, I might have thought otherwise. This was a big moment for us as coach and gymnast. He knew it, I knew it. I wouldn't return to World Cup, and once we arrived home, he wouldn't be my coach anymore.

I was unprepared for the sadness in his eyes. I acted on impulse and wrapped my arms around his shoulders. Kova reacted immediately and hugged me back just as a few flashes flickered around us. He dropped his face into the crook of my neck. His body was so warm pressed to mine. I didn't want it to end and the thought filled me with melancholy.

The bell chimed and we pulled back. The crowd bustled with excitement again and I felt it. I cleared my throat about to speak when Kova eyed me and said under his breath, "Tonight."

I nodded. I still didn't know what that meant. I just assumed I'd see him somehow.

Kova turned around and made a beeline for Coach Elena. They spoke for a moment. I glanced at the judges' table down the runway and powdered my palms then slipped on the wrist guards. The green light flashed, and I licked my lips and swallowed.

Stepping behind the white line, I asked myself what the one thing was that separated me from my competitors.

I had more to lose than them.

THE ALL-AROUND WAS A PERFECT example of how everything can change in the blink of an eye when it came to gymnastics. After the second rotation, I'd teetered between third and fourth place because of the balance beam. In the end, I'd secured the silver medal. I had been only five tenths of a point away from gold.

I smiled and told myself I wasn't allowed to be upset. I had so much fun that it was virtually impossible to be sad. I considered myself fortunate to be here.

Dressed in my Team USA sweat suit, I took it all in for the second time as I stood on the podium with Russia and China. Emotion consumed me when our flags were raised. The rich colors of my flag evoked a powerful reaction from me that was electrifying. The butterflies that had been swarming in my stomach the last two days were sprung from the restraints of my ribs and fluttered away. Quiet tears spilled down my cheeks. My heart was overloaded with feeling knowing I'd leave the Olympic Games with a handful of medals.

I glanced around. My eyes browsed over the faces who helped make this event possible. I was still in a state of disbelief and clutched the medal in my hand tighter when I saw him.

I held his stare, afraid to let go.

I had officially achieved my dream. Now I had a bigger battle to face

CHAPER 37

ow'd you do it?" Dad asked, his jovial tone causing me to look up.

He had a crystal tumbler in one hand and Sophia's hand in his other.

I shrugged nonchalantly and couldn't help but smile. Gymnastics was all I'd ever known. It was like breathing to me. When I stepped onto the competition floor, my soul came alive and I felt like I was where I should be.

"Seriously. How do you do it?" Avery asked too.

"I don't know. Guess I was born to do it." I joked.

Dad was still looking at me. There wasn't any hardness surrounding his eyes and he didn't look like he was as stressed as he had been. He just looked…happy. Really happy.

"I'm in awe of you," Dad said. He couldn't stop smiling.

I blushed. "Stop looking at me, Dad."

He mocked confusion and I couldn't help but giggle. "What? I can't look at my daughter who won a bunch of medals at the Olympics? I was captivated watching you. Now I wish I'd attended all your meets."

I didn't want him to feel bad. "You were at the ones that mattered the most."

Sophia patted the top of his hand and he looked at her.

"I can't believe the village was boring," Avery said only for me to hear.

I turned my attention to her.

"It definitely wasn't as glamourous as I thought it would be." I told her how lackluster it was. "It was like a giant schoolyard and everyone was waiting for the bell to ring. I definitely didn't see or hear about any sex orgies that supposedly happen."

"I think that happens after they compete."

I mused over her response. "I guess, but we're asked to leave to allow the other athletes to prepare. I'm thinking it happens in a hotel and not there." Not that I was looking, but I was curious after all the rumors I'd heard.

"Let's take a selfie," Avery said, and held up her cell phone.

I was sitting next to Avery with Dad and Sophia across from us. Xavier was next to Dad, but he mostly kept his focus on his cell phone. We were at a round table in a private dining room for another night of celebrating Team USA. All coaches and family were invited. Everyone was decked out, ready to celebrate. The room was filled with people mingling, and happiness permeated the air, putting a permanent grin on my face from the moment I'd walked in.

Avery held her phone up high. We said, "besties," and smiled. She took a few more pictures and then we looked at them together. She posted one on social media with the hashtag "my best friend is cooler than yours." Then she posted another with the message, "A redhead's perfect accessory—a gold medal." It was a funny one of me trying to sink my teeth into the medal.

I glanced around searching for one person.

It didn't take long. My eyes found him immediately.

Kova was leaning his elbow on a highboy table talking to a woman. He took a small sip of what I presumed was vodka in his clear glass, and I watched him like I was thirsty. He nodded a few times before he let out a real laugh and a real smile. My eyes softened with longing. I hadn't seen that type of reaction from him in months.

God, he looked so damn delicious dressed in all black. His sleeves were rolled to just below his elbows and the top few buttons of his shirt were left undone. Matching dress pants and shoes, he looked like sin in the flesh. Kova was oozing sexuality. I'd watched as he moved across the room like a social butterfly for the last hour talking to people. He never once looked in my direction. I tried not to take it personally considering my dad was here, but we had just accomplished something huge together.

"What's wrong?" Avery asked.

I bit my lip. "I feel like Kova's acting strange."

"It's probably because your dad is here."

"Yeah, you're probably right, but still. I feel like he's purposely ignoring me. Something's off. I can feel it."

"I wouldn't worry too much right now. Things are hectic here. Don't read too much into it."

I nodded in agreement even though I didn't like the negative feeling churning in my stomach. "I still can't believe you're here," I said to her, grabbing her arm. I was so happy Avery was granted permission from her parents to attend the Olympics.

"I know. I was ready to sell my soul to fly here when your dad talked to mine and said he'd watch over me. It was smooth sailing after that." She finished with a cheeky smile.

I glanced around the table making sure my brother wasn't listening before asking, "Has it been strange being so close to Xavier?"

Avery shot a fleeting glance his way. She puckered her lips before she spoke. "Yes and no. I think I make it really difficult for him. Like one minute I'll catch him looking at me like he likes me again, and I'll smile a little at him. Then the next second he looks disgusted with me. It's a little unsettling but I remind myself he thinks I aborted his baby. It keeps me from getting mad and reacting."

My heart was sad hearing this. There wasn't one person who had caused the miscarriage, but they'd never see it that way. She felt responsible, but if Xavier knew the truth, he'd feel even more responsible than her. Their truth was a double-edged sword.

Her mouth opened, then closed. She frowned and wet her lips. "We stayed up talking last night until three in the morning."

My brows shot up. I swear Xavier had multiple personalities. "You're kidding me. What happened?"

She shrugged one shoulder. "Nothing happened, we just talked about the transplant surgery, actually."

That was all she said. Nothing more. Nothing less. I waited patiently until I couldn't take it anymore.

"Okay, you're going to make me drag it out of you, aren't you?"

A sly grin spread across Avery's face. She picked her head up and looked at me with round blue eyes.

"Tell me what happened," I urged.

When Avery blushed, it was so obvious. She was light-skinned and her cheeks turned into red apples.

"He asked me to come to his room. Of course, I went. I basically fucking sprinted there. I was shocked at first because he'd hardly said two words to me since we left the States. When I got to his room, he had the fake fireplace lit up on the screen and blankets on the floor in front of it." My brows creased. That was the last thing I'd expected. "I once told Xavier I loved sitting in front of the fire and listening to the crackling wood. He had his cell phone playing the wood burning sound. It was like a beacon calling me. I went right to the floor and laid down. He did too."

My lips parted and my brows angled deeper toward each other. I was puzzled and I was sure it showed. "Who knew he had a sweet side to him? I'm surprised he did that."

She blew out a huff and said, "Me too. He said he didn't get a chance to thank me for testing to see if I was a match for you. He seemed...indebted over it."

I pulled back. "My brother?"

"Yup." She nodded. "I swear he was on the verge of crying he was so happy that we matched up. He just kept thanking me over and over. He was really sweet, and he reminded me of the old Xavier." She paused and her voice lowered even more. "I miss him."

"At least you guys didn't fight." Her eyes rolled toward mine. "Oh, did I speak too soon?"

"Girl, yes. He insisted that he's going to take care of me the entire time I'm in recovery until I'm back to myself. I told him that wasn't necessary, that I didn't need him because I had family to help. We bickered about that for a solid minute. You know what he said? He yelled in my face that he's my family and only he's going to be allowed to take care of me." I frowned, my feelings torn over his behavior. "I wasn't sure whether to swoon or be turned off," Avery said, sounding torn herself.

I glanced across the table at Xavier, who was openly studying Avery. He couldn't tear his eyes from her. My head tilted to the side as I took in his appearance. Xavier rocked that pastel preppy style well, not giving a shit if he was wearing "girl colors," as Avery's twin brothers had put it many times to taunt him. His disheveled hair complemented his lax shirt and loose tie. Funny that he loved preppy clothes when he was anything but a prep boy. He was in trouble with the law often, defensive, abrasive. There was an underlying aura of danger that followed him. He was a walking hazard. All it took was the wrong look and he'd detonate. He'd be better suited in all black, not a soft salmon color. Yet, sitting across from me, Xavier looked at Avery like he was a man drowning in love over someone he'd never have.

"How did you guys leave off?" I asked carefully, looking back at her.

"He said he wanted to see me again tonight, but I told him that's a negative because I get to hang out with my bestie," she said with a beaming smile, her shoulders shifting from side to side. I had so much love for her.

"Have you guys seen each other every night since you got here?"

She peered down then chanced a guilty side-eye glance at me. "Maybe," she drew out shyly. I laughed. "We have, but only because in order for me to go anywhere, your dad makes Xavier come with me. It's *so* annoying. Last night was the first night I was alone with him, though, like in his room alone. My heart was racing the entire time. I couldn't believe he asked me to come over, let alone set up that fake fire."

I giggled, not surprised Dad had done that. "We're in a foreign country, what did you expect? You know my dad sees you as a daughter too."

She gave me a droll stare. "I felt like I had a bodyguard. He was on top of everything I did. I couldn't breathe without him questioning me."

I grinned. "You have no chance in the Olympic village with Xavier around."

"Fucking right, man."

This time I chuckled. I didn't think I'd ever understand those two. They either had something toxic together or something profound. There was no middle ground with them. Like I'd told Xavier that day in his pool house, they were similar to Kova and me.

Hesitantly, I asked, "Do you want to see him tonight?"

Avery lifted her gaze to mine, but I stopped her just seconds after our eyes locked. Her face was blank but her eyes gave her away.

My lips twitched. "I have an idea…"

CHAPER 38

I approached Kova, who was finally alone for the first time tonight. Throwing a quick glance over my shoulder to make sure Avery was still covering for me, I stopped in front of him. He looked up in surprise and quickly surveyed the room before turning his attention to me.

"Hey," I said, feeling my cheeks rush with blood.

Kova's eyes moved down the length of my body in a sensual sweep. I wore a crimson designer dress with gold glitter scattered throughout the slinky material and matching high heels that made me feel like a goddess. The dress and shoes were one of Avery's many outfits she'd packed for the trip. She had insisted I wear them tonight.

Kova's jaw flexed and his nostrils flared as he exhaled. I was pleased with the way he looked at me.

"You look beautiful," he said, but the compliment didn't reach his eyes.

"Thank you," I said, then I got right to the point since we didn't have much time. "So… You kept referring to tonight. Did you want to meet?"

"Ah, yes," he said, his jaw stiff as he swirled the ice in his glass. "I know you will not be returning to Cape Coral for a bit." He stared down at the ice avoiding my gaze. Kova kept his elbows locked to his sides and his stance unwelcoming. I wondered if he was worried about my dad seeing us. I almost regretted coming over here now. "We have a few things that were left unsaid that I feel need to be discussed. However, if you cannot get away for, say, thirty minutes, it is no problem."

I shook my head even though he wasn't looking at me. Why wouldn't he look at me? His standoffish attitude left me with this unbearable feeling I didn't want to acknowledge. I didn't like the sudden twisting of dread in my chest.

"Avery will cover for me. What's your room number?"

That got his attention. Kova glanced up to tell me what room he was staying in, but he was so disengaged with our conversation that I had to say something.

"What's wrong?"

He looked straight into my eyes. "Nothing at all. Just catching up with a few old friends."

I nodded slowly, not believing him. I couldn't shake the unsettling feeling under my skin.

The back of my neck prickled with heat. Kova didn't say anything more. I offered him a shaky smile, but he didn't return it. There was an awkwardness hanging in the air between us. All I could do was turn on my heels and walk away.

I KEPT MY HEAD DOWN as I walked toward Kova's hotel room. I couldn't shake the gnawing feeling in my stomach the closer I got to his door. My nerves were shot after the tense moment I'd had with him before I left the dinner. Kova hadn't looked my way for the rest of the night, and I had the strangest notion that he didn't want to see me.

Maybe it was all in my head and the paranoia was getting to me. We both were risking a lot to see each other. Longing filled me. I looked forward to the day when I didn't have to hide how I felt about him.

Avery had agreed to tell Xavier that I crashed early when she went to see him. She would mention the adrenaline wore off and I just wanted to sleep. It was the perfect cover, and it wasn't a lie. It was *exactly* how I felt. I was coming down from the high of being here, and I knew everything would start to settle in my bones soon.

Standing in front of Kova's hotel room, I looked down both sides of the hallway then hesitantly raised my fist to rap on the door. My heart pounded in fear of being seen walking into my coach's room after midnight alone.

The door opened immediately and I stepped inside. Before I could say a word, Kova grabbed my elbow and kicked the door shut with his foot. He pushed me up against the wall then pressed his body to mine. With one hand gripping my hip and the other angling my jaw up to his, Kova's body was fiery to the touch and seething with something a little darker under the surface. My lips parted and I gasped as his cool lips slanted over my needy ones. His tongue slipped into my mouth and I moaned at the connection, fisting his shirt, desperately needing more of him.

I most definitely was being paranoid earlier.

My palms slid up his chest and around to cup the back of his neck. I rolled my hips against his and felt my body come alive. I relished the feeling of how strong and powerful he felt while I was in his arms. I gripped his shoulders, feeling his muscles contract under my fingertips. Kova was like a caged animal that needed to be freed. And I loved it.

Skillful lips made my knees weak. Kova devoured me with a kiss he was more than eager to give. His passion engulfed me and I reveled in the way his mouth moved over mine. The man was a damned good kisser.

Kova's hand slipped over the small of my back. A shot of electricity shot up my spine. His erection pressed into me and I sighed into his mouth.

Cupping my butt, Kova lifted me up, and I wrapped my legs around his hips. A cool breeze blew across us and I noticed my panties were damp. His palm slid into my hair, and his fingers curled around a chunk of the locks and tugged near the root. My chest pressed into his and I groaned in the back of my throat.

I broke the kiss, needing to breathe. "Kova," I said after drawing in much needed air.

My lips were swollen. His hungry mouth found my neck. I shivered as chills danced around my entire body. Kova clenched my hair and tugged it harder, exposing more flesh for his tongue to lick a wet trail to my ear. His teeth nipped my tender skin and I gasped before a sigh rolled off my lips.

"I've missed this," I whispered.

I rolled my hips in a smooth, slow wave against his hard body, silently begging for more. His hold on me tightened, and his cock teased the top of my pussy as I arched my hips back. I melted inside. I loved when he had control over us like this and still felt like an animal under my touch. Kova lifted his gaze to meet mine. His eyes gleamed. He peered at me in awe.

Kova studied my mouth. His palm cupped my jaw as his calloused thumb dragged across my lower lip. I slipped my tongue out and wrapped it around his thumb. I drew it into my mouth and bit down. Kova's nostrils flared. His body went rigid against mine. He pulled his thumb from my mouth, and my teeth cut into each crinkle of skin as he slipped out.

This intoxicating friction between us was too alluring, too dangerous. We hadn't been this close since the day we were ripped from each other. Now that we were alone, we were much more combustible than ever before.

"I wanted to do that the moment I saw you tonight in that red dress," he said, his voice raspy. *"Kravisyata."*

Why did my chest ache hearing those words?

His hand shook as he smoothed my hair behind my ear. One more glance into my eyes, then Kova stepped back from the wall and walked us over to the bed. He lowered me down. I sat on my knees and adjusted my linen cornflower blue shorts and white, flowery chemise.

"I didn't think you saw me until I walked up to you."

I lowered my eyes, not wanting to look at him, because the truth was, the way he'd acted toward me in that room made me feel invisible. Kova had treated me like a stranger, not someone I'd made a baby with.

Two fingers tipped my chin up until I was forced to meet his intense stare. He exhaled and I caught the faint scent of vodka on his breath. I wondered if he could hear how hard my heart was working right now.

Kova ran his tongue over his bottom lip, his front teeth dragging over the plumpness. "All I ever see is you. Everywhere I look, I am reminded of you. I knew the moment you walked into the room. I just did not expect to see you the way I did. And, honestly, what did you expect? I could not talk to you. I definitely could not have acted like we were more than coach and gymnast."

"That's why you ignored me? You didn't look my way once." I was still a little bothered over that. "I didn't think you even thought about me. You acted like a stranger."

Kova snorted under his breath and backed away from the bed. He dragged his hands down his beautifully tormented face as he turned and gave me his back. My body instantly missed his warmth as he walked over to the round table in his room.

I climbed off the bed and stalked after him. He glanced at me and his expression shifted into a multitude of emotions. Right versus wrong. Want versus need. Sin and morals conflicted in the storm clouds of his eyes, and my brows furrowed. I didn't like what I saw.

Kova reached for his glass and downed the rest of its contents. I watched his throat work the clear liquid, the slender muscles and veins contracting with each pull. The ice clinked together and Kova all but threw the glass back on the table.

"I'm right, aren't I? You did ignore me like a stranger." When he didn't answer, I pushed my next question through my teeth. "How do you manage to do a complete one-eighty in the span of a couple of hours? How do we go from being this close"—I crossed my middle finger over my index finger—"to this?" I separated my fingers into a peace sign. "Explain to me why you decided to put space between us, because that's what you did when you started this whole 'let us ignore Adrianna now that Olympics are over' campaign three point five seconds after it ended," I said, mocking his English. "You acted like you didn't even know me."

I was getting myself worked up and I didn't want that. I wanted to remain in control of my emotions. Being this close to him yet feeling so far away completely blindsided me. I took a deep breath. Kova had ignored me, causing my past insecurities I'd fought so hard to ignore to come roaring back in full force. And he was lying about it.

"I did not ignore you, Adrianna," he said a little stilted.

I gawked. "Yes, you did. I don't understand why you acted like I was invisible when you suggested I come here to talk. Even now, I can see the look in your eyes when you look at me. You're not as impenetrable as you think you are. I see right through you, Kova."

Kova scowled, his gaze narrowing. "You do realize your father was in that room, yes?" He stepped closer and I felt his hot breath on my face. "You do realize that I went to jail because of us, yes?" I nodded, and he continued. "Then answer me this, why the hell would I put myself in jeopardy like that again, on top of being in another country? You cannot be serious right now, Adrianna. We had a role to play. I played mine and you did too. The *Games* are over. That is it."

CHAPER 39

He was glaring at me.

I felt his words, but I didn't feel like they were coming from him. He wanted me to believe they were his, though.

It was disheartening the way he was acting toward me after our Olympic win. It wasn't an idiotic thing of me to ask him. We didn't pretend out there, there were no roles. My medals were just as much his as they were mine.

Tears climbed up the back of my eyes. I wish I didn't get so emotional. I shook my head and walked away for a second then turned back around to face him.

"If you're so worried about my father, then why did you want me to come tonight? Was it so you could tell me we're officially done working together and you have to act like you don't know me now? Is that the point you're trying to make? Because guess what, *Coach*, I fucking got it."

His eyes blazed with fire. Still, he didn't say anything.

"You've been sending me mixed signals since you got out of jail. At first, I understood. Trials came and you showed me a glimpse of the old Kova. I thought everything was okay, but really you were just giving me this false sense of hope for us. You act like you don't know me and make me think you've changed your mind about us. Then in the next minute you rip me into your room and kiss me until you steal my breath and then feed me lies. You're back to being this cold, distant man that seems to want no part of me." I pause, my jaw quivering from the tears I was holding back. "Can't you see what this does to me?"

Kova cast his eyes away. He lifted his backwards hat and ran his fingers through his hair before he replaced it. I poured out my feelings to him and he didn't even do a double take.

"Nothing has changed, Adrianna."

"You're such a liar." Kova didn't flinch. He didn't even respond, and that told me everything I needed to know. My heart pumped faster. "Kova, you're scaring me. What's going on?"

Again, no response. He just looked down and avoided my gaze. My pulse rate increased. That bridge we'd worked so hard to build was collapsing plank after plank.

"I shouldn't have come here. This was a mistake—" My heart clenched at the word. I looked at the floor and frowned. "This was a giant mistake. Everything was a mistake. I can't do this anymore." I started to feel a little frantic.

I stepped around Kova and headed for the door.

"Stay," he finally said.

I stopped immediately, wishing I was stronger when it came to him. I turned around and met his stare. He looked defeated.

"What am I doing here, Kova?" The last thing I wanted to do was fight, but I couldn't keep it in. It wasn't healthy for me or us.

I wanted to be able to talk about the past, the present, and the future with him tonight since tonight was all we had for a little while. We didn't have to sign anything in blood, but we could at least talk a little bit so there wasn't a total break in our chain.

Feeling dejected, I asked, "Help me understand what is going on. I know we haven't seen each other in about a month, but the last two days you were my supportive coach and it made me think we were okay. But now with this feeling in my heart, it's like I don't even know you."

"I was your coach because that is who I am supposed to be. I did what I had to do to help you get to the finish line. I was doing my job. I did not want to ruin your moment."

I frowned, not liking the bite in his tone. I moved closer to him. I studied Kova, but his eyes gave nothing away.

"So, you faked it? All those encouraging words, going as far as 'living with me,' they were just part of your job description?"

Kova ran his hands over his face and groaned. "No, I meant them, Adrianna, but I wish I did not."

I blinked rapidly. "How could you say that?"

He placed his hands on his hips and stared up at the ceiling for a brief moment. "I got arrested and almost charged with rape," he said after expelling a long sigh.

"I'm eighteen. It wouldn't have happened."

"Katja is still on my case. Your father… " He paused, and his eyes lowered to slits. "He still has the option to proceed with charges. There is a lot to be settled and it is far from finished. It is not so easy like you think to just jump right back to what we were."

"I knew it," I whispered, my voice hoarse. "I knew it," I said again with more conviction. Kova straightened his back and leveled a stare at me that fanned black smoke around my heart. "Keep going."

Kova's gaze hardened. His lips pursed together. There were a lot of things I'd mentally prepared for on my journey to the Olympics; however, never had I anticipated the next words to fall from Kova's beautiful lips.

"Adrianna, we cannot go on like this. I think it is best if we do not see each other until everything settles."

I reared back. The silence in the room was earsplitting. "You want time?"

He looked me in the eyes and flattened his lips in response.

My heart sank.

How could he think after something as catastrophic as what we went through that more time away from each other would benefit us? Time would ruin us. People didn't separate when things got tough. They came together and worked through their issues as a team. Their bond was unified with each challenging moment, not split down the center because there was a breach.

We are a team—I exhale, you inhale.

I had been so ridiculous.

My blood ran cold and my throat swelled. Kova had been putting distance between us. What I felt wasn't due to paranoia. It wasn't in my head. It was real. Really fucking real, and what he wanted.

I stared at him, unblinking.

My world crumpled before me.

My heart stopped beating.

All those things he had said to me that day in my condo, how he was going to leave Katja to be with me, how he wanted to live with me and my stupid fucking disease, he took it all back in the blink of an eye. All those miles we had crossed together to get where we were, they were swept away like it never happened.

Angry tears brimmed my eyelids. Kova's gaze softened and he took a step toward me. My hand flew to my chest and I clutched my throat. My brain was telling my body to breathe, but I was stuck in a state of panic. I couldn't focus enough to breathe.

He had sworn he wouldn't hurt me again. He'd promised. Yet, he did.

Then it hit me.

This was why he'd wanted me to come to his room.

He wanted to break up with me.

I leaned toward him, my heart beating frantically. His gaze didn't waver from mine. He didn't back down. He didn't say anything either. Kova was slipping away. I looked at him with resentment that he wasn't fighting harder to be with me like I would for him. I wanted to let go of him completely *and* still reach for him because I couldn't not.

"Time. You want time?" I stated again, fighting the tears. "I literally don't have the time to give you. Do you understand that? I don't have all the time in the world like you do. I'm sick, Kova. I only have now." Jesus. The look on his face matched the gutted feeling inside my heart.

His shoulders sagged and he dropped his hands from his hips in defeat. He didn't want time and yet he told me he did. I shook my head. This back and forth wasn't something I was going to continue doing. I didn't have it in me. He could either have me now or he couldn't. I was only going to get sicker, not better. I didn't have the kind of time he wanted.

I stood straight and exhaled a ragged breath. I didn't want to be hurt anymore. I didn't want anyone to make me hurt anymore. And that started with *my* choices.

I shook my head and took a step back. "It's now or never with me."

"Ria," he said, his face fell. "Please…"

I put my hand up. "Don't. I know our relationship isn't normal. I'm aware of the major issues surrounding us, but that doesn't mean you can push me away because of them." My voice shook. "I know what my dad put you through and it disgusts me you had to go through that. I'm not being unsympathetic toward you or the legal issues you're facing, but was I stupid to think we'd work through what happened? I guess so," I said, more to myself than to him.

I clenched my eyes shut, regretting that I'd snuck out. When I opened them, Kova was standing in front of me looking utterly destroyed. The miserable look in his green eyes made my heart twist with grief. He was hurting as much as I was, yet he was the one who was causing our pain. I didn't understand why he'd do this to us when it devastated him just as much as it did me.

"That is not what I am saying, but I think we need to wait for this storm to weaken before we can be anything more."

"That's not what you told me in my condo that day when you said we could be together because you had a plan. Even before that, you knew it was eventually bound to happen." I felt like I was going to shoot steam from my ears any second. "You can't look me in the face and tell me you didn't anticipate any of this. What happened for you to change your mind? I know you were arrested, but I'm eighteen now. No one can stop us."

There was so much more I wanted to add, but I stopped when I felt tears streaking my cheeks. There would always be people who wouldn't approve of us, but I never once thought that us not being together was an option. I always put him—us—first, and I thought he would too at this point.

My spine bowed, and I looked at him helplessly. "Why can't you ever put me first?"

"Adrianna, you know my feelings for you, but I have to keep your father in the back of my head. When I got out of jail, we had a meeting." I squinted at him, stunned over this news. Dad never told me about this. "Frank threatened to ruin me if I went near you beyond being your coach. He knew he did not have a leg to stand on legally, but he said he would go to the media and claim that I sexually abuse my gymnasts, and he would provide proof for people to dig deeper. He said he would release pictures of us but blur your face to protect you. He said he has connections and will make sure the story goes worldwide. I have worked with your father in the past, I do not doubt him."

I stared up at him, dumbfounded. My eyes widened and I took a step closer, angling my head to make sure I heard him correctly.

"You're scared of my dad and his empty threat? He'd never do that because it would implicate me, not in a million years, no matter how mad he is." I stared at him. "So quick to believe him," I whispered in shock. "You bought his lie. You made it your out."

Kova widened his stance. His brows lowered and his gaze turned defensive. "Everything I have worked for since I came to the United States will be taken away if we continue a romantic relationship. How would we work out if I have no gym? No name? Nothing? How could I support you, support us? I cannot make mistakes right now." The color drained from his face. "He can ruin me and you, and that is not something I am chancing."

I ground my teeth. I was frustrated because I knew my dad was using this as a scare tactic and Kova was buying it. He edged closer to me and I stayed exactly where I was.

"I have to walk a straight line and I have to do it for us. You think I want to leave you? You think I do not care about you? My fucking heart beats only for you, Adrianna. It kills me inside. I want to ram my fist through a wall over and over because of this shit we have to go through. I am trying to do what is right. Whether you like it or not, the right thing is time. Are you not sick of living in this fantasy we have created? Do you not want the real thing? I do. And I will do everything I can in my power to make that happen for us."

"I'm not trying to be dramatic, but you don't seem to comprehend that I don't have that kind of time. I was supposed to go home and start treatment. What if the dialysis doesn't work, or I have the transplant and my body rejects the kidney? I know these are slim possibilities, but that's how my life is at the moment and how I have to think now. I can't wait around for you because that's not fair to me. If we're careful, we could have now, you just don't want to."

My heart was about to jump out of my chest. I was going to be sick any second.

"You only want me when I'm at my best and not at my worst," I said, my voice shaded with disdain. "That's not what love is. I stood by you at your worst. I never gave up. I took everything you would give me, and I gave myself to you ten times over because I knew you needed me when you were going through something. Now when I need you the most, when my body is literally fighting to kill me, you feel time between us is best."

Kova opened his mouth to speak, but I wasn't done.

"You want time, Coach?" I said, bitterness dripping from my tone. "Time is exactly what I'm going to give you." I turned toward the door and shot one last response over my shoulder. "I'm leaving for the University of Oklahoma shortly after I get home. You're getting exactly what you wanted."

CHAPER 40

Adrianna," Kova called out. "Let me finish."

I wanted to lift my middle finger to him. I'd been living a dream expecting to luck out in the end. I'd set myself up, and that hurt my heart more than Kova ever could. I really was just a stupid, naive, lovesick girl.

"Come here," he demanded, and I ignored him. A string of Russian flew past his lips as I wrapped my hand around the doorknob.

More tears filled my eyes and I fought to keep them back. I was so sick of being this heartbroken girl fighting for someone who would give up on me so easily. I had allowed my view to be clouded by the illusion Kova had painted for me.

I pulled the door open a fraction and Kova slammed it shut then spun me around. He pressed his back to the door, blocking my escape. A gasp lodged in my throat. I was unprepared for the passion in his touch or the heat of his breath on my cheek.

He blinked and something adjusted in his gaze. "You are angry with me because I said we need time for everything to settle down, but you were planning to move to another state? Do you see the hypocrisy here?"

My jaw dropped. "Excuse me for assuming we would continue to be together regardless of which school I went to. We could drive or fly to each other, talk all the time, even spend time together on holidays or weekends. There's no one stopping us. It's really not that hard if you want it bad enough." I paused and shook my head. "But you don't want that and there's no reason for me to stay now."

Kova gnashed his teeth together as fire ignited in his eyes.

Finally, he displayed an emotion I could understand and handle from him.

I breathed it in and found the strength I needed. He stepped forward and pressed his body to mine, his fingers gripping my bicep.

Kova was breathing as hard as I was, but it was the way he was staring at me that reduced me to a brokenhearted mess. He looked so powerless. I didn't not want him in my life, but I refused to be put aside until the time was right.

"I never said I did not want to be with you. Do not put words in my mouth, *Malysh*." He said the words slowly and they set me on edge. "How can we be together with your father watching over every little thing we do? Please use your head for a minute and think about this. Our livelihoods are at stake."

I didn't say anything. My dad would never, ever accept us. But we could make it work if we wanted to, I was sure of it. How long would I be waiting for Kova? Until he felt like it was okay for us? The thought of watching time pass like that was asphyxiating on so many levels. I didn't want to lose him, but I had to put myself and my health first.

I lowered my eyes and grew insanely angry that this was where we were in our relationship after everything we'd been through together. "I'm sick of you," I spat, pushing at Kova's chest. He grabbed my good elbow and I fell into him. "What a regret it was to come here."

"I am right," he said, his voice filled with arrogance. "You know I am right, and you hate it. You think I want to be away from you? You think I want to even consider the idea? Never, but I am doing what I can to help you, to help us."

I needed to get out of here. I tried to shove away from him, only I didn't have the strength to, so he stayed right where he was. My chest rose and fell with rapid breaths.

"No, not this time. This time is different," I said. "You're a coward. If you weren't, you would do whatever it took to be with me."

Kova drew in a long breath. His eyes flared wide. Tension brewed between us. Men didn't like to be called a coward. It was probably one of the most insulting things to say, and I'd said it. I could feel his temper rising with each breath he took. He released my arm and I stepped back. The back of my legs hit the bed. I drew in a breath and tried to not let him affect me.

"What's the next excuse once the smoke clears? There's always going to be something working against us, Kova." I was disgusted with him and myself. "By the time you're ready for me, I won't be here."

"You are not in the position I am," he said through clenched teeth. "You have not a clue."

That set me off. I too was risking a lot to be with him.

"I don't have to be in your position to know it wouldn't matter to me!" I screamed. "I'd do whatever it takes. I *have* been doing whatever it takes. You told me you were divorcing Katja to be with me. Here I was thinking we were still okay because what we have is so strong, but really you're over here ready to let it go because you got scared." I was winded, on the edge of exploding. I wanted to punch something, and I wasn't the violent type. Kova brought out that side of me.

"You're not that weak," I continued. "You're the strongest man I know. You're just scared. You know what? So am I. I have a hell of a lot more to be scared of than you and I'm *still* fighting for us." This rage building inside of me needed to be let loose. "Tell me." I stepped forward and pushed at his chest. My eyes lowered to slits. "Tell me what it was that changed your mind. At least give that to me. I know there's more, because there's *always* more when it comes to you, Kova!" I yelled in his face, trying to rid myself of all the hurt he continued to cause me.

Kova shoved me onto the bed. I tumbled to the side and he reached for me. He grabbed my ankle and yanked me down the bed until my legs we're hanging off. I quickly sat up as he leaned over me. I breathed into his face, panting from the unexpected action.

"I cannot stand the thought of hurting you anymore!" he shouted, his eyes wide and bright.

A vein strained along the column of his neck leading down under his shirt. Finally, Kova let go.

"I will never forget seeing you on the floor that day, the blood everywhere as your fucking eyes closed shut. I thought I lost you, and I vowed to myself that I would never hurt you like that again."

He shook his head like he was reliving the moment. He looked terrified. Kova stepped away and paced the floor, but he kept his gaze on me. His aggression ate up the space between us.

"Your life means too much to me for that. I sat in jail, overanalyzing everything, realizing how much negativity I brought to your world. I decided it was best to put distance between us, except when I saw you again, I knew there was no way. Just like right now, I cannot handle the thought of not being with you everywhere you go."

I blinked and he was inches from me. Kova lowered his face and dragged the tip of his nose over my cheek until his lips hovered above mine. I found myself leaning into him, hoping he'd kiss me.

"I would give everything up for you because you are *mine* and I am *yours* and that is all that matters. We will always be each other's. No one can change that."

I leaned in closer and Kova sucked in a breath. He stepped back but I reached out swiftly and clenched the center of his shirt. I yanked him toward me and we fell back onto the bed with my legs tangled with his. I held my breath praying he wouldn't move.

He cupped my cheek and my jaw in his palms. There was a sudden tenderness in his touch. Kova looked at me. "I hate that I hurt you, and I hate that you miscarried our child. It sickens me. I hate that your father will always be between us. He will not accept us, and you cannot decide between the two of us either. A good man would have never put you in this position. I try to do the right thing, but all it ever does is backfire. You get angry and try to inflict pain on me. I bite back because I like when you push me and fight me. But this is too much for one couple."

Beads of sweat pebbled his forehead. Kova was breathing heavily, and I could feel the heat radiating from his body. I leaned up on one elbow and Kova stayed where he was on me. I took pleasure in the weight of his body on mine.

"I am better off alone." Kova lowered his voice; his distraught eyes searched mine. "And so are you. But that can never be now, can it?"

My lips parted as his words slammed into me. I let out a small whimper then flattened my lips between my teeth.

Kova stood up and reached for me, but I moved out of the way and got off the bed myself.

"Ria—"

"I'm leaving." I walked around him, but Kova was quick.

He grabbed me, his fingers pressing into my skin. I wrestled him and felt this burst of angry energy explode through me. Kova was so much stronger than I was, and I took satisfaction in the knowledge

I could use as much strength as I wanted and I wouldn't hurt him. Not unless I had a knife, which I didn't.

Kova grabbed my wrists and tried to pin them behind my back. When that failed, he spun me around so my back was pressed to his chest and he had both of my arms crisscrossed in front of me. I tried to squirm away, but he held me secured. I wished I didn't like how he held me to him.

"Let go of me."

Kova ignored me. I was no match for his strength, but still, I tried.

"Let go, Kova."

A grunt escaped my throat as the frustration mounted inside of me.

"If you don't want to be with me now, you can't have any of me later." My heart broke saying those words. "Let. Go."

Kova held me tighter. I found it therapeutic trying to fight him. It released something inside of me. My head fell back against his chest and I let out a little whimper. His face dipped down and his nose brushed my neck. His warm body enveloped me, and I stupidly relished in it. Tears filled my eyes and my body relaxed enough so Kova could let go of my wrists and bring his arms up to hug me. He embraced me with warmth and love.

"Kova."

He pressed a soft kiss under my jaw. "I love you, Adrianna."

I broke down, unable to handle a second more. "I know we're no good for each other," I whispered, admitting the truth. I leaned back into him as a tear slipped down my temple. "I know we'll never be good for each other, but that doesn't stop me from wanting to be with you."

I felt Kova shake his head. His lips brushed tenderly over my skin.

"I cannot let you go, just like you cannot let me go," he said.

The truth was like gravel on my raw heart.

CHAPER 41

Why is this happening to us?"

Kova lowered his hips to the bed and took me with him. He turned me sideways to face him. I sat on his lap with my knees pressed together and my legs hanging over his. He kissed my temple and hugged me close. I missed the feel of his arms and nestled closer. I fit like a puzzle piece against him. I could stay here for hours if he'd let me.

"All I know is that I am tired of hurting you. I will do anything to see you live a happy life. You must believe that."

I shook my head. I couldn't look at Kova just yet. What he said wasn't wrong, I just didn't agree with it. When there's a will, there's a way. Gymnastics had taught me if I wanted something bad enough, then I had to put the work in to get it. And that's how I felt about us. I was willing to do what it took. I wished he'd fight for us the same way.

"Don't you understand that time is not on my side right now? Nothing hurts more than you leaving."

Kova cupped my cheek and I finally looked at him. The anxiety encasing my chest intensified. He leaned down and kissed my tears away as they fell in rivers. I wound my arms around his shoulders and threaded my fingers through his hair. I closed my eyes as I inhaled him into me. My heart felt like it was shattering into a million tiny pieces. I was afraid to let go, afraid we wouldn't ever have this again.

Kova was my everything.

"I have thought about you nonstop since that day. I drove myself crazy when you were in the hospital and I could not be there with you." He pulled back and paused like he was struggling for words. His fingers skimmed over the hem of my shorts. "I have never felt more powerless than I did in that moment. All I felt was rage, and it resulted in a few fights while I was waiting to be released. It was part of the reason I was not released when I should have been. You mean everything to me. I resent myself every second of my life after seeing what you went through. You deserve better."

I shook my head frantically. "I'm so sick of everyone telling me what's best for me. I don't need you, my father, or anyone for that matter to make decisions for me. Let me make them, and if I'm wrong, I want to experience that for myself too. I'm the one who gets to decide what to do with my life and who I want in my life. And what I want is you, Kova. I just want you in my life."

Kova exhaled a heavy breath as his gaze bore into mine. His back bowed. He was struggling again. I could feel him wavering beneath my touch. Tipping my jaw up, I parted my lips toward his and lowered my eyes. I peered at him through my lashes. He exhaled through his nose and his chest heaved into me. Kova dropped his gaze to my mouth. I drew in a soft gasp as he leaned toward me, his tongue delicately tracing over my lips. Without hesitation, he slipped inside and stroked across my mouth in a deep kiss. Our lips fused together, and that was all it took for my body to come alive. Heat exploded around us. Flashes of desire tingled down my skin. My back arched and I moaned.

I straddled him without breaking our kiss. Kova's hands were on my hips in seconds, his palms cupping my butt as he guided me over him. Our bodies met and everything locked into place. My arms tightened around his shoulders and Kova deepened the kiss. He embraced me, clutching me desperately.

My thighs clenched around his waist and I felt his hardness press between us. It wasn't about that, though. We had something everyone dreamed of having one day, chemistry between two people that only increased the passion each and every time they were together.

Kova broke the kiss, panting heavily against me. "This does not have to be difficult. I am trying to do what is best for you, Adrianna." He paused. "Fuck," he said through gritted teeth. "I'm trying to do what is best for us."

I looked deep into his eyes. They were brimming with raw emotion. I wanted him to give into me the way I was giving into him.

"Let me decide what's best for me."

I smashed my mouth to Kova's. He kissed me back hard, brutally, putting all his feelings into the way his lips crushed mine. He kissed me like he was giving me hope and breaking my heart at the same time. This wasn't a man who wanted to leave me. This was a man who was on his knees madly in love with me, trying his hardest to right his wrongs.

"Tell me you love me," he said.

My breath hitched in my throat. I looked back and forth between his eyes, suddenly scared to tell him I loved him. My heart pumped hard and fast as he watched me, waiting, silently pleading for something he wasn't sure I could give him.

With tears streaming down my cheeks, I finally said the words he needed to hear. "I love you." I released a loud sob as soon as the words left my lips. "I've loved you for a long time."

Kova studied me, the black flecks in his probing green gaze cut right through me. My declaration stilted him into silence and his stare filled with a mixture of wonder and heartbreak. I think he always knew I loved him, but saying the words changed his reality. He wasn't prepared for the weight of those words to actually leave my lips.

Kova lifted my hand and brought it to his chest. His heart beat wildly under my palm. "Do you feel that, Adrianna? My heart will only ever beat for you. This is what you do to me when I think about how much I love you."

I felt his pulse and wondered if he knew the rapid thumping of his heart mirrored my own.

My fingers moved over the raised scar beneath his shirt, tracing over the letter. I softened. The mark was more than a binding of two people. It represented our agony and connection. Proof there was no length we wouldn't go to for each other. How were we supposed to walk away from one another when it was agonizingly clear we didn't want to?

"I love you, Kova," I said, my voice soft. "I love you so fucking much." My jaw trembled from the magnitude of emotions coursing through me.

Saying I love you was so much harder than saying fuck you or I hate you. Love was putting themselves out there to risk everything one had to give. It was the strongest emotion there was. Hate dissipated over time. People didn't reminisce over hate, they reminisced over love and the way it made them feel. Love grew and intensified over time. Love also wrecked lives.

Kova drew in a quiet breath and nestled me closer to him. Being wrapped in his arms was something I reveled in, but this time he was finding solace in holding me. His eyes closed and he took a few shallow breaths. I didn't know what the next five minutes would bring us. All I knew was that we couldn't lose each other.

"Loving you scares me," I said, opening myself up to him and the truth. "More than anything in the world."

He opened his eyes and looked at me. I cupped the back of his head and brought his lips to mine. Soft and pliable, his kiss eased the tension around me. My body pressed into his, his chest against mine, and I expelled a breath knowing this was right where I needed to be. My mind was a muddled mess, and the more I thought about our future the messier it became. There was only one thing I wanted tonight.

"Kova?" I waited until his eyes met mine before I continued. "Make love to me?"

"Are you sure that is what you want?"

I nodded. "I think it's what we need. Just...just go slow."

His brows angled toward each other. "I do not have any protection with me."

Crazy how we never really cared about protection until I got pregnant. It wasn't like we didn't know unprotected sex led to babies, we knew, we just got too lost in the passion to really care.

"I'm on birth control now."

A shadow formed in his eyes and it hurt my heart. I'd gone on birth control before I left the hospital.

"Are you upset I started the pill?"

"No," he said, shaking his head. "All of this happened because of me, and it sickens me."

I wished he'd stop blaming himself. If he didn't let go of the guilt it would eat him alive.

Kova pressed his forehead to mine and looked between us. He stilled. I fisted his shirt tighter and followed his gaze. My heart nearly stopped when I realized he was looking at my stomach.

A million thoughts ran through my mind.

I wondered what he was thinking.

I wanted to know if he felt like his chest was caving in the way mine was too.

I was scared to know if he wanted this for us, or if he was truly trying to put me before him.

His brows knitted together, and I prayed he didn't turn me away because of what had happened.

"I'm sorry, Kova. I understand if you can't...be like that with me anymore. I'm sure I disgust you after what happened—I disgust myself."

God, how I hated myself.

Kova's eyes snapped up to mine. "What the fuck are you talking about? I love every single thing about you. Everything." Kova pressed me back onto the mattress. He dropped a quick kiss to my lips then one over my collarbone. He slid further down my body and I watched him. "I loved that, for a moment," he said, kissing the spot next to my nipple, "no matter how brief it was"—he kissed just above my bully button—"my child was growing inside of you. And it makes me want you more."

I clenched my eyes shut. Kova gently placed his lips right next to the crease of my hip and thigh. It nearly ruined me when he pressed one last kiss to the center of my pelvis. My fingers threaded through the hair on the back of his head as I fought the feelings rushing through me at his unexpected tenderness and just how wrong I was.

There was this deep-seated need inside of me to know that he didn't hate me, that he still wanted me intimately, that he didn't find me repulsive after what had happened.

CHAPER 42

P ressing my lips to his, I pushed against Kova's chest to roll him onto his back before he could say another word.

I sat up and straddled his hips. Kova peered up at me, his vulnerable gaze probing mine. His hands found the tops of my legs and grabbed me.

This man loved me so much and it was ruining him. He was willing to suffer for a better us one day.

I gripped the hem of my shirt and pulled it over my head and dropped it on the bed next to us. As I reached around my back to unclasp my bra, Kova sat up and stopped me with his hands on mine. I looked at him and froze, afraid he was going to stop me completely.

He didn't. Kova unhooked my bra and the straps fell down my shoulders. I quickly fisted his shirt and pulled it over his head. The corners of my lips curved slightly at the sight of the A on the left side of his chest. Delicately, as if it were still fresh, I grazed my finger over the jagged skin. I leaned forward and pressed my lips to his chest. I was curious what Katja had thought when she saw it, because I was sure she had, but I didn't want to ruin the moment by asking him. This was about us. Our love. Our healing. Nothing and no one else needed to be brought into it at this time.

Kova's palm cupped the back of my head as I kissed my way up the curve of his neck, peppering more kisses along his jaw until I found his lips. His shoulders contracted under my touch as I rose to my knees and looked at him. His fingers pressed into the space below my butt cheeks. We stared at each other, unblinking, drinking each other in. Every lesson learned formed a new scar. I just hoped this one wouldn't hurt as much.

I stroked his jaw. His stubble was rough against my hand. My thumb brushed over his full bottom lip as his hands roamed the back of my thighs. Leaning into his mouth, I whispered, "I love you, Kova.

I want you to always remember that." Then I pressed my lips to his and savored the feel of his lips on mine, and I kissed him longer.

Kova deepened the kiss. I moaned when his hand came up and the tips of his fingers gripped the sides of my neck. He hauled me closer to him in pure desperation. His devious mouth overpowered mine. He took control of the kiss and set the pace. I panted, my lips parting. Kova wasted no time delving his tongue into my mouth with a flair that weakened my knees. He was a skilled kisser and I was needy for him.

Lowering my hips, I scooted closer, needing to feel his bare skin against mine. My nipples pressed into his chest. I sighed into his mouth from the warmth exuding from his body and wrapped my arms around his shoulders only for Kova to break the kiss.

He quietly repeated what I'd just said to him. "I love you, Adrianna. I want you to always remember that."

I reached for the elastic of his shorts. My eyes caught his Olympic ring tattoo. I could get a matching one now. He watched me, then grabbed my wrist for a moment like he was nervous. I glanced up and swallowed thickly, meeting his gaze.

Kova let go and I shifted off his body to pull his gym shorts down. His erection sprang free and laid above his hips. My eyes widened. Thick with my favorite vein, his length hung a little to the side when he laid on his back. I dragged my teeth over my bottom lip feeling the desire awaken inside of me after it was dormant for so long.

"Come here," he demanded.

Kova grabbed the sides of my face when I climbed back up his body. He kissed me as he rolled us so I was underneath him. He crushed me with his weight, and I rejoiced quietly knowing he was reaching his breaking point. My hands found his back, suddenly greedy to touch him the way I wanted to after so long. I loved feeling how his muscles contracted under my touch. He was so strong. Little sounds from me melted into his mouth. My nails scored his skin. Kova flexed against my fingers then reached between us to unbutton my shorts.

Moving to his knees, he pulled off my shorts and panties in one swift move and then halted in his tracks.

His brows lowered into a harsh frown. I followed his gaze to my stomach and my heart sank.

"Kova," I said softly. He looked at me with blank eyes. "I'm okay."

He was hesitant, then dropped my shorts on the bed. He regarded my body with contemplative eyes then looked at me again. I smiled at him with affection. We were both bare to each other now.

Kova surprised me by kissing my stomach again. I pressed my lips between my teeth and bit down. I glanced at the ceiling, fighting the emotion from his tenderness. I wish he hadn't done that. My knees pulled up and my nails dug deeper into the sheets. I expelled an audible breath trying to find the strength for this—for us. I was shaking on the inside, unprepared for the emotional aspect to hit me the way it was. Kova placed his hand over mine and loosened my fingers that were twisting the sheet. I sucked in a breath. He climbed up my body, my knees spreading wide for him.

"Ria," he said.

I shook my head. I wasn't ready to face him now.

"Adrianna, look at me," he begged.

I couldn't. I was afraid to see that he regretted me, us, this. It was too much for my heart to handle.

"My love." His voice softened, and I broke down.

Tears streamed down my temples and I sniffled, still refusing to look at him.

"I can't," I said. "I can't look at you. I don't want to see the regret in your eyes again. I already saw it once tonight when you first looked at my stomach." I flattened my lips for a second. "I don't want to see that you'll never want me like you used to."

Kova positioned his body over mine and laid on me, forcing me to look at him. "Even when I am dead, long buried, and forgotten about, I will still love you, I will still want you. That will never change. You are a part of me now, just like I am of you. We are connected for the rest of our lives." He leaned down and swept a sensual kiss across my lips. "And I am going to show you just how connected we are, *Malysh*."

Taking my arms, he bent them above my head and held both my hands securely in one of his. He captured my lips with his own and drove his tongue into my mouth determined to make me stop overthinking. He grabbed my thigh and hiked it over his waist to seat himself more comfortably between my legs. A moan purred in the back of my throat. His straining cock pressed against my hip as his kiss did wicked things to me. He moved his hand to my breast and my back arched in response. I let out a small sigh. He gave it a gentle squeeze then teased my nipple between his fingers. My body pressed into his, already begging for more.

Kova devoured my mouth, not giving me more than a second to take a breath before he was consuming me again. He tugged my nipple harder, so hard that I felt a zing hit my clit. I gasped in response and tried to wiggle my hands free so I could touch him. I needed to, but he held them down with more weight and deepened the kiss. His silky tongue twirled around mine and tugged before he let go and ran it along the roof of my mouth. Each and every time he kissed me like this, I was weak.

He slowed the kiss, then pulled back, allowing me to inhale needed gulps of air. I looked at him and my breath caught in my throat at the look of love in his eyes.

I'd been stupid to worry about how he felt about me and us. This man clearly loved me like he claimed.

CHAPER 43

I whimpered, already missing his touch when his hand found my throat.

My eyes widened as his fingers encased my slender neck. I may trust him and get turned on when he does this, but it was still a little intimidating when I was helpless.

My body writhed against his. Kova shifted to the side and his cock pressed against my pussy. He leaned down and closed the distance, kissing me painfully slow. His tongue stroked mine too sensually and I shuddered. His thumb smoothed over my pulse and carried me to another level. Kova's hips rolled into mine. For a split second my heart skipped a beat and my body tensed, but then Kova slipped his tongue around mine and I exhaled into him.

I didn't hold back the pleasure filled moan and let it roll off my lips. God, I loved this. There was something thrilling about being at his mercy and the way he manipulated my body. Silver stars danced in my vision. Little black dots floated in the distance the tighter he squeezed around my neck. It was getting harder to breathe. Still, I didn't tell him to stop. There was a dark part of me that took gratification in being choked. I liked the way he made my body go in and out of tunnels of pleasure. I liked the way he set what my body could do and couldn't do. I let him and craved it.

My mind went blank as he thrust his hips, his thick erection teasing my entrance. I attacked his mouth with mine and he growled his approval, nipping my lips and kissing me like the untamed animal he was. My heels dug into the back of his thighs. I needed more of him.

"Kova," I whispered. "I need you."

His eyes dilated. He released my wrists and reached between us to grab his cock. Kova looked down as he used the head to stroke my lips until they spread open. I was swollen and so pink. Kova's nostrils flared as he teased my wet entrance. My hips rolled back and

I angled my body to get more of him. He pressed his fist against my pussy and pushed the tip through his hand to enter me.

His hand grinded into my clit. My toes curled and I let out a long moan. "Please…"

He applied more pressure to my neck, and I could feel his palm gripping my esophagus. My chest rose, and a squeak escaped my lips. I was filled with aching pleasure it was nearly painful. Kova released his hold and all the oxygen roared back into my lungs as white-hot pleasure exploded inside of me. Euphoria barreled through my veins and I turned into an animal. I needed him desperately.

I grabbed his face and slammed my mouth to his. I dug my heels into his backside, trying to get him further inside of me. Our teeth gnashed together, but that didn't stop us. We were two passionate people and our sex only multiplied it. I turned him over and we changed our positions so we were sitting up and I was straddling his hips. Kova aligned his cock with my entrance then fisted my hair. I yelped from the initial pull but loved every second. He wrapped my hair around his fist tighter, making me arch into him.

"Only you, Kova. Only you will ever have my heart," I said honestly.

We were both on the edge yet it was painfully obvious we were hesitant to take the next step.

"I will go slow," he said under his breath, and I nodded.

Breathing heavily, he breached my entrance and pushed past that initial tight bundle of nerves. It burned a little as I stretched to fit his size. I tensed, scared it was going to hurt since it'd been awhile. My nails scored his shoulder blades and he flexed.

"Relax for me, *Malysh*," he whispered in my ear, then kissed my neck.

Kova slid inside of me a little more. My cheeks blushed as my body grew warmer. I felt like I was having sex again for the first time.

He nipped my neck. "It is me and you."

I smiled weakly at him, trying to control my breathing. Me and him. I liked the sound of that and eased myself down, taking him inch by inch.

His hand in my hair loosened and his mouth seduced me with a sweep of his lips over mine. He pulled me closer to him and rocked into me provocatively. I felt myself getting wetter for him.

He wrapped his other arm around my lower back, and I reveled in the feel of my chest pressed against his. Kova plunged his tongue into my mouth and let go of my hair. I moaned softly around his lips, madly in love with this man who was so wrong yet so right for me in every way. Kova seized my throat again and deepened the kiss so it was all I could focus on as he drove into me. With each sweep of his ravenous kiss, I surrendered myself until I let go. It was me and him, like he said, and that thought released me completely.

Kova evoked power and control through his touch, enough to distract me so he could thrust his hips against mine and drive in as deep as he could get. I gasped at the intrusion, but our kiss muffled my moans. He let go of my neck to palm the back of my head. My body tensed and I flinched, trying to move, but Kova held me snug to him and grinded me against him, creating this unbearably hot friction between us.

My thighs quivered around him. Kova let out a long, deep groan as I dragged my nails over his scalp and through his hair. I bit down on his lip and drew in a lungful of air at the same time. Kova hissed, then drove his hips harder into me. He held me down on his cock for a second. I could feel his balls tighten against my ass. His cock twitched inside me and I undulated on him.

There was this burning sensation where our bodies were joined. It was from that glorious push and pull we craved. I clenched when he drove in deeper because it hurt and he did it on purpose, but I also loved that bite of pain mixed with pleasure only Kova knew how to give. I relished it.

Kova brushed my hair away from my shoulder then leaned in and pressed his lips to my neck. I rose up on my knees, feeling how raw I was and still so tight. I sank back down on him, pushing past the pain I knew would go away soon.

His tongue dragged a wet trail up my neck. My arms wrapped around his shoulders and I delved my fingers into his damp hair, feeling his heated breath tickle my skin. I held him to me, cradling his head as he brought me higher. Kova's hands kneaded my hips. His cock was so hard and rigid, wide inside of me after so long. I thought about where his hands were, how he was kissing me, how his body felt against mine, how I loved him. My pulse hammered through my veins from the erotic note of pleasure streaming between us.

"I have missed you being in my arms," he said, looking at me like he was already lost to us.

I could feel the strain under his skin and how he was holding back. He was trying to be gentle with me.

"So have I. More than you can ever know."

I did miss him, and it was why I was suddenly so emotional. I fucking missed this man.

"Are you okay now?" he asked, and I nodded. "Are you sure? I am going to try and be gentle right now, but I do not know if I can hold out for long."

I smiled. "Don't ever hold back. I want you, and all of you."

Kova slammed his mouth to mine. Each thrust bringing us closer together, our heavy breathing the only thing we could hear. His tongue caressed me the way his cock consumed me, both taking me to new levels of gratification. He deepened the roll of his hips, reaching every depth of me he could, and tightened his arm around my back to hold me still. I reveled in his power, the way he made me feel like I was the only thing in the world that mattered to him. Sex was a way for Kova to express himself, and I opened myself willingly for him to do just that.

The friction between us heightened from the way his mound hit my clit. I trembled around him, feeling the little sparks of desire lick over my body like a firecracker each time. I could feel Kova swelling, getting harder as he was almost there. I felt every rigid inch of his cock inside of me as he increased his speed and lost control. I gasped and shuddered around him as he held me immobile then made me look him in the eyes.

"I need you." He grunted as he pushed into me. "I need you forever. How can we give this up? Do you feel this?" he asked, then slammed into me passionately and I lost my breath. "How are we supposed to walk away from this?"

I couldn't respond. Not without him hearing the tears in my voice. This beautifully anguished man was at my mercy and giving me everything I could ask for. I was a risk, we were the gamble of a lifetime, but he let caution fly because he loved me, he loved us, even though it killed him to do so.

CHAPER 44

Kova leaned into me and pressed my back to the bed.

He hovered above me and I held my breath when I met his defenseless gaze. My lips parted as he slid into me with precision and held himself there like he needed this more than I did. My back arched, my nipples pressing into his bare chest.

"I do not want to be the one to ruin your life," he said, and the hitch in his voice sent a shiver down my spine. His honesty broke my heart. He couldn't ruin my life even if he tried. "I do not want it to get worse for you, but fuck, Ria, how do you go on without your other half?"

"You don't."

He kissed me deeply. His tongue was wicked, his kisses devouring me until I was breathless. My hands roamed over the strength in his back, and I took pleasure in the firm muscles and how beautiful his body was.

Kova hiked my leg over his back to drive deeper inside of me with ease. My thighs quivered and he went even harder. I gasped and clenched my eyes shut as he reached so far back it actually hurt. My breath hitched in my throat and I tensed for a second from the pain in my stomach. Kova took me with purpose. He was on a mission to not only have me, but to take what he could. He was a desperate man.

His hips bucked against mine like he was in dire need to be deep inside of me. My nails marked his back as I took what he gave, and I gave him what he so clearly needed of me. I tried not to think about the fact that this might be our last time together.

Kova muttered in Russian but I couldn't make it out.

For the first time in a while, pleasure rose in my blood. My hips surged against his, and the feeling intensified inside of me. We both moaned at the same time in breathless anticipation at the connection. We felt too good together.

Holding onto Kova's biceps as he took me, I kissed his shoulder, the honey curve of his neck, and every inch of his skin I could reach. My inner thighs were wet with both of our desires. His lips found my neck, and my head rolled back in euphoria. My body tingled. I was on the cusp of craving and need. I found myself chasing what only he could give me.

"I cannot lose you," he whispered so low I almost didn't catch it.

Kova's fingers pressed into me. He was speaking in Russian again, but it was a mumbled mess. His body was like this emotional wave crashing into me, shaking violently as if he was lost to something bigger than us.

He pulled out and dropped his weight onto me, then he laced his fingers with mine and stretched our arms above my head. I felt that telltale feel of an orgasm climbing. My mouth fell open and I moaned in pleasure. This man… What he did to me… My toes curled and I wrapped one leg around his from the pressure between my hips.

"Tell me you love me." Kova demanded, but I flinched when he surged back inside me. He was going so deep. "I need to hear it, Adrianna," he said, his eyes clenched shut like he was the one in pain. "Tell me you love me the way that I love you. It is me and you, *Malysh*." His forehead creased with harsh lines. "Me"—he withdrew and surged in slowly, then let out the sexiest moan yet—"and you."

I attempted to speak, but Kova kissed me ruthlessly, pulling my bottom lip into his mouth and tugging on it. We were two passionate people who were both the best and the worst kind of people for each other. And yet, we couldn't stop. We were addicted to one another.

He squeezed my fingers tighter and brought our joined hands to the sides of my head. My back bowed in response, and I clenched around his fingers, holding on for dear life when I felt the burst of pleasure slice through me.

The orgasm rippled from me and I exploded around his cock. My hips began thrusting into his, desperation glided my clit over his dick, fast and quick. I inhaled. Kova hovered over me, riding me until I saw stars and felt the bursts of energy kiss my skin. He dropped his head to my breast and tugged on my nipple with his teeth. His tongue twirled around it and latched on, pulling on the sensitive tip. A blooming heat spread through my limbs. My pussy clenched around him again, and I was floating down from oblivion.

His cock twitched and his thrusts quickened. Kova ran his nose along the line of my jaw. He grunted in bliss, and I could tell he was getting close to finishing. His back bowed as he fought his release, but I wished he would just let go already. Kova withdrew from me and sat up. His hands reached for my hips and guided me onto his lap. He glanced down to line himself up with my entrance, and froze to a standstill.

I frowned and followed his gaze, curious as to why he stopped. When I looked down, my heart dropped. He was staring at my stomach again.

His lips tugged down.

"I'm okay. Keep going." When he didn't move, I lifted his chin and nipped at his lips. "Kiss me. Kova, please kiss me, I need you."

He finally met my gaze. My stomach tightened at the pure anguish in his eyes. Color seemed to drain from his cheeks.

"I cannot do this to you."

No.

He looked down again. The back of his knuckles grazed gently over my skin. His eyes lifted with an unspoken apology and I felt the final straw snap inside of me.

He exhaled a swoosh of air, then said, "*Prosti—*"

"No," I said firmly even though emotion clogged my throat. My heart dropped into my gut. "Do *not* say that."

"I am sorry," he said, his chest heaving rapidly as if he was struggling to breathe.

I gripped his arms tighter and held onto him for dear life. "Kova, I'm fine. I promise I'm okay. Please don't stop." I pleaded with tears in my eyes now. "Please, Kova. I love you. We need this. I need this. Don't let your mind go there. We're here, we made it." When he didn't budge, my voice shook with panic. "Kova, I'm begging you, don't do this to us."

He looked at me, but it wasn't enough.

Cupping my face, Kova pressed a kiss to my lips before laying me back and rolling over off me. He placed his hand on his stomach and stared up at the ceiling, looking like he was absolutely wrecked.

I broke down and covered my face as I lost myself witnessing his state of emotion.

"I am always going to be a source of pain for you," he said, more to himself than to me. His voice was gut wrenching.

I cried harder, quieter, consumed by the obvious shift in our relationship that struck with force. Pressing my knees together, I drew in a long breath as I watched him sit up at the end of the bed. Kova dropped his head into his hands and didn't move. Each second that passed with his back to me was another layer stripped from my heart. Every breath he took was one he chose to take without me.

I pulled the blanket over to cover my chest and then wiped my eyes with it. I sniffled when he stood up and pulled his shorts on.

"I love you, but this is too big for us to overcome this time, Ria." He faced me with tears in his eyes. "It is only going to get worse. Oklahoma is a good idea. Knowing you are close to me, I would have to find you."

I couldn't take another minute of this and cried out. My heart was about to pump out of my chest and explode. All I could do was try to catch the shattered pieces with slippery fingers.

"I do not want this to end, but I do not see another way for us any time soon. I cannot—*will not*—keep putting you through all this hurt. I refuse to continue doing that to you. Being in your life while you are going through treatment would only bring more agony."

"You think leaving will make me happy? Don't you understand that the thought of life without you breaks my heart? I don't think I can survive without you, Kova."

He studied me for a moment before replying. "You are much stronger than you think." He was shutting down, withdrawing from the conversation, but his next words obliterated my heart. "I think you should go back to your room."

Kova stepped into a pair of shoes after putting his shirt on, then reached for his cell phone and room key on the dresser. He slipped them into his pocket. I curled onto my side, the chilly comforter cooling down my cheek. Pulling my knees up, I hugged myself as I watched him walk toward the door.

This didn't feel real. This wasn't us. Not after how far we'd come.

Kova was walking away from me. He was taking everything that I willingly gave to him with him. I allowed it, though, because I loved him. I loved him with every bone in my body, and there was not a single thing I could change about that, or would change.

The further he got from me, the more I held my breath. Stopping with his hand on the knob, Kova tilted his head down then to the side. He lingered, then looked back at me.

My lungs seized from lack of air. My stomach was a mess. I wanted to scream at him or call him a coward again, anything to make him stay and fight through this hardship with me.

"Please don't go," I whispered.

He turned back to the door and opened it. A gasp of air expelled from my lungs.

I closed my eyes shut and broke down in his room after hearing the soft click of the door shutting. I knew he wanted us, that wasn't a question. He just didn't want us bad enough to walk through the fire to get there.

CHAPER 45

Somehow I had made it back to my hotel room.

I had no memory of how, or changing out of my clothes, or retrieving my notebook. Everything had blurred into one.

I'd been writing for over an hour, sobbing my eyes out. My tears smearing some of the ink, but I couldn't stop my hand flying across the paper.

I wrote down every emotion I felt from the moment I walked into his hotel room to now and described what it did to me. Writing was cathartic. I understood why Kova liked to write. It was private, intimate, real. No one judged me, no one gave terrible advice. It was just me and a blank page, allowing me to express whatever the hell was going through my head. I realized through the painful words how much I held inside of me.

Pages and pages later, I was still shedding tears trying to understand how it came to this. It was nearly two in the morning when the door opened and Avery walked in. Our eyes met. I was still a sobbing mess and the sight of her devastated me further.

Avery rushed over to me just as I covered my eyes. My head tipped back. I released a tight breath, suffering all over again.

Wrapping her arms around me, she held me as I cried on her shoulder. She comforted me without saying a word. Avery had been with me through everything from the beginning. She had a notion of what I felt right now. There was no need for me to say anything, she knew.

"Oh, Aid," she said, her voice full of sadness. "Don't cry. Trust me, crying will get you nowhere. You'll realize it wasn't worth it."

I wanted to believe her, but I couldn't, not with this agony pulsing inside of my ribs. It told a different story. I was completely blinded by heartbreak and couldn't see anything beyond my pain.

After a few moments, I pulled back. Avery reached for the box of tissues on the nightstand and plucked a few then handed them to me.

I kept my head down and blotted my eyes. "I just don't understand," I said. "It doesn't make sense. He wanted me to wait. Why would he want to wait? It's not like he said give me six months to clean this up, or one year, he just said we needed time. Time is an infinite number, and a self-imposed deadline can be pushed back. Kova is a perfectionist. By the time he comes to me, I'll already be dead and buried."

I could feel Avery studying me. I looked up at her through my lashes. Her lips were flat and twisting with sorrow as she looked into my eyes.

"I tried calling you. How long have you been here? I would've come back in a second if I knew you were like this."

I blinked. I didn't recall hearing my cell phone ring. "I don't know where my phone is," I said. God, I sounded so empty.

Avery frowned. "Are you sure you brought it back with you?" I nodded. Avery got up and looked around. She came out of the bathroom holding it and looking at the screen. Her thumb moved up and down as she read.

"You have a bunch of messages."

I didn't care.

"Hayden and Holly both sent you congratulations." Her voice trailed off. "Wow. Homeboy gave a play-by-play of you as he watched the event on TV." Her eyes widened. "Okay, now Hayden's just annoying me with all these messages. Holly said congrats and that she loves you. She said you looked so happy on the podium. You even have a message from Reagan."

I sniffled, trying to be grateful I had friends like them, but I felt nothing.

"Congrats, Red, I knew you had it in you all along. Too bad you didn't medal in beam. Nice job, though." Avery observed me with a blank stare. "That was from Reagan."

A partial laugh escaped me. "I figured that."

"Do you want me to message them back for you? I can pretend I'm you."

I nodded. "Thanks." Even though I was upset, that didn't mean it was okay to ignore their messages. I felt bad, but I didn't have the mental fortitude to handle responding to them right now.

Avery put her knee up and sat on the edge of the bed, typing away. After a few minutes, she put the phone down and looked at me. The air was chilly, yet I didn't move to pull the blanket over me. I felt like in some way I deserved to suffer in the cold when I despised it wholeheartedly.

"I'd give up my medals not to feel this heartbreak anymore." I blinked, staring straight into her eyes. "I'd even give up going to the Olympics."

Her shoulders slumped forward. Avery frowned, then said, "Hey. You worked hard for those. Don't say that."

"What happened with my dumb brother?"

"Don't change the subject."

I eyed her resolute expression and knew I wouldn't be able to turn the topic. After a few quiet seconds, I said, "Then how do I stop feeling like this? I feel so empty inside, yet I feel everything all at once. This is worse than when I found out about the marriage."

That took me so long to accept and get over. I couldn't imagine how long this would take.

Her brows furrowed like she was bothered. "I don't like that you'd give up something like your medals in exchange for him after how hard you worked for them. You almost sacrificed your life for them." She took a deep breath and exhaled. "You're my best friend, and I feel it's my duty to tell you that if Kova makes you feel this way, then I think you need to reevaluate what *you* want. He clearly has other plans right now, not that I agree or disagree with them, but you need to think about you where he's concerned. What do you want? You know what he wants," she said, hitching her thumb over her shoulder. "The *you* that I know, would never think like that. Those medals are your whole life, and you'd give them up because of a guy?" Avery gave me a droll stare. "No. Nope. Not happening. I know right now is hard for you. I'll be here every step of the way to help you, but you need to change that attitude right now."

"What do I do, then? I feel so hopeless inside, Ave."

I sniffled again and leveled a stare at her. My stomach was hollow from anguish. It'd been hours since I had dinner. The thought of eating now or anytime in the near future made me sick. Hello, emotional stress.

"What did you do?" I asked. "I'm sitting on the edge here wanting to erase every memory so I never have the chance to feel like this again."

Sympathy filled her crystal blue eyes. "That's what happens with your first love."

My jaw trembled. Kova was my first everything. He was a devastating love I'd never regret.

"It took me a while to realize the only way to stop that emotion gnawing away at you is to live with it. Receive it, accept it, and move on. I'm not saying tomorrow, I'm not saying to never think about it, I'm just saying you don't want to waste your days away pining after something you can't have. You need to live your life and find something new that makes you happy. We fell in love, we had our hearts broken, and we'll move on like so many others have."

"Why does anyone want to fall in love if it ends like this?"

Avery smiled sadly at me. "Sometimes the most heartbreaking memories are the most heartfelt ones we can never let go of. You had a good time, and you'll remember that feeling it gave you. You'll smile and wonder where that person ended up and how their life is going. Nostalgia will hit and you'll smile. There's something to be learned. It's why you hold onto them."

I glanced down at my hands, musing over her words. I was twisting one end of the tissue into a sharp pointed edge. There was something somber about that. People wanted to remember the good times that were filled with kisses under the rain. It was when one felt the most alive.

"In some strange way that helps," I said. I glanced away, feeling the sorrow settle over me once again.

"I can't stand to see you like this. Yeah, I like Kova, and I think you guys would be good together. But seeing you like this kills me. It makes me despise him. Honestly, I want to kill him. He isn't worth this, Adrianna. Not to see you like this, ready to give up your Olympic medals."

I fought back my tears. I heard Avery loud and clear. I thought about what Kova had said to me and how I felt his tone in my heart. He mimicked my feelings exactly, yet he'd still walked away. I didn't understand.

"Why didn't he fight for me?" I asked, my voice small. "He didn't even try. I wanted him to so badly. All he kept saying was that we needed time. Time is the same thing as walking away. Seriously, Ave, do you really think my dad is going to be cool with Kova even in a year? Obviously not."

Her shoulders fell. "Would it have changed your mind if he had?"

I bit down on the inside of my lip. Avery sensed my indecision and leaned in to hug me. "You know, sometimes I feel like I'm stuck in the twilight zone when it comes to you and Kova. I find myself cheering for him when I know I shouldn't. Call me crazy, but I don't think he didn't *not* want to fight for you. You guys have been through a lot, and I've seen the way he looks at you when no one is around. That's not someone who gives up easily. I think Kova is really trying to do what he thinks is right for the both of you. I think he would've fought for you only if he knew he could win. He can't win right now. Why drag out the bad time? It could only make things worse."

I pursed my lips together, fighting the emotion and shifted my eyes to Avery. Her crystal blue eyes weighed into mine. That sounded like Kova. I wanted to believe her, but it was hard to when I was so passionate about us. It went back to that whole "if there's a will, there's a way" thing. I felt like he had no will, and I think that's what crushed me.

"Kova doesn't know that for sure. That's a huge risk to take."

"As much as it hurts to hear this, I think he did the right thing, even though it's killing the both of you. You're strong, he knows that. He knows you'll get over this." She paused and pressed her teeth into her lower lip. I could sense her hesitation when she sat up straighter. "The next couple of weeks are going to suck monkey balls, not just because of Kova, but because of your health too. Your life is about to take a huge turn. I feel like you should take that time to go through the motions and think about yourself and what you want. Reflect, heal, and all that shit. That way you give yourself time to figure out how to navigate your new life. Find who you are." She stared me in the eyes. "That's when you'll see just how fucking amazing and worthy you are."

Tears filled my eyes. I seriously loved my best friend. My jaw wobbled as I let out what I'd secretly been holding in. "I think... I think I'm really just scared, Ave. I'm scared I'm not going to get to live a full life. If I wasn't sick, then I feel like I'd be more understanding, but that's not the case. I want to live right *now*. Tell me I'm insane— we both know I am—but I think I need to live to get me through what I'm about to do, and that's with the people I love most." Tears streamed from my eyes and my voice squeaked. "I'm not asking for a lot. What if he comes around when it's too late? All that wasted time."

Her eyes hardened and she pointed a finger at me. "Don't even utter shit like that. I'm serious, Adrianna. You know I'm always going to be Team Ria, even if you're wrong, but you have to give Kova a chance to come back from this too." She was a little upset with me. "You know I'm right. Just say it," she said, grinning now. "Ave, you're always right."

A smile twitched my lips. I regarded Avery in a different light tonight. We'd always had this funny, easygoing friendship. The last couple of years we'd grown a lot, and now I was seeing her in a way I never had before. My head tilted to the side. Avery had this fiery ball of courage that she hid in her back pocket. There was a tenacity about her, and she inspired me with it.

"Did you let go completely?"

Avery looked away for a long moment, then back at me. I knew her answer before she even said it.

I smiled sadly at her.

"He's got one chance left. When he's ready, he's ready."

"Are you just going to wait?"

"Psh," she said. Her smile was filled with amusement. "That's a negative. I'm too young to wait around for love. If it happens, it happens."

I smiled back, but I didn't believe her. Avery was putting on a strong front, but I'd give it to her. She was trying to lift me up, and it was working.

When Avery spoke again, her voice was low, and there was a slight tremble to it. She couldn't look at me. "I feel like when people are looking for love, it never happens. I also feel like when they're waiting for it to knock on their door, it'll never happen either. I don't want to be like that, so I'm just gonna live and see where I end up and have fun. I want to spread my wings and fly against the wind. Life is too short to eat fat-free ice cream and sugar-free cake."

She was seriously winning me over.

"Did you think it would come to this?" I asked her. Tears blurred my eyes once again. I wanted to stop crying.

"No," she said quietly, and grimaced. "Honestly, I never saw this coming. I feel bad about it." Leaning into me, Avery gave me a big bear hug, then looked at me and said, "I think you need to ask yourself who you are without Kova."

CHAPER 46

There was an enormous feeling of loss that no one had prepared me for after the Olympics.

It had hit at the end of the first week.

An emptiness settled in my chest and built a fortress around the outer layer. I didn't like the barren feeling that spread like black smoke through my heart chambers, and I used sleep as a way to avoid it.

This time three weeks ago, I was standing on the podium accepting the team gold medal. Now I was getting out of the shower hardly able to stand because of inflammation in my body. My ankles were sore, my toes looked like sausage links, and my cheeks were often warm to the touch. I was *so* out of breath, and the exhaustion wrecked me. I couldn't catch a good deep breath no matter how hard I tried. It was like my body had said that's enough and took over and released everything I'd been fighting to keep at bay for the last few years and unloaded it.

I'd achieved my dream…but no one talked about the after.

The first week home was spent sleeping, and then more sleeping. Dad was staying at Sophia's, but they both came over throughout the week to check on me and have dinner at night. We hadn't gone back to Amelia Island because I had a doctor appointment set up two days later and Dad felt it wasn't necessary to drive to Cape Coral right after. I was glad. I didn't want to be stuck there. Surprisingly, I felt more at home here than I did there. I'd missed my appointment, and the ones scheduled after that. Dad had reassured Dr. Kozol that I was okay and that I would be in within the next few weeks.

The second week I still hadn't cleaned anything or even unpacked my bags. Sophia actually came over and did that for me. She offered to hang up my medals, but I told her it wasn't necessary since I needed to start packing up my condo anyway and wanted to bring them with me. I slept a little less but not by much.

Today marked the end of the third lonely week home, and the deadline of when I was supposed to announce to the gymnastics world that I was committing to the University of Oklahoma.

The school was aware of my health and was still willing to take a chance on me after I'd told them I couldn't take a full load the first year. They even granted me a late start due to competing in the Olympics, so long as I could catch up on my assignments. I should be elated, but I couldn't find a smidgen of joy. There were no rays of sunshine in my veins. No excitement when I got a swag package of clothes in the mail from the school. Not after how depressed and alone I'd been lately.

I'd gone through spurts of depression in the past, but I'd never felt depression quite like this since I've been back. It made me think I'd never truly experienced what depression was until now.

My ache for Kova increased with each moon. It was worse in the middle of the night. I missed him so much and longed to hear his voice. Tears fell at any given moment. I was alone, missing my other half.

There was no more Kova and Ria.

I wondered if his heart hurt the way mine did.

If I was on his mind the way he was on mine.

If he felt my loss the way I felt his.

I wondered if he'd picked up his phone to call me like I had him numerous times only to not go through with it.

Kova had been on my mind more so this week than the last two, and I think that was because my time here was coming to an end. He had known about my commitment to Oklahoma before anyone else had, but he didn't know that I hadn't left yet.

It was strange. I hadn't felt the need to tell him I was actually here. We'd both made a decision that night in his hotel room. Being home and looking back on that night, writing and reading my journal, it killed me to accept that our minds were set and we weren't budging.

I don't think it would've mattered if he knew I was here or not. Kova wanted time, but I didn't have it to give.

Seven days from now I would be in another state living on my own again. I was both anxious and nervous about that and thought Dad would initially be against me moving so soon, but he was actually relieved. He figured the further away I was from Kova, the better.

I turned off all the lights then locked up my condo, finally leaving for my very much delayed appointment. I made my way downstairs and stepped outside. Dad was already waiting for me with Sophia. Pulling my jacket tighter, I opened the door of his sleek Mercedes and slid into the back seat.

Within the hour of arriving, I had vials of blood drawn, ultrasounds completed on various parts of my torso, and numbers were input into the computer to track my overall health. We were sitting across from Dr. Kozol ready to go over my new treatment plan. It was like any other appointment I'd had with him in the past, only it wasn't. Dad and Sophia were here, and something about that made this appointment feel so much more final.

"Congratulations, Adrianna," Dr. Kozol said, taking me away from my thoughts. "The whole office was cheering you on. We're so proud of you, even though you defied doctor's orders."

I chuckled and dipped my chin to hide my blush. I was honest and told him I'd taken lots of Motrin while I was away. He continued, "We had every television on in here, holding our breaths. You had quite a few people in tears watching you accept the gold medal. I must say, for someone who is as ill as you, you're a true fighter and a sight to watch. You made it look so easy, like nothing held you down. I'd never guess you're as sick as you are."

"I've been sleeping since we got back. Believe me, it came with a price, but it was so worth it."

He angled his head, giving me a knowing look. "I bet. Your exam tells me you had a pretty bad flare up. Luckily it happened after you got back."

Dr. Kozol asked me a handful of questions, then went on to address that he'd found a doctor in Oklahoma he felt was capable of handling my case. He told us how he'd spoken in depth with him multiple times and what his plan of attack would be. It was similar to my current one before I'd decided to move. Though he was confident, he also suggested we get a few opinions of our own, just to be safe.

I listened to Dr. Kozol tell Dad step by step of what to expect within the next few months. I'd read about this phase online so many times I was having nightmares about it and it hadn't even started yet.

"Expect dialysis three to four times a week, lasting anywhere from three to five hours each time." Dr. Kozol stacked some papers together. He pulled a pen from his coat pocket then began writing something down. He looked up at me when he was finished. "During that time or after you leave, your body will cramp from the fluid being pulled from your body during dialysis. That's the stuff your kidneys couldn't process any longer. Most patients complain of leg cramps, though some say their entire body aches. Everyone is different and only time will tell." He tipped his head and bore his eyes into mine. I felt like I was about to get yelled at from my dad. "Make sure you take it easy and don't overdo it. If you're postponing the transplant surgery, then you need to treat your body like a temple during this time."

"Okay." It was all I could say. I swallowed, though my throat was dry. That was a lot of time to sit and do nothing while my body was cramping up.

"Take the nausea pills I prescribed you since we know they already work. You'll have nausea most of the time, and drugs will be given to hopefully prevent flare ups. Your blood pressure will likely dip. That'll be monitored so you don't pass out from not being able to catch your breath from something as simple as carrying groceries to doing a light jog."

That worried me. I already had a hard time catching my breath, which he was aware of. Now I was going to need to be extra cautious that I didn't pass out and hit my head and die in my new apartment alone.

"She'll be taking a year off from sports to work on her health," Dad said to Dr. Kozol, then he turned to me. I told him I would take a year off. That didn't mean I actually would. I was estimating six months, at most. "Your priority is your health. Nothing else. There should be no reason for you to exert yourself. All you have to do is get up and go to treatment. That's it."

I nodded vehemently. Dad was right, and I had to remind myself that I had a very strong and solid support system. He was making it possible so that I wouldn't have to worry about anything except my health and attending the few classes I was taking.

Dr. Kozol continued. "Some people will either gain or lose a substantial amount of weight, so watch for that. Some patients claim they have newfound energy after dialysis starts. No two patients are the same. Log your symptoms in a journal so you can track how you're feeling." He looked at Dad. "If you want to have a driver on the back burner for her, it wouldn't be a bad idea. Occasionally there've been patients who are too physically tired to drive after.

Of course, Dad loved the idea and said he'd set something up just in case.

I thanked Dr. Kozol and apologized to him for all the times I had been difficult. He chuckled and said he liked the medical challenge I brought to his desk. He also added that I probably aged him ten years while I was under his care.

My future wasn't going to be pretty for a bit, but one day it would be again. I was confident that it would be, even if the only thing I had to look forward to wouldn't start for about eight months or so. I wouldn't give up sports completely, it just wasn't possible. However, I would be smart about my decisions. Light jogging maybe, and some light weights. No actual gym, though. No Motrin, nothing that could hold me back. I only wanted to go forward from here. Moving to a new town alone would be a challenge too, but I was a little excited about that. I wasn't sure how I was going to handle everything on my own in the beginning, yet I knew exactly what I had to do in order to live.

I was going to live. I had to for me. I hadn't achieved my dream of Olympic glory only to give up now.

CHAPER 47

L ike every other night of my last week here, Dad and Sophia
brought over takeout.

They made sure it was food I could eat on my special diet.
Dinner was really the only meal I ate since I slept most of the
day, so I made sure to eat everything they brought over.

"Did I bring enough boxes?" Dad asked, taking the last bite of
his steak.

After we ended with Dr. Kozol, my dad picked up boxes then
dropped me off at my condo. He was flying out in a few days to
negotiate a new business deal, and Sophia was going with him.

They both planned to meet me in Oklahoma two days after I
arrived to help me get settled and go to my first doctor's appointment.
Dad had insisted that Sophia stay and be there for me after he left
until I got used to the side effects of the treatment, but I wanted
to do it on my own. It was something I needed to do on my own.
Maybe she could stay a few days, but that was it.

"Yes, I have plenty. I should be able to have this place packed
up in a couple days with a day or two to run last-minute errands."

"How have you been feeling…otherwise?" Dad asked, dragging
out his question uncomfortably. I watched his eyes do a quick sweep
across my body and I knew what he meant by that. "Every time I
see you, you look like you're hardly sleeping."

Though the part of my life that haunted his eyes was in the past,
it was still very much in the present for me and lingered like a bad
odor in the air. It was going to take time to dissolve.

"I'm honestly doing well, just catching up on all the sleep I missed
out on. Dealing with the aftermath, of course, but otherwise, I'm
really okay."

Dad regarded me. I held his stare, willing him to believe me.

"I can help you pack, if you'd like," Sophia offered. I looked at her.

"I'd like that. Thanks," I said, giving her a smile.

I didn't want to pack, and I sure didn't want to do it alone where I was lost to my thoughts. I'd either get nothing done from being depressed and not having the energy to do it, or I'd cry over the shitty hand I'd been dealt.

Dad's voice caught my attention. "When you get off the plane, look for the chauffeur to take you to your apartment. Your SUV won't arrive until the following week. Your apartment is right outside of campus and within walking distance of everything you could need, at least that's what student services told me when I spoke with them. The driver will have your house key, and the place will already be stocked with food."

I smiled, grateful that Dad was still willing to support me after everything. He could've kicked me out. I was eighteen, after all. Standing, I took the plates to the sink. They didn't usually stay after the sun set.

"Let me get this," Dad said quickly, and stood with me. He waved my hands away. "Go relax with Sophia on the balcony, or something. It's cooler out now."

"Dad, it's still like eighty degrees outside."

"It's better than ninety-three."

Dad carried the empty containers and plates to the kitchen. I was kind of happy that he suggested I hang out with her. Sophia came into my life at the worst time, and I've been wanting to thank her for everything she's done to help me.

We both took a place on the love seat on my patio. Sophia angled her body toward me and brought her knee up.

"How do you feel about the move? College? Are you getting excited?"

I nodded and shrugged at the same time. "A little bit. I think I'm starting to be okay with it…with things."

Sophia's eyes softened with compassion. She knew I wasn't just talking about going to college.

"Whatever is meant to be will always find its way," she said like she was so sure. "You'll see. I know what you're about to do seems scary, but I think you're going to discover just how strong you are."

My voice was small. "I don't feel strong. I feel really weak." I swallowed and opened up a little. "I'm scared."

Her eyes were empathetic. "Francesca used to tell me the same thing. She had a fighter's heart and I envied that about her. I didn't have the same ambition as her, obviously."

I felt bad that she viewed herself as someone weak. To give up a child because she knew she couldn't give it a proper home is not something a weak person did; however, I understood her sorrow completely.

Sophia continued, her brows smoothing out as she thought about Francesca. "She'd say she didn't know who she was or what her purpose was in life anymore. She was physically weak all the time, said her head was foggy a lot. She forgot things so easily, or couldn't focus on one task long enough to finish it. She was much sicker than you, though. Much sicker." She paused, staring off like she was stuck in the past. "It's going to take time adjusting to this new lifestyle of yours." Sophia rolled her lip over her bottom teeth and worried it a bit before returning her gaze to me. "I didn't mean to ramble and tell you a morbid story about my sister."

I shook my head, letting her know I appreciated it. "It's totally okay. I'd rather know what to expect, even if it is kind of sucky." She gave me a small smile, and I reassured her once more. "Tell me whatever you think is helpful. I know Francesca and I have different illnesses, but they're still similar in many ways. At least I won't be going crazy over the side effects."

Sophia nodded her head, her tender doe eyes expressing her feelings. I studied her. She appeared apprehensive about something. I decided I would start a conversation and open up a little more to her. She was trying…and so was I.

I licked my lips nervously. I wanted to tell her how I was really feeling inside. I wanted to make sure what I was feeling was normal and that I was supposed to go through these motions. A part of me hoped she had sound advice to give.

"I've had a lot time to think since I got home. I should've gotten up and gone about my usual day. I should've started packing and preparing to move. I should've had deep tissue massages post training so I didn't lock up. Instead, I let myself go. I couldn't do anything because all I did was think about *him*." I eyed her to see how she'd respond to mentioning Kova in the way I did. "Every day, all day, my thoughts have revolved around him. I wasn't even awake long and I still managed to think about him the majority of the time. I even dreamed about him. The strange thing is, he would be so angry to know I wasn't taking care of myself, that I'd gotten weaker. He wouldn't have wanted me to feel the way I have been." I sighed heavily. Saying these things aloud was vastly different than thinking about them. It made me reflect on myself. "I normally never succumb to these feelings, but I've been having a really hard time lately. All I do is lie in bed." I blinked rapidly, feeling the tears climb my eyes. "As the days passed into weeks, I realized that the reason I was sick was because of me."

Sophia had tears brimming on her eyelids. She didn't respond just yet, and I had more to get off my chest.

"I wasn't trying to make myself sick, I just missed him so damn much that I couldn't do anything else. How did you do it? How did you get over my dad if you loved him so much? How did you not think about giving me up? How do you wake up and not allow yourself to think about it?"

Sophia angled her head to the side. Her eyes were guarded. "I never got over him, and I never stopped thinking about you. Why do you think I'm here?" She smiled softly. Now I felt bad for asking her that. "You don't have to stop thinking about him, but you can't wallow in your feelings the way you have been either. That's not healthy. You have to pick yourself up and heal, and the only way you can do that is by learning to love yourself first. After that, you take each day one at a time."

I shook my head, not understanding how it could be so easy. "One second I know I need to leave and the next I want to stay. I know what I'm supposed to do, but I'm scared of the unknown. How did you leave the person you loved?"

She shrugged one shoulder and shook her head slowly. She wasn't even sure herself. "It's easy to fall in love when it's not the right time. Walking away is another story."

I let out a breathy laugh and glanced down. "It sucks when it's the first time."

Fuck. I hated heartbreak.

"Your time may never come, or maybe the stars will align when you least expect it and it'll happen. It took me too long to see that I had to do what was right for me to be happy and healthy in order to attempt a life with him or you again one day. I think you already know what you have to do, Adrianna."

I glanced away, my jaw was trembling. "Then why do I feel like this? I'm so torn. If I think it's right, then I'm wrong. My gut is just making me sick."

She blinked and her eyes lifted to mine. "You feel doubt."

"Yes," I said immediately. I was totally doubtful, and it was wrecking me inside.

Sophia shook her head. "You're not doubtful, you're emotional. You shouldn't doubt your decision, but you should be emotional over it."

Tears fell from the corners of my eyes. She was right. I twisted my fingers together.

"That feeling you have deep inside of you? Go with it. Trust it. It's okay to be emotional, even upset."

"I feel like I have two gut feelings." I laughed but I was being serious.

"You have to work on trusting yourself more."

I looked at Sophia. It was still strange to me that this woman was my biological mother and I had only just met her. She helped me at my lowest and was willing to stay by my side despite the baggage I carried. She didn't judge me or humiliate me, or make me feel bad for my choices. Sure, she probably had tons of thoughts running through her head, but she kept them to herself. She just listened and gave advice when I needed it most.

I couldn't recall one time Joy had ever been there for me in the way Sophia had. Before recently, I couldn't recall my dad being there much either. I realized during my time with Sophia that I longed for guidance, to have a parent tell me what I was going through was normal and that I was going to be okay. My heart was pounding in my throat. I wanted a real relationship with Sophia, and I hoped she wanted that too.

"There are no words that describe the gratitude I have for you." Taking a deep breath, I released it, and said, "I want to have a relationship as mother and daughter…if you want one with me. Even though you weren't part of my life until recently, you still didn't have to help me and be there for me like you have been." Pausing, I licked my lips nervously. "Thank you for coming into my life when I needed a mom the most."

"If it were up to me, I would've been in your life since day one. With that being said, I'm not going to focus on what I lost out on. I'm going to focus on the present and what I have in this moment and every day after. If you want me in your life, I'll be there. I want it more than anything, but I want it at your pace and when you're ready. I'll always be waiting. Do whatever you need to do for yourself. Don't worry about me, your father, your coach, your friends. You have to live the life *you* want. It's okay to not have all the answers right now. As long as you're trying to be the best version of yourself, that's all that matters."

My eyes dropped to my hands. Sophia's words moved me deeply.

"You have no idea how much I really needed to hear that." I smiled bigger and then sniffled. I looked up at Sophia.

Leaning closer toward me, Sophia said, "We lost out on a lot of time, and while I try not to think about it, it still breaks my heart. I don't want to waste another second with you."

I hoped she understood just how much I wanted a mom and one who wanted to be there. I'd take anything at this point. It would be so nice to be able to call her up and just talk. Avery had that with her mom, and I longed for that myself. Now that she was in my life, I wanted to know everything about her. Everything I missed out on.

"Tell me about your sister, about your parents. I want to know everything."

Sophia laughed. It was a full-on belly laugh that caused a wide smile to spread across my face. This was good, really good.

I sighed. My heart felt like it was in a good place for the first time in a while. I definitely couldn't open up about Kova to Sophia the way I did to Avery, but that's why Avery was my best friend, and Sophia was my mom.

"All in good time," Sophia said, growing serious. "Have you finished reading the book?"

Before I could answer, Dad opened the sliding glass door and stepped outside to join us.

"Not yet. I've been saving it to read on the plane." I paused, thinking about the hours I was going to spend at the dialysis center. "If you can recommend any more books, let me know. I'm going to need them."

Her eyes lit up. "I have plenty to recommend, and even a few at home I can give you. Reading is good for the soul and helps you escape reality for a little while." Sophia looked up at Dad. "Ready to go?"

Dad nodded. "I've got a late-night conference with Asia I can't miss. I need to head back to your place soon and use your office."

Sophia stood up and straightened out her shirt. She looked at me and said, "I'll be here around nine tomorrow morning to help pack."

Until then, I was going to lose myself in my journal and just write out what I was feeling.

CHAPER 48

Can I see you?

My heart lodged in my throat.

I was pretty sure I stopped breathing for a whole minute. Rolling over onto my stomach, I crumpled up my blanket under me and held my phone between both hands. I reread the single text message over and over until my eyes were blurry. It was still early in the morning and I didn't sleep well last night with everything on my mind. I could be hallucinating.

This was the message I'd been waiting on for weeks.

Now I wasn't sure how to react to it.

On one hand, I was excited to see that Kova was finally thinking about me. On the other, I was apprehensive to see him after the way we had left things.

Without wanting to look too eager, I put my cell phone down. If I responded immediately, then he'd know I was waiting. I didn't want to give that to him. We'd gone a month with no contact, I could hold out a little longer.

Not reaching for my phone was more of a struggle than I thought it would be. I turned over and got out of bed. My bones cracked and my lower back ached a little when I stood. I groaned inwardly and stretched my arms above my head. I took a long shower, then poured out the first nine pills of the day, and his message was still there.

I guess I wasn't hallucinating after all.

I stared at the screen trying to think of the right response. Butterflies took flight in my stomach knowing I'd be seeing him again.

Biting my lip, I finally texted back.

ME

How about tonight? My place?

He responded immediately. He'd been waiting. I smiled, taking satisfaction in that.

COACH

I will be there at 8.

COACH

See you later.

I checked my watch.

It was 7:57 and I was edgy with impatience. Kova would be here any minute.

I shook my fingers out. My nerves climbed as the clock ticked by. I'd dropped Dad and Sophia off at the airport earlier. We'd said our goodbyes, and I drove back to my condo, sweating to death from anxiety that I was going to see Kova. Would he still be *that* Kova? Would I still be Ria to him?

I had kept busy with the last of the boxes I had left to pack, then took a quick shower since I'd gotten so clammy after the drive home from the airport. I'd dressed and even added a touch of mascara to my lashes and a plum tint to my cheeks. The blush helped offset the dusting of freckles on the bridge of my nose.

I walked into the kitchen and grabbed a bottle of water. I'd been so parched lately, but that was due to not getting the daily ounces of water I needed since I was sleeping twenty hours a day. I'd have to start counting my meals and fluids again just to make sure I was getting the proper nutrients. Uncapping the bottle, my hand shook a little as I brought it to my mouth. I took a long pull then recapped it. Kova was going—

Knock. Knock. Knock.

My eyes widened as heat instantly prickled down my spine.

My heart froze.

I stared at the door for another long second then walked around the kitchen counter, nervous to answer it. While I had no idea which version of Kova stood on the other side of the door, I was excited and couldn't rub the smile off my face. I brushed a lock of hair behind my ear before I reached for the knob. Inhaling a deep pull of air, my heart was pulsating in my throat as the door opened and our eyes met.

He was still as handsome as ever.

I wasn't going to hide how I felt toward him. Not at this point. He could see through my gentle gaze and soft smile. I was looking at him with a love no one would ever stand a chance against. Kova was my everything and he'd never doubt it.

Sophia was right. I was emotional over my decision.

It'd been almost one full month since I'd last seen Kova. I didn't love him any less. He was similar to the ruined man who had left me behind in his hotel room, only he wasn't. Something was different about him. He looked ragged and worn down, but there was a peaceful aura around him in the midst of my chaos that soothed me. I was drawn to it.

All these feelings hit me at once as my eyes shifted back and forth between his.

The stupid man that I loved so much was looking at me with a stare I hadn't felt the weight of in so long. The plea in his gaze made me want to do anything for him again. He blinked and the struggle was there. He was dying inside without me, like I was without him. Kova was trying so hard to do what was right. The problem with that was he forgot about himself and what he wanted too.

I pushed the door back and welcomed him in.

I had to break the craving I got when Kova looked at me. I was all the things he needed from someone to give him, and I liked that I was. It made me feel good about myself because I grew stronger when he did. He was an addiction that I would always chase first.

"Adrianna," he said, and I felt my cheeks blush.

I locked the door, then slowly dragged my eyes up to his. "Hey."

"It is good to see you. I have missed you." Kova raked his eyes down the length of my body. "You look good."

"Likewise."

My ears were warm. I slipped my hands into the back pockets of my shorts and rocked on my toes and heels. I was nervous to take the step toward him even though that stupid organ in my chest was begging me to.

"How did you know I was here? When we were in Greece, I told you I was leaving."

Kova's response was a subtle curve to one corner of his lips. I didn't bother pushing the question. He had known I was here, he just took his precious time.

"What did you want to talk about?" I asked, changing the subject. I gestured toward the chairs at the breakfast counter. He raised a brow. I had boxes sporadically placed around my condo. "I actually have something I wanted to talk to you about too."

Kova took a seat and angled his body toward me. I caught a drift of his cologne and faltered in my step. Desire prickled down my arms and I blinked. I exhaled a breath. My palms were clammy, I was restless for his touch. My chest rose and fell so quickly as a flood of emotions came roaring back into my heart. This was going to be much harder than I'd thought.

Just as I was about to sit next to him, Kova reached out and hooked a finger around my belt loop. With a tug, he spread his legs and pulled me to him. I inhaled a gasp. My hands came flying up and pushed against his chest when our eyes met. The connection was automatic for me. My fingers curled around his shirt and I felt the pull. I leaned into him, needing to close the distance.

Hugging me with his legs, I was just inches from Kova and eye level with him. My lips parted as I peered through my lashes at him. His stubble was much thicker than he usually wore it, and there were faint purple circles under his eyes that I hadn't noticed at first. The tips of my fingers brushed across his collarbone. I did it again, and Kova's palms warmed against my back, pulling me toward him. His touch scorched my skin, flames of desire coaxing me to let nature take its course. The back of my hand grazed his facial hair.

Our lips were seconds away from meeting. "*Malysh*," he whispered.

I pulled back and frowned at him. The curtain lifted, the smoke cleared, and I blinked. That was why I was in this predicament in the first place. He called my name and I came running. Over the past month, I was forced to reassess a lot of the choices I'd made. I felt different inside now. My views had shifted.

I took a small step back, but not so that we had to stop touching. "What did you want to talk to me about?"

His head dipped to the side and he peered up at me with alluring eyes. "I spoke with an attorney on what the best course of action was for my marriage. I filed for divorce."

I blinked. Wow. *Not* what I'd expected.

"I don't understand," I said, my throat a little dry.

"I told Katja I no longer cared what she had on me. I was running worried and she thrived off that. When I showed her I did not care about her threats and actually filed, it was not a thrill to her anymore. I have a long way to go, but the divorce process has been started."

His brows knitted toward each other when I didn't respond. Kova had already told me he was filing for divorce because Katja had gotten pregnant by another man. It was his way out for all the blackmail she had on him. It wasn't for *us*, though. "I told you before Frank found us that I was going to," Kova added when I'd remained silent.

Kova filing for divorce should've relieved me, even made me feel giddy, not this sense of indifference unfurling inside of me. I was supposed to leave, and he just threw a curveball at me.

I studied Kova. Was I supposed to say congratulations?

"When did you file?"

"Two weeks ago."

He'd filed two weeks ago and it took him that long to reach out to me. Something about that crushed me.

"Where is Katja? Where does she live now?"

He shook his head, confusion filling his eyes. "At my house," he said, then he sobered up. My hands fell from his chest and I tried to take another step back, but Kova caged me in. My pulse sped up.

"And that's where she's been with you since you got back, right?"

The happiness Kova had walked in with was slowly dissolving into thin air. His shoulders hardened and his brows creased together like he was offended I could insinuate anything more.

"You question my love for you," he stated, quiet and low.

I shook my head. "Never."

I knew Kova loved me, and that no one would ever love me the way he did.

"What do you want me to do, Adrianna? I am trying to make the necessary changes for our future. Is that not what matters?"

I wasn't expecting the knife to slice through my chest the way it did. I wanted to yell back and demand to know why he waited two weeks to see me. If he wanted time knowing that I didn't have much of it to give, why didn't he move quicker if he was sticking to his plan? I was trying not to be nitpicky but that was weeks wasted that we'd never get back. Weeks we could have spent talking things out and figuring out life together. Hearing that he was still living with Katja hurt me. It didn't matter that he'd filed for divorce if he was still living with her.

If Kova was serious about us, he could've gone to a hotel or rented a condo. Anything to prove he was putting me and him first because it was something he wanted for us. But he hadn't.

Without an ounce of emotion, I said, "If the divorce is what you want, then I'm glad for you."

CHAPER 49

Kova pulled back, a tinge of worry etched his forehead.

His eyes shifted quickly between mine. "It is what you wanted too, yes?" he said.

"What I want shouldn't sway your decision. The decision should only be yours, Kova."

His worry deepened. "The decision *is* mine. You knew I needed a way out and why I had to stay married. We talked about this and you agreed with me. Now that I have filed papers you have a change of mind? What happened? I do not understand why you went backward instead of forward."

I was one of those angry criers. I could feel the tears rushing to the surface threatening to spill over. The last thing I wanted to do was to shed more tears.

I couldn't figure out what I was most angry about, though. Was it that Kova wanted time? Or the fact that I was sick and I resented myself for it?

My hands were resting on his spread thighs. I could feel the tears clogging my throat. I didn't change my mind, we just didn't agree with what the other wanted. I drew in a breath through my nose. My eyes closed shut and I clenched them to hold in the tears.

"What is it?" he said, his voice grave.

"Did you just think you could ignore me for however long you needed to, then come back and act like time didn't pass and everything would be fine and I would be waiting here?" A sharp ache shot through my chest. "A quick update and then it's goodbye for a little while again? Because I had a lot of time to think during these four weeks, and after the way we parted, I was under the impression you were completely done with me."

His brows shot up, his eyes widened. Kova's voice was bold. "I said I needed some time. We both do."

I shook my head in disagreement. "Time is infinite. You can't tell someone you need time and expect them to wait until you get your life together."

My pulse hammered away in my neck. I was proud of myself for standing up. We both remained quiet until Kova spoke.

"I want you. You want me. Is that not enough for us to hold on to for now?"

He looked at me with his heart on his sleeve. I shook my head, regret filling my veins. It simply wasn't enough. We'd learned that the hard way and we'd both suffered. It was now or never. It had to be.

"You've had me on your time since we started," I responded, my words were just above a whisper. "You had me when you pulled me from the first meet. You had me when you got married. You had me the months following when I was devastated that you could lie to me the way you did and hide your marriage. I don't think you understand the magnitude of what that did to me." I paused. "You had me when Katja paraded around your gym humiliating me, rubbing your marriage and my poor health in my face. Still, you had me when I got pregnant. But now that I have to step away from gymnastics for a little while to work on my health, you want more time…" I shook my head and said, "It's always when you're ready for me and never the other way around."

Blood drained from his cheeks. He leaned back. "That is not true," Kova said, his green eyes flaring. "I want you always. There is much unfinished business left to take care of and too much outside noise. We would be fighting every day like we are now and grow to hate each other. I cannot stomach the thought of that."

We'd always had shit between us and still managed to make it work. I wanted to stomp my foot because it was no different now.

"You had me through the good, the bad, and everything in between. Anytime you needed me, I've been here. Where were you all the times I needed you? That's right. You were playing house with your wife."

His back straightened with indignation. "That is not fair, Adrianna," he said, his voice low but steady.

"Maybe not. But I've given you more than enough time. I've been waiting for you to choose me since before you made Katja your wife, because even back then when it first started between us, my feelings for you were that strong. I waited, though, for different reasons. Mainly because I was so young. I thought that was the issue, but I'm learning it's more than that."

Kova's eyes softened with pure unfiltered rawness. His face fell. I think it was starting to really hit him that I wasn't changing my mind. He couldn't give me what I wanted, and that killed him. It killed me too.

The barefaced truth was I would do anything for him.

It wasn't that I thought he wouldn't do anything for me, but he had to think about it first. I didn't.

That was the difference.

"I am trying, Ria," he said dejectedly. His fingers let go of my belt loops and found the back of my thighs. His palms were warm to the touch. Kova leaned forward, his back bending over so he could look into my eyes and plead with me. His eyes were so vibrant and green. "Please believe me. You have every part of me. No one has ever had me the way you do, and no one ever will. I am doing the best I can, given the situation."

Guilt ate through my lungs, squeezing them tight. I moved my hands from his thighs to his biceps. My thumbs glided over the veins. I pressed and watched the vein compress and expand.

"I want you now. I want you on my time. I don't want to wait around anymore for you. I love you and you love me. Couples fight and then they make up. They learn from mistakes and it brings them closer. Isn't that how it happens? I really think in the end we would be okay.

"I want you to be mine and only mine, and that means not living with anyone else if it's not me in the meantime. I want you to be committed to me unconditionally. Can you give me that? Give yourself to me completely the way I can give myself to you?"

God, the look in his eyes was going to ruin me forever. It was seared into my heart. I knew his answer before he did.

"I didn't think so," I answered quietly for him.

There was no animosity between us. Just brokenhearted words neither of us expected. Kova was trying. I just couldn't give him more than an inch without it eventually leading to another heartbreak. That would require more than I had to give.

"I didn't hear from you for a month. Is that what we are now? A monthly check-in?" I said, trying to step away again.

Kova pulled me closer and dipped his head into the curve of my neck. He exhaled a heavy breath and it prickled my skin. He held me tight and I let him because even though he'd hurt me so many times, I didn't know when I would see him again. My arms wound around his shoulders and it was my turn to dip my face near his.

"Do not dare reduce us to that."

"Actions, Kova. I can't give a title to something without cause. You gave it to me."

"Adrianna, you are not being reasonable." He stressed against my collarbone. "Sit back and think about what you are holding against me. My hands are tied."

Pulling back, I had to look at Kova when I said what I needed to say next. He had to see how much his decision had crushed me, how it ultimately changed me. I hoped one day I'd be able to forget it, but I wasn't sure how when anytime I thought about my time at the Olympics and who was on that journey with me, I'd always, and forever, think of Kova. He didn't just leave a footprint on my heart. As always, Kova went the extra mile and carved it out of my chest with his chalk-covered hands and took it with him.

"When you saw me break down in that hotel room... When I finally needed you for once, you walked away."

His eyes hardened and his body tensed under my hands. "Let me refresh your memory that I was there for you after training and during recovery. I took care of you when you could not on those nights. I even became certified to treat your Achilles injury and bought proper equipment just for you. You hid your illnesses from me and would not let me be there for that, so I had to be a piece of shit and push you to open up to me because I knew you needed me. I let you use a knife on me because you needed me. So do not dare tell me I have not once been there for you. I have plenty of times. We are not so different, Adrianna."

Warm tears fell from my eyes. I burst out crying. Kova knew more about how I felt about my illnesses than Avery. He knew my darkest fears and how I was scared it was going to kill me at a young age.

That was the hardest reality to accept, that I was going to live this next chaper of my life on my own.

Kova dragged me a little closer again. He was right. We weren't so different, and he *had* been there for me.

Wrapping his arms around my back, he pressed the tips of his fingers into my sides as he hugged me. I whimpered softly until I got myself together to look at him again.

Kova reached out and used his thumbs to wipe away my tears as I said, "I can't keep getting caught up in us holding out for more when all it does is make me sicker in the end." Exhaling a deep breath, I said, "I put too much into us."

He looked at me, his brows lowered. He seemed concerned. I gestured to the space between me and him. Emotion cracked in my voice and my chin wobbled.

"The old me wouldn't have hesitated to give you exactly what you wanted." My lips pressed together. Kova squinted at my mouth. "I had to make a choice." I shook my head, feeling miserable. Kova finally dropped his hands from me, mine fell to the tops of his thighs again. His lips parted in what I would assume was disbelief. "You mess with my mind too much. You're all I think about almost every second of the day. I get so consumed in *you* that I forget about *me*. It's taken enough of a toll on my life." My voice shook. "I love you—"

Kova pushed the barstool back and swiftly stood. He looked terrified. Utterly terrified. I could feel the fear pumping in his chest.

"Adrianna, stop," he said. "Do not say another word," he warned.

I kept going even though it was going to hurt him. I had to get it out and this was the only time we had.

"I love you, but I need to get my mind right and my health right, and I realized I can't do that near you. The more I stay around you, the more destruction it causes to my life." I paused, and he held his breath. "I wanted you to be all in, but you wouldn't. I didn't want to have to question us as a couple in between dialysis appointments. It had to be all or nothing for me. You made your choice, and so did I."

His eyes widened and his lips parted. I swear I could hear his heart beating. "What are you telling me?"

My heart lodged in my throat, and more tears brimmed my eyelids. I took a step back. Kova looked down, confused, then back at me. This next part was going to be so difficult.

"I need to focus on me."

"What are you saying?" He demanded through a harsh whisper. "Say it."

I stared. With tears streaming down my cheeks, my voice was so small and dripping in defeat.

"This is goodbye."

His hand came up slowly to cover his mouth, his eyes bore into mine. "I refuse to accept this." His words exposed the shake in his voice, and once again, I almost yielded. "Absolutely not."

"You have no choice but to accept it. I've already made up my mind." I paused. "In two days when I board my plane, I'm leaving us here and saying goodbye to what we once were."

The anguish filling my chest was almost too much. Whoever said "sticks and stones may break your bones but words will never hurt" was a total fucking liar.

Kova's lips parted and I felt his shock reverberate through me. His wild eyes held me immobile. He ate up the space between us in three strides, his gait heavy with determination. He closed the distance and I placed my hand on his chest to stop him. A gasp escaped my lips as he cupped the back of my head and brought his mouth to hover above mine. Kova leaned into me as he pulled my body to his.

"Don't make this harder than it needs to be," I whispered. "Please." He shook his head, his beautiful eyes pleading. Hot air swept across my cheek as he exhaled through his nose. I knew what he was thinking—we were already passed that point. Kova pressed closer to my lips and I arched back, curling into him.

"No." It was all he said. "No." His voice shook a little this time. "Not this."

Kova pressed his nose into my cheek, and his hands traveled my back. He picked me up and wrapped my legs around his back. His fingers threaded through my hair and cupped the back of my neck. He held me to him for dear life. Heat flooded my body, and a soft sigh rolled off my lips. I felt his sorrow and it consumed me. I exhaled and melted into him, missing him so much already. He swept frantic kisses across the slope of my neck. My thighs squeezed around his waist in response and I held him to me just as tight.

I loved this man with every part of me, but that wasn't enough to stop me from executing the hardest thing I had ever done in my life.

Kova pulled back and met my gaze. He couldn't take his hands off of me. The startling revelation in his eyes was much harder to witness than I'd expected.

"You are leaving me," he stated.

My lips puckered and tears blurred my vision. The creases between Kova's brows deepened with each second I didn't respond.

"I'm leaving us."

Kova shook his head. His gaze bore into mine and it twisted my stomach. This was a total blow to his gut and it showed.

"What does *us* mean? Define it, Adrianna."

My shoulders fell. "Why are you bothered by this? It's what you wanted, isn't it? The time you so badly needed?"

He pulled my lips closer to his. "Not if there was a chance I could not ever see you again," he responded immediately.

My nostrils flared. "While you were making decisions that worked for you, I made a decision for myself. The time you needed away from me was enough time for me to reevaluate my life."

A breath hitched in my throat. The moment the words left my mouth I regretted them. I was finally understanding why people lied to their loved ones. Sometimes the truth hurt more.

Tormented eyes regarded me.

Shaking my head with regret, I said quietly, "Times up, Kova."

He didn't hesitate.

Kova pressed his lips to mine in a no-holds-barred kiss. He inhaled me deep and drew me into him like I was the air he breathed.

Like he didn't want to let go.

CHAPER 50

Kova's fingers pressed into my waist, and I clenched his shirt in my fist. I kissed him back without reservation.

Our lips fused together too perfectly, the stars only ever aligning for us when our bodies did. It wasn't fair, it was a cruel existence that tortured our emotions, but it was how we communicated.

Kova's grip on me tightened. I arched into him with a small gasp as his tongue delved into my mouth. A moan vibrated in the back of my throat causing Kova to escalate his assault on my mouth. I kissed him back with just as much vigor, arching my hips against his. Kova noticed and responded with a skilled stroke that made my toes curl. I was getting lost in the man who was my everything and that I was inevitably walking away from. He was my awakening and my reckoning.

Breaking the kiss, I whispered, "I'm sorry."

"You are just going to give up on us? Just like that?" His grip tightened like he was afraid of my answer.

My jaw trembled at the defensive tone in his voice. "I'm not giving up on the idea of us, but I am letting go of us right now."

"No," he whispered sharply and shook his head. "I know what that means. Please," he begged, "do not do this. Whatever you want, it is yours. Tell me and I will honor it."

Tears trickled over my pressed lips and down my chin. His gaze was a kaleidoscope of emotions. It hurt to see him in pain like this, to know that for once it was me doing the hurting.

His eyes were glossy with tears. This was the second time I'd seen an emotion this powerful on Kova. It rattled me. The last time this happened, he'd found out I was pregnant.

"It's too late," I said, my decision final.

Without saying another word, Kova slammed his mouth to mine. He savagely kissed me like his life depended on it. His hands were all over my body, the warmth creating a carnal glow throughout me. I jerked forward to kiss him back and bite his lip. He touched every inch of me he could. The desperation in his touch was what took me by surprise and revived the flame I'd gone breathless to blow out. His tongue plunged into my mouth and wrapped around mine in a sweep of untamed passion. His kiss was a feeling, an erratic pulse. Kova's hand captured mine. He squeezed my fingers, pressing our joined hands against his heart where the letter A would be for the rest of his life.

"Fuck everything. I am going to sell the gym and come with you. Where you go, I go. It is us, Adrianna. I would rather fight with you every day than risk never being with you again."

I gasped, shock ricocheting through me. Burning stones were tossing around in my stomach. Kova was going to give up what he loved. Had I been wrong about how he felt about us all along? My heart clenched at the thought.

No, I wouldn't go there. I wasn't going to backtrack because he said something I wanted to hear.

"You can't do that," I said. "You can't, Kova. I won't allow it. You love that gym."

He pressed his lips to mine. "I love you more, and if that is what it takes, then so be it. I do not care if you tell me every hour that I am being a dickhead, or that I am terrible at expressing myself, or that this was a mistake. As long as we are together, then say all you want. I know where your heart lies for me. But if it will chance ever being with you again? No. Absolutely not."

He kissed me again until I was breathless. I allowed it by pressing the back of his head so his lips crushed mine. Desperate lips and painstakingly slow hands showed that what we had was real. I never wanted to let go of him. What I wanted, now, was to change my mind.

My breathing labored to wheezing and that worried me, but not enough to stop. And that was my biggest flaw right there that could eventually cause me my life—I stopped thinking about *me* when I was with *him*.

This feeling, though, this connection, the chemistry driving us together, it was once in a lifetime and why I allowed it to devour me.

"You're just making it harder," I said, breaking the kiss, and Kova groaned.

Flattening my hand, I pressed on his chest to push him back to put space between us, only I fisted his shirt and tugged him to me.

"Fuck," I whispered under my breath and dropped my head on the curve of his shoulder. I couldn't let go, damn it. I was scared to, because the truth was, I didn't want to. I honestly didn't want to let him go.

Taking my jaw into his hand, Kova tipped it back until I was forced to look at him. His thumb pressed under the center of my chin and his palm cupped my throat. The gesture was tender but his touch longed for love. Kova stared into my eyes. He fought to steady the tremble in his hand, but I felt it.

He exhaled, and like always, I inhaled.

Then Kova gave me a soul-searing kiss that almost made me change my mind. His lips suctioned over mine and he breathed me into him like I was his last dying breath. His kiss evoked the unusual love we had for each other, and I loved that it did. It made it that more ours and ours alone.

"Do you not see it yet, *Malysh*?" His eyes were frantic. "I bleed my emotion silently, and you express yours with hunger. It is a give and a take, a perfect balance, which makes us right for each other. We need each other."

Just not right now, I thought as more tears surfaced. He'd only changed his mind because I set the ultimatum.

Kova placed me on my feet and turned away. I watched as his hands came up to the back of his head and he laced his fingers together. Frustration bloomed a shade of red under his white knuckles.

He turned around and I almost lost my breath. Konstantin Kournakova was a beautiful tragedy I'd never forget.

"I am going to accept the offer I got for World Cup from Danilo. He can have it all," he said with determination. "I will talk to my attorney about rushing the divorce, and I will give Katja whatever she wants to be away from her. You want to say goodbye forever? No, that is not happening. It is a done deal, the gym will be sold. I had already started the preparations. I will just move it along quicker." Kova paused, then caught me by surprise. "I am coming with you."

I shook my head, he wasn't understanding.

CHAPER 51

My chest ached. I didn't want him to make these decisions because of my tears. I wanted him to make them based on his own feelings and experiences, the way I had.

"Don't. Don't do that. Don't give up what you love for me," I argued.

"It is done. I am selling World Cup."

Goose bumps broke out over my arms. He made it sound like he was so sure about it.

"It's too late for that," I said miserably. "I'm going alone."

The look on his face had me drowning in grief. Kova hung his head between his shoulders. I could feel his suffering pouring into me and it was wrecking my heart. I walked over to him. He wrapped his arms around the small of my back and hugged me so tight I could feel the subtle shake under his muscles.

"I do not want to live without you."

My eyes closed shut, seeping with tears. "Our love makes me sicker, Kova."

My face was folded into the column of his neck as he gave me a hug. Kova didn't respond for a long minute, maybe two. He was sinking in anguish with me. We stayed in each other's arms as reality fell upon us.

Our love made me sicker. Our love ultimately tore us apart.

I wiped away the tears under my eyes and took a deep breath. His suffering mimicked mine and it made this that much tougher. Kova's gaze was glossy, brimming with dread.

"I know it is selfish of me to try to stop you, but love is selfish, and, *Malysh*, I have never loved anyone or anything as much as I love you. If you are leaving, then so am I."

My stomach clenched. The words I longed to hear were too late.

Shaking my head, I was brutally honest. "I don't want you to come with me."

He didn't blink. He didn't even move for a long moment. His lips pressed together and he subtly nodded his head. His form became blurry in front of me.

"Can I at least take you to the airport?"

I sniffled. "Yes."

Cupping the sides of my face, Kova bent down. My hands found his hips just as he pressed one last kiss to my lips.

"Just know that this is not what I want. It is going to be the biggest challenge of my life to see you walk away, but I will. I will give you what you want and hope our love only grows from the distance into something that will force us to come together and be impossible to walk away from again one day."

He kissed me hard, then briskly pulled back and spun around. Kova didn't stop, not even when he flung the door open and marched out with my heart did he turn around and look back at me.

"TELL ME I'M DOING THE right thing," I cried into the phone a couple minutes later. "Because if I am, why does it hurt so bad?"

The first thing I did was call Avery. I could barely see the screen from the fat warm tears pouring out of me to find her name. The waterworks were turned up high and I was hiccupping into the phone.

"You had one job, and you ended up screwing your coach." A sad laugh escaped me at her dry humor. "What happened?"

I sniffled and pulled my knees up to my chest, nestling further into the corner of my couch. I stared out the sliding glass door at the swaying palm trees, rewinding the story from the beginning for Avery. I broke down multiple times and asked her repeatedly if I was making a mistake. She insisted it was par for the course and encouraged me not to feel bad about it.

"You're doing the right thing. It takes courage to defy your heart. If your health wasn't in jeopardy, then I'd say you need to give yourselves a fighting chance. But I can't. There's too much at stake, and if Kova did anything to risk your progress, I would personally kill him."

My teeth worried my bottom lip. "It just feels… I don't know…" My voice was distant.

"It's going to feel like that for a long time," Avery said, knowing what I meant.

I was nauseous. My nerves were so bad I felt like they were burning a hole through the lining of my stomach. How long was a long time? He hadn't even been gone for more than an hour and I wanted to run to him.

"I told him he could take me to the airport."

Avery groaned.

"What does that mean?"

"It means there's a ninety-nine percent chance you're going to change your mind now. I kind of wish you didn't agree." She half joked, half laughed. "Tomorrow when the movers are at your house, all you're going to be thinking about is saying goodbye to Kova the following day. That anticipation is going to build and you're going to give in."

"Maybe I'm supposed to cave." I countered. "Everywhere I look, I see him. I smell him. I *feel* him, Ave. My heart is saying don't do it." I was drowning in heartache and beginning to doubt my choice now.

"Now's not the right time to think with your heart, chica. Look at where your heart's taken you the last few years," she said sympathetically. "Yeah, you're essentially walking away from someone who can never be replaced. You'll never have what you have with Kova with someone else. And you know what? You don't want it with anyone else. So in a way, you're walking away with assurance that this is how it's supposed to be for now, and that one day it will be worth it because there isn't a world that exists where you two aren't together."

My stomach was churning into tighter knots. "This is going to suck," I muttered.

"Tomorrow when the movers are there, just call me. Call me eighty-seven times if you have to. I just want you to think first before you make any decision."

"I will. Do you think he'll show up tomorrow?"

"I think when you told him everything, including your love is making you sicker, that put shit into perspective for him. Aid, even *I* felt that, and I don't even love you like that." We both laughed. "But you know why it hurt when I felt it? Because it's the damn truth and it fucking sucks. Kova knows that, that's why he didn't argue with you. So, no, I don't think he'll show up."

"Aren't we too young to feel heartache like this?" I joked, then rubbed at the tightness in my chest. Wiping my eyes with the back of my hand, I sat up a little straighter and exhaled.

"I'm learning that there are no rules in the game of love." Avery was wistful.

"I'm forfeiting now."

We both laughed again then said our goodbyes, with a promise that I'd call her first thing tomorrow. I was still suck in the corner of the couch with no will to get up.

Slouching down, I clicked on the picture icon on my phone and scrolled through photos I'd saved of Kova and me, looking for a specific one. I didn't have many, but I had enough that even in spite of my broken heart it still held memories I never wanted to forget.

I stopped scrolling when I found it. I stared, unblinking at the image that brought tears to my eyes. Only, I wasn't looking at just the image. I pictured myself standing in the room watching the pair take a selfie together. They were at ease with each other and I found myself longing for it. She was a tiny, happy thing snuggled in his strong arms. He was protective over her, though she didn't know it yet. Laid back and in love were a few words I'd use to describe the feeling on his face as he lifted the phone, and with a few clicks, he captured this photo.

It was the day he came to my hotel room after I had to attend and watch the meet he wouldn't allow me to compete in. He'd pulled me onto his lap after and asked what I'd learned. I'd resented him leading up to that day until understanding had dawned on me. His motives were genuine, the outcome constructive, but the way he delivered them was usually questionable. It was a day I would never forget. I thought it was when I really started to feel something for Kova.

It was also when he'd said we were a team, exhaling and inhaling together. I was his weakness and he was my strength. We inspired each other, and we pushed each other to be better people than the day before. He was the beast beneath my beauty, pushing me, he'd said.

It was all true, and that's what broke me down.

Tears filled my eyes. The longer I stared at the picture, the more I longed to feel safe in Kova's arms again.

Pressing down on the image, I saved it as my wallpaper.

CHAPER 52

startled awake and sat upright, listening.

I thought I heard a bang.

Blinking my blurry eyes, I glanced around and yawned. I must've fallen asleep on the couch. I spotted my cell phone on the floor and realized that was the sound that woke me. I picked it up and checked the time. It was close to midnight. I tucked it into my stomach then curled onto my side. That space in between just falling asleep and really sleeping was—

Knock, knock, knock.

I froze, my hand clenching my cell phone tighter. My body instantly warmed. Staring at the front door, I knew who stood on the other side without having to guess. I breathed and felt goose bumps pebble my skin.

There was a small part of me that secretly hoped he'd show.

I placed my phone down and stood on unsteady legs. I crossed the carpet and reached for the knob. I stilled for a moment. My heart was pounding in my throat. I didn't have to open the door. I could pretend I was asleep. It would be the right thing to do, and then I wouldn't feel guilty about lying to people about him. He knocked again, this time a little heavier.

My heart was racing.

I swallowed thickly and asked myself what *I* wanted.

Without a second thought, I reached for the lock and unbolted it.

Holding my breath, I pulled the door open and found Kova leaning against the frame. Both of his elbows were pressed against the sides to hold him up and his legs were crossed at his ankles. His head hung miserably between his shoulders and he was staring at the floor.

I didn't have to say anything, and neither did he.

My stomach was a knotted mess seeing him like this.

I felt his despair coming from a mile away. I was sure he felt my sorrow when I was looking at our pictures earlier and reminiscing. My fingers twitched. I knew if I took one more step it would change the course of the night for us. The knots in my stomach were growing. I could be strong in my personal pursuit, but I could also be human and allow us one more night. Kova came to me. He was leaving the choice up to me.

I reached for him.

Stepping forward, I wrapped my arms around his lower back and hugged him. His elbows fell and he engulfed me with his body. I pressed the side of my face to Kova's chest and closed my eyes. I heard his heart beating rapidly and tasted his bitter anguish on my tongue. Stepping closer, my arms tightened around him.

Kova rested his cheek on the top of my head and hugged me with a passion that pushed down my walls. I inhaled and felt his heat spread through me.

Home.

This was home for us.

"I wish I did not love you the way I do, Adrianna," he whispered. "I wish I was a stronger man."

Tears sprung to my eyes and I clenched them tight. His tone almost brought me to my knees. Kova was gutted. There was a rawness in his voice that sounded like he'd been crying all night. I knew exactly what he meant, though. We had no right to love the way we did.

I lifted my head from his chest to finally see his face. My stomach twisted as our eyes met.

"You're the strongest man I know."

His eyes were rimmed a pale pink. Kova was a robust man but the weakness in his indecisive gaze left me feeling for him. I had the notion that he was ashamed he was here, but not embarrassed. It was an inkling in my gut, but I'd feel the same way if it were me.

Rising up on my tiptoes, I ran the pad of my thumb over his lower lip and tugged it to the side. I watched it plop back and did it again, feeling hungry for his lips on mine.

My other hand cupped the side of his jaw and I brought his mouth toward me. My body arched perfectly along his. Kova held me closer.

Need surged through me and I pulled in a deep breath. Just before I pressed our lips together, I whispered, "Let's finish what we started."

Our lips met. The words burned my throat and my heart sank with reality.

This would be our last night together and I realized how much I wanted this for me, for him, for us. But I also realized how deeply it would hurt in the end.

The kiss deepened and I held my breath, my heart racing with desire. Kova nodded without separating us and I almost fainted with excitement. I couldn't hold back and plunged my tongue into his warm mouth. Kova met me needy stroke for hungry stroke. His silky tongue was the most illicit.

Our bodies aligned and he tightened his arms around me. This kiss wasn't a painfully hard one, it didn't fill me with anger or sadness. It was a kiss that longed for more days watching the sunsets together.

It was a kiss that was supposed to be felt forever. And boy, did I feel it in my chest.

My back arched and I lifted a leg to hook it around Kova's leg for more stability. He got the hint and hoisted me up instead. My legs wrapped around his waist and I gripped him between me. I felt so tiny, protected, and loved in his arms.

"Come inside and lock the door," I said quickly before my lips were back on his. "Don't forget the chain," I added.

I knew where this was going, and so did he.

There wouldn't be any talking, just breathless pants and naked bodies making sweet harmony together between damp sheets.

And I was okay with that. I needed it, he needed it. I was impatient for him and squeezed my thighs around him. The only time we were ourselves and open with each other was when he was deep inside of me and I was at his mercy. It was carnal and it was glorious. I loved what our bodies did when no one was looking.

Kova walked inside and kicked the door behind him then turned to secure it before he carried us away to my bedroom. Our lips didn't separate and his tongue never stopped caressing mine as he held me with one arm under my ass and the other hand tangled in my hair.

He didn't bother to flip on the light, we didn't need it, I'd accidentally left the bathroom light on earlier and it provided a soft glow in the bedroom. He brought us to my bed and held me closely as he leaned over and laid me down in the center. He covered me with his weight and twisted his tongue around mine. We moaned in harmony at the feel of our bodies pressed together. I ground my hips erotically against his, not holding back tonight. Kova reciprocated, and he let out a hearty groan when I rubbed my pussy down his thigh. I was already so wet for him.

Only Kova could intoxicate me with a kiss.

His elbows boxed me in. My hands gripped his backside with need. I pressed my fingers into him and felt him contract under my touch. The only sound in the room was that of our lips. Kova kissed me with a sensuality that I was sure was only seen in movies. We had a full-blown hot and heavy make out session that was probably some of the best foreplay we'd ever had while he still had his hat on backwards and we were both fully clothed.

"I want you all night."

Kova dusted kisses on my jaw and sloped down to my neck. He moved the collar of my shirt to the side and kissed whatever he could put his lips to.

"Yes." I sighed, arching my chest into him.

My fingers reached for the hem of his shirt and pulled it up. Kova moved just enough for me to drag it over his head and then his mouth was on mine again. I got the feeling he was scared to stop kissing me and made sure to meet me stroke for stroke until he took my breath away.

Blindly, I felt around my bed for his hat. That broke the kiss, which almost made me giggle. He looked at me and I answered the question in his eyes.

"I always loved the hat on you."

Kova replaced the hat and regarded me. Soft eyes roamed over my face just as my hands found the waistband of his shorts. I didn't pull them down yet, I just wanted to feel the planes of his back one more time.

Dragging my hands down the length of his back, his muscles contracted under my fingers as he kissed me. I reached around to his lower stomach, running my fingers along the crease of his flesh and the seam of his elastic shorts. His hips flexed as I glided my nails along the deep grooves of strength.

I pulled back and ran the tip of my tongue over my bottom lip then pressed my teeth down. I dragged them over and glanced nervously into his eyes.

"What do you want to say," Kova asked gently. "Tell me."

I became shy, but for a valid reason. He could reject me and I wasn't sure I was prepared for that.

Kova adjusted his legs and I felt his cock slide against my thigh toward my pussy. My back bowed and my legs spread wider to feel more of his length.

"Will you stay the night?"

He smiled faintly and dropped his gaze to my lips. Kova nodded then found my lips again. Relief coursed through me and I could breathe. I twisted my legs around his and gasped as he surged forward and crossed over my clit. He kissed me until we were both panting in desperation, then he pulled back and climbed off the bed.

I watched him, curious what he would do next. I was hungry for him and already missed him on me. He toed off his shoes, then hooked his thumbs in his shorts and shoved them down. I pushed up on my elbows and watched in fascination as he stepped out of his shorts. His cock sprang free, the crown glistened in the dim light. Desire pulsed through me, and I pulled my knees up and my toes curled under me.

Kova cupped his sack and adjusted himself. I drew in a shallow breath, still in a bit of disbelief that he was here. He palmed his length and my lips parted as he twisted his wrist and gave himself a good squeeze. I pressed my thighs together and wetness coated my pussy. I drew a breath in through my nose and arched my back. A soft moan rolled off my lips. For a brief moment I wondered how I was going to live without him and why I was doing this to myself when I felt so strongly toward him. Kova waved two fingers at me to look up. Heat bloomed under my cheeks as our eyes met.

"Are you sure this is what you want?" he asked.

I swallowed and nodded.

"Say it."

"I want you," I said, curling my toes tighter.

His eyes bore into mine. "Tell me again. Once I start, I will not stop."

A smile tipped my lips. This was one of my favorite sides of Kova. "Make love to me."

His gaze darkened. That was all the confirmation he needed. Kova extended his arm and grabbed my ankle. He yanked me down the bed, and in the blink of an eye, he had my shorts and panties off and on the floor. He climbed over my body and I sat up, putting my arms in the air for him to remove my shirt. He tore it off and unhooked my bra in a flash.

"I am desperate and crazy for you." A gasp lodged in my throat. My heart ached. "This is not goodbye sex. Do you understand me, Ria?"

CHAPER 53

Kova gave me a quick kiss then reared back and grabbed my hips. He flipped me over to face the bed and jerked my ass up. Heat zipped down my spine. My arms moved to the sides of my head and I spread my fingers out for balance. He tapped the back of my thighs and my knees automatically spread wider. A sigh rolled off my lips. Moving the hair from my face, I peered over my shoulder and caught a glimpse of Kova. His eyes were on my exposed sex. He made me feel desired the way he stared. I clenched and imagined his fingers on my clit. My pussy contracted and his eyes lowered.

"Arch your back." I did, and he growled. "More, Adrianna." He demanded. "I know you can do better than that."

A wistful grin spread across my face. Of course, I could. I just wanted to hear him say it.

I curved my back and gave him the view he wanted. He palmed my ass cheek and goose bumps pebbled my skin. I pushed my ass into his hand wanting more and watched as his jaw flexed in appreciation the sharper the angle was. His thumb grazed over my swollen lips. Pleasure glazed my pussy and Kova used it to tease me. A moan escaped my throat.

Lowering himself, Kova gripped the top of my thighs to hold me still. He disappeared from view and placed his flat tongue on my pussy. My jaw dropped and I gasped, feeling pleasure drip from me toward his mouth.

"Yes." I sighed.

His fingers dug into my legs as he pulled me to him and gave me a long, thick lick with his tongue. Chills danced over me and my eyes fell shut. He caressed my clit until my hips were moving into his face, then he penetrated my entrance and stroked me until I was reaching behind me and wrapping my fingers around his wrist. He was tormenting me.

Dragging his tongue higher, my pussy clenched knowing where he was going. One of his hands left my thighs and he pushed down on my lower back to spread my knees wider. It felt different at this angle, more intense and better. I liked when he put pressure on me so I couldn't move much. There was something arousing about it.

With a last sweep over my pussy, Kova kept his hands where they were to hold me steady and dragged his wet tongue that was mingled with my pleasure and his saliva toward my ass. I fisted the blankets as mortification burst under my cheeks. I was beyond embarrassed I liked when he did this to me. A squeak pushed past my lips and he tasted me slow and deep. I rocked into his face, sighing and moaning, wanting him to tear me up like the animal I knew he could be.

His mouth left and clamped down on my backside and bit me. He quickly released my skin and lapped at the sting with his tongue. He did it again, this time tugging my skin between his teeth until he heard my small inhale. He let go and moved his way up my back, biting me and pulling my skin between his teeth. He left me gasping and breathless, feeling the zing all the way to my clit. I shivered.

I watched him stand from the corner of my eye and his hand slipped between us. His fingers found the sensitive nub and I whimpered, needing him desperately to fill me. Kova leaned over and pushed my auburn locks away from my face. He fisted my mane and wrapped it around his hand. My neck kinked to the side and I waited. He leaned in and the warmth of his chest heightened the chemistry between us.

"I am going to fuck some sense into you." He bit my ass again. "Then I will make love to you, and knowing I cannot change your mind, I will still try to prove that you and I are it, Adrianna."

Kova pulled back and palmed his cock. Dragging the tip up my wet pussy to my entrance.

"There is no way I am putting one more thing between us tonight, *Malysh.*" Then he drove into me bare and pressed down on my lower back until I was in a butterfly position.

Thank God I was flexible, and not just because my hips were flat to the bed. He hit a different angle and the pleasure was too intense for my body to process. Low hips caused my clit to grind into the sheets. I felt pleasure seep from me, and I exploded. I orgasmed immediately, spasming around his cock. The sheets were bunched in my hands and I was trying to hold onto the bed from how extreme the pleasure was. Lips parting, I moaned as I rocked into him shamelessly soaking up my climax.

"Beautiful," he said, the heel of his palm gliding up my spine.

I shivered when his fingers wrapped around the front of my neck and applied pressure. My back bowed and he dug his fingers into my throat to draw out the orgasm. A very pleased sigh spilled from my lips and I smiled lazily.

Kova was pressed to my back, his cock still deep inside me. "Nothing like being able to watch you use my cock to come on me." My pussy spasmed in response to his dirty talk, and his dick twitched. I was so soft and wet for him and I didn't want him to leave my sex. "I bet you needed that." I nodded, panting. He pulled out just a fraction then pushed in too hard. "I bet you need more, though. Am I right?"

I tried to look at him as much as I could from this angle. Reaching behind me, I felt for Kova's face and guided him to turn so he had to face me. I lifted up just enough to capture his lips with mine and kissed him with gratitude. He loved me so good and I was thankful. It'd been so long since I had a proper orgasm, and with everything going on the last couple of months, I was overdue. I felt drunk from coming so hard. I pulled his tongue into my mouth to suck on it. Kova growled into my mouth and squeezed my neck until my lips popped off his with a pant and I was falling into a black hole of pleasure.

"Move down just a bit." Kova instructed. "There. That is it." His hand reached under to feel where our bodies were joined and then higher where my tender clit was. My teeth bit into my lip and my feet flexed in pleasure. I bent my knees to my sides, and our joined bodies just hung off the bed. I shivered. If it weren't for Kova's strong thighs to stop me, I'd fall off. I was at his disposal to do as he pleased, and it excited me.

Kova leaned over me again, this time bringing his knee up and resting it over mine. He adjusted himself inside of me and got seated

deeper than usual. At least that's what it felt like. I savored the feel
of his body on me, hoping this night would pass slow. If what I was
imagining was what Kova planned to do, then it was going to be
incredible.

Bent at his hips, he stood on one leg as his hands reached for mine.
He moved over my wrists and interlocked our fingers together, then
brought them down to our sides. He positioned me on the mattress
with his weight and rolled his hips into mine with a slow, divine
tenderness that made my whole body quake. His fingers tightened
and I heard the whisper of a grunt in my ear. Kova exhaled in bliss,
and I felt it wash over me. I wish I could see his eyes right now. I bet
they were closed, and he was deep in the moment.

His legs were long enough for him to stay bent over me and his
cock fully seated inside. Something about this position made me
defenseless. It evoked too much emotion from me and I couldn't
process it all at once. Being under Kova was a thrill. His movements
were animalistic the way he mounted me from behind. His hunger
was deep, and I was anxious for him to devour me. His hips surged
above mine, dragging them to thrust into me until I felt the top of
his sack at my pussy. I clenched around him, my stomach tightening.
My clit rubbed the bed as he pushed forward, and I sighed loudly.
Kova's lips found my cheek and he pressed frantic kisses to me while
he drove his hips painstakingly slow into me. He bit my puffy bottom
lip and I reacted by wrapping my lips around his into a breathless kiss.
Nose brushed nose while tongues danced erotically around the other.

My body was shaking under his. Kova bent the leg he was standing
on to get under and ground in deeper. He reached the peak and
we gasped at the same time. We both held still, unable to move as
we lost ourselves to the exhilaration. I was aching for release and I
kept contracting around his shaft. I was trying to wait for him, but
I wasn't sure how much longer I could hold out before I started
screaming his name.

Kova turned our joined hands over and placed our wrists under my
chest to prop me up a bit. It gave him leverage to drive into me. My
heart sped in anticipation. I couldn't think properly *and* try to fight
release at the same time. Kova leaned up behind me and dropped
kisses to my shoulder blades. He pressed his lips to the center of my

back and stilled. I held my breath as he dropped his forehead to the back of my neck. He let out a heavy sigh and it blazed down my spine.

We didn't move. The only sound was heavy panting and damp bodies grinding back and forth.

"We cannot get closer than this, *Malysh*."

His voice... The anguish in it seized the oxygen in my lungs. Kova wasn't just talking sexually. I felt the depth of his words and the way he held me under him as he said them. He believed it and there was something so incredibly fulfilling about it. Something flashed in my mind and I got emotional for a second. I wondered if it could ever be better than this, and if I wanted it to or not.

Kova had experienced a myriad of life events with me in a brief period of time. Emotional highs and extreme lows, the way we tried to disentangle ourselves only to keep running back. Tears began to climb my eyes.

Kova was right. We were closer than ever before and the energy in that alone made the blood in my veins rush for him. My body tingled and my neck arched back wishing I could make this exact moment last forever.

"Kova," I whispered. I didn't even recognize my own voice. I held our hands closer to my chest. "I... Oh... I..."

"Tell me."

My pussy clamped down on his cock and I squirmed under him. His groan was deep, sensual and it heightened the chemistry. His chest was damp on my back. Kova was a man who was lost to pleasure.

Drawing in a nervous breath, I needed to find relief. "I love you."

Kova pushed back and that only made the moment that much more intense. He exhaled and his breath tickled down my back. His cock twitched and he dragged a breath in. My clit touched a different part of the bed and I moaned at the coolness. I was on the edge and needed him to finish us already before I exploded.

"I am coming inside you," he stated.

"Yes." I sighed in euphoria. I imagined him coming inside me and I gasped.

His width felt larger than usual and I briefly wondered if he'd had sex since after us. The thought disappeared the second I felt the spark of pleasure deep in my pussy. I gripped our hands so I could buck my hips back. I almost squeaked when he hit a new spot. I wanted more. I *craved* more. Little moans spilled from my throat and then he was rearing back and moving his hips forward into me, driving them with a one-track mind. I was going to be raw by the time we were finished.

"The last time I came inside of you was right downstairs." My heart clenched. "Remember that, when we were outside? My cum was dripping down your leg," he said, his groan guttural, and that was it.

I exploded around his cock for the second time. "I'm sorry… I can't hold on."

Kova tensed, he held his breath, and then he was rocking into me with a swift hardness. His dick jerked and he was coming inside. He let out a loud sound between a pant and a guttural groan, and it made my pussy tighten so I was riding the swell with him. Another pant, and it was in the back of his throat and filled with so much pleasure that I was almost jealous.

My flesh tingled with rapture. I closed my eyes and allowed myself to fall in a cave of depraved thoughts with him. It was decadent and tempting, and where I came alive. The intimacy wasn't a casual affair. Far from it. The intimacy between me and Kova was about truth and what would ultimately connect us forever. We could tell each other anything, and he told me his truth the way he made soul-searing love to me.

I could feel Kova's orgasm as he unloaded inside of me. My pussy was slippery from his thick fluid. Hearing him find release was orgasm inducing. Feeling his cum spill out of me as he mounted me from behind was an experience I'd never forget.

I was free-falling still when Kova finished and swiftly pulled out. He grabbed my hips and shoved me further up the bed and flipped me over. A breath escaped me and my body opened to him. Kova climbed over me and crushed me with his weight. His lips devoured mine and his tongue was needy. I kissed him back and cradled myself around him. The inside of my thighs were sticky, and his heavy cock lay pressed between us, wet and burning hot. There was something about the way we were tangled that made my heart rush with love.

His kisses would be the death of me.

Fingers in my hair.

Damp bodies.

Starving kisses.

Legs straining in ecstasy.

He. Did. Not. Stop.

Kova's passion was all-consuming. He was going to make sure I felt him for eternity.

CHAPER 54

Kova turned over and took me with him.

I laid on top and felt the cool breeze blow against my back. I shivered and Kova wrapped his strong arms around me. His warm embrace transported me back in time when we had experienced this a time or two when there was no outside noise and it was just us.

My eyes watered. I was beginning to understand what Kova was trying to explain to me that I was so bent against. Because right now, when there was not a single thing that could interrupt us, it was harmony in the soul. This was peace. This was true bliss in every aspect, and really, how it should feel.

It was how it needed to be.

I lifted my gaze to meet Kova's. Sparkling emerald green and gunmetal gray stared back at me. He released my legs from his and I dragged them up to straddle his waist. My tongue ran over my swollen lips and heat flamed my cheeks when I felt myself leak his pleasure onto his pelvis. It was so warm and thick.

A smirk tugged at Kova's lips that made my heart stumble. He lifted his hips slightly to glide over my clit. I gasped then clenched, feeling more of his cum ooze from me. He liked it and my cheeks deepened in color. I wondered if I had ever seen his filthiest side.

Palming the back of my head, he brought my lips to his and gently kissed me. My body was exhausted and I was beginning to feel tired. The tips of his fingers dragged lazily up and down my spine. I purred into his kiss. Kova used his other hand to reach behind me and drag two fingers coated with his release over my clit.

"Kova, I'm a little sore," I said against his mouth. "Give me a minute."

He ignored me and rubbed the sensitive ball in circles. I squirmed on top of him, feeling out of breath. My nipples brushed across his and my body was on fire when he traced my folds. My toes curled and I tried to hold back from feeling too much. His fingers dipped into my pussy and pressed along the walls of my sex. He withdrew and dragged them up to my ass. I clenched.

"Let me play with you," he asked gently, his voice rough. I nodded and rested my head on his chest. "I like touching your pussy. If you need to come while I am, go ahead. Rub your clit on me, *Malysh*. But let me have this."

My legs spread wider for him and I closed my eyes, exhaling. He pulled my hair off my neck, and I dragged lazy circles around his chest. The heel of his hand cupped my ass as his fingers delved into my tender sex. My hips widened and I exhaled a sigh. Kova breathed and his stomach stroked my clit. I let go and let myself just feel.

"I forgot how small you are on me. I miss it," he said, twirling the ends of my hair.

"I didn't expect you tonight."

"I will not apologize for coming here."

A sad smile tugged at my lips. I was glad he couldn't see it. "I would hope not."

Kova stroked me softly, twirling his fingers into my pussy the way he was twirling my hair. I felt the budding of an orgasm and was immediately humiliated. I didn't want to come like his on him. My thighs squeezed his stomach and he sensed I was close.

"I need you to know something," he said, his voice a touch urgent.

I swallowed, shamelessly rubbing myself on him. My body was pulsing with need. He played my pussy like a violin and made the sweetest sounds as I orgasmed. A long moan left my lips. I was so wet that I felt it trickle down his stomach and along my thigh. Kova noticed and growled in approval.

"I think I have loved you after the first week and I did not know it. I do not regret a single day with you. I only wish I had not been so determined to keep you away. I wish I would have just acted on what I felt for you first so we could have had more time together."

He continued touching me. My breathing was labored and my heart raced. Kova slipped his fingers from my pussy and pressed on the puckered hole, and I stilled.

"Inhale." When I did, he said, "Exhale." He pressed a little deeper. "Relax."

He coaxed me to loosen up. I was weak for him, and my entire body was charged with electricity. My clit tingled and I was suddenly awake with craving.

My mouth fell open and I dug my nails into his chest. "You don't resent me for what happened?"

Tears coated my eyes again. I didn't have to say it for him to know what I was talking about.

"Never," he said, appalled I'd ask such a thing. "If anything, it makes me love you more." He drew his knees up and I felt his cock touch the back of my thigh and drive over my ass cheek. My skin heated. "Your strength is what makes you so damn magnetic. Regardless of what happened that night, I do believe it was how it was supposed to be in the end, as much as it hurts to say it."

I nodded, unable to say the words. I knew what he meant, still it didn't hurt any less.

I started to cry. "I was so worried you'd hate me or find me ugly. I didn't think you wanted me anymore, and then I started to get paranoid—"

"Look at me."

"I didn't give you a choice!" I spoke over him, crying a little more. "I wasn't going to give you a choice."

"What?" he asked, confused.

I was so sorry it broke my heart.

I had to get it out.

I was a horrible human.

Kova sat up and took me with him. "Look at me, Adrianna." His eyes were glowing as he looked at me in awe. I sat in his lap, my body shaking as I cried softly. I tried to look away, but he wouldn't let me. Whatever he was going to say, or whatever he was going to do, he wanted me to trust in him.

"I had made up my mind that I was going to get rid of our baby and then I lost it." I hiccupped. "I didn't even ask you what you wanted. I'm so sorry. God, I'm so sorry."

Kova grabbed my chin and pulled it forward to press a peck to my lips. He pulled back and I drew in a shaky breath. He looked into my eyes, then kissed me the same way again.

"Sometimes you talk too much," he said quietly against my mouth. "You worry too much too."

I inhaled another shaky breath. I frowned. I was so confused.

"I am not mad." He planted another kiss. "I could never resent you." Two kisses. "I understand why," Kova said honestly, and it shattered my heart even more. "The miscarriage is not your fault, and as for the abortion, your decision was the right one. That does not mean I did not want our child, it was just not the right time for us, Adrianna. That is all. Nothing more, nothing less. Please, for me, stop making yourself sick over it. We do not need to keep discussing it."

Tears streamed from the corner of my eyes. I shook my head. "But how come you don't say anything about it? Why don't you even look sad?"

A shadow crossed his eyes. "Because I see how you are dealing with it and I am not adding to your sadness. The truth is, the whole thing"—he swallowed thickly—"fucking kills me, Ria. You have no idea what it does to me and what *we* lost. I am wrecked inside."

Kova took my wrists and guided them over his shoulders. He brought me closer to him then reached between us and palmed his length. His erection moved over my overstimulated clit. Always eager for him, I lifted my hips for Kova to push into me. My lips parted and our eyes met as he pushed all the way in. I sighed. Kova held still and so did I. His nostrils flared and I held my breath. We didn't move.

A moment later, he brushed a lock of hair behind my ear, and said, "If I felt any of those negative ways about you, would I still want to make love to you? Would I sell my gym? I am willing to go against your father for you. Truth is, I would do anything for you, Ria. I would probably kill for you, that is how much I fucking love you." He thrust in and growled. He was so hot inside of me, burning me up. "You always told me actions speak louder than words. Now that I am finally making moves, you question it."

I closed my eyes, feeling guilty.

"No, look at me. You want to know what I feel and how I am dealing, look at me when I tell you."

The demand in his voice caused me to shiver. I moved my hips, needing to feel him. Kova was right. I did ask, and here I was unable to handle it. I met his gaze.

"I cannot even get mad because I created that stress in you. All I can keep doing is trying to prove that you are my one and only forever love. One day I hope you believe me."

A gush of emotion pushed through my lips and I whimpered. "I do believe you. That's the thing, I do believe you. I'm just... I don't know what. Emotional, I guess."

Kova's hips surged forward and my eyes fell heavy from the wonderful blooming heat in my pelvis.

He continued when I couldn't speak. "I love you, and I never stopped loving you. I never will." He rocked harder into me. "Remember that. Remember right now when you question my love for you next time, because I know you will."

I smashed my lips to his and my arms tightened around his neck. Divine fullness filled me, but my heart was still aching. I was so stupid to doubt him. Every time I thought about Kova, my fear was he didn't want me anymore. How many more times did he have to tell me he loved me for me to finally believe it?

"I'm sorry," I cried against his mouth. I said it again as I greedily took his length. "I'm so sorry."

He shook his head, his voice frantic. "Stop. There is nothing to be sorry about."

I was sorry for more than just what happened. Mostly, I was sorry I was leaving him behind.

"I'm sorry," I whispered.

Before I could say it again, Kova spoke a few lines in Russian under his breath, then he kissed me. A sharp pang sliced through my chest at the familiarity of this moment.

Prosti.

All the air left my lungs and I abruptly broke the kiss and we stopped moving.

This was nearly the exact thing as that awful night. Kova came to me and apologized in his native tongue for hours while we made love. The only difference now was we were aware of the outcome, and it was me who was saying sorry.

We really were one in the same.

"Prosti," I said. I licked my lips and looked down.

My voice was quiet, broken. I was truly sorry for my decision even though I knew it was going to wreck us.

He tipped my chin up, and his intense eyes bored into mine.

"Ya ne mogu predstavit' svoyu zhizn', ne vidya tebya kazhdyy den.'"

My chin trembled. I waited for him to translate.

"I cannot imagine my life without seeing you every day." Kova's hips pressed forward and my jaw fell open at the delicious pressure between my legs. "I love you, Adrianna."

I inhaled, trying to steady my tears. "Promise me you'll never stop?"

I was such a hypocrite.

Kova sealed his response with a kiss. My hips moved over his in a slow wake, painting every inch of the way he felt pushing inside of me to memory. I had no right to ask him to keep loving me after I left, but I had to do it, and I needed to know he wouldn't forget about me.

Because the truth was, I would never forget about him, and I hoped that would be enough one day.

Wrapping his arm around my lower back, Kova guided us until my back was on the cool mattress. My hips widened and Kova seated deeper in my pussy. My heels drove into the bed and my neck arched, the back of my head pressing into the bed from the blissful pleasure. I let go and sighed, feeling so good.

"Tell me you love me."

Grabbing his face between my hands, I pressed a kiss to his lips. "You had me the first day when I walked into World Cup. I could never not love you, Kova."

His dejected smile crushed my heart. "I am going to make love to you now, *Malysh*, and I am not going to hold back. You are going to see how much I need you. I am not going to stop until your entire body feels how much I love you," he said, sinking deeper.

And that was what he did.

Kova took control of my body for the rest of the night while he made soul-searing love to me. There was no hurry to his kiss. He didn't drive into me like the intoxicating animal he could be. I didn't try to fight him or taunt him just to get a rise out of him.

We were just two lovers immersed in each other with desperate moans and shuddering bodies, wishing time would slow and the sunrise wasn't on the horizon.

CHAPER 55

I thought about Kova the entire time the movers had been in my condo.

My decision plagued every second of the long day, and it caused an awful headache from the stress. I couldn't stop thinking about the night before and how much my life was going to be so different a week from now. Mostly, I thought about how badly I wished things were different. My head was a mess and I wanted free from my thoughts.

Something he'd said stuck with me. I too couldn't fathom a life with him not around. He'd been the one constant in my world, and I was closer to him than anyone else. Any time I tried to imagine a life without him, this massive gray cement wall appeared before me. It left me feeling uneasy, which made me even more anxious for tomorrow.

I thought maybe Kova would've stayed the whole day too, but when I woke to an empty bed and a little note saying he'd be back to take me to the airport the next day, I was conflicted. I fell asleep with his arms holding me and our legs tangled together between my damp sheets. I was pretty positive we didn't move until he left. Now that he was gone, I was missing him so much and wished he had stayed. However, the other half of me knew it would've just been harder to say goodbye when it came time to leave. A warm ache began between my legs. I could still feel his lips on my back, his nails digging into my ass cheek as he gripped it, the way his thumb stroked the front of my throat as he came inside of me. Chills rolled down my arms and need pulsed through me.

Kova hadn't been joking when he'd said he was going to make me feel his love. I had felt it from the moment I woke up. I'd called Avery a couple of times to vent. I'd decided not to tell her anything about Kova showing up and staying over. It was something I wanted to keep for myself.

I glanced at the time over the stove. Thankfully the movers had been running behind yesterday. It was late by the time they'd finished and I was already exhausted from the night before that I fell asleep shortly after I took a shower. I slept in as much as I could until I got up to pack the last few things in my check-in bag. I had only an hour to spare before Kova arrived.

My knee bounced and I bit my bottom lip until it was raw. I was a mess and paced the floor, looking for last minute things to tidy up. Kova would be here soon and I needed to calm my racing heart and steady my hands.

I told him I'd meet him downstairs, but he said he had something for me and asked if he could come up. There was no way I would tell him no, so now I was waiting—

My heart dropped into my gut when I heard the knock. I wiped my palms down my distressed jeans and walked toward the door. God, I was so nervous that I could feel my heart beating in my throat. Heat broke out over my skin in anticipation. The closer I got, sharp knots twisted in my stomach.

Reaching for the door, I took a deep breath and unbolted the lock to welcome him in.

Kova turned around to face me and I felt a fissure along my ribs.

Oh, God. I couldn't handle it. My heart was on fire, and all these emotions I'd slept on were climbing to the surface again. He looked like shit. There were dark circles under his lackluster eyes like he hadn't slept since he left here.

Before I could think better of it, I closed the distance and stepped into Kova. His arms immediately wound around my body and hugged me to him. My eyes closed feeling his warmth surrounding me. I heard something drop behind me but I didn't bother looking. Not when Kova held me like he needed me.

"Adrianna," he whispered in pure agony.

I pressed my face into the column of his neck and squeezed my eyes shut. Kova tightened his arms and I savored the feeling. I wasn't sure I could do it.

"Tell me I'm making a bad decision," I said, breaking down. "Tell me I'm being stupid."

Kova pulled back and looked into my eyes. He came in and shut the door. The back of his hand brushed over my cheek. My lips trembled. His eyes were glossy and rimmed with a tint of pink. The facial hair helped hide the hollowness of his jaw. Kova was in a much worse state than the other night. I didn't know how I was going to get through another second knowing he wasn't mine anymore, and I wasn't his.

"I think it is a terrible fucking decision. The absolute worst you have ever made." His voice was raw. "But you made the right decision," he whispered, sounding like he was on the verge of cracking.

I released a ragged breath. Kova reached for my side braid and ran his thumb down the fishtail design. I wanted desperately to reach out and touch him again. I ached to, because later today I'd be hundreds of miles away and wouldn't be able to.

"Your hair has gotten so long," he said. I think it was more to himself.

"I'd cut it to my shoulders if it wasn't so thin now."

I was quiet, reflecting. His eyes flashed to mine. Kova liked my hair.

"I used to think my hair gave me headaches." He looked at me in confusion. "It was so heavy when I tied it up in a knot. I thought it was giving me raging headaches from the weight and pull of the rubber band. Now I know it was the lupus because I never wear my hair up anymore for that reason and my head still pounds."

Kova wrapped the braid around his fist and gave it a gentle tug. The corners of my mouth twitched at his playfulness. I lifted my gaze to his and my knees almost buckled.

The distance and raw emotion in his eyes choked me up.

His regret tore at my heart.

His desperation and hunger ran along my skin and sunk into every pore.

Kova was drawn. Lost. I felt him dying inside at the knowledge there was nothing we could do to save us. His defeat stripped me bare. It overrode who he was as a person, and that was upsetting. I didn't want to lose him.

Helplessly, he dropped my braid. "I wanted to give you something before you left."

I wiped my eyes, then dried my palms on my thighs as Kova retrieved the bag he brought in. I'd forgotten about it and realized that was the sound I heard behind me when we hugged.

Kova walked over and placed it on the kitchen counter, then reached inside. Once I got home from the Olympics, I hadn't been able to wear the necklace and bracelet set he'd given me for my birthday since Dad and Sophia were often around. I didn't want them to question me, or worse, take it away. I packed it first and told myself that once I was settled in Oklahoma I would never take it off.

I gasped and covered my mouth when my eyes landed on our spiral bound notebook. A memory flashed through my mind and I stifled a sad chuckle.

"Why did you laugh?"

I looked up at him. "Do you remember when I had this idea and what you said to me?" A crease lined the space between his brows. "You said it was the worst idea and you didn't want to do it."

His eyes flashed and he gave me a lopsided grin. He remembered.

My heart was thumping at the sight of it, wondering who'd had their dirty hands on it and read our personal letters. These words were ours, and ours alone. It upset me thinking someone read the personal thoughts I fought so hard to get from Kova.

"Where did you find it?" I asked. I hadn't seen it in months, not since Katja stole it and did who knows what with it.

"I got it back from Katja."

My skeptical eyes lifted to his. "What did you have to do to get it?"

He lowered his gaze. "Before I left here the other day, you said something that stuck with me. You said our love makes you sicker."

My jaw trembled and my nostrils flared trying to hold in my emotions. I had regretted saying that immediately after it left my mouth.

"You are right," Kova said quietly, like it was final, and that filled me with dread. "Our love does make you sicker. I hate myself for it because I know I am a huge part in that." He shook his head, struggling to finish. "That was it. It really hit me just how sorry I am for what I put you through when I married her. I broke you."

I moved closer to him, but he stepped back and put his hand up. I frowned.

"You didn't break me. I'm still here."

He lifted his eyes to mine. "I broke you that day, and you were not the same for a long time afterward." My heart ached hearing him confess his most private thoughts. "Regardless, you will never understand how sorry I am for what I did. I thought I lost you for good and made it my mission to fix it. I wish I could void out that part of my life like it never happened." Kova paused, his eyes were glistening. "But then I wonder if we would be where we are now…" His voice trailed off. "So, when I left here yesterday, I picked up a bottle of vodka on my way home and started to pack her things once I got there."

"Kova, you left early in the morning."

He gave me a knowing look. "I was drunk all day." I chuckled sadly under my breath, and he continued. No wonder he looked like shit when I opened the door. "To be completely transparent, I felt bad for her and thought giving her time was fair. I thought I was doing the right thing for both of you. The situation is not so easy to walk away from and start over. Katja and I have a lot of history. I did her wrong, she did me wrong." He paused, then finally handed me our notebook. "There is no reason for her to live with me, even if we are in the process of a divorce, not if it means I am going to lose you forever. You mean too much to me to chance that. I did not mean to upset you with that decision. I was just trying to do right."

My chest was hollow. "Kova—"

"No, let me finish."

I closed my mouth and my shoulders drooped. He was so resolute in us that fresh tears streamed down my cheeks. The dark circles under his eyes now had a cause. He'd been relentless in his pursuit of us. I think I loved him more for that.

"I packed up everything in the bedroom she slept in. I got her a hotel room for two weeks, then I changed my locks and froze her accounts. Katja has plenty of cash and can afford it, or she can make the bastard who got her pregnant pay." Kova glanced away and ran his tongue over his bottom lip. "They were planning to blackmail me and use our affair against me to get what they wanted."

My brows rose as fury flowed through my veins. I was stunned into silence. How heartless of them. I didn't have a leg to stand on, but I was not a vindictive person either.

Kova didn't care about money. He probably would've given her anything she asked for because he was guilty himself and that sickened him. He'd struggled with us until I pushed him to snap. With help from Joy, all Katja focused on was revenge. It was easy when someone was whispering in their ear the whole time.

"I learned their plans shortly after I was released." Kova paused, then said, "I know you are skeptical when it comes to Katja, but I need you to know I am no longer living with her."

My brows lowered. He was right. I did feel a different way when it came to Katja and how he treated her. I wasn't sure I could ever let go of those feelings unless he was completely separated from her and they never spoke again.

"How did you manage to do all of this so quickly? What about World Cup? Please tell me you didn't do anything drastic."

He looked right at me and said, "I told you I was going to accept Danilo's offer. Madeline and Danilo are a good team and kept the gym running smooth."

CHAPER 56

ears welled in my eyes.

"Why would you do that? That gym means so much to you. I wish you hadn't."

World Cup was his everything. It was his second home. Where he was himself. It made me sick to think he'd sold it for me.

Kova shook his head vehemently, though his inconsolable gaze didn't match the tone in his words.

"Enough. I am not talking about it anymore. It is done and contracts have been signed. The gym is not worth more than you." With a jut of his chin, Kova gestured toward our notebook. "Take that. All the pages are intact."

My thumb dragged down the silver spirals thinking back to the day we started this. I flipped through and the pages fanned out. I caught the faint sent of Kova in them and I drew in a quiet breath. I held the book close to my chest and my eyes closed. There were so many memories in these pages that I wanted to hold on to forever.

"Thank you."

Kova reached into the bag and pulled out something wrapped in black tissue paper with scotch tape all over it like it was a decoration. He flipped it over and there was an envelope attached to it. Taped down, of course. My lips twitched.

"I do not know how to wrap," he said, self-conscious of his wrapping skills.

My brows shot up as Kova handed it to me. "You have a gift for me?"

He gave a blasé shrug. I glanced down and eyed the white envelope. I reached for it, but Kova stopped me.

He massaged the back of his neck. "There is, ah, a letter I wrote for you. I wrote it the other day. Do not open that now"—he pointed to the black tissue paper—"or read the card. Open it when you are settled…in."

He couldn't even finish the words. I choked up inside and looked away, letting out a breath.

"Do you want me to call you after I do?" I asked.

A shadow passed through his eyes that made my stomach flutter nervously. It was short-lived, but I'd caught it, and I didn't like what I saw.

"Just read it first."

I shifted on my feet. "I feel like you don't have anything of mine to hold onto now."

Kova's green eyes glittered under the bill of his hat. He placed his hand over his heart, right where the A was that I'd carved.

"I have what I need…for now."

A blush crept up my cheeks. I averted my gaze, more eager to read his letter.

I was so touched by his thoughtfulness. "This notebook means a lot to me. I looked forward to your letters. It was one of the few ways you'd tell me what you were thinking. I used to reread them at night. Sometimes I would laugh, like when you said you loved cotton candy. Other times I'd cry a little reminiscing, or just feel bad. I hated that this disappeared. I didn't think I'd see it again. Thank you for getting this back. Do you think Katja shared it with anyone?"

"She did not show anyone. Trust me on that."

"Why are you so sure?"

"Because she was hysterical over what I had written for you when I had not once shared myself like that with her. I did not speak to her the way I spoke to you." He paused. "She was humiliated and swore she did not have it in her to show anyone. I believed her."

My heart was racing so damn fast.

Avery was right.

I wanted to cave right now and say fuck the consequences and do anything I could to be with him, but I couldn't do that.

"Do we have time? I have one more thing for you. This one you can open."

I blinked and checked the time over the stove. "Yeah, we have a little more time."

Kova reached into the bag again, this time retrieving a black velvet square box. He studied it for a moment, his thumb stroking over the top.

"I wanted to give you this at the Olympics, but the timing did not feel right."

I flinched. My heart hadn't recovered from that night yet. Kova looked at me like he wanted to say something. Instead, he placed a quick kiss to the top of my head then handed me the box.

My heart was fluttering wondering what else he gave me. I shot him a half smile then lifted the top to reveal a thin chain with the five Olympic gold rings clasped together. My lips parted in awe and I gasped. "Kova," I whispered. Tears welled in my eyes. The charm was positioned off center so the symbol would rest over my left collarbone. The pad of my finger grazed the shiny metal as I stared at the circles.

I tilted my head up and sadness clouded his features. I blinked a few times. "It's so beautiful."

"May I?" he asked. I nodded.

He stepped closer and bent over, squinting his eyes. "I did not want you to mark up your skin. At least, I hope that you do not. I thought this was a better alternative." He released the necklace from its holder then placed the box on the counter next to us.

I smiled to myself remembering how I had once told him I hoped to have a tattoo like his one day. That felt like ages ago.

Kova stepped behind me. I lifted my braid and felt him exhale across the back of my neck. He raised the necklace and laid it over my chest. His fingers shook as he clasped it together.

Kova arranged the necklace then placed his hands on my shoulders. I peered down. My skin was creamier than usual from lack of sun and it caused the gold to stand out. His fingers splayed down the chain and grazed the delicate symbol that lay near the slant on my neck.

"Seeing you up there was the best day of my life," he said.

I swallowed thickly and my stomach clenched. I would forever hold this moment close to me. He had his set of rings, and now I had mine.

Leaning back against his chest, Kova slid his arms around my hips to embrace me. He pulled me to him and his large body engulfed mine. His arms were my security.

"Are we really going to do this?" I asked, my voice shaky.

I scooted closer and turned slightly to the side, resting my head on his bicep that was the perfect height as a pillow. I pressed my face into his arm and inhaled softly. We folded into each other and held on tight. My heart filled with warmth. He smelled like home. Kova leaned down and placed a kiss to my cheek.

Kova had once said there was no Kova without Ria, but the truth was there was no Ria without Kova.

Neither one of us had truly been living until we connected with each other. I'd taught him how to find true happiness, and he'd showed me how strong I could be. He'd prepared me for the battle I would soon face, and I was ready.

"Thank you for the necklace. I like your idea much better."

"I had it custom made. It is engraved underneath."

My eyes widened. I leaned forward to look, but he tugged me back. "Look at it later," he whispered. "Stay with me a little longer."

A soft smile tipped my lips. I nestled into Kova and absorbed his essence when it dawned on me. "What if I hadn't made it to the Olympics?"

"I had something else picked out for making the National team, but once I knew you were chosen for the Olympic team, I rushed the order."

"I love it so much," I said, my voice throaty. "I'll never take it off."

Kova kissed the space under my ear, his nose grazing my cheek. After a few last moments together, his next words twisted my stomach with instant nausea.

"Let us get your luggage."

I tensed, tightening my grip on him. My heart started to pound. His raw voice wreaked havoc on my heart. Tears instantly rose to my eyes and I squeezed them shut. I sniffled and anxiety swelled in my throat.

After a few moments I finally responded, and Kova dropped his arms.

Inhaling a deep breath, I walked to get my belongings. I'd only lived here for a couple of years, yet these walls held enough memories to last a decade. I wished I could take them with me.

I turned off the lights and my knees weakened. This was getting more and more real and I was beginning to question if I could actually go through with it or not. I loved him with all my heart.

Walking back into the living room, I found Kova near the front door. He had my World Cup duffle bag over his shoulder and my large rolling suitcase in one hand. He extended his arm and I faltered in my steps and stopped walking.

I stood across from him and my breathing labored. My chest was spasming in one breath and constricting in the other. Eyes widening, I felt the onset of a panic attack starting. Kova's eyes narrowed and I tensed, feeling the pressure intensify. My fingers flew to my throat and I was instantly scared. I tried to push against it with a slow pull of oxygen and it only backfired. Lips parting, I stared at Kova, trying to swallow and I couldn't.

Kova dropped my bag and stalked over to me. He grabbed my upper arm and yanked me to him. I gasped and my chest expanded right before he gripped the back of my neck and slammed his lips to mine. His hard kiss was intended to snap sense into me, and he instructed me to breathe as he let go of my arm and wrapped his around the small of my back. His fingers loosened on my neck.

I listened, steadying myself.

Kova gave me one more kiss and reached for my hand, tugging me behind him. "I love you. Now let us go."

I locked up my condo for the last time.

Timing, man. It loved to fuck with me.

CHAPER 57

Walking down the hallway, Kova pressed a quick kiss to my shoulder.

I leaned into him and placed my other hand on the fold of his elbow. He kissed the top of my head as we made our way toward the elevator together.

I had a gut feeling he was scared himself despite trying to seem like he had it under control. Kova kept me glued to his side and kept giving me little kisses.

Neither one of us spoke while we walked to his car. Once my luggage had been stored away, Kova opened the passenger door for me. I turned to thank him, but he was purposely looking elsewhere. He blinked, noticing me but still didn't look. I pulled back, feeling the pinch in my heart sharpen until I saw that his eyes were glossy.

I didn't say anything and took my seat.

The drive to the airport was exceptionally quiet. We didn't waste the time talking. We laced our fingers together over his console and I rested my head on his arm as he drove the forty-five minute distance. He kept his gaze on the road the entire time. I couldn't see his eyes behind his sunglasses, but I noticed the harsh lines around his mouth.

Time passed too quickly and we were exiting the highway.

"You can do the drop off so it's easier for you," I suggested.

"I will park."

My stomach cramped. I had a feeling he was going to say that. I wanted him to park, but I also didn't.

It took no time to park and check in my suitcase. Kova took my hand and didn't let go. We walked into the terminal and checked the departing times. Kova looked at his watch then looked over my head. He read the signs, then he took a step and I followed.

It was funny how emotions worked. Kova and I knew there was no point in trying to make light of our situation with feeble talk.

There was nothing either of us could say that would bring even an ounce of comfort. The fact was the end result wouldn't change. I was still leaving.

I eyed the escalator knowing Kova couldn't go with me past that point.

The closer we got to it, the warmer my blood heated. My heart viciously attacked my ribs. I watched the moving stairs climb and realized I didn't want to do this.

I was going to be sick.

Kova tugged me toward an empty luggage area. He dropped my duffle bag then turned toward me and cupped my face, encasing us under the lip of his hat. My hands automatically slid under his arms to hug him tight.

My emotions were already elevated and they broke the moment Kova pressed his body to mine. Tears seeped from my eyes as he swept a kiss across my mouth. His lips were damaging, and his fingers wrapped around the sides of my head and gripped me. I drew in air through my nose and fisted his shirt in my hand. He didn't want to say goodbye.

Kova ripped away, his eyes pierced my heart and his voice held me hostage.

"Understand something, Adrianna." A soft whimper escaped my lips. "I will come for you."

I was shattered.

Completely shattered inside.

I never thought we would come to this. Nodding, my jaw trembled in his palms. I wanted to make him promise he would come for me.

Drawing in a breath, my words shook as I cried softly. "I wish things were different and you were coming with me."

He didn't respond. He couldn't. Tears blurred my vision again. I glanced over my shoulder at the escalator. Once I stepped on, there was no turning back. Knowing I was running out of time, I started to panic.

I looked back at him. "You said you sold the gym. Come with me," I whispered.

"No, *Malysh*."

My heart sank. Kova's eyes shifted back and forth over mine. I'd seen him suffer in the past, but nothing compared to how he was now. He was bleeding love and drowning in it…like me.

"You are going alone."

"But you said you sold the gym," I said, a cross between a beg and a whimper.

My eyes filled with fresh tears and his gaze softened. Heat bloomed in my cheeks from the blood pumping through my veins. I was scared to leave him. Scared to leave us. Scared to go on this journey alone. Scared I'd get too sick to live with him.

"Come with me," I begged. "Please."

Clenching his eyes shut, a low growl pushed through his chest.

"I'm scared I'll never see you again," I said, baring my heart. "And if I do, what if you've moved on?"

Kova slammed his mouth to mine and plunged his tongue between my lips. He let go of my face and hauled me to him. He said I love you without breaking the kiss. His fingers grasped my braid, twisting it as he deepened our love.

My heart dropped.

I knew what this was.

This was a goodbye kiss.

Kova was kissing me goodbye.

Unleashing his emotion, Kova kissed me ruthlessly, passionately, all him. There was no shame in his fiery strokes that stormed my mouth. I fell into him, and released a sigh savoring this moment.

Kova severed the kiss and shoved me away. I stumbled back, stilling in shock. My jaw fell open and I stared at him, unblinking.

All I could hear was the sound of my heart beating in my ears.

No.

"This is not over, Adrianna. It will never be over between us."

I shook my head vehemently and ran to him. Kova caught me, but he didn't let me speak.

"This is only goodbye for now," he said.

A breath hitched in my throat. Kova's lips were on mine again, and I knew in my heart it was the last one.

He broke the kiss again and took a step back.

Tears were flowing from my eyes. I couldn't stop crying.

This was it.

He was leaving, and so was I.

"No." I panicked and ground my teeth together. My feet carried me to him. "I'm not ready to leave yet. I just need a little more time."

Reaching up, Kova brushed a loose lock of hair behind my ear, his knuckles grazing my cheek. He eyed me with empathy. One corner of his mouth quirked up and his eyes glistened with unshed tears. I stepped closer, needing to feel his body pressed to mine one last time.

"My dearest *Malysh*," he said with the utmost affection. "I love you, and I will always love you. Do not ever forget that."

My lungs ached for air. My heart was a burning stone in my gut making my knees weak. Any second, I was going to crumble to the floor.

Kova held me close and our lips met one final heartbreaking time.

We pulled apart. Kova threw his hands in the air and spoke something under his breath that I didn't catch. My eyes caught the subtle shake in his fingers. He placed his fist to his mouth, his eyes pleading for me to go.

My face slowly fell as his response settled over me.

He wanted me to leave. No—he needed me to leave.

"Go, Adrianna. Just remember I am coming for you. And once I have you, I will never let you go again. That is a promise I intend to keep."

I liked his challenge.

Kova gestured with his head to the area behind me. We were standing across the room from the escalator.

"Leave, Adrianna."

CHAPER 58

t was on the tip of my tongue to ask him to walk me to the escalator.

I didn't. After all, I was doing this for me, and that meant I had to walk away on my own.

Bending down, I picked up my duffle bag and placed it over my shoulder. I blinked my eyes rapidly trying to stop the tears. His chest rose and fell and his hands were clenched, hanging at his sides.

My heart, how it ached for him. We were saying goodbye. Did he even realize he was giving me the strength I needed to walk away? He was the push I needed to keep going, the firm voice and bold eyes encouraging me to be better.

I inhaled a deep breath and turned around. Each step I took, I drew in a quick breath—faster, harder, tighter. I thought about my decision one last time and if this was what I wanted. I looked inside myself, really questioning what I truly wanted.

It was so easy to convince myself that I was making the right decision by leaving for Oklahoma, but in this moment it was so fucking hard to stay positive. A part of me knew I needed to leave, yet the other part wanted Kova to take me back home and never let me go.

Swallowing thickly, I gripped the railing and stepped onto the lifting stair. I turned to look over my shoulder to find the man who held every part of me in the palm of his hands.

There was an emptiness in my heart the moment our eyes connected. A real void that only he could fill. Cold, hollow, damp. Soft tears streamed down my flushed cheeks. I couldn't believe this was really it.

I didn't care if he saw me crying, or anyone else for that matter. Gymnastics had taught me so much through the years that transformed me into the person I was now.

I learned self-discipline at a young age, and that money couldn't buy everything.

As an early teen, I had discovered that I needed an abundance amount of patience to accomplish a dream.

The deeper I got into the sport, I'd decided how to receive criticism and if I was going to use it in a constructive manner or cause me to crumble.

My goal had drained me, pulled tears from my eyes, and ripped back layers and layers of my skin to prove a point. But it had never made me second-guess myself. I never questioned if I couldn't handle something. It was where I discovered how strong of a person I really was.

There was so much more to gymnastics than how many back flips somebody could do.

I went to Kova for one reason, one goal. I had a dream, and he said I was going to fight for it. He showed me how to thrive and conquer, that giving up wasn't in my vocabulary because you don't just challenge your body with a dream, but you challenge your mind too. He taught me that a little fear was okay, but to always trust in myself. I came to Kova with a dream of going to the Olympics, and he gave it to me. The least I owed him was unveiling my true emotions and not hiding myself from him.

Now our time was over.

Halfway up the stairs, I clung to the railing harder, and Kova pressed a tight fist to his mouth again. I was about to go out into the world on my own, taking what I'd learned from the sport that had captured my heart as a kid. Kova dropped his head for a spilt second then looked back at me. I knew that look in his eyes all too well. He'd reached his point of no return and was already succumbing to the darkness in him that made him who he was. He fought it while I embraced that part of him and drew it out. He'd fight it now too until he couldn't anymore. Kova was an emotive man who deeply ached to express love and feeling with someone who he truly connected with. I was that person.

Our gazes never wavered the higher I went. We were too afraid to look away, not wanting to break the connection.

Stepping blindly onto the platform when I reached the top, I slowly walked in the direction of my gate, still watching him through blurry eyes.

Kova stayed where he was, rooted to the ground and fixated on me. We only saw each other, and all I could hear was the roaring sound of my heartbeat in my ears the further I got away from him.

Kova's lips parted and my heart plummeted as he took one step in front of him only to stop.

This was too much.

My jaw trembled and my teeth clamped down on my lower lip as his head dropped between his shoulders and he faced the floor. He couldn't stomach to see me walk away.

Gripping my duffle bag strap in search of courage, I turned and stared straight ahead, letting the tears fall freely in waves. There was no way to disguise the pain of losing a loved one and I wasn't going to even try. I was going to let myself feel every emotion to remember that this was real and it would never be forgotten. I was leaving someone I loved behind. There was no reason to shut the door on those feelings.

Kova was as devastating as a tornado.

A quiet sob escaped my lips. I puckered my mouth together.

I thought back to the first time I saw him again as a teenager at World Cup, how he stole my attention and took my breath away. We were inevitable then and we didn't even know it.

Kova had supported me and pushed me to be better than the day before. He believed in me and showed me how to succeed with the right skills, not just in the gym but in life. Even on my worst days when I wanted to give up, he encouraged me to do more, try more, knowing if I didn't give it my all, I'd regret it. He was the flame to the fuel in my veins. He saw the drive in me and ignited it.

Blinking my eyes, I felt a fresh need course through my body.

A new goal sprang to life.

It would be the riskiest one yet.

I was my new goal, and my incentive to thrive would be Kova. It was going to hurt so good.

That was how I was going to view us—a risk worth taking while I got better, healthier. Because I would. I refused any other outcome. I wasn't going to let lupus and kidney disease steal me any more than I already had, not when I had a lot of life in me left to live.

I took a seat near my gate away from people and placed my duffle bag on the floor near my feet. I reached inside and pulled out the gift wrapped in black tissue paper with the envelope attached to it.

I carefully tore off the envelope and accidently pulled back some of the tissue paper. The scent of his cologne bled from the paper as I slipped his note out of the envelope and unfolded it.

Sniffling back the last of my tears, I wiped my eyes with the back of my hand.

My Dearest Malysh,

I was scared to want you. I still am.

Damn it. Fresh tears instantly filled my eyes.

Do not feel bad for the decision you have made. Even though it kills me, I do not regret a fucking thing. Every moment with you was worth having all the way until now, even the bad. If that was all the time I was allotted with you, then I will die a happy man. I hope it is not, though. I hope that when your mind wanders to the past, you think of us and the connection we made. I hope our goodbye opens a door for us to spend a lifetime together. This separation is one of many boulders for us to overturn. I want to be the one to help you lift them when times are tough, but I understand why you want to do it alone. After all, your fight is what I love about you.

You were right to leave.

When I came to your hotel room on the night after the meet I had pulled you from, it was then that I started to write about us every single day. What you made me feel, what you were going through, how I saw you through my eyes. Your strengths, my weaknesses. Our ups and downs. How I learned you were sick and keeping it from me. When I realized I loved you, and how I knew you loved me before you said it.

I smiled at that. I'd only allowed myself to love him in the dark until I couldn't hide anymore.

It is all there in my journal. Every thought, every feeling, they are yours.

I gasped, my hand flying to my mouth to cover it. Tears welled in my eyes. Kova gave me his private journal.

Read one page a day, no more.

Our time is not over, Malysh, but it is for now.

Ya lyublyu tebya vsegda I naveki.

X

Kova

I smiled sadly to myself and felt a fresh tear slip down my cheek. That was the first time he'd signed his name.

Taking out my cellphone from my bag, my screen lit up with the picture of us from that night in the hotel room. It felt like ages ago but the feelings came rushing back as if it happened yesterday. I decided to send him the picture.

He'd know why I'd sent it.

I shouldn't have thrown away my burner phone. Oh well. If my dad was monitoring my messages, let him see it. What was the worst that could happen at this point? I was leaving.

Just as I was about to slip my phone back into my bag, it dinged. I slid the screen open with my heart in my throat and grinned at Kova's response.

A black heart emoji.

I rolled my lips between my teeth and tasted my salty tears. It was so Kova, and I loved that.

Something happened when Kova came along. He changed me for the better, he gave me strength and helped me see my worth, even if it was a struggle at times. He also hurt me more times than I wanted to count, but I wasn't going to focus on moments that would only harden my heart.

The way we understood love started with pain. Our love story wasn't an easy one, so our ending wouldn't be either.

There were no hearts and rose petals about it, no white picket fence and butterflies. No children. No happy ending. But it was raw, it was real, and it was ours. It was tragically beautiful. No one could take that from us.

I didn't think either of us realized how deeply intertwined we truly were until we had to go our separate ways.

It was utterly devastating.

3 ... 2... 1... Happy New Year!"

The small crowd in the student center went wild. I huddled in the corner, regretting letting my teammates rope me into coming. I still had months before I could join them in the gym and competitions, but the coaches had thought it would be a good idea to come on board now and build the camaraderie. It turned out to be a good thing and had helped to occupy my mind for a while. I didn't have that team bond with them yet since I hardly knew them, but it felt nice to be included. It was a good start.

Avery knew what New Year's Eve meant to me and who I thought about.

I'd flown home for three days to spend the holidays with my family. Avery flew back with me the day after Christmas and has been here ever since to support me. Three days was all I could handle knowing I was in close proximity to him. The temptation was too strong to see him. There wasn't a doubt in my mind I would have borrowed Dad's car to drive south.

"Happy New Year, bestie!" Avery said excitedly, wrapping her arms around my shoulders. I pulled back and forced a smile on my face. "Still thinking about him?" I nodded solemnly, dropping the phony smile.

"Do you think he thinks about me as much as I think about him?" I asked, my voice small. Sometimes I wished I didn't think of him as much as I did.

"I do." She nodded. "He can't not be thinking of you," she said.

"Really?"

"Yes," Avery said, and I actually believed her. "I think it's as hard for him as it is for you."

I hoped so. This was agony.

Not incorporating gymnastics into my daily routine was a tough adjustment. Same with not incorporating him. I knew it would be hard, especially while going through dialysis. Just not this kind of hard. I reminded myself daily that this wasn't forever and that I would go back to the sport that I loved with every fiber in my body soon. I would take what I learned from him and apply it. Fortunately, I had the absolute best friend in the world by my side even if she was living states away. Like Avery had said, "I'm only a phone call away." And she was.

"I'm going to miss you when you leave," I said, pouting. "Who's going to braid my hair and read sex scenes with me out loud?"

We giggled. I'd convinced Avery to read a romance novel a few months ago and the rest was history. She said boys were better in books. I agreed. Even though we both loved the steamy scenes, her way of putting a smile on my face was to narrate a book while I was at dialysis. She had come to three sessions with me and my cheeks bloomed with heat. It was the three best sessions I'd had.

After I'd arrived in Oklahoma a little over a year ago, Dad and Sophia had flown in to help me unpack and get settled. Sophia ended up staying then for close to a month. I'd initially wanted to go at it on my own, but after my first few dialysis treatments, I had to admit it was nice to have her help. Once I'd felt confident I could make it to treatments and care for myself afterward, she returned home to Georgia. We spoke and texted all the time. Truth be told, the month she'd spent here was exactly what we'd needed to work on our bond. I was really happy to have a mom who wanted me. There was a part of me that longed to be able to say my mom was my best friend.

As the New Year's celebrations continued, I wanted to creep toward the exit and drop the empty smile from my face. All day I'd reminisced on the past, and as the day had drawn to an end, my veins had filled with a vibrating need for the one person who wasn't here. I hadn't heard from him since the day I left. He'd said he'd come for me, and while I desperately wanted him to, I was partially relieved he hadn't yet.

Avery left a couple of days later and I already missed her so much. Some days, like today, were lonely. I didn't regret my decision to move here, but it wasn't easy either. Life lessons and growing up and all that jazz.

I retrieved a bottle of water from the refrigerator and took a sip as I sorted through the mail I'd left on the counter earlier. I smiled at the postcard Avery had sent from Florida.

Working on my holiday tan in the sun. How's the snow?

She could be such a brat. Avery wasn't a fan of the cold weather and almost bailed after she arrived here. Apparently Oklahoma had one of those rare cold fronts where it felt like negative three degrees. She said she wasn't built for cold, and I'd have to agree that I wasn't either. However, it was where I felt I needed to be.

I flipped the grocery ads aside and revealed a padded yellow envelope. My brows furrowed wondering who had my address and what I received.

Turning it over, my heart stilled at the familiar writing on the label. Chills raked down my arms. My stomach twisted into knots and I sat on the stool before my legs went out from under me.

It had been sixteen months since I last had any form of contact with him. I'd counted.

I had zero shame.

Quickly, I tore open the package and saw three journals inside. Lips parting on a gasp, I pulled them out along with a letter attached to the top one. Each journal was wrapped in black tissue paper bound with a green sticker that reminded me of his eyes.

My Dearest Malysh,

Enclosed is my soul.

X

Kova

With shaking hands, I lifted the first journal and lost myself in his words.

It started from the day I left.

He wrote about his divorce process, my dad dropping the charges against him, selling World Cup… He was raw and honest, and I found myself tearing up every few pages. I missed him every day, but I never realized I missed him this much until I stayed up all night reading the journals. At times the pages were filled with his dark thoughts or ramblings that I couldn't make sense of. I gathered he'd had copious amounts of vodka those days when he penned his feelings. Still, I savored them. They were his thoughts, ones I begged him for when I was in Georgia. I would take what I could get. It was a little view inside his head and I was grateful for it. My heart ached and relief flooded through me. He still loved me. He hadn't come for me yet, but he still loved me. I was somewhat okay knowing that.

The second journal turned slightly personal. I cried a lot.

> I do not know who I am without her here. I thought things would smooth over once the divorce proceedings began, but they have not. It has only worsened. I miss her and I do not know how to handle these thoughts raging through my head without her to talk to me. It is painful. Strange enough, she could look at me and know my head was filled with chaos and iron it out for me. She would push, half the time I hated it, but I always felt better when I spoke to her. If only I realized that then.

> I need her more than anything in the world, but I know I cannot have her. It is not right, but fuck, I am dying inside without her. I want to run to her and take her in my arms and never let her go. They say you do not know what you have until it is gone, and now I understand that sentiment more than ever. I never should have let her leave.

> What a fucking mess my head is.

> I am alone, stuck in this house with the walls closing in on me. I want to burn it to the ground and leave. I should go back to Russia.

> I hate Russia. It is too far from her.

> I have nowhere to go, and yet all I want to do is runaway and leave.

> Everywhere I look, I think of her. I see her. I smell her. I wish I did not. She is hundreds of miles away, yet she feels right here with me.

I lost ~~you~~ her. I feel like I lost ~~you~~ her for good and I do not know how to handle this. I am going out of my mind.

I hate myself for causing her pain. I want to numb myself from feeling. Board up my windows and shut the world out. It is better that way and how I used to live, until her.

Why did she take my black and white world and splash it with color? I wish Frank never called me, and I wish she never stepped foot in my gym. The moment I saw her was a punch to my gut. It is still fresh, like it happened yesterday.

But then I would never have experienced love and laughter. She showed me that. She changed me for the better. I think, anyway. I cannot tell. Did I ever do the same for her?

I hated myself for feeling what I did when I saw her again. She was not a child with pigtails anymore. I was repulsed and sought my therapist immediately. I did everything in my power to keep her at arm's length but the temptation was too much for us to combat. I did not have this reaction to Katja, and I questioned why not so many times until I eventually gave up. I tried with Katja, but my heart was with her. Always with her. After I experienced life with her, there was no going back. I was sold and I desired every second with her.

Some things are not meant to be explained.

She is my other half. That is all, and I will not question it further.

I woke sick to my stomach, reaching for her. It makes no sense since we rarely were able to share a bed, yet it does not matter. I know what I feel and what I want. I need to touch her to know she is real and what we have is real. This gnawing feeling in my stomach that she needs me will not go away. I keep thinking I am going to see her, then I wake up and reality hits me. Does she need me?

Fuck this, I am going.

No, I cannot. I said I would give her time, and that is a promise I planned to keep.

FUCK. I want to fight for her now and show her we need each other. She stood by my side when I needed her the most. I should be by her side as she begins the hardest journey of her life, and I am not. She does not want me there and I have to respect that.

I let her down.

I have to believe the one thing I did right was let her go. I tell myself that often.

But the truth is, she is stronger than me. She said goodbye.

She let me go. For her. If that is not strength, I do not know what is.

I love her more for it.

Frank may have dropped the charges, but that does not change a thing. He and I will never be the same. There is no friendship, no acquaintance. Nothing. We are strangers.

Does it bother me? Yes, it does. Immensely. I want to rectify it, but I know there is not a single thing in the world I can do or say to fix this. I am not looking for friendship or forgiveness. I am not sure what I want from him. He was a good friend, and I ruined the bond between us. That is not who I am. I let him down, another person who trusted me, and lost faith in me.

Was it worth it? Ten times over. I would do it again in a heartbeat for her without remorse. Only this time it would be ten times better. I would love her harder, prove to her she is my world and that we need each other. I would love her first.

Love, what a finicky thing it is. It made me do things I did not know I could to another person. So many regrets, so many highs. I hate myself.

I guess I want to apologize to Frank for hurting him, but I will never apologize for loving her. And if he asked me if I could go back and change history, I would tell him no.

I guess there would be no reason for Frank and I to talk in the end.

The divorce was finalized and I drank myself into a stupor for a solid week, just like the night I married her. I should have found relief I am no longer tied to Katja, but all I felt was loss. Loss over her, not Katja. I should have said no to Katja from the start, but there were too many forces working against us.

I ruined three lives, and I am still without her. I am no one without her. What is life without her?

Katja had a baby boy. I am glad that

Chaper of my life with her is closed for good.

🤸🏃🤸🏃🤸❔

There is a beast pounding against the walls of my chest desperate to break free. I hear his voice in my head, his negativity is eating away at me. My world is so dark and the vodka does not quell this hunger.

I wish I did not love her as much as I did. I wish I could turn off the feeling. World Cup used to be my safe haven, a place where I could release my stress in the dark and alone. I joined a gym, but a regular gym does nothing for me. Ethan said I should attempt CrossFit, but flipping over a tire does not motivate me. The one thing that has helped has been running as far and as fast as I can until my legs give out.

🤸🏃🤸🏃🤸❔

I am a hostage to my emotions. I fear one day I will not break free from them.

I shut the journal and held it close to my chest, sinking against my headboard of my bed. I closed my eyes and exhaled. There was too much sorrow in his words for my heart to handle another page. I wanted to call him and make sure he was okay, just hear his voice to know and then hang up. But I wouldn't.

The nights were the hardest for me. It was when my mind raced with thoughts and my heart beat a little faster. I wondered if I hurt us both for my decision to leave. I wondered if we could ever come back from this. Sometimes I wished I could fast forward the days and months just to see if it was all worth it in the end. I didn't have this feeling that something wasn't going to happen, I just didn't like the unknown.

CHAPER 60
TWO YEARS LATER

I t was a week into the New Year, and just like the year before, a padded envelope arrived. Only, this time it looked bigger. I rushed into my condo and ripped it open. He'd sent four journals this time.

My Dearest Malysh,

I am a man still in love with someone I have no right to love.

X

Kova

I was so engrossed in his writings that I hadn't noticed two hours had passed. I needed to eat something and take my medication before I was due to meet my personal trainer. I'd started competing again months ago, but these days I didn't push myself in the gym like I used to. My body simply couldn't handle it. Instead, I played it smart and when I felt worn out, I stopped and took a break. Thankfully my coaches were understanding and didn't ridicule me otherwise.

Before I left, I decided to read a few more entries. I couldn't not, knowing I had a long night ahead of me. Even though I'd been taking my training slower than I wanted to, it still wore me out. I knew once I got home I would crash and I wouldn't be reading anything else.

However, that all changed when I picked up the third journal. I canceled my training session, knowing I would be in no position to work out. I wasn't prepared for the way his entries switched from him writing about how he felt and his life, to writing directly to me.

I found myself in a sea of emotion and longing. My chest ached and tears gathered in my eyes as I continued reading his entries.

As you know, I sold World Cup. I cannot even walk inside the gym without thinking of you, despite Madeline and Danilo requesting for me to come back. I have not coached since you left. I cannot bring myself to. It reminds me too much of you. Of us. You are everywhere I look inside of that gym. The day you left you took every part of me with you. I am now an empty shell of a man and nothing more.

I rushed the divorce with Katja because I was afraid of losing you rather than leaving her on my own when I wanted to, before it all came to a head. I made rash decisions when it came to us being together, always assuming I was doing the right thing. I acted out of fear instead of consideration. I know now by doing that, I never truly saw you. It kills me that it has taken me this long to finally grasp what you meant when you wanted me to put us first. I thought I was. I only wish I had understood when you were still here with me.

I know now that I am not half the man I thought I was. You trusted me with your heart, your body, and your soul. You showed me unconditional love, and what did I give you? Nothing. I gave you nothing but painful memories and tears that soaked your pillowcase at night. You must know I have a plan to fix all of the damage I have caused you.

Every day I miss your touch. Every minute I miss hearing your voice. Every second I hold out hope for us.

One thing I refused to miss was your return to the sport that brought us together in the first place, so I came and watched you. I purposely hid from you, but I was there in the stands as you lit up the room with your passion for gymnastics. You only competed on bars and floor. O bozhe, what a sight that was to see you again. I watched you. I watched the people watch you with nothing but awe on their faces. I am so proud of the gymnast you have become. You left a mark on your teammates and the spectators that day, the same way you left your mark on me.

It was then that I realized I needed to fix me before I came for you. What I am saying is, I need to find me too in order to be enough for you. I must work on myself to be a better man. I wish I could have you by my side as I figure out who I am, to help me fight this battle raging inside of me to find the truth, but you have already done so much for me, and if you can do it on your own, then I can too. Do you remember when I told you that you inspire me? That has not changed. Your strength gives me strength. I admire the fuck out of you. I was a wreck when you left, but you leaving was the right decision, and the best thing you could have done, not just for yourself, but for me as well. I am glad you left even though every damn second without you makes for a very lonely, miserable world.

I will come for you, but only when I am the man you need, one you can be proud of. One that will never hesitate to put you or our love first. Until them, I will take the time I need to work on myself to be good enough for you, and then, only then, will I come for you. That is a promise I intend to keep. You were once a reflection of me for a short period of time, but now I want to be a reflection of you for the rest of my life. I will come for you, Malysh. And once I have you, I will never let go. I just pray you accept me and have not lost hope in us before then.

I am a man of many flaws and too many sins to atone for. The regret I live with on a daily basis eats away at me. I pray one day you have it in you to forgive me for how badly I have treated you. I will not make excuses for my behavior. I will own them and face them like a man. We had many odds working against us. I just hope I did not chase you away forever. Please, you must know, it was never my intention to cause you pain. I do not want to lose you. You are my other half, and well, I need you in order to be me. I am not whole without you.

You say I left an indentation on your heart. You have done the same with mine.

I see it every day when I look in the mirror.

It is us against the world. I took you for granted, but I promise you I will never do that again. Please just give me a little more time. If *you send me away when I come, then I will respect your wishes, but I pray that is not the case.*

Until I see you again.

Ya lyublyu tebya vsegda I naveki.

I NEVER CONTACTED HIM AFTER receiving the journals last year, and still I wouldn't contact him after getting these. The ball was in his court. It was his move to make. He'd said he would come, so I would wait for the day he decided to show up.

I think back to his entry of how he felt the decisions he made in moments of fear were right at the time. His regret suffocated me. They were right for him, and maybe a little for me. He shouldn't have regret because I too had made decisions in the moment thinking they were right. It was a sweet-and-sour taste on my tongue. My decision to leave wasn't one made out of fear for him or us…I had done it for me. Okay, maybe a little for us. It was a moment of clarity I knew we both needed. If I had acted in fear, then I would not be in Oklahoma now.

He said he gave me nothing. But he was wrong. He helped give me my dream…and myself.

CHAPER 61
THREE YEARS LATER

I stared up at the screen and awaited my score. My veins filled with electricity and my knees were shaking with adrenaline. My smile was plastered across my face. I'd been competing for two years now, but this was my first televised meet since the Olympics, and I was a ball of nerves. I wanted to prove I still had what it took to be on the team, but it was hard when I knew all eyes were on the girl battling kidney disease and lupus. The support this university, my teammates, and my incredible coaches showed me was invaluable. I competed my heart out. That was my gift to them for what they gave me.

Since officially returning to the sport, my worries were laid to rest once I had sat down with my coaches and we devised a safe plan for me to compete. Committing to Oklahoma was the best decision I ever made. I was iffy when it came to the bigger competitions because I was scared to fail and let my team down. They all reassured me that if they didn't believe in me they wouldn't let me risk it. He'd always told me I shined under pressure, but I didn't have him here with me and I wasn't sure I could pull it off again without his words of encouragement. My new coaches were stellar, I wouldn't complain, but they weren't him.

I glanced toward the crowd. I knew Dad and Sophia were somewhere in the stands. They'd refused to miss this day and booked their flights the moment I was given the schedule for the season. A part of me couldn't help but wonder if he was in the audience too. My heart said he was here.

The crowd cheered, breaking my wayward thoughts. My teammates engulfed me in a hug and tears once again filled my eyes. I was my own worst critic and their support meant the world to me. These women were the best part about joining the gymnastics team.

I looked back up at the screen in disbelief. My vision blurred and my jaw trembled. I scored a nearly perfect score. I couldn't believe it. I wondered if I would ever stop getting emotional over gymnastics.

Shortly before I began training again, I started seeing a therapist once a week. I felt it was something I needed to do in order to stay healthy as a whole. I didn't want to kill myself for a medal, and it was so easy for me to. I was older now, still living with life-threatening illnesses. I wanted to prosper and fly, and I wanted to do that by accepting what I was physically capable of and being okay with it. Reaching out for help didn't mean I was weak like I had once thought. If anything, it made me stronger. My score told me I'd made the right choice.

My coaches high-fived me as I dropped down by my duffle bag to remove my grips. My smile faltered a little, my happiness dimming. I was over the moon with my score, but it just wasn't the same without him here.

IT WAS THE NINTH OF January and I was on edge.

His package should have been here Saturday and it wasn't.

I waited in the lobby by the mailboxes, trying not to pounce on the mailman as he slowly stuffed the slots full. Finally, after an eternity, he closed the metal doors and locked up. And I was right there, opening my assigned box before he even walked away. I rifled through my mail where I stood.

No package.

My heart slipped.

My hope died a little.

Another day went by, and another, and another. The week came to an end and still nothing. I tried to go about my life, putting on a smile for everyone around me when I was crumbling inside. A second week had come and gone, and my misery was replaced with anger. On a whim I opened my messaging app and typed in his name.

ME

> I'm going to assume my journals were lost in the mail.

I waited for his response. After ten minutes, I texted again.

ME

I know you read my message. It says read.

I sent him a screenshot and circled where it said "Read" beneath my message. Within seconds, the little dots appeared on the screen telling me he was typing. I held my breath, hoping he'd send a response the size of the Bible back.

COACH

I do not want to interfere with your life.

I groaned inwardly. Of course, he'd be short with his words.

ME

I can make my own decisions, thank you very much. Now send me my journals, Kova.

ME

I looked forward to the package. I read the journals all the time.

The little dots didn't even appear. My chest ached when he didn't respond. Suffocation clawed at my throat.

ME

I need them. Please. Give them to me.

Still nothing. His lack of response was like a punch to the gut. How could he ignore me? My heart thumped erratically. I tried not to cry, but it was fruitless. My heart still ached for my other half.

ME

They help me. Please.

Another week passed and no texts, or journals in the mail. I tried not to succumb to the darkness. I'd come too far to go backward now—surgery on my Achilles, dialysis a few times a week, balancing my diseases while killing it in the collegiate world of gymnastics and attending school. By all outward appearances I was at the top of my game, but appearances were deceiving. I was good at faking it too.

I was dying inside. I never stopped loving him, but I guess he stopped loving me. That was a hard pill to swallow. He said he would come, and I told myself that I would wait for him. Exhaling, I righted myself.

A couple of my teammates had talked me into attending a party with them tonight. It wasn't something I did normally. I was young, single, why the fuck not go out and act my age for once. I needed to stop dwelling on the package I hadn't received and let go for once in my life.

After an hour or so, I found myself refilling shot after shot of vodka and fending off horny college guys. I had zero desire in interacting with any of them, even in my inebriated state. There was only one person who stirred my blood, and I was drinking his poison.

He said he'd come for me, but he never did. He lied.

My chest rose and fell rapidly. Tears were threatening to spill. I refused to cry and pulled my phone from my back pocket, squinting at the home screen. I pressed the wrong buttons a few times before I found the message icon. I was sure I'd regret this in the morning, but it wasn't morning yet and the alcohol gave me the liquid courage to text him.

ME

I went to a dumb drat part and I drunk and now I hate you. I seriously hate u.

ME

Why did you have to make me fall in love with u.

ME

Where are the jounrals?

ME

Send me MY journals, Konstantinn. You know they are mine.

ME

They were never yours to begin with.

I woke the next morning to banging in my head and a twisted stomach. Immediately I checked my phone, forcing back the bile rising in the back of my throat.

I waited all night for a text. He never responded. Taking my phone, I threw it across the room and let it hit the wall. I fought back the tears and clenched my shaking fingers into fists.

The hangover was a blessing in disguise. It allowed me to forget the aching in my heart. I knew better than to drink, especially on my medication. But I needed one night to cut loose and forget the pain of loving someone from afar.

The banging returned and I shook my head under my pillow. Big mistake. I groaned through the raging migraine I was dealing with, my stomach churning once again. I shot up and ran for the bathroom, making it to the toilet before I was vomiting clear liquid and the Taco Bell I'd consumed before passing out last night. I was never, ever drinking again. Or eating Taco Bell.

After I expelled every last drop I could in my body, I stood up and gargled with mouthwash, then rinsed my face before walking back to my room to crash. I halted in my steps when the pounding returned, and I realized it was coming from the door. My brows furrowed.

Bleary-eyed, I stumbled to answer it. The sooner I could make the noise stop, the faster I could climb back into bed and pass out. I wanted to go back to sleep and pray this was all a dream.

Reaching for the knob and bolt, I opened the door and sobered right up.

Heart instantly racing, my lips parted in absolute shock. I blinked rapidly.

After three years of no calls, no texts, nothing so much as a picture, just yearly journals filled with his thoughts and desires, except for this year, the stupid Russian who'd claimed my heart years ago stood in front of me.

My lips parted further. Tears immediately welled in my eyes.

"*Allo, Malysh.*"

EPILOGUE
THIRTEEN YEARS LATER

KOVA

"Come, Lili. Come to Daddy."

I stayed squatted as I waved my fingers, encouraging her to take a step.

Her chunky bowlegs were apprehensive as she attempted to walk to me for the first time. Drool fell from her toothless smile and plopped on the chalky floor next to her purple toenails. Mia, her older sister, had painted them for her when she was sleeping because she does not ever sit still any other time.

I had four daughters, all gorgeous, just like their mother. And all under the age of six.

I was fucked.

Double fucked.

I was cursed, certain I had pissed someone off in another life. I do not even joke anymore that God was testing me. I knew he was.

Lili picked up her stubby leg. Just like the time before, I held my breath and hoped this would be the first step she took. My knees were screaming in rebellion staying in this position so long, but I held still if that meant seeing her walk.

"Da, Da, Da," she babbled.

More slobber fell to the floor. Lili had a slight Russian accent, but my wife insisted it was just baby speak. I firmly believed she was wrong, and I told her that often. It made her heated and she would argue; she was even more beautiful when she was fired up.

Lili mumbled again, the enunciation in the back of her throat. Totally Russian there and not that American baby speak.

"Yes, Lili, *Da, Da, Da*," I said, heavy on the Russian enunciation.

Lili squealed. She lifted her knee and balanced on one leg, her toes curling into the floor for support. My brows rose and I encouraged her again to take another step, holding my breath. I wiggled my fingers and made a funny face trying to make her come to me. All my daughters have taken their first steps inside our gym. I was hoping Lili would too.

Her cherry chocolate hair was tied up in some messy thing I did for her. She tried to pull it out and whined because she could not accomplish it. I gave her a stern look and she dropped her arms with a pout. My wife had been trying to teach me how to do their hair since Mia was born.

No matter how much I tried, I still could not figure out how to do it without ripping hair out.

Looking at me with massive amber eyes, Lili began to lean too far to the side. I reached out quickly and caught her, making a big splash about it so she would try again. I planted a huge, loud kiss to her cheek. Her eyes twinkled and she giggled as I stood her up again. Lili was the first of our daughters to attempt to walk by eight months. Something told me we were in trouble with this one.

"Lili, come Lili. Come to Daddy, *malyshka*."

She shrieked excitedly then took a step. I held my breath as she placed one foot in front of the other and stayed upright. She hesitated, and I gave her a little push, telling her to keep trying. She did it again and I waved my fingers impatiently just as she took two steps and fell into my arms.

I heard a gasp behind me and quickly turned around, blindly standing Lili up.

My wife. I smiled seeing the happiness written across her face

"Is that my girl walking?" my wife cooed.

I glanced back at Lili and let go, watching as she took three steps this time before falling into her mother's arms with a shriek. She scooped up Lili and held her tight to her chest, right above her growing belly. Lili's fat feet dangled on the sides of her waist.

Our gazes met and my stomach tightened. I will never get over the fact that this beautiful woman was now my wife. How I fucking loved her to the ends of the earth.

Her eyes shimmered up at me and her soft smile made my heart pound.

"*Allo, Malysh*. When did you get here?"

This was my favorite time of the day that I looked forward to after we said our morning goodbyes—when Adrianna brought all of our daughters to gymnastics practice. It was one of the very limited things she could do while being on bed rest. While she should not be doing anything at all, I knew I had to give her something, otherwise she would take the directions lightly and overdo it. She could take the girls to and from school, and she liked to bathe and put them to sleep. That was it.

I reached out to palm Adrianna's belly and stepped close to her with Lili sandwiched between us.

"Just now."

She smiled and rose up on her tiptoes to give me a kiss, but Lili gave her a wet one first. There was slobber all over my wife's cheek and she laughed. My lips twitched seeing her happy.

"Why? Did you miss me?" she asked, and she angled her brows.

"You already left me once, just making sure you were not making another run for it. I never know with you."

Her eyes lit up ready to retaliate and she punched my stomach. I grabbed her hand and held it tenderly. I looked down at her with nothing but love. I do not let her live down the fact that she left me.

My palm skimmed along her pelvis to feel her rounded stomach. Her shirt was too short and showing part of her lower belly. I loved that little space of skin on her. For someone so small, she wore pregnancy extremely well. Adrianna claimed to enjoy being pregnant, and since I loved seeing her grow with my child, it was a win for the both of us.

Breaking apart, Lili rested her head on her mother's shoulder and then placed her thumb in her mouth, twirling hair around her finger.

Though each pregnancy Adrianna glowed more than the previous one, it came with a steep price. I did not want her light to burn out and I was terrified it would. Our growing family was a heavy burden on her body, one I did not wish to keep chancing. We were fortunate enough to have made it this far after several specialists had agreed we most likely would not.

When we were told that Lili's pregnancy was the last her body could handle, Adrianna had cried her eyes out for days. We knew this would come one day. She was not ready and had begged me for one more baby, hoping it would be a boy this time. She did not want that choice to be taken from her again.

She wanted one more chance to give me a son on her terms. Our terms.

I felt we were blessed to have our daughters and I had told her it was not necessary, but Adrianna had this incessant need to defy all odds.

We had argued about it at first. A lot.

Adrianna was the love of my life. We had walked through fire and hell to get here. I had told her she could fight me all she wanted but I was not changing my mind. Call me selfish, I *was* selfish. I wanted her to stay healthy to be with our family. I was not going to lose her for good this time, because I knew I would never survive living this life without her again.

Lili had only been born about two months prior before she went on this emotional tirade. Her hormones were making her crazy. Of course, I could not tell her that. However, I had told her she was being irresponsible and that we had four gorgeous children already and was that not enough for her.

She had slapped me.

The woman *loved* to slap me.

She would not talk to me for a full two weeks, though every night she came to me.

I had tried to put my foot down, but she was adamant. My wife had this endless need to push her body to the limit. It drove me absolutely insane, but I loved her so fucking much that I had eventually caved and we tried for one more baby.

Surprisingly, it had not taken long to conceive.

Adrianna loved to remind me it was meant to be and the reason why it had happened so easily.

I wanted to give Adrianna the world, not hold it back from her. I felt like she was taking a huge risk every time we conceived, but it was hard to say no to her when I knew all she wanted was a big family.

Our doctors were confident she could carry to term one last time, but she was still labeled as high-risk.

As I approached the golden age, I had this constant fear inside of me that something was going to happen to her and my kids. It consumed me. They were little spitfires who took after their mother, and they were my world. I was already wrapped around their boney little fingers, which was why I planned to keep them locked up until at least thirty-five. No public schools. No cell phones. No boyfriends. Adrianna laughed every time I brought it up because she thought I was kidding, but I really was not. I could already feel my blood pressure rising just thinking about who I would have to fight off. It almost made me feel bad for being with Adrianna when she was so young.

Almost. Not entirely.

"Where are the rest of the—"

Before I could finish, Mia, Svetlana, and Nastia came barreling into the gym, running straight for me in a race of who could get to me first. Squatting down again, my knees popped and Ria winced at the sound. I opened my arms as Lili squealed behind me at seeing her three sisters.

"Daddy!" I heard about eight times in the span of three seconds right before they plowed into my chest.

I pretended to fall back on the floor, and they giggled in response, falling over me dramatically. I glanced above their little heads at Adrianna. Our eyes met and she smiled down at me. I loved the sound of our girls' high-pitched laughs. It did shit to my heart that I could not explain and made this life that much sweeter. Leaning my head up, I gave them tons of animated kisses and they chuckled even more. I never knew how much I could love like this until my wife gave us children. Now I felt like I was going to erupt from it.

Nastia jumped on me again and I grunted in response. My wife covered her mouth and tried to stifle a laugh. I could see the smile behind her hand. At this rate, I would not be able to give Adrianna any more kids even if I wanted to if they kept kneeing my dick all the time. I wrapped my arms around the three of them and held them until they were giggling from my tickles, begging me to stop.

At first, we had been concerned if Adrianna could get pregnant after many failed attempts. She had said it was karma and a constant reminder of what we had endured as a couple. She was never able to fully let go of losing our first child and had nearly damaged herself emotionally in the process. It had wrecked me to see her so miserable.

All of Adrianna's specialists had gathered in one room to discuss if she could get pregnant at all when we had decided we were ready.

She had not had a regular period for years, and the doctors were concerned about the health risks she could possibly undergo being pregnant with stage four kidney disease. The medication she had been taking for years had caused harsh side effects. She was not the same. The medication damaged parts of her body that would never be able to recover.

After a year of trying to conceive and false pregnancy tests and tears I kissed my way through, we had turned to fertility drugs.

It had not been easy for either of us, her more so. Adrianna had been brokenhearted when we filled the prescription for the first time. She had blamed herself for the pregnancy she lost all those years ago, saying it was her fault she was unable to conceive naturally. I had kissed her all damn night and let her cry on me until she fell asleep, and when she woke with fresh tears the next morning, I stayed right where I was and held her until she stopped shaking. It had fucking devastated me to see her like that, but I stayed strong because she needed me. I owed my wife everything for the life she gave me. If she had wanted a baby, then I would move mountains to give her one.

Weeks had gone by and she began to feel inadequate as a woman, that something was missing from her. I had told her she was crazy and to calm down because she was perfect the way she was—biggest mistake I ever made as a husband. The moment I had said to calm down, she exploded.

Apparently, women did not like to hear those two words together.

We had considered adoption from Russia—her idea—but I was not ready to give up on having our own children one day, even if we were only granted one. I had never wanted little hellions until Adrianna had put the idea in my head. Now I cannot imagine my life without them. I wanted a plethora of them.

"Daddy! Throw me in the air," Nastia demanded, her red ringlets falling in front of her eyes.

"Me too, Daddy!" Svetlana, Nastia's twin, screamed like a hyena in my ear.

I winced, going deaf for a split second.

Yes, twins.

Both my wife and I were still perplexed over it. We knew twins were a strong possibility because of Sophia combined with the potency of the fertility drugs, but we did not anticipate them.

"Again, Daddy!" Nastia said, elbowing her sister out of the way.

"How are you feeling?" I asked and stood up. I gave the kids one last toss each in the air. "Girls, go change and warm up." They dashed off. They loved gymnastics.

Adrianna's dreamy smile took my breath away as she peered up at me. I fucking loved this woman. The light was shining through the large window showcasing the dusting of freckles across the bridge of her nose. The older she got, the more pronounced they became. I wrapped my arm around her shoulder and held her close to me.

"Great? Amazing? Wonderful?" She smiled bigger, then yawned. "I slept most of the day. Thanks for taking Lili for me."

"*Malysh*, I am not *taking* Lili for you. She is my daughter too."

She pouted and I had the urge to kiss her lips deep.

"I know. I just feel bad because you have to work."

I shook my head. "You know World Cup is family. We rotated events—I took her to vault, Danilo took her on floor, Madeline had her on bars, then she ended on balance beam with me."

She grinned, and her eyes lit up. It was the little things we found satisfaction in now.

Madeline and Danilo had phoned me one night explaining that they wanted to expand World Cup, and that they wanted me to come back and coach. They had sweetened the proposal by allowing me to buy my way back into the gym. I countered back with adding Adrianna to the offer.

When I had returned to World Cup with my wife, I was placed under scrutiny. They had no idea we were married, let alone together. It did not faze me one bit, and I had answered every question they asked. I was proud of us and refused to hide what I felt for Adrianna ever again. I knew how it looked, we had heard it all, but that was then, and this was now.

Adrianna, on the other hand, did not have the same reaction. She had been uncomfortable, edgy, like everyone looked at her with disapproving eyes.

It was not until she had become pregnant with our first daughter that everyone had a change of heart. The whole gym shifted and we suddenly became one big family. They saw her go through the emotions of longing to have a child and failing, how her chances had been so slim. They saw how she leaned on me, how I cradled her when she was finally pregnant. They saw how strong our love was during one of the hardest times for us, and it had lifted the curtain for them.

"Need any help today?" she asked eagerly.

I knew where she was going with this. "I got it covered."

Her eyes dropped and a laugh rumbled in my chest. "Tell me you love me." I demanded, my eyes penetrating hers.

"Never," she said with a smile on her face. "Come on, Coach, let me help a bit. It's not like I'm asking to make a comeback. Maybe if you let me help, I'll make it worth your while and we can go into your office like old times…"

She loved to be in the gym as much as I did.

"Go put your feet up in my office. Call a friend or buy some shit online. But I do not want to hear that your blood pressure dropped again or see you rushed off to the hospital."

Her eyes flared. "That was one time, three pregnancies ago."

"And I never want to relive that moment."

Her eyes dropped lower now. Just as I was about to add something else, I saw Svetlana, or as Nastia called her, Lana, stop walking and drop her head. I peered around Adrianna and frowned as I watched her stand alone in her metallic pink leotard. She balled her tiny hands in her mouth, her creamy fingers twisting against her teeth. She was our little pixie of a girl with untamable red curls and sabal eyes. Svetlana was noticeably smaller than her twin.

I nodded with my chin and we both looked at her.

"Svetlana, idi syuda I skazhi mne, chto ne tak."

My children understood both Russian and English, at my wife's request.

Her little feet padded across the floor. Svetlana glanced up with tears shimmering in her innocent eyes.

"What's wrong?" my wife asked, handing me Lili before kneeling down.

We had a rule. When one of the girls needed us, we would give them our undivided attention, if we were capable in the moment, of course. Between their close ages and female emotions, we did not want them to feel we favored one over the other.

I also was trying to prevent meltdowns before they happened. That was a lot of female hormones under one roof.

"I do not want to do the bawance beam." Her little voice squeaked.

I had a good chuckle over her lack of contractions. Every once in a while, my kids sounded like me and I found it hysterical. Now I understood why Adrianna made jokes about it.

"It is scary. Can I just do the other ones and not that one today?"

"Are you still thinking about when you slipped off yesterday?" Adrianna responded, and Svetlana nodded, her chin staying tight to her chest.

Reaching for her, my wife picked up Svetlana and cradled her to her hip. She sniffled and placed her thumb in her mouth. Normally I was against Adrianna picking up the children while she was pregnant, unless it was Lili, but I never said anything when it came to Svetlana.

Her muscle tone had been very weak since she was born. She had to be supported for a solid two years by us holding up her and her neck. Adrianna and I had worked diligently with our daughter to build muscle tone through play.

Doctors firmly believed that Svetlana's hypotonia was actually caused by muscular dystrophy.

Svetlana had no idea gymnastics was more about rehabilitation for her than the actual sport. We did not want to push her to do the balance beam. We both had agreed that if our kids did not want to play the sport, then they did not have to, but for Svetlana who actually liked gymnastics, it was part of her therapy. We gave her a nudge on all the events. She needed gymnastics to live.

"I guess I'll be on beam for the next hour," Adrianna said happily. She planted a kiss to my lips then waddled away. It was a struggle for me to let her go, but our daughter needed her, and, well, Adrianna needed this too.

For the next hour I watched while my fearless wife helped coach our daughter. Tonight I would have to make sure I take the girls so she can get a little extra rest. It was rare when she told me she was tired and wanted to relax, but I knew how much the pregnancies drained her. She was my other half—I felt what she did. Adrianna was determined to be there for her kids. I loved her so much for that and did not want to take it away from her, so I had to be creative about making sure she did not overdo it. Like taking parent duties the entire night. Svetlana was still in pull-ups, and Mia was already fighting us about staying up later. Nastia never liked to sleep and half the time she would climb into Mia's bed. Putting them to sleep could be exhausting, especially if you were pregnant.

After Adrianna had undergone the transplant surgery, the last thing we had expected was to conceive again. We had not even given it a thought, truthfully. Mia had been a newborn when Adrianna's kidneys failed and she was rushed into surgery. She had fought hard to be able to be a mother to our daughter while recovering. Adrianna was, to this day, trying to do her best to keep up with our girls despite being placed on bed rest. I could not take that from her.

Juggling World Cup, my children, and a very pregnant wife was a challenge. Danilo and Madeline took my teams while I stayed with my wife twenty-four seven. Luckily, Sophia stepped in and offered to help. The woman was a godsend, a true blessing. She did not have a single mean bone in her body and often reminded me of my late mother, who Svetlana was named after. I would like to think they would have gotten along well.

Lili was now sleeping in her stroller a couple of feet from me while I was coaching the elite girls on beam. I overheard Adrianna walk Svetlana through her fears and encourage her back onto the lower balance beam. She told Svetlana stories of how she used to be scared and said it was okay to feel that way because one day it would go away.

Like mother, like daughter, I thought. They both hated the balance beam.

"*Dade,*" she said, standing on the floor beam. "*Ya smotri.*"

My lips twitched and I walked over to her. She wanted me to watch her. Svetlana's Russian was mixed with English and typically backwards. We did not have the heart to correct her yet. She was too cute for words when she tried to speak.

Grabbing both of my wife's index fingers for support, Svetlana slowly walked the beam. Her legs shook and her fingers were screaming red from holding onto her mother. I shot a glance over her head to my wife, and our eyes locked. I was not sure if it was possible to fall in love with someone a little more every day, but I did with her. She was a wife, a mother, my other half. My world revolved around her and our children.

Our soft smiles mimicked each other's, but there was a sadness inside of me I was hiding from everyone, including Adrianna. Seeing Svetlana walk the balance beam without tears was a big moment for us.

Svetlana was the runt of the twins. Nastia had crushed her in the womb. We had initially thought she was just a lazy baby with floppy limbs, but when she continued to miss the milestones while her twin surpassed them with flying colors, we took her into the pediatrician to have her examined.

Adrianna was neurotic these days and took the girls in for every little thing.

"Come on, baby girl, you can do it." Adrianna encouraged softly.

I could hear the tears in her voice that she worked hard to hide. She was terrified she was going to pass her illnesses down to her children, and she felt responsible in some way for Svetlana's disease.

We both had deep fears we did not speak of.

That did not mean we were not aware of them. We were. And we addressed them without making it obvious. It was how we worked, otherwise it was too easy for the both of us to slip into darkness and spread ruin. Communication was key, Adrianna had said.

Adrianna's gaze was fixated on Svetlana's feet, watching her step one shaky foot in front of the other. That way if she slipped, my wife would catch her before she had the chance to fall so she did not lose her courage. We planned to incorporate calf raises into her practices to help steady her ankles.

Svetlana glanced up, her dark eyes glimmering. Her cheeks had the cutest dimples when she was really happy, and right now they were all I could see.

My daughter glanced into my eyes and I nearly lost my breath. My children were my life and I felt this need to protect them at all costs. I never knew this kind of love existed.

Letting go, she held her little body as tight as she could, then walked straight to me.

"You did it, my sweet *malyshka*," I said, then scooped her up into my arms. I held her tight, giving her an exaggerated kiss on her cheek. She giggled and kicked her legs excitedly against my stomach. I held her back to support her. "I am so proud of you. Soon you will be doing flips off it."

"Mommy said she was scared."

Her lisp melted my heart.

"She was, but you know what? She had a really good coach who helped her overcome those scary thoughts and showed her that she was strong enough to handle it. Those scary thoughts only stay if you let them."

Her round eyes looked at me. "Wike you, *Dade*."

I grinned, hoping Adrianna heard the accent. "Exactly."

"Mommy said she used to do fwips."

"She did."

Svetlana sucked in a breath like she had a lot to say. Her brows rose and she tapped my shoulder. "Mommy said you can do fwips too. Fwip, *Dade.*"

"*Dade* is a little old for that now."

Putting Svetlana down, I told her to rotate to the next event, but she would not budge. She stared up at me with huge eyes that flickered with optimism like her mind was spinning. She reminded me so much of Adrianna.

"I want to do fwip like Mommy," she said, and threw her arms in the air like she was describing an explosion. My lips twitched. Most words that included an L in the spelling, Svetlana said them with a W sound. It was too adorable. "I want to do big fwips wike mommy one day. Big ones, *Dade*." She paused, then said more so to herself, "I wike big ones wike dat." She was watching an elite tumble across the floor, mesmerized by her twisting in the air. Her eyes widened, her voice a collection of bouncy tones and innocent words.

Svetlana wobbled to the side. I reached out instantly to steady her. She fell often and had bruises all over her milky skin. One would think we beat our kids.

I squatted down in front of her and looked at her. "Remember, if you ever feel like you are going to fall, just squeeze your butt and your tummy. It will help."

She blinked at me. "Wike when I try handstands."

It was a simple rule in gymnastics, but it made me so fucking proud that she remembered. "Yes, exactly like that. Now go tell your sisters about the flips you are going to do one day. While you are there, tell Mia to lose the attitude or she is working bars for one week without grips."

Svetlana nodded. "Okay, *Dade*," she said, then turned around and ran in the direction her sisters were in.

Little brat gave her sister a hug and did not tell her shit.

"A really good coach, huh?" my wife said, sidling up next to me when our daughter was out of ear distance.

My brow peaked. "Is it not the truth? Am I not a really good coach?"

"Maybe." I could hear the smile in her voice.

I looked at her. She shrugged one shoulder indifferently and crossed her arms in front of her chest. Her breasts were swollen and full, and exactly where my eyes fell. They had been full like that for years, ever since her body started going through maternity. She was rounder and softer in all the right places, and I could not keep my hands off of her.

Like right now. I wanted to drag her into our office and make her ride me until she could not stand.

I stifled a growl. Maybe I would take her up on her offer from earlier.

"Kova."

My eyes snapped to hers. The sounds that left her lips made me feel weak for her.

"Come. We have a matter to discuss in my office."

After asking Madeline to look after Lili, we walked together, and when we reached the office, I stepped in first and moved to the side. Before she could blink, I was pulling her to me and kicking the door shut so I could press my lips to hers. A soft gasp of surprise feathered her lips and then I was kissing her speechless.

"Wife," I said, growling against her mouth.

Her lips turned up in a smile against mine. "Husband."

It did not get any better than this.

"You know how much I love seeing you nurture our daughters, yes?" She nodded, arching into me. We were looking at each other. Her body was so warm and inviting against mine. With my hand on her stomach, I said, "And you know how I love to see you grow with our child, yes?" She nodded again, her smile growing bigger. She made my fucking heart race when she looked at me like that, like I was her entire world. I craved this look every day the sun rose. "Then you know how much I want to be inside of you, yes?"

She purred like a damn cat and my cock was erect in seconds. My tongue traced her lips and her gasp was hot, immersed in desire. Fisting my shirt, she leaned up on her toes to reach my mouth. My hands smoothed over her belly to the crease at her thighs. I cupped her ass, my fingertips digging into her with need. I swear she wore these little linen shorts to torture me. There was hardly any material, but she insisted they were the only comfortable thing to wear because she was hot all the time. Her little ass was heavier now, and her thighs swept into a tender touch that made me want to dive between them and spend all night there.

My hands swooped to the front of her expanding belly, the pads of my fingers gliding gently over the C-section scar from the birth of our twins. She hated this scar, along with the other one she did not like to talk about. The transplant one. I told her that I loved her even more for them. They were battle scars and she should wear them proudly. She is still working on that.

Her legs spread automatically, and she rolled her hips up toward me. A growl escaped my throat. I loved when she became needy for me. Our bodies were not our own when we were like this. My fingers slipped inside her elastic shorts, making a beeline straight to her clit. She let go of my shirt, breaking the kiss to yank down my shorts. I smiled against her lips, nipping at them. Her sex drive when she was pregnant was worse than mine.

"You do this to me on purpose." Her voice was a breathless whisper.

I played innocent. "All I did was kiss you *allo*."

"Yeah, right. You kissed me like you wanted to fuck me." She bit my chin.

The corners of my mouth curled up and my eyes bore into hers. She made me the happiest man on earth, and not because she was stroking my cock with purpose and focused on a steady execution, but because of the feeling she gave me every time I looked at her.

"*Malysh*, I want to fuck you all the time."

Her wispy giggle made me harder. "Babe, you know I'm always wanting sex now. You can't do that to me," she whined. "Give me five minutes? We have time before the appointment. I need you."

My brow peaked. She rubbed her sweet body all over me. How could I deny her? I never had been able to in the past, and now that we were married, it was even worse.

Plus, she was right. We had time to spare.

Clearly, I did not need much convincing.

Within seconds, I was on the couch positioned against the corner with Adrianna sitting on top of my lap with her back against my chest. Our shorts were gone, her legs were spread and knees bent and pulled up, and I was deep inside her pussy, driving into her wetness. It was easier for her in this position and the one she preferred.

With one foot on the floor and the other propped on the cushion, I rocked into her, building a steaming surge of pleasure between us. I fisted her hair to one side as I struggled to contain the pure warmth of euphoria from being inside of my wife. I exhaled across her neck and she let out a loud and hearty moan like she had been waiting for this moment. It gave my cock a heartbeat of its own and skyrocketed my need for her.

"Do whatever you want to me," she said, already feeling enraptured. Her head fell back onto my shoulder.

I smiled against her neck and nipped her. "I always do, *Malysh*... I always do."

Taking her left hand in mine, I placed it where our bodies were joined and laced our fingers together. Her diamond wedding ring cut into my palm as our fingers glided over the wetness together. Her hips reared back into mine. She had yet to take the ring off, not since the day I pushed it on her finger.

"Go deeper." She moaned, her fingers tickling the space under my dick. I thrust in deep and she took my sack in her hand. I tensed, feeling my balls tighten as she caressed them like silk. "How do you always make it feel so good every time?"

"It is my goal to drive you out of your mind when I am inside of you."

I groaned in her ear at the feel of her soft fingers caressing my skin. Cupping the back of my head, she turned to the side and pulled my lips to hers. My wife was feisty when she felt our bodies fused together.

I could not see past her belly, but I had a vivid imagination. I reached around and my palm ran circles on the inside of her thigh, and she quivered in response. I gave her a good grab and her legs widened willingly. It was one of those things that made her hot for me. She liked the pressure on her leg because it teased her pussy.

Adrianna drew in a slow breath the deeper I went. Her swollen pussy soaked my balls, her pleasure dripping over them. Her sex tightened around my cock and squeezed me so hard I almost shot inside her.

"Feel that?" she asked.

I moaned my response. "Of course, *Malysh*. Any deeper and I will split you in two."

Her hips began moving on their own, her thighs clenching. Her moans fought to break past her teeth biting into her lip. She was needy as hell when she was pregnant.

"No, no, no." I gritted the words out through my teeth, trying to hold her back. Sometimes she made me come before I could stop it. "We still have a minute left."

She whimpered. "I need to—"

"Shhh, I know what you need," I said.

"Oh, Kova."

My name was like a sin on her lips as her pussy leaked all over me. She tugged the hair at my nape, but I made her work for it and yanked away, taking pleasure in the sharp pain she caused. Our bodies moved in harmony. I was sliding into her with ease.

"I'm so glad I married you," she said, and it caused me to loosen my lips and laugh.

"As am I, *Malysh*."

"Maybe I have an addiction problem," she said out of the blue. "Like I'm addicted to sex with you."

I shook my head and grinned. "You know what problem you have? You talk too much during sex. You always have. Shut your mouth and let me have my way with you."

"Yes, sir."

I kissed her neck, then slapped the inside of her thigh, chuckling under my breath. She hissed, her pussy clenching around my cock.

Her hand came up and wrapped around my bicep to hang on. It was how I knew she was close. She needed to hang on to me.

"Straighten your legs," I said, my voice low.

Binding her ankles with mine, I held her legs down and stroked her clit until she was dripping and straining on me to let go. I lifted my hand in the air only for my palm to come down and slap her pussy as I drove in until I was balls deep and she was squirming.

Her pussy tightened around my cock and she began spasming, letting the sexiest purrs escape her throat. The heat of her body liquefied on me and Adrianna was riding the wave. She tried so hard to rock into me. She let out a sigh and my eyes widened. I was lost to the pleasure and slapped my hand over her mouth. The last thing we needed was someone knocking on the door. Her hips pumped back into mine and she was like this tiny little ferocious animal in heat.

Her teeth bit into my fingers, her entire body shook with such extreme pleasure, and it caused me to unload inside of her. My hands trembled from sheer desire as I poured my seed into her. There was something about knowing my cum was inside of her that turned me from animalistic to caveman. Always had since the first time I came inside her pretty pussy. I pinched her nipple and my body folded into hers as she drained my cock.

"I feel like stars are dancing on my skin," she said, her voice in a dreamlike state.

I knew that feeling all too well.

"No, this is just us, Ria. It is what has always been there since day one."

"Do you think it will ever go away?"

"I hope not."

She paused, panting. "Same." She cupped the back of my head and smiled up at me before bringing my lips to hers for one last kiss.

Once we cleaned up and dressed, we were on our way to the gynecologist office to find out the sex of our last baby. Juggling four kids was not easy. We were basically pros at quickies these days and jumped at the opportunity when it arose. It did not help that I had a wife like Adrianna. I wanted to be in her and around her all the fucking time.

The doctor walked in and went over her vitals before she was pushing a wand with a clear lubricant over my wife's belly.

Thank fuck her vitals were good and her blood work came back normal. Normal for her, anyway.

The doctor turned the screen our way and pointed between the legs that were wide open to reveal the gender. "It's right there," she said.

Chills covered my arms. I leaned in and Adrianna rose up on her elbows to peer at the screen. My jaw dropped. I had been so certain God had a vendetta against me, maybe my debt was finally paid.

The doctor printed out a few ultrasound pictures with some comments to explain what we were looking at.

She did not need to explain this one. It was obvious.

I was exuberant on the walk back to the car with a little pep in my step, whereas Adrianna was quiet. I opened the door and helped her sit inside, then I looked at her melancholy eyes. Adrianna leaned into me sadly.

"What is wrong, *Malysh*?" I asked, stroking her hair away from her neck.

She shook her head, unable to answer.

"Is it because the doctor said the baby could be over ten pounds? You are having a C-section again so—"

"It's not that," she said quietly.

I thought for a second when it hit me.

"I thought you wanted a boy."

We were actually having a boy. Finally.

A healthy boy ahead of his due date by a few weeks, actually. He was already so big, bigger than the girls.

She lifted her head and her green eyes shifted back and forth between mine, filling with tears. Her lips turned into a frown and my chest started to feel tight from seeing her like this.

"Adrianna? Sweetheart? What is wrong?"

"I just…" She stammered, her chin wobbling before she burst into tears. I wrapped my arms around her. "I just… It just hurts to name him after my dad when he's no longer here anymore. He wanted a grandson so badly, you know? And now all these feelings are back and I'm just really upset."

Her tears were falling faster now and I had nothing but my shirt to offer her. She couldn't stop crying, so I lifted the hem and gave it to her. She wiped her eyes and then sniffled.

Frank had gone into cardiac arrest three months ago and passed away suddenly. Adrianna thought she was good at hiding her grief, but I saw it every day and mourned her loss with her.

He loved all his granddaughters equally and spoiled the shit out of them, but he wanted a grandson. He wanted to be able to teach him golf and watch sports with him.

It had taken a while, but after Mia was born, Frank finally accepted us. Adrianna had joked that first he did not want us to be together, then he was telling us to have more kids. In the end, he had nothing but love for his daughter, and wanted to see her happy.

"I just can't believe we finally get a boy and he's not here. It's so unfair."

Her voice was so small and she trembled against me. All I could do was hold her closer to me.

"*Malysh*, please do not cry."

Adrianna sniffled and burrowed her head against me. She wrapped her arms around me.

I stroked the back of her head and played with her hair. "It is bittersweet, but that seems to be our theme, yes?"

She nodded quietly.

"You can change the name, you know," I told her gently.

She shook her head and looked up. "No, I don't want to change it. I'm just sad he's not here to see we finally have a boy. He won't get to hold him…" Her watery eyes studied mine. "Unless we should name him after you." She paused, then said, "We should probably do that. How about we make one long name?"

"You allowed me to name the twins after my mother. Whatever you name our son, I will be happy with. I promise."

Her chin quivered and she looked so fucking adorable. I kissed her lips, and she said, "Really? So, if I wanted to name him Konstantin Frank Rossi-Kournakova you would be okay?"

"I think it sounds like a mouthful, but if it is what you want, then yes."

Her lips puckered and I returned the gesture knowing she was purposely baiting me. Her face was pinched, twisting with indecision. She was quiet for a long moment, visibly torn between names. Truly, I did not care. I would be happy either way.

Cupping her face, I smashed a kiss to her lips.

"How about we decide when he is born? That way we can look at him to see which name fits him best," I offered. I did not want her stressing out over this right now. We had time. "Just want to add again that I am okay with whatever you want to do."

She leaned up and pressed a kiss to my lips, then let out a heavy breath, and nodded. Gratitude blanketed her face. "Thank you," she said softly. "I'm ready to go home, hubby. Let us go get our babies."

LATER THAT NIGHT WHEN MY wife and kids were long asleep, I took out my journal and penned my thoughts for an hour or so.

Only when I filled a journal was Adrianna allowed to read my entries. She loved to see what I was writing, and was always trying to peek over my shoulder. She too now had a journal and traded with me. She only filled one over the years, though, because she was so busy with the kids.

Adrianna shifted in her sleep and whimpered under her breath. She rubbed a spot on her stomach and scissored her legs. I placed my pen down and reached over.

Carefully, I slid a pillow under her growing belly and then one between her knees. Our bed was overflowing with foo-foo pillows she had accumulated over the years.

Picking up my pen, I started writing again.

Countless times I lined the pages with words of how I saw her with our daughters and the way they adored her. It was beautiful and I never wanted to forget the feeling they gave me or the look of utmost love in their eyes. Each daughter had their own journal that Adrianna and I wrote in. It was something we would present to them when they got married one day. Some people had pictures to capture memories, we wrote letters.

Turning to the side, I placed the pen and journal on my nightstand. I shut off the light then scooted underneath the sheet until my wife's head rested on my chest. I pulled her in as close as she could get with her growing belly between us and tangled my legs with hers. I wrapped my arm around her and kissed the top of her head. She sleepily kissed my chest before throwing a heavy leg over mine and sprawling across me, kicking the sheet off her body. She nudged her head into me until she was comfortable. The woman was like an inferno. Her body was scorching hot and twisted in an uncomfortable position. Yet she looked so peaceful, so I did not dare move. One thing I had learned was to never wake a sleeping Ria, even if I was sweating.

I stroked the small of her back and she let out a soft breath. I never held her from behind when she was pregnant. Adrianna said her back got too sweaty for that nowadays. Half the time she only wore a T-shirt—usually one of mine—and a pair of panties to bed because she was too hot for anything else.

I gazed down at my wife under the soft glow of the low light she left on in the hallway for the girls if they needed us at night. She was the most remarkable woman, and for some reason, she had chosen me.

"I love you, *Malysh*," I whispered, and hiked her leg up higher on me. Her legs jerked all night looking for cool spots.

She mumbled under her breath and stretched over me again. "I love you forever."

My lips twitched. She had no idea how off key she sang that response. I was pretty certain she had no idea she had.

I hugged her tight to my chest, feeling a torrent of heavy emotions rush through me. Our anniversary was a few weeks away. I had a feeling she would be more emotional than usual simply due to her pregnancy, and the perfect time for me to convince her to name our son Frank. Frank Konstantin. I knew it was something she wanted. I did too.

Adrianna was the love of my life. Her happiness was a radiance I was drawn to. I planned to give her a life to remember, one where she was smiling and glowing all the time.

Time.

Our love tested time.

What I would not go through to have a thousand lives with her.

Looking back, I had no idea how we made it to this point. We should not have. The foundation of our story began with lies and deceit. Our relationship at the time had been filled with more sorrow than happiness. Yet, here we were, and in love more than ever.

I had joked that God was testing me, but the truth was, he had been watching over me the whole time. He gave me her.

Adrianna rocked into me, a soft whimper falling from her lips. Her hand flew to her stomach and she inhaled, holding still. I brushed her hand away and gently rubbed her stomach until she was breathing normal again.

"Relax for me, *Malysh*," I whispered, then kissed the top of her head.

THE END.

ABOUT LUCIA FRANCO

Lucia Franco resides in South Florida with her husband and two sons. She was a competitive athlete for over ten years – a gymnast and cheerleader – which heavily inspired the Off Balance series.

Her novel Hush Hush was a finalist in the 2019 Stiletto Contest hosted by Contemporary Romance Writers, a chapter of Romance Writers of America. Her novels are being translated into several languages.

She's written over a dozen books and plans many more for the future. When she's not writing, she can be found swimming in the ocean or getting lost in her butterfly garden.

Find out more at authorluciafranco.com

Made in United States
Troutdale, OR
05/13/2024

19843017R00266